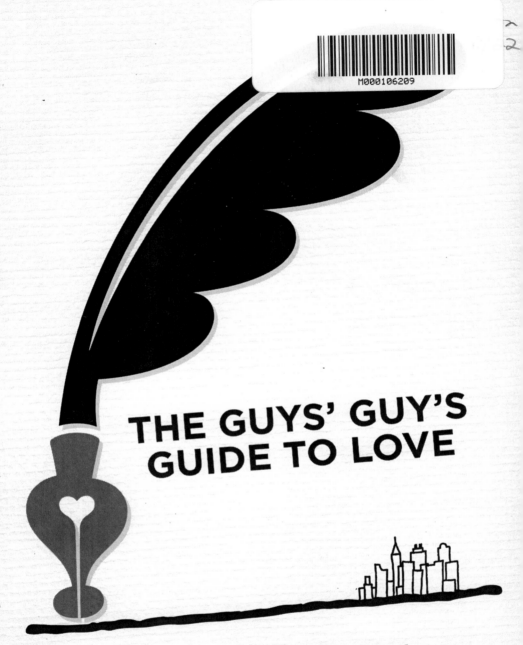

THE GUYS' GUY'S GUIDE TO LOVE

A NOVEL BY ROBERT MANNI

LIVE OAK
BOOK COMPANY

Published by Live Oak Book Company
Austin, TX
www.liveoakbookcompany.com

Distributed by Live Oak Book Company

For ordering information or special discounts for bulk purchases, please contact Live Oak Book Company at PO Box 91869, Austin, TX 78709, 512.891.6100.

Design and composition by Greenleaf Book Group LLC
Cover design by Chris Lenox

Publisher's Cataloging-In-Publication Data
(Prepared by The Donohue Group, Inc.)
Manni, Robert.
    The guys' guy's guide to love : a novel / by Robert Manni. — 1st ed.
       p. ; cm.
    ISBN: 978-1-936909-25-4
    1. Man-woman relationships—Fiction. 2. Advertising personnel—New York (State—New York—Fiction). 3. Love—Fiction. 4. New York (N.Y.)—Fiction. 5. Love stories, American. I. Title.
PS3613.A66 G89 2011
813/.6   2011938397

Print ISBN: 978-1-936909-25-4
eBook ISBN: 978-1-936909-27-8

First Edition

For Mom and Dad

Thanks for everything . . . the conceiving and the believing.

"The rock's easy, but the roll is another thing . . ."

–Keith Richards

# ACKNOWLEDGMENTS

I gave myself ten years to be writing this passage and I do so with appreciation and gratitude for the many people who have supported me. I believe that we all come from the same source and that this story is ours to share.

I met Steve Armour at the New York Writers Workshop. Steve feels the rhythm, music, and beat in a story and has an ear for language and great comedic timing. These are gifts, and I thank him for helping me keep my story focused on an unwavering, classic trajectory. Steve is my teacher and my friend. We wrote the TV pilot based on this book and had so much fun and received so much positive feedback that Steve has already been commissioned to write his first movie. Amazing, and there's more to come from us. Thank you, amigo!

I have another teacher: my wife. We've only been married for a short time, but she has helped me elevate my thoughts, vibrations, and manifestations. She also reminded me that "the flavor is in the fat" while I was working through the final edits to this book. I love Uni Manni.

Many thanks and love to the very creative and passionate leaders of my GGG2Love team—Mara Wedeck and Stephanie Wang. They have selflessly and generously dedicated themselves to putting together a wonderful marketing plan. I am beyond grateful for their wonderful contributions. Special thanks also to Scott "Sherpa" Swanay, Colin Lange, Chris Lenox, Dave Bassiri, Rick Markert, and Dan Wakefield.

Thanks to Hobbs, Bryan, Amy, and the team at Greenleaf Book Group for making this project happen in short order.

More thanks to Tom Manni; Sanjay Sanghoee; Bill and Debbie James; Susan Dalsimer; Dr. Tony De Marco; John Krieger; Charles Salzberg; Doug, Chris, and Greg at EUE Screen Gems; Reiki; The Rolling Stones; the Jersey Shore boardwalk; Terry Asis; Tim Tomlinson; June Clark; Mickey Rourke for inspiring a comeback; Aloun, Kevin, Media Bob, John Fante; Lawrence Block; New York City; Vince Laraia, Leonard Soloway, all of my angels; my hilariously devilish friends and colleagues in advertising; and to everyone who listened to my story, read a passage, and gave me encouragement.

ONE LOVE!

CHAPTER 1

Buzz~

Max Hallyday sat at a small table in the Peninsula Hotel's rooftop bar, ignoring the iPhone zitzing in his pocket. He gazed beyond the tables of fashionably dressed women sipping brightly colored cocktails and looked deep into Manhattan's canyon of gleaming skyscrapers.

Buzz~

It's probably Veronica, he thought, but he couldn't answer. No time for another fight. His new client was minutes away, and he needed to be at his best.

Buzz~

Max drummed his fingers on the table. *What if that is the client? Better take a look.* He yanked the phone from his pocket and saw Veronica's name. Before he could stop himself, he pressed the button, opening her text message.

Need 2 talk.

He flinched. *Hey! What's up?*

Confused. Something's wrong.

?

With us.

Max's face tightened. *Us?*

We want different things. U r holding on 2 the past.

What past?

Ur old job.

Max shot up and began snaking his way through the maze of tables. *Felt bad leaving Goodson. I'm at HHI now . . . right?*

U r not sending right signals. Goodson Advertising—not hot.

What do u mean?

I hooked u up 4 ur new job.

And I'm here! Max hit send and ran his hand through his choppy black hair. He glanced sideways and noticed he was precariously close to the ledge.

R u? U complain. I need more.

More what??

More of everything.

Max frowned. *Everything?*

Need U to take charge.

Max scoffed as he typed. *Take charge of what?*

Us, the agency . . . everything.

I'm on it!

R U? Not good at this.

Max frowned again. *Good at what?*

Can't do this anymore . . .

What r u saying?

Max—I'm sorry. B strong. GTG.

As the screen turned black, Max clenched his jaw. He kicked the short wall, and then stared down at a battalion of taxis racing down Fifth Avenue. For a fleeting moment, he imagined himself sprouting wings and floating off into the blue. But he knew there was no escape. He checked his watch. No sign of his client, Layla Korindopolos, but she was sure to arrive any second.

He waved, and then blurted something to a waiter about water. A glass was in his hand almost immediately. Max took a long drink and trudged back to his seat. It was a brilliant, cloudless afternoon in May with the sun glistening off the apex of the Chrysler Building. New York City was majestic and beautiful.

At thirty-six, Max was still a young man. He was hungry, optimistic, and unwavering in the pursuit of his dreams. But Veronica had blindsided him. She was smart. And successful. And so damn seductive. How could she do this? Beads of perspiration appeared on Max's forehead. Hearing laughter erupt from a table of women to his right, Max swung around, wondering what was so funny. When the women stared back, he caught himself and feigned a smile and a halfhearted wave. *Pull it together*, he thought. *Your client will be here any minute.* Then he remembered that he'd invited his best friend, Roger Fox, to join them. *Dammit. He's already a handful on his own.*

A moment later, Max recognized Roger ambling through the entrance. As always, Roger appeared rakish and cool, stylishly attired in a tropical-weight gray suit and a lavender silk tie. His lean athletic build, hazel-green eyes, squared jaw, and self-assurance were magnets for the women celebrating springtime at the rooftop oasis. The Cheshire Cat grin that spread across his suntanned face only added to Roger's good looks. Heads turned as he sauntered through the crowd. Max shook his head and wondered what it would be like approaching life so effortlessly—putting in half the effort, yet receiving twice as much in return. Life seemed too easy for Roger.

Roger spotted Max peripherally, of course, but with the precision of a submarine's periscope, he swiveled his head, scanning for potential conquests. At ten o'clock, a statuesque brunette and her two friends—locals, probably married. At two o'clock, though, three well-heeled blondes. He checked their hair, dresses, bags—definitely out-of-towners looking for action. He steered a course to Max's table by way of the blondes.

"Max," he called, pausing long enough to receive admiring once-overs from all three women. Then he joined Max.

At six-foot-four, he towered over his friend, now slumped in his seat at the small round table. Roger pulled up a chair and studied Max's face.

"Hey, *amigo*. What happened? You look like a member of the Addams Family," he said, patting Max on the back. "C'mon, is this how Hornsby Hammerhead's newest VP mans up for his new client?"

Max balled his fist and met Roger's knuckles head on with a meaty thud. "I'm okay. Tough day, that's all. I just need to clear my . . ."

"Good, because, baby, it's springtime," Roger crowed, waving his hand at the now crowded space. "Check out this talent. We need cocktails," he added, signaling a waiter with two long fingers. When he ordered gin and tonics, Max waved him off and asked for water.

Roger tapped his foot and surveyed the scene. "Talk to me about

Peacock Beverages and this client of yours. What's this about healthy booze?"

"It's like I told you. Peacock is launching a new line of spirits. They're infusing vodka, rum, and gin with herbal extracts, botanicals, and all-natural flavors."

"Cool. I never realized vodka and rum were good for you."

"Good for you or not, I've tasted them and they're going to be huge."

"So what's the plan?"

"It's simple. You're here to talk about sampling ideas—that's all. I want Layla stoked about her products and fired up about investing in our advertising. They're putting a pile of money behind the launch and there'll be plenty to go around. But first, I need her committed to a new campaign. When the time's right, I'll make sure you get a shot at selling her ad space in your magazine. Just not now—got it?" He took a deep breath and drained the glass of water.

"Sure. So is she . . . ?" Roger asked, raising an eyebrow.

"Yeah, Layla's attractive, very put together, but more important, she's a pro—intelligent, without the drama."

"Perfect. Then what's not to like about the new gig?"

"I'm still torn about leaving Goodson," Max said, checking his watch.

Roger shook his head. "Please, not this again."

Max put up his hand. "Henry Goodson let me do my job. It was about results, not process. HHI told me I could manage my business, but they sold me a bill of goods. I know it's a global conglomerate, but advertising is supposed to be fun. I deal with so much bureaucracy, it's like I'm working for the DMV," Max said.

"You gave Henry Goodson's agency seven good years. Now you're making big bucks. That's all that matters."

"I like the money, but I'm not going to sell my soul to get it. I need to handle things on my own terms. At Goodson, I ran my game," Max said, leveling his eyes on Roger's suntanned face.

"Wake up and smell the vodka, dude. You're forgetting that Goodson Advertising doesn't pay that well. And Henry didn't always come through with our bonuses."

Max looked down at his empty glass. "It's a small shop. Henry did what he could for us. Remember, he cut you a break when you got busted nailing that intern on the roof deck."

Roger shrugged. "Do you want to be the guy who devotes his career to shilling Bobalooie Bubble Gum? HHI's the hottest agency in New York—probably the world—and liquor advertising is cool. We're—I mean, *you're* going to make a killing when these cocktails take off."

"I hear you," Max said, "but I'm slammed. No time for anything but work. Like tonight—Cassidy and I have our meeting for The Children's Literary Club of New York. I'd like to be there. And I'm so exhausted I can't find time to work on my stories."

"Cassidy can handle the club. And once you come to terms with your new gig, you'll have plenty of time to write about Peter Rabbit or whatever. It's game on, dude." Roger took another swig from his drink. "Here, you're all sweaty," he added, holding out a damp napkin that he unwrapped from under his glass.

Max shook his head.

"A round of golf this weekend will get your head right."

Max didn't respond.

"What's with you?"

Max handed Roger his phone. "See for yourself."

Roger tilted Max's iPhone to block the sun's glare and began reading. "Order me another," he said, shaking his glass so the ice tinkled. His eyes lingered on the screen after he read the message thread a second time. When the waiter arrived with his drink, Roger handed the phone back to Max.

"Wow. That's cold," he said. "A kiss-off by text. *Ouch.*"

"Yeah. I know Veronica comes on strong, but I gave her space. A lot of good that did me."

"Strong? V's a super Type A. She's got that Westchester meets Upper East Side thing. She's got it all, but thinks she's falling behind."

"She's from Ossining," Max said, glancing toward the entrance.

"Whatever."

"Okay, maybe I was hooked on her looks and the sex, but I never tried to change her."

ROBERT MANNI

"Hmm, I can see how she could be addictive," Roger said, stirring his drink. "Maybe being so available was the problem."

"Huh?"

"When guys try too hard, it shows. Chicks are hardwired to smell fear. And desperation's a major turn-off."

Max shook his head incredulously. "I wasn't desperate. I was paying attention."

"Okay, you paid attention, and went shopping, and watched Kate Hudson movies together. And how did that work out?"

"Thanks for the pep talk," Max said, seeing Veronica's text flash through his mind. "So, not being available is the key to success with women?"

"That's the tip of the iceberg, Max. It's going to take a special woman to understand a guy like you."

"As opposed to understanding the guy who doesn't stick around long enough to rumple the sheets," Max offered.

"*Amigo*, I *know* women."

"How much can you know? You're a wham-bam machine."

Roger shook his hand. "I love women and I get what they're looking for."

"Let's have it."

Roger cleared his throat. "Women are drawn to the rugged individualist."

"Like Mr. Brawny, the paper towel guy?" Max cracked.

Roger laughed. "If you were really paying attention, you'd know women go for dudes with the kind of self-assurance that says they really dig the girl, but can live without her. *That* drives women crazy."

Max looked across the city skyline. "Maybe. I'm just not feeling it today."

"You'll be fine after you let Veronica go. Who knows? Maybe you'll get another shot at the title."

"Think so?" Max asked, turning back to the table.

"Probably not," Roger chuckled.

"I'd like to go to my happy place now," Max said, dryly. "You know, since Veronica's so high on herself, Cassidy calls her Victoria."

Roger chuckled. "No question, the girl is lingerie model material."

"Yeah, but there's pressure dating a woman with her looks. The

6

THE GUYS' GUY'S GUIDE TO LOVE

last time we were makin' it together, I almost wish I'd known it really was the *last time*." He tilted his chair back. "Would you want to know if it was the last time you'd be making love to the most beautiful woman you'd ever been with?"

Roger furrowed his brow. "As long as the sex is awesome, who cares? Men and women spend way too much time analyzing one another. Remember that," he said, gesturing at Max.

"Are you knuckle-wagging me?"

"I am, *amigo*. Now, pull it together. This is business, not a Deepak Chopra conference."

"There's my client," Max said, wiping his face and motioning toward the entrance, as an immaculately dressed woman with handsome Mediterranean features strode through the door. She had shoulder-length, raven-black hair, highlighted by subtle shades of red. Her curvaceous figure was wrapped in a white tailored Gucci suit accessorized with a matching handbag and an oversized pair of white- and gold-framed sunglasses.

"Not bad," Roger said. "Legs aren't that long, but . . ."

"Chill."

"Built kind of low to the ground . . ." Roger clicked his teeth. "She's no thoroughbred, but *damn* she's stacked."

"We're not betting on her in the third race."

Layla Korindopolos was the daughter of Nikola Korindopolos, the notorious international business mogul. Despite her privileged life, Layla was a sharp-minded and capable marketer. Max respected her and knew that her being tabbed to direct the rollout of Peacock Beverages' new line could result in Layla securing an increasingly powerful position in an exploding category.

"Whoa. Impressive rack," said Roger.

Max shot him a look. He smoothed his suit and straightened his cobalt-blue tie, remembering that it was a gift from Veronica. She said it matched his eyes.

"Ms. Korindopolos," Max said. "It's great to see you."

"Max," she said, taking his hand confidently and smiling. "How are you? And, please—it's Layla." She looked around the crowded scene and took a deep breath that swelled her breasts. "Such a gorgeous day."

Roger was stealing a peek at her cleavage when Max turned to him.

"Layla, this is Roger Fox. Roger, this is Layla. Roger works for *Plates* magazine. I've asked him to join us. Roger's got some interesting ideas for sampling your products."

Layla removed her glasses and studied Roger through dark, almond-shaped eyes. Roger broke into his most disarming smile and placed his left hand over hers during the introductions.

"It's my pleasure . . . Layla." He slipped his business card into her hand and added, "Can we offer you a cocktail?"

"Of course."

As Layla inspected Roger's card, Max searched for the waiter. It was time to take charge of the situation before Roger forgot whose client they were entertaining.

"I called earlier," Max said. "The hotel carries all of Peacock's products."

Layla nodded her approval. "Good. I'll have a glass of Chardonnay. Gentlemen, order as you please."

"I'll go for another Tanq—" Roger began, before Max kicked him under the table.

"Two Peacock gin and tonics," Max interjected. "Roger loves Peacock gin. Isn't that right, Roger?"

"Absolutely. Did you know that the bar at *Plates'* gourmet kitchen is fully stocked with Peacock's line?" Roger asked.

Layla smiled. "You gentlemen have excellent taste. Roger, I'm sure you're an expert on the city's restaurants. Tell us what's new."

Taking his cue, Roger showed off his acumen about the latest trends in New York's constantly evolving palate, sprinkling his gastronomical recitation with the first names of a select group of its best-known chefs. Once he'd secured her attention, he leaned in and whispered the secret to his favorite dish—the plum-sake-poached torchon of foie gras and coriander-anise-crusted, seared big-eye tuna served at the Biltmore Room on Eighth Avenue.

"Sounds delish," Layla said.

"It was, but sad to say, they closed awhile back. Tough business, restaurants."

Max let Roger prattle on, grateful for having a moment to think, before his phone buzzed. He slid it onto his lap and opened a new text from Veronica.

Thinking about b 4. Sorry baby. Didn't give u a chance—need 2 talk.

Max took a slow breath. *With client.*

Want 2 hear ur side . . . no promises.

Max smiled inside. *C u at 8?*

K. No later. U like surprises, right?

Of course! B there at 8 sharp.

U better . . .

Max tucked the phone away. By now, Roger and Layla were discussing the merits of gourmet food trucks and Asian tapas.

"Why don't we have dinner at the Chambers Hotel?" Roger asked. "The hostess is holding a primo table for us at eight. It's on *Plates*."

Max did a double take. "I'm sure Layla has plans, Roger. Plus, Town closed in November."

"They've opened a new place. Different menu every night. You'll love it. They even have steak, Max," Roger said with a smirk.

"Oh, I love farm to table. Great wine list, too," Layla said.

Max hesitated. "I have someplace I . . ."

"This sounds like fun," Layla said. "I had to reschedule dinner with my father, so I'm game. I'll be in and out of the office with field sales starting tomorrow, so tonight is a good time to discuss our launch strategy. I have news on the budget, too," she added.

Max squirmed. Between Layla, Veronica, and Cassidy's book club, he was about to be triple-booked.

"Are you sure? I'm not certain they take reservations, and I wouldn't want you to have to wait. You know how the traffic gets when . . ."

"Max, please," Layla said with a laugh. "I'll be fine." She turned to Roger and smiled. "Thank you, Roger. It would be a pleasure to join you gentlemen. Shall we go?"

Max looked over at Roger, now grinning innocently. Layla excused herself to make a phone call.

"Nice going," Max said.

"She has good news on the budget."

"Let's just go," Max responded resignedly.

Roger shrugged. While exiting, Max waved Roger and Layla ahead, telling them he'd catch up. He slowed down to call Veronica.

No answer. He pursed his lips and dialed Cassidy Goodson. Moving faster to keep pace, he was short of breath by the time she answered.

"Max? Is someone chasing you?" Cassidy asked.

"Very funny . . . something's come up."

"I thought you'd be here by now."

"We're having dinner with my client . . . so I can't make the reading."

After a long pause, she said, "Serena can cover for you—for the third time."

"I'm really sorry," Max said. "You know how it is with clients."

"I do know," Cassidy replied. "I'm tap dancing and spinning plates getting this magazine launched. Talk about pressure."

"I knew you'd understand."

"Is anything wrong?" she asked.

"No, no, I'm late, that's all."

"Is this about Ms. Victoria?"

"It's *Veronica*. Why do you keep calling her that?"

"Because she's all about the garters and teddies."

Me too, he thought.

"Hey, are you still there?" Cassidy asked.

"What?"

"Have you considered what we talked about?"

"The men's column? It's like I told you—women don't want to hear the real truth about guys. We're not very interesting. We can survive on ketchup, toilet paper, ESPN, and a six-pack. How exciting is that?"

"You said the column was a great idea. And I told you that you can write whatever you want, as long as it's about guys."

"I'll think about it."

"You owe me for being a no-show again," she said. "I've got to go set up the tables now. Sorry you can't be here."

As soon as he hung up, Max felt like kicking himself—disappointing Cassidy had become a habit. But he knew she had things under control. His phone pulsed. Veronica.

U call?

Yes—B4.

I've been trying on a few little things . . . all black.

10

Max tightened his grip on the phone.

Something unexpected has come up.

Oooh, tell me more.

The client. Taking her to dinner.

Her? Dinner?? Where???

From Peacock. Some new place in the Chambers Hotel. Roger's here.

Chambers Hotel?

Yes.

I want 2 go there.

We will. Promise.

I need action, not promises.

Max hurried to catch up to Roger and Layla, who were already standing at the hotel's entrance. As Max approached, a pitted-faced man in a dirty raincoat staggered toward Roger and Layla. Layla leaned back when she caught a whiff of alcohol on the man's breath. He started to show her an umbrella—a tattered version of the second-rate kind New Yorkers buy on the street when caught in a sudden downpour. Roger stepped between them.

"Excuse me, sir," the man mumbled. "Want an umbrella? It's going to rain."

"It is?" Roger said, looking up. The skies were clear, with the exception of a small cloud to the west. After a quick side glance to make sure Layla was watching, he said, "Well, we better buy an umbrella then. How much?"

"Five bucks."

"I only have a ten."

Max rolled his eyes as he took in his friend's performance.

Roger pressed the bill into his palm and the man's face lit up. "Good evening," Roger said, before glancing at Layla, who smiled as the man shuffled away.

"Shall we?" asked Max as he held the door open for Layla. As she swished into the lobby, Roger admired her backside. He shot Max a quick nod toward her direction, eyebrows raised.

Max rolled his eyes again and reached for his phone. Roger flicked Max's shoulder, whispering out of the side of his mouth, "Put that away and join the party."

"Yeah, yeah," Max said, following Roger inside.

They passed the hotel's intimate bar and descended the steps to a dining room anchored by a large communal table. Roger whispered something to the pretty Asian hostess. She tossed her hair back and laughed, leading them toward a relatively private table in the back.

"I love the energy," Layla said, facing the bustling scene. Max peeked at his phone again. Veronica had aborted their last text message. He tapped her number again. No answer. Roger pointed out the ladies room to Layla and held her chair.

Once she was a few tables away, Roger turned to Max. "Will you stop with the *Angry Birds* already? You've got a smoking hot client here and she deserves a little TLC from her agency. How about we show her a good time and then sell her something?"

"That was Veronica sexting me."

"I thought you said it was over," Roger said.

"Maybe not."

"Well, if she hits you up again, tell her *mañana*. Or better yet, let me talk to her."

"Don't think so," Max said.

"Then hand me that wine list," Roger said, proceeding to flip through the pages. After closing the leather-bound book, he signaled the sommelier and quizzed him relentlessly before settling on a high-end Napa Chardonnay and a rare vintage Bordeaux.

Max heard his phone beep. Veronica again.

"Hey, she's on her way back," Roger warned. "Shut that down."

"One sec," Max said, desperately working his fingers across the keyboard.

Remember that black bustier and thong? The one u said made my tits look enormous?

Of course!

Then y aren't u here?

Trying. Need more time.

The black heels with the ankle straps?

B there by 10.

Taking me 4 granted?

9:30.

I need someone who does whatever it takes. Let Roger deal with the client. Leave now.

9 on the dot.

Don't bother. This isn't working.

Max's face flushed. Roger poked him under the table.

Max slipped his phone back into his jacket pocket. They stood when Layla returned, her lips now shimmering with gloss. Beads of sweat reappeared on Max's temple, and he was sure Layla was staring at them.

"Max," Layla said, touching his arm lightly. "Are you all right?"

Max straightened his tie and assured her that he was fine. Roger gave Max a get-it-together-now face when the menus arrived. When the headwaiter descended on the table, Max tried to listen, but he didn't hear a word about the specials.

Roger peppered the waiter with detailed questions about the ingredients used in the foie gras terrine appetizer. Layla listened intently and savored her wine before deciding on the cod with chamomile, fennel, and ramps. Roger ordered the swordfish and stared Max down when the waiter turned his way.

"And you, sir?"

Max hadn't opened his menu. "Sirloin. Medium rare."

"No sirloin this evening, sir. We do have a steak frites."

"Fine. And I'd like a salad with . . . whatever dressing."

"We actually have a few variations today . . ."

"Surprise me. I love surprises. I've been getting them all day," Max said, forcing a smile.

"Have you told Roger about our new line?" Layla asked, eying Max curiously.

"Just the highlights," Max said. "What's been written about them in the trades. I thought that since we're here and Roger works for a new epicurean magazine, it might be a good time to brainstorm ways for sampling your line and matching the products with food."

Roger tapped his foot, eager to chime in. "*Plates* would be honored to introduce your products into the city's top establishments. We can develop a range of terrific recipes for drinks, dinners, and desserts, too. Do they have a name yet?"

"Well, there's one we're considering. These spirits are very elegant—great packaging and a frosted bottle. It's been difficult to come up with a name that captures how precious they are. But we need to make a decision very soon to stay on schedule. We're considering *Holy Spiritz*. What do you think?"

"*Holy Spiritz*? I love it. A blessed choice," Roger said.

Max cleared his throat and gave Roger a quick, sharp glance. "*Holy Spiritz* is provocative, and certainly worth considering," he said, steepling his fingers. "But do you think it might be a bit strong? There could be PR issues with consumer advocacy groups. Layla, would you allow my team to develop a list of potential names that are similar and still supportive of your strategy, but sound less ecclesiastical? We'll conduct the research and, of course, include *Holy Spiritz* in the testing. We want the strongest name recognition for your brand and a smooth, successful launch without the potential for negative press."

Max held Layla's gaze across the table and watched the corners of her mouth slowly turn upward. "That's exactly the kind of thinking I want from my agency. Excellent, Max. You're right. The branding process needs to be handled with the utmost care." She turned to Roger. "Could you pour me some wine? I'd like to try the Bordeaux."

Roger barely avoided knocking the bottle over as he reached out to fill her glass. Max looked over at Roger, who feigned a smile back.

"I'll have more wine, too," Max said cheerily, holding out his glass.

Roger filled it dangerously close to the brim until Max held up his hand.

"One more thing," Layla said, swirling the deep red wine. "I'd like the agency to develop the ad campaign concepts while I'm out next week."

Without a name for the brand? Max thought. When he saw the unwavering look on her face, he said, "Of course. I'll ask our teams to put together some directional ideas."

"I want real campaigns, not rough ideas. We need a quick turnaround. Can you do it?"

"Definitely."

"Good. I have some ideas, but I'll set the budget after I see the work. I think your agency will be pleased."

Max nodded. After finishing his wine, he excused himself from the table. Inside the men's room, he leaned over the sink and splashed cold water on his face. The color was finally returning to normal. He dried off, took his phone out, and tried contacting Veronica again — first by phone, then text, and finally e-mailing her. No answer. By the time he'd plodded back to the table, his insides were gurgling and his stomach was raw. The moment he sat down, the waiter slid a platter of steak frites under his nose.

Roger continued pouring it on for Layla, reeling off potential food and liquor matches for her new products: a Vietnamese vegetarian medley paired nicely with the vanilla bean and aloe infused rum, and the lobster ravioli with a pink sauce made from crème fraiche and strawberry vodka. Max sighed. His client was charmed by Roger's performance, and Max wanted to get her out of there. Right now.

As Roger guided Layla through the dessert menu, suggesting more eclectic ideas that paired food with her products, Max excused himself again. He stepped into the foyer to call Veronica. It was after ten. He held out hope that she was still decked out in lingerie antici-pating his arrival. No response. He put the phone away. *It was over.* Max dragged himself back to the table where Roger and Layla were laughing with the waiter as he tried valiantly to field Roger's endless questions about today's desserts.

"Can you tell us something about the breed of cows used in making the curds for the various flavors of ice cream? Are Holsteins favored in a particular climate or season?" Seeing Layla's smile, Max was comforted that at least his client was enjoying the show.

"I'll have the milk bar crack pie," Max said, yielding to the waiter's recommendation when it was his turn to order.

Over espressos, Roger continued working Layla, piling it on even more than usual. After requesting the bill and a second espresso, Roger waxed on, ignoring the check. Ten minutes later, Max finally picked up the tab and frowned at Roger, who avoided making eye contact.

Outside, Max flagged down a taxi for Layla while she stood by, still laughing with Roger. It was approaching midnight and Max was ready to crash. As he held the cab door open for her, Max noticed the man who had sold Roger the umbrella leaning against a building, guzzling from a bottle wrapped in a paper bag.

Roger said, "Layla and I can share the cab."

Max tightened his grip on the door handle. "Aren't you going west, Roger? Layla lives on the Upper East Side."

"We're fine, Max," Layla said.

"Then please, take this one," Max said, smiling tactfully and air kissing Layla on both cheeks. He glared at Roger as he cut in front of Max and slid into the back. The moment the door closed, the taxi bolted into the night.

Roger maneuvered his long legs in the backseat. He shifted his body, facing Layla as they pulled up to the tall, black cylindrical building at the corner of 66th and Second Avenue. Roger leaned in carefully, making warm, steady eye contact.

"I really enjoyed tonight, and I'd like to help with your launch any way I can," he said. "Why don't I set up a dinner and give you a more personalized introduction to the *Plates* experience?"

The driver looked back in his mirror.

"Well, that's quite an offer," she said. "You certainly appear to be an expert in your field."

"I do my best," he said earnestly. "How should I contact you?"

Layla stepped out into a light rain. She automatically tucked her bag under her arm, looked back, and said, "Google me, Roger." She smiled to herself as she walked away.

When the next cab pulled up, it was drizzling. Max climbed into the backseat and hit Veronica's speed dial again, but his call went directly to voice mail. He slumped back, staring through the grimy window as the taxi rumbled to the West Side. Fat raindrops began splattering the street as the lights of the city flashed by the window, wet and weird on the glass.

Max sighed. "Shit, it's only Monday."

CHAPTER 2

Cassidy Goodson and her friend Serena de los Reyes emerged from the depths of Brooklyn's Borough Hall subway station into a perfect Sunday afternoon. They'd just finished a marathon yoga session at Serena's studio in Park Slope, and Cassidy's fair skin glowed.

"You're still upset," Serena said, studying her friend's face.

"I can't help it," Cassidy responded, adjusting her yoga mat under her arm. "He's working so hard in a new job and she nukes him with a *text*!"

Heads turned at that remark, not that Cassidy, in her faded jeans and tight T-shirt, wasn't already getting her share of looks. With her lean frame, light brown wavy hair, and pale blue eyes, she had the all-American appeal of a leading actress on a sitcom—the kind of woman mothers hope their sons will bring home for Thanksgiving dinner.

Serena, wearing one of the boho-styled ribbed tanks she sold in the boutique adjacent to her yoga studio, also turned heads. This afternoon, her jet-black hair was pulled into a tight ponytail. Her baby-blue top and matching track pants showed off her athletic curves as the two women strolled along Montague Street.

Entering Noodle Pudding, they were greeted with smiles from the staff and were seated immediately at a table by the window. Cassidy had been away on business for Serena's birthday, so today she was treating her best friend to lunch at her favorite Italian bistro. Following another endless winter, the restaurant doors had been swung open, letting in a light breeze that circulated a scent of fresh pesto throughout the room. Cassidy balanced her tortoiseshell glasses on her nose and took a cursory glance at the specials board. She didn't open the menu, reaching for the breadbasket instead.

"That class was awesome," Serena said in a velvety voice that carried a hint of an accent.

"I still can't keep up with you," Cassidy said, shaking her head.

Serena looked up when she heard Cassidy snap a semolina breadstick in half. "God, you really are upset. You're eating carbs."

"I can't help it. She's unbelievable," Cassidy said.

"Who?"

"Victoria."

"Veronica," Serena said, rolling her eyes.

Cassidy shrugged.

"Listen," Serena continued. "Maybe she's got the looks and the smarts, but some women are never satisfied. When the time comes, she'll go down hard."

"I know, but it bugs me that she's still pulling her shit and getting away with it," said Cassidy. "What's happened to her since we worked at *Face Front* is amazing. We were a kick-ass team."

"Look, nothing's happened to her. She is what she is. She's got the bitch gene programmed into her DNA."

Cassidy half-nodded. "Yeah, but she helped me get transferred into editorial."

"Come on, girl. We've been over this. Someone who can sell the way you can should know why she was pushing you out of her department."

"But I wasn't a threat, and you were running the show. You taught us everything."

"Didn't teach her to sleep with the publisher. Or to screw me out of my job."

"But look what you've got now—a great business, without the nonsense," Cassidy said, now flipping open her menu. "She just pisses me off."

Serena unfolded her napkin. "Are we going to order, or just bitch about the bitch?" She waved, and a waiter came by, scribbled their orders, and retreated to the kitchen.

"So, how do you like the new neighborhood?" Serena asked.

"Feels like home already. I mean, it's only three blocks from my old place, but the view of the city's awesome. Now, if only I could find time to invite people over and enjoy it."

"Like a hunky guy?" Serena suggested, laughing.

"I'm so crazed at work, that's the last thing I need."

"Maybe it's the only thing," Serena said.

"And you?"

"There's no one in the pipeline right now," said Serena, pulling off a piece of fresh bread after the salads arrived.

"I know. It's too bad that men act crazy around you."

Serena laughed. Although it had been two years since they worked together at *Face Front* magazine, the two women had forged a strong, lasting friendship. They both preferred the relative tranquility of Brooklyn's picturesque brownstones and tree-lined streets to living in the maddening buzz of Manhattan.

Three days ago, Serena turned thirty-eight, but she maintained the exotic look of a former fashion model with her dark, smoldering eyes and flawless caramel skin.

Serena watched Cassidy poking at her salad. "God, you really are upset over this. Max is a sweet guy, but considering the company he's been keeping, maybe he had it coming. You know, a very smart woman once said, 'The only thing worse than a man you can't control is one that you can.' "

"Whatever, but I don't like her hurting him. Let's hope what goes around . . ." Cassidy's voice trailed off as the entrees arrived. "I'm taking him kayaking on Tuesday."

"Oooh," Serena said, arching an eyebrow. "Romance on the high seas."

"Oh, no," Cassidy said. "We tried romance before. Remember? I ended up crying into my Krispy Kremes for a week."

"He just couldn't deal with dating the boss's daughter. But you're both free and single now, and you work at different companies."

"Yeah, and we're also friends now. And I like that. Besides, I've got this magazine to launch."

"A magazine can't give you what you need, girl," Serena said, grinning. "Why don't you stop over at his place, loosen his belt, and see what happens?"

Cassidy pointed her fork in Serena's direction. "Max had his chance. He needs to decide what he wants and go after it. He gets so close to putting it all together and then something always happens."

"One thing you don't want happening is him getting back with *Victoria*," Serena said, her eyes narrowing as she twirled her pasta.

Cassidy half-smiled. "Veronica. After what she put him through, he's got a bad case of the New York City guy virus: emotional unavailability." She held out her goblet of Barolo and Serena clinked it with her sparkling water.

"Enough about them. How's the magazine? What did you finally name it?" Serena asked.

"*My Radiance*. And I'm doing everything I can to set the bar higher than reporting on starlets dancing on tables in their bras and panties," Cassidy said with a chuckle that revealed her dimples. "But there'll always be the obligatory celebrity features. Young Hollywood sells."

"Why don't you create your own celebrities?" Serena suggested. "Find experts on things that interest women."

Cassidy's face brightened. "That's what we're thinking. There are plenty of smart women we can showcase. And I want articles about men, too, and from their perspective. Like a guy shooting from the hip about how men lure us to bed or how they feel about getting dumped by someone like Victoria. Women might like a peek into a man's world, even if it is kind of weird."

"A regular guy's perspective."

"We'll demystify the species, assuming we can refer to men as a species," Cassidy mused.

"Personally, I don't see guys being all that mysterious, but you might be on to something. You're going to need the right male voice— someone who'll tell women why guys ask for your number and say they'll call, and then don't. Not that it's ever happened to me," Serena said, smiling. "What about Max? Doesn't he write stories?"

"I've asked him, but he told me that if he revealed men's inner secrets, he'd have to kill me," Cassidy said.

"Too bad. Maybe when his head clears, he'll change his mind."

"If he ever gets over her."

"Make him get over her," Serena said, picking up her menu. "I want something chocolate."

Cassidy sighed as the waiter took their plates away. Her phone rang, so she unzipped her tote and reached around inside. Too late. A beep sounded when the call went to voice mail. She listened to the message as Serena scanned the desserts.

"Hmm, flourless chocolate cake or chocolate panna cotta?" Serena asked herself aloud.

Cassidy dropped her phone. The color had drained from her face.

"What's wrong?" Serena asked.

Cassidy fumbled for the phone and threw it into her bag. Her eyes darted to the door. "That was Beth Israel hospital. It's my Dad—his heart. He had chest pains and they rushed him to the emergency room. Here . . ." She tossed some bills on the table and grabbed her mat. "I've got to go."

"I'm coming, too," Serena called out, following behind her. The two women rushed outside and jumped into a cab waiting at the light.

CHAPTER 3

"**S**o, you got voted off the island," Roger said, leaning back into his leather chair. He was using his Sharpie to tap the opening riff of "Honky Tonk Women" on his coffee mug. "You knew what you were getting into. Veronica's a barracuda gnashing through a school of minnows. Give yourself credit. Most guys don't have the balls to date a woman like her. And you survived."

"Right," Max said into the phone from his office across town.

Roger closed his door and switched on the speakerphone. "I've been worried about you, *amigo*." He took a sip of his latte. "So, have you heard from . . ."

"Layla?" Max replied.

"Ah, no. Veronica."

"Oh. We talked . . . a little. Like I told you, she says we need distance. I'm still not sure what happened."

"Did you ask her what she wanted?"

"Maybe she wants a rugged individualist," Max said.

"*Thattaboy*," Roger declared. "*Amigo*, you can't win with chicks like Veronica. They go all out trying to change a dude into their ideal mate. Then, after you've morphed into the submissive pussy you thought they wanted, they dump you. They know that the alpha male of their dreams would never put up with their self-loathing. This is tricky shit, so stop beating yourself up. Plus, women in the big city have busy lives. They don't have much use for us guys except when they snuggle in front of the tube or get horny."

"At least I don't need batteries," Max laughed, shaking his head.

"You need to keep moving. Let's try something new to take your mind off your mistakes."

"Gee, thanks, coach."

Roger ignored him. "How about knitting? There's this joint downtown where the chicks hang out to stitch and bitch. We can take a class."

"Do the alpha dogs knit?"

"Yes, *amigo*. It's about gravitas, and taking risks, and not giving a shit. When those needle-clacking lonely hearts see two studly guys practicing their art, they'll be all over us. You can knit Uncle Roger a sweater."

"I don't need to purl a pair of cabled booties to meet women."

"But you need to if you want to get laid," Roger said. When Max didn't respond, Roger added, "So what's new at Hornswoggle? Are they still working you like a farm animal?"

"Well, I have a new boss. I haven't met him yet, but he sends me dozens of e-mails every day. I'm constantly revising my revenue projections for him instead of building Layla's business."

"Just ignore him and do what old Henry Goodson taught us. 'Own the client relationship.' Then the new *el jefe* can't fuck with you. Plus, you already have both hands full with Layla, and that ain't bad."

"This guy has already fired two senior account people and hasn't replaced them."

"More opportunities for you to shine," Roger said. "That's why they're paying you the big bucks. My bankroll didn't make weight until I left Goodson."

"Maybe this is my wake-up call. At Goodson, I ran the business and we produced great creative. That reminds me, Henry's still in the hospital."

"That's too bad," Roger said. "Henry's a good dude." He checked his watch. "Hey, *amigo*, I need to finish a few things before I head up to the stadium. Sorry about your ticket. Clients again. I'll make it up to you. Promise."

"Of course," Max said evenly.

"I'll represent for both of us tonight. *Ciao*."

Max strolled down the hallway and overheard a group of colleagues fretting over an impending crisis on a new brand of potato chips. He smiled to himself, wondering what kind of calamity could possibly be looming for bags of salty snacks. Moving at a crisp pace, he nodded to the eager smiles and "hi-how-are-you's" from the fresh-faced account coordinators penned in the rows of cubicles leading to his office. Max liked these energetic young workers, knowing that many of them had been handed their entry-level positions by virtue of being the spawn of a client or an agency business partner.

Since taking the job, Max had witnessed an underlying sense of paranoia from his peers that permeated even the most mundane day-to-day dealings. When he'd ask a fellow account director about their business, the answer was served up mannequin-like, in the same flavor of vanilla.

"Things are great."

"My client is so awesome."

"They loved our ideas."

The transparent "I love my job" mantras that HHI's employees parroted sounded like they were read from cue cards. And Max understood. There was always the possibility of being overheard—or worse, being wrong. During departmental meetings, Max listened to the politically charged agendas of the top executives. This was a dramatic change from the weekly free-for-alls at Goodson. As the leader of his team at Hornsby Hammerhead, Max constantly encouraged his staff to introduce fresh ideas, but his subordinates offered little and waited for him to lead the way. It was safer to agree, even if they secretly believed he was wrong and hoped he'd fail.

Max plopped down in his chair, opened his calendar, and fluttered his lips with a long exhale. He was slammed for the entire week through seven o'clock Friday evening. Foremost in his thoughts was Kent Gloss, Hornsby Hammerhead International's newest Executive Vice President, and Max's new boss. Gloss had recently joined the agency under a fanfare of press, following his meteoric rise at a rival shop. He'd built a reputation around a bare-knuckled management style and an impressive record of new business wins, and was considered one of the top young rainmakers in the industry. He was also notorious for manipulating the media. He'd been dogged by rumors that he often leaked negative information about the competition—inaccurate reports that weren't debunked until after the damage had been done. But he kept winning new business and that was all that mattered.

Gloss called meetings when it suited him—at any hour, on any day. He phoned executives early Sunday mornings and arranged conference calls for Saturday afternoons. He was a brash Brit in his early forties who was driven to succeed at any cost. In his current state of mind, Max was apprehensive about meeting Gloss the next morning. At six forty-five, Max shut down his laptop and then lost himself in the crush of people on Madison Avenue.

As he walked down the fourth floor corridor of Beth Israel Medical Center, Max heard laughter emanating from the room at the end of the hall. When he reached the doorway, two nurses stood giggling next to Henry Goodson's bed. Henry was propped up, holding court with the women. The Yankees game flickered silently from the television perched across the room.

"So you're telling me that no one's ever drunk champagne from a bedpan?" the man with the gentle eyes and white goatee asked. The women broke into laughter again as one of them placed a dinner of steamed chicken with brown rice onto Henry's plastic tray.

Seeing Max at the doorway, Henry raised his arms in a welcoming pose. "Ladies, this is Max Hallyday, one of New York's top account executives. Max, say hello to my guardian angels."

The two middle-aged women smiled broadly as they greeted him. After exchanging pleasantries and refilling Henry's jug of water, the nurses waved goodbye and returned to their rounds. Henry looked up warmly as Max approached. Despite his sallow complexion and confinement to the hospital bed, Henry's eyes were clear and blue like his daughter's.

"Good to see you," Henry said. "How's the job?"

"Fine, fine. How are you feeling?"

Henry was spry and congenial at sixty-three years of age—a runner who, until recently, had still been logging fifteen miles a week. A survivor of the Sixties, he'd seen it all and experienced more than most. When it came time to make his mark on the system, Henry had emerged from the fray with his values intact and a thriving creative business.

"I'm doing okay, son," Henry replied in a measured, much-less-animated tone than usual.

Max studied his eyes. "Take your time and get well."

"They need me back at the agency," said Henry, catching his breath. "I want to get my ass out of here by the end of the week. I'm feeling much, much better."

Max looked around the drab hospital room. "So business is okay?"

"We're fine. Losing good people like you creates challenges, but we'll survive," said Henry, shifting his pillows beneath him. "This new job will be great experience for you. You can learn a lot at HHI. I see they've hired Kent Gloss. Smart."

"You know Gloss?"

Henry nodded. "I know of him. Despite what you may have read, he's a juggernaut for new business. He must be highly intelligent, and from what I know about his tactics, I wouldn't want him sniffing around my accounts," he said with a slight smile.

Max ran his hand across his mouth and took a seat.

"You look a little tense, Max. How about some prune juice?" Henry said, holding out a paper cup. "That'll loosen you up."

Max smiled. "I'm fine. Really."

"I hope so." He bumped his fist against Max's knee. "You know how valuable you were to me. I can't pretend otherwise. You did a great job managing the bubble gum . . ."

"Bobalooie."

"Right, you made a nice profit for us on that account, and it's keeping us afloat."

"Just doin' my job."

Henry waved dismissively. "You did more than your job. You put your heart into your work, and I'm not sure you know that. You built solid relationships—that's what counts. But, advertising's all about change. We'll keep growing. That's as soon as I get myself out of here," he said.

"You'll be home soon," Max said quietly, picking up the remote control. "Watching the game?"

"Of course. You don't think I was really listening to you? Turn up the volume."

Max smiled and clicked to the Yankees–Red Sox game. Yankee Stadium was sold out and the fans were fixated on this latest chapter of their rivalry. The moment after Mark Teixeira tied the score by depositing Josh Beckett's pitch into the right field bleachers, Max's cell phone lit up. He checked the number. It was Roger, calling to rub it in about attending the game. Max beamed when he heard the crowd's roar in the background.

"Red Sox suck!" Max barked into the receiver. "What's up, man? Hell of a game." He covered one ear, barely making out his friend's voice over the din of the stadium.

"Dude, where you at?" Roger yelled.

"With Henry. We're watching the game in his room."

"Tell him I said hi, and that he needs to get better right away. Sorry you couldn't make it. We're having a blast," Roger said.

When the crowd quieted down, Max heard a woman's voice in the background—and he froze. *No*, he thought. *It couldn't be.*

Roger said, "Hold on, the beer vendor's here." Max thought he heard the same woman's voice again before Roger returned and said, "Hey, dude, A-Rod's up. I need to see this. I'll call you tomorrow. *Ciao.*"

After Roger hung up, Max stared at the television, perplexed. Before replacing the phone in his leather jacket, he considered calling Roger back, but instead dialed Veronica's number. His call went to voice mail. He clenched his jaw while plinking out a text message.

V, it's Max. Just checking in 2 see how u r doing. What's up? He waited, never taking his eyes away from the message panel. When he was about to close the phone, she replied.

Hey! What's up?

Where r u? He hoped his intuition was wrong.

At the game.

Max felt his face turn red. He banged the railing on Henry's bed, causing the older man to sit up abruptly.

"Sorry, Henry. I can't believe they called that pitch a ball." *Glad u r having fun*, he typed. *Am I interrupting?*

There was a long pause. *With friends. Glad u r okay and not mad.*

Of course not. I'M SO FUCKING HAPPY!

???

Sorry, just wanted 2 say hi. Take care.

Max closed the phone. After some more small talk, Max made Henry promise him a speedy recovery and then said his goodbyes.

Back in his apartment, Max's mind flashed between images of his ex cavorting with his best friend and thoughts about his brief relationship with Cassidy. Seeing Henry in bed with a failing heart was depressing. Max grabbed a beer and dropped onto his couch. *Was I too abrupt with Cassidy? What was so wrong with having a relationship with the boss's daughter?* Henry had been cool about it. Max thought that he had cut off something that felt good, without really giving it a chance. But, he had made a choice—the hot girl, the hot gig. *Too late to go back now*, he reminded himself.

When his radio alarm blasted him out of bed at five fifteen, Max dragged himself to the bathroom and fired up the shower jets all the way. This was a key meeting that required focus. Aware of Gloss's powerful position, Max wanted to be viewed as an indispensable member of his team. He wondered if Gloss would want him working on new business. Under normal circumstances, a new hire like Max would be given time to get his account running smoothly before being pressured into additional duties. But nothing at HHI was "normal circumstances."

While toweling off, he couldn't shake his discomfort with his new agency. The environment seemed toxic—maybe too toxic—but for now, Max was determined to make it work. After forty crisp push-ups, he quickly dressed, and with his hair still wet, tore open a Clif Bar on his way out the door.

Max didn't waste time searching for a cab. Like any savvy New Yorker, he knew that when it rains, taxis vanish like dreams. The E train was almost empty when it pulled into the 34th Street station. Max sat alone, attempting to translate the Spanish language ad for a roach control product. When he exited the subway, his blazer and pants were damp and his stomach was knotted up. But when he entered HHI's world headquarters, Max rolled his shoulders back and reminded himself that he was a vice president at Manhattan's hottest advertising agency.

Studying his face in the mirrored walls of the elevator, he saw how it was changing from boyish good looks to a more chiseled, masculine countenance. He tugged down the lapels of his jacket. This was his moment to shine. When the elevator doors slid open to the thirty-eighth floor, he walked confidently toward the corner office.

Gloss's stone-faced assistant inspected him and then traced his finger down his planner. "Hmm, I don't see anything. Oh wait, here it is." He buzzed his superior. "Mr. Hol-i-day. Yes, he's late. Shall I send him in anyway?"

Max glanced at his watch. Six thirty sharp. He narrowed his eyes. "It's Hallyday, by the way," he said as the assistant gestured toward the door.

Kent Gloss was seated behind a large desk in the far corner of the spacious room. Thick curtains were draped across the windows, rendering the office dark except for a small lamp glowing on Gloss's desk. An oversized framed print with THINK in bold letters hung directly across from Gloss on an otherwise bare wall. Gloss was hunched over his speakerphone in the midst of a caffeinated rant. His buzz cut compensated for a dramatically receding hairline and flecks of gray at the temples, and his sharp, pointed features were restrained behind black-framed glasses. He was stylishly dressed in a tightly-buttoned black suit. Sensing Max's presence, Gloss turned and pointed to the chair in front of his desk. Max slowly entered the office, listening to Gloss's call.

"Yes, Crimmins, the information I gave you is one hundred percent accurate. Another scoop for you, mate," Gloss said sharply. "Now, about those seats for the Dalai Lama benefit in September. Yes, you heard me correctly. First row for His Holiness." He examined his cuticles while listening to the voice on the other end of the line. "Blast it, Crimmins! It's three months away. Get them." Gloss frowned, hanging up the phone. "Bloody trade press." He looked down and scribbled some notes.

His Holiness? Max wondered, glancing around Gloss's office. Its sheer size and the furnishings were impressive. There were two sets of handcrafted miniature soldiers displayed on a table adjacent to Gloss's massive desk. One of the armies was British. The other appeared to be Huguenots. Max ran the tip of his finger over the helmet of one of the soldiers. He looked up to find Gloss sizing him up from behind his desk.

Gloss was thin, but wiry, and his movements were rapid and bird-like. His stare was intense, reminding Max of a crow. Gloss reached his boney white hand across the desk. Max shook it, searching Gloss's hard black eyes for something to read in them, but they were blank.

"Don't touch those," Gloss scolded, nodding to the toy soldiers.

"Oh, sorry. They're cool."

"Yes, they are. So Holiday, you're the new man on Peacock."

Max wasn't sure if this was a question. "It's Hallyday," he replied.

"Of course. Let's not waste time then. I have a hard stop at seven," Gloss said, leaning back in his chair. "All right—the drinks sector is expanding rapidly and adding these supposedly healthy ingredients is fucking brilliant. Right, mate?"

"Yes, and we're working on new campaigns . . ."

"I know," Gloss said, waving him off. "I've had a look at the ideas. Not a bad start, but you need to buckle down."

Max was surprised Gloss had already reviewed his account's creative work on his own. As he watched the impassive look on the Brit's face, he knew that connecting with his new boss and developing a rapport with him was going to be a challenge. Gloss wanted something, and it wasn't about becoming Max's new friend.

"I see you have a solid background in the sweets sector, Holiday. They tell me you doubled the billings with your client at Goodson."

Max smiled tightly and shifted in his seat.

"You're aware that HHI will benefit greatly as soon as we establish a presence in the category?"

"Sweets?"

"Yes, Holiday. Sweets. We need a confectionery account, and with your experience, you're the man to go get it. Any ideas?"

Max braced himself. "Tooka Wooka Inc. might be in the market for a new agency."

"Tooka Wooka is shite. They only spent a few million last year. How's your relationship with Bobalooie?"

"They have a long-standing partnership with Goodson."

"How solid can it be after their top account man left the agency, eh?" Gloss asked, getting a cocky tone. "I checked the figures. You did some job there and *your new agency* can use revenues like that."

"I don't think Bobalooie's looking to change agencies."

"Don't you agree that having our resources at their disposal would benefit them? We can do it all for them—the adverts, PR, digital, social media. One-stop shopping."

Max wasn't enjoying Gloss's line of questioning, but there was truth in what he was suggesting. Bobalooie's management had not been pleased about Max's departure and they made sure that Henry became aware of their concerns. They didn't have time for loyalty.

"Holiday, I know you're a company man. And I'm sure you don't wish anything negative for your former agency. But you're on my team now. And I have to feed our shareholders and their bloody bottom line or we're all fucked. I can see you're busy with Peacock, but I need more from you. I want that Bobalooie account in this agency by the end of the year. Right?" He glanced at his oversized watch. "Bio break, mate."

Max's eyebrows shot up. He hesitated, unsure how to respond.

"The *loo*, Holiday," he said dismissively. "Now—think about what we discussed and get started. I want that bubbly gum account in this agency. Oh, by the way, welcome aboard, mate. Cheers," he said, rising from his chair and herding Max out of his office.

CHAPTER 4

On a bright Sunday morning, Roger Fox winked at the doorman on his way out of a faceless high-rise on East 80th Street and York Avenue. He stretched out his long arms, yawning, and walked west toward his pad across Central Park. It had been a long night.

Roger loved weekend mornings in the city, especially after spending the night in a beautiful woman's bed. As he sauntered along the quiet city streets, he passed blocks of upscale shops and restaurants, beauty salons, and creature comforts that attracted a significant portion of the more than half a million single women living alone in New York City. Despite the pricey high-rise rentals and condos, women from all over the world continued to pour into Manhattan in record numbers. Roger laughed to himself, thinking, *Keep 'em coming.* He'd spent the past ten years exploiting these gals. For a hit-and-run artist like Roger, they were targets wearing their hearts on designer sleeves, and they couldn't be easier to pick out if they had bull's-eyes painted on their sling backs.

Before last night, he'd never experienced a hint of uncertainty about bedding a new woman. For Roger, sex was clinical: a cut-and-dried process. And although he found the Upper East Side an especially fertile hunting ground, Roger picked up women everywhere.

Like a young boy, he kicked an empty beer can as he padded along, recalling his recent conquests. Until last night, they had been so easy. Like last weekend, at a hotel bar in Murray Hill, he'd seduced a lonely business traveler in from Ohio, hoping for romance in the big city.

Upstairs in her room, while occasionally glancing at a Telly Savalas movie, Roger had happily ravaged the weary traveler. She'd moaned while crouched on all fours, stripped down to her pair of heels and a thong.

And on Tuesday, he'd finally gotten his revenge on that priggish media buyer who delighted in flaunting her power over him, when after hours, her flirty assistant gave Roger a blow job while he sat smiling in her boss's chair. Then, on Thursday, the surgically enhanced divorcée at his gym—the one having trouble with the settings on the hip and thigh machine, had come home with him. After smoking a joint, Roger gave her an oily massage and soon had her writhing around his king-sized bed. For Roger, as long as the women caused that stirring sensation below his waist, life was good.

In bed, Roger was the master of the game. He would first synch his energy to his conquest, carefully working her body with soft, sensual caresses until she was primed for his onslaught. He always waited for the perfect moment—when she'd exhale and surrender to her desires for passion and true love. That's when Roger would sink into her and build slowly with deep, confident strokes. Once the woman let go, he'd step up the pace and overwhelm her until it was an out-of-body experience, with Roger observing both the woman and his performance. For him, it was always the same: surreal and empty. Inwardly, he wished that he, too, could experience the pleasure he was witnessing. However, Roger remained locked outside, lacking emotion or joy beyond the fleeting elation from the powerful surges that flowed through his muscular body when he climaxed. Somewhere deep down, Roger was aware of his inability to be open to love, and he desperately wanted that to change. But for now, love was elusive—a way of forgetting.

But this Sunday morning was different. Last night he'd met his match—a woman capable of seizing the power. She was a beauty and she knew how to take charge, never letting him turn her into a conquest. She was hot, but she had maintained her cool, even when letting herself go. This one was different.

In Roger's eyes, the quality of the sex determined his potential for love. And on this beautiful spring morning, Roger was feeling optimistic when he entered Central Park, where the trees and spring flowers were bursting with promise. As he continued along his path west, he whistled, "The Girl from Ipanema" and decided that he wanted to see her again. Definitely.

Last night's date had begun like many of his Saturday night affairs. Roger offered to pick her up at her place, but she insisted that they meet at an upscale Mexican restaurant in the Flatiron District. She strode into the bar at seven sharp, where Roger was nursing a margarita and checking out the bubbling scene. Her arrival shifted his awareness. All heads turned as she moved gracefully across the room, expecting and accepting the stares of both the men and women at the bar. The crowd parted as she made her way directly to Roger, where she planted her moist, full lips on his cheek and lightly cradled the back of his neck with her hand. She gave him a light squeeze and gently smiled.

Her pearl-white teeth lit up a wickedly delicious mouth. She was dressed in a body-hugging emerald halter that outlined her full, per-fectly shaped breasts. Her lush blonde hair, parted to the side, fell onto well-proportioned shoulders and set off clear chestnut eyes. Her arms were well toned and her tight black jeans accentuated legs made even longer by a pair of open-toed Blahniks with sharp heels. She had Roger's full attention.

Their margaritas were strong and flavorful. As they waited for their entrees, Roger sat charged with sexual tension. He hoped their small talk over dinner would serve as a prelude for the naughty sug-gestions he planned to whisper in her ear later following drinks at a nearby lounge.

They knew many of the same people in their business. Selling advertising space was a lucrative but highly competitive game. After first crossing paths during Roger's short tenure at *Face Front* maga-zine, they worked for competing media properties.

After their entrees arrived, she smiled and took a sip of her drink. "I can't understand why you're still selling print. Magazines are going the way of the dinosaur. Digital advertising has taken over."

"No doubt. Digital sales are growing like wildfire, but ads are ads. The last time I passed a newsstand, people were buying magazines. And as soon as I close a few more key accounts, *Plates* will be the hot-test publication in the epicurean category."

"But isn't it difficult for a new publication to break through? *Plates* is off to a good start," she said, "but it could take years to become a household name. Can you afford to wait?" He feigned wincing, so she added lightly, "Sorry. I'm sure you'll do fine."

He watched her closely, considering her comments. *Does she have an agenda?* His decision to stick with selling print advertising was debatable, but he enjoyed the wining, dining, and schmoozing that came with the territory. Maybe the magazine world didn't move fast enough for her. So what? It was sales, and Roger could sell anything. Even her. Tonight. She was so damn hot that he didn't care if her comments had been pointed.

"We'll both kick ass," he said assuredly. "Another margarita? These are *muy excellente*. I can taste the fresh kiwi. All-natural is a major trend for spirits," he said before downing what was left of his drink from the salt-rimmed glass. "They're mixing booze with healthy ingredients now, or so I've heard," he added, immediately regretting his comment.

"One *muy excellente* margarita is enough. My trainer would kill me," she said, filling her lungs so her breasts protruded. "So tell me about these new drinks. Which company is selling them?"

Roger rubbed his nose, stalling to come up with a response. "I'm not sure, but they sound interesting. I'm sure everyone will be selling them."

"But, who is the first mover? Where did you hear this . . . in the trades?"

"Yeah, maybe . . . I think so. You'd have to ask someone who works in the category."

She narrowed her eyes and smiled. "You're not holding out on me, are you, Roger? That would make you a very naughty boy."

Roger grinned, considering the prospects. *Oh good*, he thought. *She wants something. Leverage!* "I'll see what I can find out," he said, signaling for the check. "Let's get out of here and grab a nightcap. The Darby sound good?"

"I've got a better idea. Let's go back to my place."

He searched the room for the waiter and pulled out his wallet. It didn't make a difference where they were going, as long as they ended up in bed.

Roger took mental notes as he entered her apartment. The eggshell white walls were lined with her own acrylic paintings. She favored vivid colors, but the artwork lacked an underlying energy. Set against the white, the paintings merely added a semblance of texture and brightness to an otherwise chilly living space. Most of the tastefully chosen furniture was made of deep walnut, but the pieces were larger than the rooms could comfortably accommodate. Roger thought they'd look better in a house. After she excused herself, Roger wandered into the kitchen and looked around. When he opened her refrigerator, the bright light hit his eyes. He crouched down, frowning as he canvassed the glass shelves past the single-serve packages of tofu, bottles of Perrier, containers of low-fat yogurt, and an opened bottle of Chardonnay. Then he spotted her two courtesy six packs of beer—Corona Light and a German import. A promising sign, but unfortunately there were no ingredients for throwing together a hearty breakfast or even a sandwich. Roger closed the door and called out, "Hey, do you have anything to drink besides beer?"

"There's a bottle of Goose in the freezer. Is that okay?" she called from another room. He smiled while pulling the frosty vodka from the icebox and two shot glasses from her cabinet. He stopped, now hearing a rhythmic clicking in the hallway. As the sounds grew louder, he quickly poured two shots. He turned and she was standing in the doorway, hands on her hips, wearing a black lace bra with a matching garter belt ensemble, and a pair of five-inch stilettos.

She flashed a wicked look. "Save room for dessert?"

His eyes scanned her up and down, admiring the smooth curves that complimented her lightly muscled arms and legs. He took a deep breath and then smiled while holding up a shot glass in each hand. This wasn't Roger's usual Saturday night fare. This was Veronica Sparks at the height of her powers—and Roger was going to spend the night exploring her magnificent body.

CHAPTER 5

After leaving his office, Max stopped at his apartment and took out his bike to ride along the Hudson River Park to Chelsea Piers. The skies had cleared following the rain, and a glowing sun brought a jolt of energy sorely needed by the city after another long winter that had painted Manhattan's stony face a shade grayer than usual. As he pedaled, Max considered the recent events at work and in his personal life and tried to keep things in perspective. Once the creative teams came up with a campaign for Layla's line of drinks, new revenue would flow into the agency. That might temper Gloss's fixation with the Bobalooie Bubble Gum account, and maybe he'd leave Max alone to build his business.

Max was still bothered by Veronica's text and hearing a voice that sounded disturbingly similar to hers when Roger had called from the Yankees game. Of course, it didn't prove anything. They could have attended the game separately or been part of a group of media cronies out carousing and burning through their expense accounts. *But, God—stabbed in the back by both of them at once?* Just the thought made him sick.

As the rush-hour traffic whizzed past Chelsea Piers, Cassidy greeted Max with a hug, holding him an extra moment. "Everything all right?" she asked.

He smiled. "Better and better."

With the water temperature in the frigid fifties, they changed into rubber wet suits, fleece top liners, paddle tops, and sneakers before reconvening dockside. Max took notice of Cassidy's athletic figure, but shook his head when he saw her Red Sox cap.

"How can you wear that?" he asked, pointing at the traitorous display on her head.

"Hey buddy, I'm from the other half of Connecticut," she responded, laughing.

Cassidy spent several minutes explaining the basics of kayaking to Max. In the background, a line of town cars turned into the piers, dropping off executives destined for an evening cruise around the Hudson on the corporate vessels docked along the waterfront. As he listened, Max watched the motorcade crawling behind Cassidy, thinking he recognized a few agency types meeting their clients at the dock. As Cassidy stressed the importance of maintaining balance, a sleek black limo crept by and stopped at the curb. The voluptuous figure of the woman emerging from the vehicle looked familiar, and for good reason. It was Layla Korindopolos stepping out of the backseat. She straightened her dress and slipped on her sunglasses while hurrying to the dock. Max held his hand up to Cassidy.

"What?"

"That's my client over there," he said, pointing at the dock.

Cassidy turned to catch a glimpse of Layla's backside as she pranced up a ramp leading onto one of the yachts.

"In the Chanel suit?"

"Yeah. Guess everyone's got the same idea today."

"So let's get out there. Ready?"

"I was born ready."

"Grab that handle and let's shove off."

After sliding their kayaks into the murky Hudson, Cassidy led the way as Max paddled close behind. She turned back to him frequently while navigating toward deeper waters. Max was a good athlete, but this was a new sport that required coordination, not just upper body strength.

"How's it going?" she called, watching him gamely struggle to keep pace.

"I'm cool. Let's paddle down to the Jersey Shore."

"You're doing great," she said. "Be careful of the currents and wakes. They're pretty random."

"No problem," Max said, as his vessel teetered beneath him.

Pretty soon Max was struggling to keep up with Cassidy's experienced strokes. Noticing him falling behind, Cassidy slowed down. Once he caught up, they skimmed along the water together, matching stroke for stroke. The late day sun sparkled off the river, bathing their silhouettes in shimmering light. They stopped a few hundred yards from the river's edge to admire the city's skyline and smiled at each other before resuming their paddling.

"I can see why you like to come out here," he said. "I thought I was fit, but I'm already winded. You're in awesome shape."

"I'm glad you like it . . . the kayaking," she said with a short laugh.

Their view to the south was partially obstructed by the buildings making up Chelsea Piers. As they glided along, they heard the bellowing of a large yacht opening its throttle as it pulled out from the southern tip of the piers where the larger boats docked. The roar of diesel engines and the accompanying swells wobbled their kayaks. Despite Cassidy's calls to Max to follow her along the coastline, Max lost control and his kayak turned sharply toward the yacht. Fighting the chop, Max tried his best to maintain balance while drifting into deeper waters. But he'd gone too far off course and was caught in the path of a tugboat boring directly down at him. The tugboat's captain saw the lone paddler and cut back his engine, but it was too late, and he barely avoided Max's kayak, now wobbling precariously in a series of cascading wakes.

When the water surged up against the small fiberglass craft, Max saw Cassidy wave at him and paddle furiously in his direction. He tried to turn his kayak, but another wave hit the aft side and rocked it. That was the last thing he remembered before he capsized.

Max tried staying calm under the water, but quickly found himself flailing his arms. Although he was wearing a life vest, he was trapped inside the capsized kayak. While struggling to set himself free, he held his breath and felt his lungs tighten. He swallowed a mouthful of water, began to choke, and then flashed forward to tomorrow's humiliating *New York Post* headline: "Ad Man Dies Ass Up." He wriggled, trying to free his vacuum-sealed legs and saw red, then gray. As his world darkened, he thought he heard a voice calling from above. He felt a hand grasp his wrist and hold it firmly, which somehow helped him slide out of the kayak. When his head broke the water's surface, he spit out water and gasped. As he sucked for air, his chest ached, but he was all right. Cassidy maintained her grip on his wrist as he bobbed in the water.

"Max, *Max*! Are you okay?" she called out. He nodded weakly. "Grab the oar," she said. "I'll get your kayak. The preserver will keep you afloat."

Treading water, he relaxed his body and regained his composure. He watched Cassidy catch his kayak from ten yards away and hold it steady with her oar.

"Max, can you make it over here?"

He took another deep breath before slowly swimming to her. Throughout the ordeal, the tugboat idled nearby. After two unsuccessful attempts, Max finally climbed back into his kayak. The tugboat's crew had amassed along the railing, looking down at him and shaking their heads. After the captain waved, he slowly opened up the throttle and chugged off. Max looked upriver and glimpsed a yacht in the distance steadily churning along a northern course. He made out the name: the *SS Apperitivo*, *Plates* magazine's corporate yacht.

"So I guess we won't be kayaking together again anytime soon," Cassidy said between spoonfuls of Manhattan clam chowder.

Max placed his empty mug on the table and searched for the waiter. They were seated in a booth at the brewery located in the sprawling facility, nursing bowls of hot soup and frosty steins of beer.

"Your butt looked cute sticking out of the water," she added.

"I try to look my best when I'm drowning. And thanks again for saving my ass," he said, crushing a handful of oyster crackers over his chowder. "So how's your dad? They let him go home yet?"

"He feels better, but . . ." She stirred her soup. "Your visit cheered him up, by the way. He really cares about you."

"I care about him," Max said, digging his spoon into the steaming bowl.

"You haven't been yourself lately," she asked. He shrugged, and she added, "You need to forget about her. You can do better."

"Than Victoria? You think so, huh?" he said. "Hell, I should have known it was coming. For the past few months all we did was argue about stupid things."

"Is that what you want?" Cassidy asked, placing her spoon on the edge of her plate. He looked at her and she looked back, and for a moment they both remembered what it was like when they were together. And it was good. Cassidy waited for Max to say something, but he didn't. She sighed inwardly, rearranged her features, and put on her friend face. "So, are you finding time to write?" she asked.

"Nope. I'm too damn busy now. HHI isn't what I expected. Maybe I shouldn't have taken the job, but I've got to make it work. It's like you always say; I need to find time for other things."

Cassidy studied him and then tapped her spoon on the table. "The column for my magazine," she said emphatically.

"Ah jeez—not again."

"C'mon, I need someone to give women the inside scoop on men in the city. Like how they date and how players like Roger operate."

Max gazed at a boat slowly pulling out from its slip and shook his head. "A column about him?"

"Guys like Roger take whatever they want and don't care who they hurt. Think about it. Have you considered that he might have been on that boat with your client?"

"That's crazy," he said flatly.

"Do the math. She shows up at the corporate dock and the next thing you know, it's ahoy matey, there blows the *SS Apperitivo*."

"Oh, come on. *Plates* throws those little get-togethers on their yacht all the time. Plus, Layla doesn't impress easily. She's been there, done that."

"Yeah, well she was *here*, and his company's boat was out *there*," she said, pointing toward the river. "And where's Roger? Didn't you tell me that you could go kayaking tonight because Roger canceled on you? And that he was entertaining a client? Think about it."

"You've been watching too much *Law and Order*," he said, fiddling with the plastic wrapper from his crackers.

"Hmm," she said, half-smirking. "Then why did you tell me about that phone call from the Yankees game?"

Max tilted his head. "C'mon, Cass."

She reached over and touched his hand. "Max, you know I'm right. This could work. You can use the column to turn things around."

Max silently examined Cassidy's long, slender fingers resting on his hand. She quickly moved her hand back to her lap. "Roger says his rough riding days are coming to an end," he said.

"Then you need to get started."

"What if these women don't like what they read? They only want to hear the good stuff, and this won't be pretty."

"Just tell the truth. It'll be a public service. You can even write about dating women like Veronica," she said. "I'm sure Roger knows all about her type."

Max responded with a scowl.

"Oh, I didn't mean it that way," she added, biting her lip.

"So, all I do is hang with Roger and expose his tricks for getting girls into the sack? And all the women who read your magazine will want to thank me personally?"

"Something like that, but let's not get ahead of ourselves," she said.

Max peered into Cassidy's eyes. "You really want me to do this, don't you?"

"Yes—for me, and for yourself, too."

He swallowed some beer thoughtfully, and then said, "You can't put my name on it."

"No problem. We'll use a pseudonym. How about Dick?"

"Very funny."

"Max? Is it a yes or no?"

"For you?" he asked.

She nodded. "For me."

"Okay, for you I'll do it."

"Really?"

"Yep," he said, smiling back. She leaned over and planted a kiss on his cheek before adding, "And you'll be reporting directly to me."

"You've thought this out, haven't you?"

"You bet," she said.

"I see. So what do we call this column?"

"Hmm, how about 'The Modern Man's Dating Tips for Women'?"

"Is this for *The Saturday Evening Post*?"

She punched his arm. "You're the writer," she said, laughing. "Come up with something."

Max mulled it over while sipping his beer. Then his eyes lit up and he snapped his fingers. "How about 'The Guys' Guy's Guide to Love'?"

"The guy's guide to what? Say that again."

"The Guys' Guy's Guide . . . to Love."

Cassidy mouthed each word slowly and grinned. "You need to get dunked in the Hudson more often."

 CHAPTER 6

Roger awoke with a pulsating headache and his stomach churning from the previous night's sugary cocktails. He rolled over and rubbed his belly, opening an eye to check the alarm clock. In two hours he'd be playing golf with Max at Leaping Frog Country Club in Neptune, New Jersey. He pushed himself out of bed and washed down three Ibuprofen with a can of Red Bull. At eight fifteen, a bleary-eyed Roger was behind the wheel of his silver turbocharged Saab, emerging from the Lincoln Tunnel under crystal-blue skies. Max slouched in the passenger seat, sipping a large Dunkin' Donuts Coolatta. As Roger opened the sun roof, Max flipped through Roger's digital library in search of road music.

"What are you up for?" Max asked, scrolling through Roger's iPod Classic digital music collection. "Kings of Leon? Raconteurs? Jay-Z?"

"Too stimulating. I still have a headache."

"Perfect," Max said. "How about a Bavarian polka festival?"

"Save that for the ride back to the city—provided you break one hundred. Pick something mellower."

"Let's see," Max said. "Zamfir, king of the pan flute?"

Roger laughed. "Well, he is a classic, but keep scrolling. There's a Bobby Darin playlist in there."

Max slid Roger's iPod into the console. A moment later, a crisp version of "Hello Young Lovers" bellowed out of the speakers. Max adjusted his golf cap and took a long sip of his coffee-flavored drink.

"So how are you feeling after your Poseidon adventure the other day?" Roger asked.

"I'm taking a break from kayaking," Max replied before turning to Roger. "Listen, we already covered this, but Layla's my client, my only client, and I can't have you sneaking around with her behind my back. You can sell her pages in *Plates* after I nail down a new campaign. No new advertising means no ads for your magazine. Got that?"

"Of course, *amigo*. My bad. I should have told you."

"Okay. If you screw things up with her, we both lose."

"Why make it sound like that? I was looking out for our best interests. I wanted to get her pumped up about working with you after your meltdown at that restaurant."

Max stirred his drink. "Knowing that you have my best interests in mind is comforting," he said evenly. "Now stay away from her."

Roger looked at Max out of the corner of his eye, and for the next few minutes neither one spoke as Bobby Darin reprised the chorus to "Mack the Knife."

"So now that you're a *swingle* again, how's it going with the ladies?" Roger asked, breaking the silence.

Max pushed back his hat. "Not sure. I'm still recovering from being run over by a Mack truck named Veronica."

"You'll be fine," Roger assured him. "Has she been in touch?"

Max arched an eyebrow as Roger pushed down on the accelerator and bolted past an SUV. "I told you," Max said, "Veronica said we need distance . . . and I keep asking myself if we were really in love."

"Or lust. Maybe you just liked sleeping with her," Roger suggested.

"That's an understatement. Now the snakes in the grass will come slithering out of their holes and go after her . . . don't you think?" Max said, eying Roger.

Roger revved the engine and shifted gears, his eyes fixed on the road. "She probably scares most guys off," he said. "Women. They're predictable in their unpredictability. Out of the blue they'll turn on you—sometimes it's because you're not paying enough attention to them; other times it's because you're paying too much attention—as you learned. Most guys are clueless. They never see the end coming until it's too late and it's been staring them in the face for months."

"Tell me more. I like pain."

Roger chuckled. "Hey, *amigo*. Ever hear about the Seven S's?"

Max shook his head and sucked the bottom of his drink through the plastic straw.

"Remember that Hawaiian chick I told you about—the one I met at the sales meeting?"

"Yeah. Her orgasms were so explosive, housekeeping had to bring up extra towels."

"That's her—the gusher. The second I saw her, I knew she loved to bone."

"How's that?" Max sat up slightly.

"Her ankle bracelet . . . and that fuck-me tattoo spread across her lower back. *Bull's-eye*. Dead giveaways. Anyway, she told me that her girlfriends keep this list to decide who they sleep with."

"The Seven S's?" Max asked. Roger nodded and Max said, "Okay, cut the suspense. Let's have them."

"I'm not sure if they're in any special order, but here they are: single, smart, sexy, sensitive, sweet—let's see, that's five—sensible and self-sufficient."

Max mentally ticked them off and asked, "What's the difference between sensitive and sweet?"

"Excellent question, Luke Skywalker. Sensitive means paying attention to *her* needs, not being a wuss and crying over *The Lion King*. Sweet means being nice—you know, to old folks and small animals. But it can also be code for pussy-whipped. Remember, they actually don't like that."

"Right. I think she forgot an S."

"An eighth S? Give it up."

"Self-assured."

"Nice. See, you're all over this. We just need to hook you up."

"Maybe I'll pick up a few moves from the master—that's if he hasn't already retired his lightsaber."

"You don't need my bullshit to get laid," Roger said. "You're Horndog and Hammerhead's newest bull shark."

"I'm serious. How about a little skull session after golf? I need some nuggets. You know, the good stuff."

"We'll see. I wouldn't want to corrupt my little grasshopper," said Roger, breaking into a wide grin while darting through traffic. "Beautiful fucking day. Let's play golf."

While Bobby Darin lamented about his dream lover, Max slipped on his sunglasses and slid down in his seat. Five hours later, he and Roger pulled their cart up to the eighteenth hole of Leaping Frog Country Club, where Max maintained a membership. After changing their name from Halevy when he arrived in New York, Max's father had traveled frequently on business and then died quickly following a vicious bout with pancreatic cancer when Max was in high school. His father had never found the time to properly teach Max the game. But he had loved competition and instilled in his only son the importance of believing in himself and being creative when faced with challenges. He constantly reminded Max to "make it happen." After his death, Max took a summer job at the driving range. He slapped balls after hours under the lights before finally scraping together the funds for a junior membership at Leaping Frog. Each year, Max would somehow find the cash to maintain his membership. It turned out to be a wise decision because when the club was sold, the new management upgraded it into one of the county's top courses.

On the final hole, Roger ripped his tee shot two hundred and sixty yards up the sloping fairway. Max, scrambling to break one hundred, pushed his drive into the right rough, but scrambled to hole in at five. After pitching his ball gently onto the green, Roger two-putted for par and pumped his fist triumphantly. On the ride back to the clubhouse, Roger tallied the scores, confident he'd won another twenty dollars from Max.

Roger's father had also been a golfer. He was Roger's mentor and course companion at Deal Country Club until his sudden death at age fifty-two. Roger still played golf intermittently, but had not retained the same passion for the game since his father's passing.

Roger counted Max's strokes. "Dude, what'd you shoot on seventeen?"

"Five, including the penalty stroke."

"Okay—you shot one hundred. Sorry, man."

"Let me see the card," Max said. After adding up the scores twice, he scoffed. "Better check your math on the front nine. I shot ninety-nine and you owe me twenty bucks."

Roger grabbed the card and totaled the scores twice before tossing it into the cart. "Damn, your handicap is too high," he said. "Next time I'm not giving you all those strokes. Let's grab some beers."

"Since you're buying . . ." Max said, hopping out of the cart.

Inside the clubhouse lounge, Roger and Max stood at the bar rehashing their round.

Roger waved to the peroxide blonde working the tap. "Two drafts. Frosty mugs."

After analyzing the back nine holes, Roger placed his sunglasses on the bar and signaled for another beer. Max switched to iced tea and ordered a turkey wrap.

When the bartender asked if Roger wanted anything from the kitchen, he shook his head.

"So, where were we before our round?" Max asked. "Discussing the seven or eight S's?"

"Yes, *yes*! Their little checklists. It's like *Jeopardy*. The dude with the most points keeps playing until some new guy beats his score. Did I ever e-mail you that article about portfolio dating?"

Max shook his head.

"Women segment men by type and deploy them as needed. Straight friend for lunch, mover for a hookup, et cetera."

"So, we're more specialized now. Like relief pitchers in baseball."

Roger nodded. "Yep, and women are intuitive, too. They've got this fucking hyper radar that tells them when something's not right. That's a problem."

"And maybe that's why *Charmed* is still airing on cable," Max mused.

"Ever ask divorced women when they realized their marriage wasn't going to work?

"Nope. Why?"

"Their answer's always the same—*when they were walking down the aisle*. Women have a sixth, seventh, and eighth sense."

"They see dead people?" Max asked in a loud whispering voice.

"Dead relationships. Women know the truth, sad as it is, but the little darlings still maintain hope that we'll change. That's *their* weakness," Roger said.

"Having faith?"

"They should know better. Men don't change."

"Some men evolve," Max offered.

"Really?" Roger scoffed at the notion. "If you're paying attention, did you notice that women communicate differently?"

"How so?"

"Say you go out with a woman three or four times, and for some crazy reason you never bust a move on her except for a few smooches at the end of the date. You know what she's thinking?"

"I'm gay?"

"No, she's thinking there's something wrong with *her*. She'll bring up sex, but she'll talk around the subject. Sex is totally her decision. She decides right away if she wants to sleep with you. So if she lets you stick around, it's up to you to make it happen. Of course, most guys blow it, but chicks are patient. They'll wait until the right guy convinces them to drop their drawers."

Max rubbed his chin, considering Roger's logic.

"But I digress," Roger continued, "what does a woman say to let you know she's ready?"

"For sex?"

Roger nodded and then knocked back his beer. "Remember, women love boning, but they play these games so they don't feel slutty."

"Maybe she'd ask me the same thing I'd ask her—do you want to have sex?"

"No. *No!*" Roger said, waving for another beer. "She'll say something like, 'Where do you see this relationship going?' That's code for 'Why don't you fuck me, dummy?' "

"I've actually been asked that . . . not the thing about dummies."

"And you thought she wanted you to sign your life away, when all she needed to know was if you'd stick around after she slipped off her thong."

"So what's the right answer?"

"It's whatever she needs to hear to get her to peel her panties. Make her feel special. Tell her you've never felt like you do when you're with her, but *always* leave yourself an out. Otherwise the dreaded commitment talk rears its ugly head. Avoid that at all costs."

"I'm sure you do," Max said, laughing and pounding on the bar. "What else?"

"Always notice three things about a woman—her shoes, her bag, and her hair."

"Really?"

"Yeah, women all have a deep relationship with food and with their hair. Forget about food, because that's when the 'Do you think I look fat?' talk surfaces. Never go there. You can mention their shoes and get a smile. And check out the bag to see if they have coin, but don't say anything about it."

"Why not?"

"That's so not alpha male. You get demerits for that."

"Oh."

"But always speak up if you notice even the slightest change in their hair. They lap that shit up."

"You are twisted, cynical, and fucking amazing." Max laughed out loud.

"Oh, I almost forgot. Gotta invest in the love bank."

"The love bank?"

"You can never make too many deposits into the love bank," Roger said. "The love bank is real, and again, it's all about the little things, like taking charge and planning the date—*cha-ching!* Or letting them vent about their jobs without solving their problems for them. They don't need us for that." Roger shook his head and mouthed "no." "We're there to listen, entertain, and make them feel beautiful. That's how you get laid."

"What's your secret to mastering the rules?"

"Chicks want to be swept off their feet, so I take charge of the situation. I maintain a laser focus on my leading lady of the moment and make things happen as quickly as possible. Then I move on to the rest of the herd."

"How considerate of you."

"Put away your violin, *amigo*. Women are way stronger than men. And you have no idea how brutal they can be to one another. They make sure we don't see the real ugly shit they pull, which is usually over some guy. If they seem uptight, it's because they've invested so much into the relationship. And most guys are so fucking self-absorbed that they miss out on all the love that could be coming their way." Roger glanced at his watch. "Gotta go. Why don't you come over tomorrow night? We'll down a few more brews and I'll reveal the secrets to online dating, Roger-style."

"You're still into that? I thought you were already the king."

"Every king needs a queen, and there are thousands of ladies-in-waiting online. Those dating sites are still the ultimate distribution system for female talent. Where else can you sit at home scratching your nuts, plinking at your laptop, and scoring dates with hot women? It's like fishing in well-stocked trout ponds in early spring. And it's always springtime online. Plus, there are no rules and—"

Max pushed the check in front of him. "Thanks, Roger. I had an awfully good time."

Once outside, they donned sunglasses and traipsed across the steaming asphalt parking lot.

"Why don't I drive?" Max asked, tossing his golf shoes in the trunk.

"No way," Roger said. "I'm cool."

"You've had five beers. Lemme drive."

"I've got Altoids in the car. Hop in, Buzzkill."

Roger could hold his alcohol, but Max knew better than to tempt fate on the roads of New Jersey. Roger patted Max's shoulder, assuring him that he was fine before sliding behind the wheel and gunning the engine.

As Roger backed out, Max remembered how they had met. It was during a high school junior varsity basketball game between Roger's Rumson squad and Max's Red Bank High School. Roger was a star forward and top scorer. Max was his team's point guard. He excelled at handling the ball and dishing out passes to his teammates. During a switch off, Max slid over to cover the taller Roger. The score was tied when Roger set up on the lane, waiting as the ball was passed his way. He caught it, pivoted, and turned, inadvertently driving an elbow into Max's face. Max's hands shot up, thinking his nose had been broken. His teammates charged the court and one threw a roundhouse right at Roger. He ducked sideways, avoiding the punch. It landed hard on the other side of Max's face. Then all hell broke loose.

During the mayhem, Roger threw his arm around Max, whose nose was spurting blood. Roger carefully led him to the sidelines and sat him down near the stands. Roger took off his jersey, held it to Max's face, and cracked jokes until the school physician arrived. Fortunately, Max's nose was only dislocated. After it was adjusted and bandaged, Max insisted on returning to the game to shoot his two free throws. He sank them both, but had to come out of the game again when blood began seeping from his nostrils. His team went on to win by a two-point upset. After the game, Roger congratulated Max for his gutsy performance, and they soon became friends. Roger found Max's integrity and determination intriguing, since he'd never been forced to tap his internal reserves the same way. And since things always seemed to fall into place for Roger, Max often wondered why the stars aligned for certain people. Despite their differences, the two young men maintained a strong connection partially driven by their competitive natures.

Instead of making the right onto the ramp for the Garden State Parkway, Roger turned left into a convenience store parking lot and hopped out. He returned toting a twelve pack of Yuengling beer under his arm.

Max protested. "You must be kidding."

"We'll be on the Parkway in a jiffy," Roger said, sliding behind the wheel and popping open a cold can.

Out of nowhere, a Neptune Township police cruiser zipped into the lot and blocked their exit. Roger's car was impounded an hour later. Max called for a taxi to take them to the train station. Roger brushed off the incident, assuring Max that his mother's boyfriend, a prominent local attorney, would straighten things out. Max nodded, but said nothing.

During the ride back to the city, the two men barely spoke. Max checked his phone, cringing each time another e-mail from Gloss showed up in his mailbox. When they exited Penn Station at Eighth Avenue, Max swung his golf bag over his shoulder and turned to his glum-faced friend.

"Hey, I just thought of a ninth S," Max said cheerfully.

Roger made a dour face. "You're getting good at this. What is it?"

Max stopped at the corner and grinned. "Sense of humor. See you tomorrow night."

CHAPTER 7

Stepping onto one of the three floors that housed HHI's creative department, Max was again struck by how quiet his new agency was compared to Goodson. The plastic plants and hermetically sealed windows were a far cry from the environment at his former employer. At Goodson, windows were opened, Frisbees sailed down the hall-way, long-legged interns on Rollerblades whizzed past his office, and whiffs of pungent smoke occasionally seeped out from under the doors of young creative teams brainstorming ideas for a new cam-paign. At Hornsby Hammerhead, a handful of high-powered suits called the shots. Max loved working with the creatives—art direc-tors, copywriters, producers, and the digital whizzes. If an agency were a bakery, they made the cookies. They came up with the ideas, and without them, there was no agency.

Max knew his role. He was the man in the middle, an enabler who set up the clients and his creative team for success. That was the job, and the perpetually revolving door of executive churn served as a constant reminder that advertising was a fickle, right-now business. The bottom line was that if his creative teams failed to come up with ideas he could sell, an account person—even one as talented as Max—could find himself out of a job. And right now, Max was on the clock to deliver the right campaign for Peacock Beverages' line of new-age spirits.

After reviewing the agency's creative reel, Max requested Bette Johnston, a creative director who'd produced a strong portfolio of ads for fragrances, beverages, and fashion. Bette was a well-put together lipstick lesbian who'd worked at HHI for the past decade. When Gloss took over, he viewed Bette as a carryover from the previous management and left her unassigned. She made too much money and it was a matter of time before she'd be pushed aside in favor of younger, more affordable talent.

When Max knocked on her open door, a fugue emanated from the music system on her console. Bette motioned him inside with a faint smile. She was dressed in a black linen tunic that offset her auburn hair and pale complexion. "So how's the booze business?" she asked. "Got any samples? It's five o'clock somewhere."

"Sorry, I'm dry right now. We don't have any product yet."

"So what are they called?"

Max cleared his throat. "For now, *Holy Spiritz*."

"Oh Jesus," she said dryly.

"Got a few minutes?"

"Sure." Bette doodled on a pad while Max walked her through the creative strategy for Peacock's marriage of clear spirits and new-age additives.

"How many campaigns do we need?" she asked.

"For now, three," Max began, rubbing his cheek. "I think we should explore concepts focused on the holistic aspects of the brand and the name, *Holy Spiritz*. Maybe you can tie them to heaven or nirvana or whatever."

"I asked you how many campaigns, not for your ideas."

"Sorry, but we're under the gun, and you and I need this to work," Max said, looking at Bette. "Can I share a few other potential directions with you?"

"Potential directions? You're something."

"We might try a second campaign that focuses on the ingredients. You know, 'the finest spirits made from glacial waters and winter wheat, expertly blended with nature's finest homeopathic blah, blah, blah.' "

Bette remained impassive. "What else?"

"That's all. But we'll need one more. Why don't you push the envelope and see what you come up with?"

She eyed him, tapping her pencil. "You're sure about that?"

Max wondered if challenging a wounded creative to go wild on a brand of alcohol was wise. "Yeah, go for it," he said. He closed his pad and stood up. "Bette, I don't think we want Gloss involved in this."

She allowed the corner of her mouth to curl upward. "I hear you. We might as well have some fun before we both get fired," Bette said.

When Max emerged from the 96th Street subway station, it was still light outside. Dressed in jeans and a plaid shirt, he walked north up Broadway toward Roger's digs on West End Avenue. He stopped by a deli and picked up some sandwiches and two coconut waters.

Roger met him at his door in a canary yellow polo shirt, maroon soccer shorts, and leather flip-flops. He was holding the neck of a half-empty bottle of Corona and an unlit joint dangled from the side of his mouth.

Max laughed as he gave Roger the once-over. "Where's the keg?" he said before following Roger inside where a Rat Pack–period Sammy Davis, Jr. song was bellowing from his state-of-the-art sound system.

Roger lived in a large corner one-bedroom on the twenty-second floor, with an expansive view across the Hudson River to New Jersey. The living room was well furnished with a fifty-inch LED television tuned to ESPN with the sound muted. A copy of *The New York Times* was strewn across Roger's oversized leather couch and empty beer bottles decorated the glass coffee table. A massive palm tree anchored one corner of the room, and black and white tropical-themed photos adorned the walls.

"Hungry?" Max asked, digging into his bag of food and following Roger into the kitchen. He tossed Roger a sandwich. Roger peeled back the waxed paper and studied it before stowing it in the refrigerator.

"Don't you eat anything besides turkey?"

"I had steak last week."

"Right," Roger said with a fast smile. "Wanna hit?" he added, holding out the joint.

Max waved it off.

"Brewski?"

"I'll start with this," Max said, placing his iPhone on the counter. He popped open a coconut water and then chomped a dilled gherkin spear. "I need fuel." Max frowned when an incoming call wobbled the phone.

"Getting that?" Roger asked.

Max peered at the screen and shook his head. "Nah, I'm off duty."

Roger shrugged and relit the joint. He inhaled deeply and placed the roach on a crystal ashtray. "So what's new at Hornswoggle and Hammerhead? Things getting any better?" he croaked, exhaling a thick stream of smoke through his nostrils.

"I try to think of it as a journey, but it's like the Titanic."

"C'mon dude, you're swimming in the big pond now," Roger said before draining his beer and reaching into the refrigerator for another.

"Bigger pond, bigger sharks," Max said.

"And the new boss man?"

"Aiyy," Max said, as a small beep announced a text message. He grabbed the phone. "That's him. Again. I think he's going after the *Guinness Book of World Records* title for e-mailing, texting, and phoning one person the most times in a day. Unfortunately, I'm that person." Max typed a brief reply and then shut off the phone. "I don't trust him."

Roger relit the joint. "That sucks. So how's your writing?"

"I had to put my kids' stories aside for now," Max said. "Cassidy asked me to help her with something she's doing for work."

"The girlie magazine?" Roger asked. "Why do they need someone to tell them how to do everything? Can't they make decisions without consulting a bloody committee?"

"That's what they do. Anyway, Cassidy wants to put out a more intelligent *girlie* magazine, and I'll bet she can. You know, she could be running her dad's agency by now."

"Yeah, she's a sharp one, all right. A bit anal, but she gets the job done," Roger said. He nodded to the living room. "Ready to take a deep dive back into the world of online dating?"

Max nodded and grabbed his phone.

"Be forewarned, *amigo*. Things have changed, and you'll need a seasoned guide to catch the mermaids roaming the digital waters," Roger said dramatically while lowering the music.

"Sure thing, Cousteau," Max replied while scanning the collection of music lining Roger's bookshelves. "What's with all the bossa nova? Are you hosting a carnival?"

"There's something about that beat that helps the ladies let go."

"Does everything have a sexual payoff?"

Roger ignored the question. "Let's get you a taste of Uncle Roger's skills," he said, disappearing into his bedroom. He returned with his MacBook. After booting up, he clicked on his bookmarks and opened one of the many dating websites he had saved.

Max scrunched his face as he watched Roger log in. "Who's McDucky?"

"That would be, MrLucky."

"Lame."

"It's better than Snake Eyes, which is what we're going to call you. Now pay attention."

For the next few minutes, Max quietly observed Roger navigate through the profiles, peppering his tutorial with cutting comments about the women.

"These ladies play hardball, Max. If you're not prepared, they'll chew you up like Flintstones vitamins," said Roger.

"Think so? It doesn't look like much has changed. These women are looking for relationships. I'm seeing honesty, trust, and emotionally available all over these profiles."

"They may *say* they want a relationship, but most of them are on these sites every freaking day," Roger said. "I'm surprised these sites don't offer pension plans."

"You said they're patient. Maybe they're just looking for the right guy."

"Maybe they *like* looking. Trust me. There are plenty of female players here juggling dinner dates," Roger said. "And they have a lengthy list of demands—salary, height, *Is he daddy material?*—right down to the shoes. And because they're online, they think they're shopping at Amazon.com. If you don't make their grade, you're gone with a keystroke. There's always plenty of fresh male meat waiting to be filleted. This is empowering for them."

"You make it sound so clinical."

"The next time you're on a date, see how they interview you. It's like you're applying for a job at Goldman Sachs. By the time you've finished a glass of Cabernet, you'll feel like you've been stripped down to your Def Leppard tattoo. It can be brutal," Roger said and then grinned. *"But,* if you play your cards right—like Uncle Roger does—you can get laid. A lot."

"I'm sure you can meet some pretty cool women on this site. Their wanting to meet a guy who's honest and available sounds reasonable, especially if they've been taken advantage of by some ass-clown players."

"I like that, *amigo.* Give them that 'I'm sensitive to your needs' angle. I want you working that," Roger said with a wink.

Max laughed as Roger scrolled through the myriad profiles, occasionally pausing when one caught his attention.

"Here's one—'PLEASE DO NOT BE LIKE MY EX-HUS-BAND. IF YOU ARE A COUCH POTATO AND DRINK TOO MUCH, DON'T REPLY. ME—I LOVE ITALIAN FOOD, DIS-NEY WORLD, CUDDLING, MOVIES. AND PLEASE CHECK YOUR BREATH. THERE'S NOTHING WORSE THAN A MAN WHO DOESN'T TAKE CARE OF HIS ORAL HYGIENE.' What do you think? Is 'SLEEPING IN STATEN ISLAND' the one for you?"

"I floss," Max said, chuckling.

"Her profile is all caps. Psycho."

"Look—she likes animals," Max laughed, pointing at the screen.

"Probably keeps her pet water moccasin in the bathtub. And here's the killer—no photo."

"What if she's CEO of a corporation and doesn't want people seeing her online?"

"Nah," Roger said. "She's 'self-employed.' That's code for *un*employed. Oh yeah, and she wants a traditional relationship. That means you pay for everything."

"You don't need her money," Max said, polishing off his drink.

"Do the math. Her money is her money and *your* money is her money, too."

Max yawned. "I've seen enough. What would you like me to do, Captain?"

"First, you create an intriguing profile. Each step of this process takes marketing savvy and you're a natural. Before I began hustling, I read over fifty women's profiles to find out what they're looking for. And you're right—most of them want to connect with a nice guy. That's why I keep two profiles."

"Two?"

"MrLucky works for the female players—they're all about hitting the clubs and expensive restaurants. They want dudes who throw their cash around. These chicks know they're top shelf and they demand a tribute. It's worth the investment, though, because they're not uptight about sex."

"So you have one profile for the good Roger and . . ."

"And another for the player, *playa*."

"Greedy bastard," Max said. "So let's see them—the nice Roger first."

Roger pulled up a profile with the username, Saint in the City. His primary photo was a close-up of his face with a two-day growth, his eyes staring pensively into the distance. The copy detailed a passion for old movies, as well as his love of the ocean, samba, and discovering out-of-the-way cafés. It also touted his curious mind, emotional availability, and desire to share his life with one woman.

"Who the hell is this guy?" Max asked with a laugh.

"Hey, man, I'm all of those things—not all of the time, but . . ."

"That's quite an elastic version of the truth. You're sure you're ready for a one-on-one relationship?"

Roger cleared his throat. "Of course."

Max looked at him dubiously. "Let's see MrLucky."

Roger clicked on the other profile featuring a photo of him in a black turtleneck with tussled hair and sporting a devilish grin. He described himself as a successful, adventure-seeking professional with passions for skiing in deep powder, spur-of-the-moment trips to Vegas and the Bahamas, and sampling New York's hottest restaurants and lounges.

"MrLucky attracts the top-shelf arm candy, but unfortunately these ladies drain Uncle Roger's bank account fairly quickly," Roger said.

"What kind of response do you get from these?"

Roger clicked to a page filled with the small green-light icons that had been sent by interested women.

"Wow, they like MrLucky," Max said, scanning three pages of headshots of attractive women. Roger smiled and clicked to his other profile.

"Check out the Saint in the City."

Max recoiled in surprise and said, "There must be hundreds here."

"That's this month," Roger said coolly.

"No pun intended," Max said, "but how do you keep up with all of this?"

"Easy. After I put each candidate through the Roger filter, only the fittest and most talented survive."

"Sounds like a XXX-rated *American Idol*. Do I want to know about the Roger filter?"

"Any woman who has the words *no* or *don't* in their profile gets deleted. I only deal with women whose cups are more than half-full and whose cup sizes are overflowing. Then I imagine what they would look like covered with oil and . . ."

"I get the picture. I'll have that beer now," Max said, stepping over Roger's legs.

"Grab one for me," Roger called out.

Max returned from the kitchen and said, "Let me drive. Maybe I'll have beginner's luck."

He revised the search criteria and included women from the outer boroughs. The two men sat quietly as Max scrolled slowly through each page, occasionally stopping to re-read a woman's profile before moving on.

"Dude, if you read every damn word, this is going to take forever," Roger said. "Look at the pictures and go with your gut."

"The girls from Brooklyn seem laid-back," Max said.

"I know what you mean. Maybe that's because we're from Jersey. Hey, how come all of these chicks are pushing forty?"

"I typed in women in the thirty-five to forty category. I wanted to see if they're looking for different things."

"Besides sperm and a paycheck?"

Max laughed. "I know that money and career are mission critical, but it's the same for guys. In New York, you are what you do."

"Then you're in luck," Roger said.

"Thing is, I don't care what a woman does for a living, as long as she's passionate about it."

"What about Veronica?" Roger asked. "She's a type A business-woman who craves money."

"Being focused is good. I like that. But V's engine is in overdrive twenty-four-seven," Max said.

"She runs so hot that you got burned."

"Maybe," Max said, shooting a sidelong glance. "V's too smart for this," he added, nodding to the computer screen.

Roger stood up. "I guess you know what turns her motor on," he said coolly, looking down at Max. "Time out," he added, burping loudly on his way to the bathroom.

Max continued flipping through the profiles and stopped abruptly when he spotted a familiar face. He put his bottle on the table and clicked on the woman's profile.

Roger reappeared a few minutes later, still zipping up. He plopped down next to Max. "Whoa, who's she?" he asked.

"Nobody. Well, I kind of know her, but she's not for you," Max said, clicking to the next profile. "Check this—a bodybuilder from Benson-hurst. Nice pecs. And she loves anything in zebra or leopard print."

Roger nudged Max aside and clicked back to the previous pro-file. He carefully studied the slightly blurry photo of a dark-haired woman with deep-set eyes, full lips, and delicate cheekbones.

"Exotic. I dig the long hair and that naughty mouth. Looks Latina. *Muy calor.* Why are you hiding her from Uncle Roger?"

"She's a friend of Cassidy's."

"And I'm *your* friend," Roger said, his eyes glued to the small photo. He read her username aloud. "Higher Ground. She looks familiar."

"She worked at *Face Front* a few years ago, maybe when you were there."

"I was only there for a few months. She's hot."

The two men quietly read through her profile. Higher Ground was looking for a man who was confident, funny, intelligent, open-minded, and emotionally available. She professed a love for the city, travel, and cozy cafés, and described herself as athletic and toned, an owner of a boutique business, and living with a rescued greyhound.

"Finally, a chick who doesn't say she's equally comfortable in jeans or a little black dress," Roger mused. He clicked again in the hope of finding additional photos. "I need to see her body," he said, but the only other image was a photo of a speckle-coated dog sniffing a flower.

"She doesn't take any crap from guys," Max said.

Roger gulped his beer. "Hey, cool it with the judgments. I'm everything she's looking for." He clicked the green-light icon next to her picture, signaling his interest in her, and said, "Let's see if she responds."

"Roger, please don't screw with her."

"Want a fresh one?" he asked, nodding to Max's empty bottle.

"I think I've taken in enough for one night." Max stood up and headed toward the door. When he turned to say goodbye, Roger was in the kitchen, digging into the refrigerator.

"Hey Rog, don't forget that other S," Max called out.

"Another one? Are we in double digits yet?" Roger asked, brandishing another bottle.

Max pointed at the bottle. "They want you sober."

CHAPTER 8

"**P**luto isn't a planet," the freckle-faced kid called out, waving his hand back and forth from the third row.

Max looked up and paused, searching the faces of the children's book club that were gathered in a circle on the rooftop patio above the offices of Goodson Advertising. He was reading a short story he'd written about the friendship between the moon, the planets, and the stars.

Max recognized the young boy, still frantically waving his hand, and smiled. "Liam's right, everyone, but this part of the story took place many, many years ago before Pluto joined the Kuiper Belt. We're actually going to find out more about what happens to our . . ."

"Pluto's not a planet," the boy shouted again.

"That's correct," Max said, laughing inside. He picked up the story again and went on without being interrupted. When he finished, the kids cheered. He smiled and waved as he stepped down from the small podium.

Cassidy and Serena met him with warm embraces. A handsome, olive-skinned young man with dark eyes stood at Serena's side. He looked like he was in his mid-to-late twenties. Max gave him a nod before Serena introduced him.

"Max, this is my cousin, Alejandro Trebilcock. Alejandro's staying at the beach with us this summer. He's from Chile."

Hearing the name, Max unconsciously raised an eyebrow, but smiled and offered his hand to the younger man. Alejandro's long black hair was pulled into a ponytail. His chiseled face and gently cleft chin gave him the exotic look that New York's fashion magazines search the globe to find. He had a wiry, V-shaped physique, with swimmer's shoulders that tapered down to a thin, rock-star waist.

"They liked your story," Alejandro offered with a broad smile.

"Thanks, man. I like it when people listen to what I'm saying, even if no one's over three feet tall," Max said. He felt he could finally relax after another grueling day servicing his accounts and jumping through hoops for Gloss. He exhaled and gazed up at the sky. "Check out the moon. It's red."

Alejandro tilted his head back. "They say spirits come out under a red moon."

"Maybe they're right," Max said. "I've been working with spirits all day."

Alejandro gave him a puzzled look.

"Forget it. Why don't we all get something to eat?" Max suggested.

After falling in behind the kids in the chow line, Max leaned toward Cassidy and said, *"Treb-il-cock*? Are you kidding me?"

"Something wrong with that?" Cassidy asked, laughing and shushing him with an elbow as the line crept forward.

After the four grabbed snacks and soft drinks, Cassidy picked a table close to the stairs so she could hand out event brochures as the families departed. Max returned to the chow line after wolfing down a turkey burger and a diet soda. He'd stopped abruptly to retie the laces of his running shoes and felt what could only be hot dogs, a cardboard tray, and a small boy smack into him from behind, in that order. Max twisted around to inspect a bright red and yellow stain splattered across the back of his white shirt. A five-year-old African-American boy stared up at him, just about to cry.

"It's okay, buddy," Max said. He plucked a piece of hot dog off his shirt, rubbed it into the gooey stain, and shoved it into his mouth. "Mmm," he said, rubbing his belly. "Want some?"

The boy looked at Max like he was crazy, but his tears passed.

"Let's grab some napkins and a couple more hot dogs," Max said.

As he took the tray from the boy, dropping it into a nearby trashcan, an African-American man in a designer suit appeared and asked worriedly, "Jimmy, what happened?"

"We're good," Max said. "A little accident with the franks. That's all."

"Big accident, looks like," the man said. "We were hoping Jimmy might grow up to be a wide receiver for the Giants. But after that drop . . ."

Max laughed and wiped his hands. "Not so fast. I'm a Giants fan, too, and they can always use help. By the way, I'm Max Hallyday. Nice to meet you."

"Brenton Banks. Jimmy, say hello to Mr. Hallyday."

"It's Max, Jimmy."

Max held out his hand and the boy took it. "I liked your story."

"Ouch," Max said. "That's some grip, Jimmy."

The child laughed.

"Max, let me send that shirt to the cleaners," Banks said.

"I'm fine. Really."

"Well, I'd like to do something. Do you have a card?"

"Let's see," Max said, while digging into his pocket. "Here's one, without the mustard. I'm in advertising. Come to think of it, maybe it should have mustard on it."

"Thanks for understanding," Banks said, laughing. "You better get back to your group. They're looking this way and the ladies seem to be having a good laugh."

"They love physical comedy. Nice meeting you, Mr. Banks."

"Brenton."

"Right. Take care, Jimmy," Max said, smiling and patting the boy on the shoulder. He walked off toward the men's room, brushing a piece of hot dog bun off his khakis.

Cassidy had been grazing on a salad while observing the little mishap. She smiled now, watching Max trudge to the bathroom, checking over his shoulder for updates on the back of his shirt, hoping the stain would magically disappear. As Alejandro and Serena stood in line for seconds, Cassidy sipped her seltzer and watched the polished-looking man gather his son into his arms. She'd noticed him earlier, of course—who wouldn't, with his athletic frame, expensive clothes, and photo-model child—and she'd seen him finding excuses to look her way.

Handsome man, she thought. *Beautiful boy. Handsome father . . .*

As if he felt her eyes on him, he looked over and smiled, took the boy's hand, and walked toward her. Cassidy arranged the brochures and then turned the clipboard with the registration forms facing out.

"Excuse me," the man said, taking a brochure. "I just wanted to say thank you for putting all this together."

Cassidy looked up into his handsome face, outlined by a close-cropped beard and steel-gray eyes. "Thanks. It's my pleasure," she said. She smiled at the boy. "What's your name? I'm Cassidy."

"This is Jimmy," Banks said. "Say hello, J-man."

The boy grabbed a brochure and turned away.

Banks shook his head with a short laugh. "Sorry. I guess he's at that age when women have that effect on him."

Cassidy smiled, watching the boy.

The boy flapped the brochure. "My mommy has a girlfriend," he said.

Cassidy's eyes flew open, but Banks just gathered the boy close to his legs. "Yes, she does," he said. "And we want her to be happy, don't we?"

The boy nodded and wrapped himself around his father's leg.

Banks grinned at Cassidy. "Life in the twenty-first century, right?"

Cassidy laughed. "I guess so," she said.

"I'm Brenton," he said, extending his hand.

"Glad you enjoyed the reading, Brenton" she said, shaking his warm, strong hand as Jimmy swung around his father's hip. She opened a brochure. "Maybe Jimmy would enjoy our Rock 'n' Read event next month in Central Park. There'll be lots of celebrities, singers, and kids' book authors attending. Fun for all ages," she added cheerily.

"What do you think, little man?" Banks asked, looking down at Jimmy.

The boy nodded, and Banks leaned over and filled out the registration sheet. "Will you be there?" he asked without looking up.

"I'll be there."

"Then so will we," Banks said, suddenly catching Cassidy's eyes.

His appreciative look caught her off guard. He took Jimmy's hand. "Let's go, buddy." He waved at Cassidy. "See you soon."

Cassidy smiled at the boy and waved as Banks led him away. She watched them walk off, admiring the father's tall frame and self-assured gait. Before reaching the door of the stairway, Banks paused and turned back to her, holding up the brochure. "I guess all the information I need is right here," he said.

Cassidy blushed, knowing she was caught staring and that her cell phone number was listed on the top left-hand corner of the pamphlet. "How about I just see you at the event?"

Banks nodded. "Sounds good."

"And don't forget to bring Jimmy," Cassidy added.

At a few minutes past nine, the sky grew dark and the gathering broke up. Max, Cassidy, Serena, and Alejandro hopped into a cab and headed to Serena's apartment in Brooklyn. Everyone congregated in the kitchen. With Memorial Day weekend only a week away, the women discussed their summer plans while Max and Alejandro retired to the living room. Alejandro bounced a tennis ball to Serena's dog, Chili. The dog, a brown-and-white-speckled greyhound, inspected it before picking it up and slowly walking it back to Alejandro. He gently placed his hands on her back, patiently holding her as Chili panted.

"Is that a Vulcan death grip?" Max asked.

"Just a little Reiki for our friend. She's old. The energy's good for her."

"*Ray*-ki? What's that?"

"Reiki's a relaxation technique. It allows the energy to flow through the body's meridians and eliminate blockages. When your *chi* flows, it helps keep you healthy. I transmute, or channel the healing energy in through my crown chakra and out of my palms."

Alejandro moved his hands in a series of fixed positions around the dog's body. "She loves this. It relaxes her. My hands heat up a bit when I'm doing my work."

Alejandro put his hands out and Max touched them.

"Wow, you could reheat pizza with those mitts," Max said. "Does Reiki work with people, too?"

"Of course, as long as the person is open to receiving energy."

Max scratched Chili under the chin and asked Alejandro about his background.

"I became a Reiki Master and teacher about five years ago. I run a small clinic back home where I also practice Jin Shin, qigong, and other ways of using universal life force energy."

"So what brings you to New York?" Max asked.

"I decided to take our winter off so I could enjoy your summer."

"Have anything planned?"

Alejandro broke into a wide smile. "I surf."

"In South America?" Max asked.

"Everywhere, from Chile's La Puntilla—which is quite ragged—to the Pauba, Brazil shoreline and Trujillo, Peru. It's all good. In fact, I entered a surfing contest this summer in New Jersey."

"I read about that." Max pointed to a pillow on the floor. "So, does Serena make you sleep there?"

"No, no," Alejandro laughed. "But I like it. The pillow is made with buckwheat husks."

"I'm sure that makes all the difference," Max said with a laugh. He checked his watch. "I'm slammed with meetings tomorrow. Let's see if Cassidy's ready."

When they returned to the kitchen, Serena was gesturing broadly as she commented on the relative importance of the size of a man's hands. A few minutes later, Cassidy and Max bid their good nights and climbed into the back of a cab. The first stop was Cassidy's apartment in Brooklyn Heights before Max returned to the city.

When the taxi turned onto Cranberry Street, Cassidy touched Max's arm. "So, any word from . . . ?"

"She says we need space."

"How does that make you feel?" Cassidy asked.

"Spacey. I don't want to talk about it."

"Fine," she said.

"Serena looks awesome," Max said.

"Yeah, her studio's going really well. She's finally left the magazine business behind."

"Is she seeing anyone?" Max asked.

Cassidy looked him up and down. "Who wants to know?"

Max shrugged. "With that body, I guess a lot of guys want to know."

Cassidy punched his arm. "I thought you were still getting over Victoria."

Max put up his hands. "Hey, I'm just making idle chitchat."

"Is that so?"

"Besides, you were checking out Alejandro's bod pretty seriously," he joked.

"He's very attractive." She winked back.

"He sleeps on the floor."

"He's a healer. He heals people," she responded defensively.

"And dogs. He's too pretty. I think he's a woman."

Cassidy rolled her eyes, half-smiling. Then she whacked his thigh. "Hey, where's my column . . . Dick?"

"It's Rod."

"Same difference," she said.

He reached into his leather brief, took out an 8x11 envelope, and handed it to her.

She smiled. "Good boy."

The cab stopped at the corner and idled. Cassidy grabbed her bag and looked at Max. "I knew I could count on you," she said, leaning over and kissing him on the cheek, letting her lips linger briefly before pulling away. "Good night, Rod," she said as she stepped to the curb.

Max smiled, enjoying how pretty she looked bathed under the light of the street lamp.

Serena cleaned up the kitchen, and on the way to her bedroom, side-stepped Alejandro lying on the floor with a blanket covering his side. Chili was curled up with her chin draped over Alejandro's ankle. Seeing them look so peaceful made Serena smile contentedly.

After washing her face, she stood facing the mirror in a sheer silk T-shirt. Although there were a few stray strands of gray underneath her long sleek mane of black hair, she maintained the exotic beauty and high cheekbones of a model. As a teenager, she'd had a short stint on the runway after being discovered by a local photographer while sitting on her front stoop. This led to her being lured by a renowned Latin American international recording star into spending two years traversing the globe with his entourage. Although her basic role was arm candy, her worldly education approached a level that most coeds only dream about. Serena's keen self-awareness wasn't built on class-rooms and memorization. It came from a life on the road.

After a year into the relationship, the singer hinted incessantly that he wanted a baby, so eventually she became pregnant with the star's child. But soon he lost interest and continued playing the part of Lothario at every stop on the tour. Through cloaked threats and offers of a substantial cash payoff, Serena was pressured into having an abortion—a decision that left her heartbroken. She wasn't bitter and didn't want to carry any trace of him. But since then she'd har-bored a basic distrust of men, and as a result, had never married. Now she longed for an opportunity to find a loving partner who'd want her just as she was without making her change or do things his way. Maybe when the time was right, she'd want a child.

Twenty years later, she still displayed the polish of a woman whose beauty had been her business. In baseball parlance, even though she was a veteran, Serena could still bring it. And she knew it.

Serena padded to her room and checked her e-mail. She scanned the discount offers from Groupon and Victoria's Secret, as well as correspondence from her friends in Miami. Before shutting her com-puter down, she signed on to her favorite online dating website. There were only a few green-light signals in her box—a relatively slow night for someone as alluring as Serena. The first one was from a man refer-ring to himself as the King of Brooklyn. He looked like a guy from the neighborhood, and he had a penchant for Vegas and Atlantic City. *Delete.* The second was from someone calling himself Big Brain. He professed a love of nonfiction and cooking, but he didn't post a photo and his job and marital status were blank. *Delete.*

She yawned before opening the last of the new green lights. A handsome face lit up the screen. His piercing eyes, sensual mouth, and wavy, sandy-brown hair were worthy of investigation. She took a spoonful of chocolate sorbet and began reading. His profile was well written, and he stated that he was ready for a relationship. His passion for samba, the ocean, and discovering out-of-the-way cafés intrigued her. She studied his eyes. They seemed kind. And he was quite good-looking—*muy guapo*. *Worth a shot*, she thought, licking chocolate from her lips. She took a breath and hit "send," returning a green light to the Saint in the City.

CHAPTER 9

At five fifteen, Veronica's radio alarm blared to the sounds of Hall & Oates singing "Maneater" on her favorite FM station, which featured a mix of eighties and nineties music. Like clockwork, each morning she'd slide out of bed, drop down into a full plank position, and nail twenty perfect push-ups. Then she'd march into the kitchen and grab her waiting cup of coffee, before scanning *The New York Times* and *The Wall Street Journal* from her iPad. After changing into work-out clothes and tying back her blonde hair, she'd meet her trainer at the gym on the top floor of her building.

But this morning Roger Fox was in her bed, and Roger didn't like getting up early without a very good reason. Waking up next to Veronica was a very good reason. But it was Monday, so Veronica didn't have the time for an encore of the previous night's sexual gymnastics. After the alarm sounded, she brushed Roger's hand off her thigh.

"Staff meeting," she said in a clear, sharp voice. He groped at her like a giant squid as she slipped out of bed.

Still half asleep, he mumbled, "Come back. Uncle Roger's got something for you."

On her way to the bathroom, she took a quick peek back at him lying naked under the sheets and said, "Wasn't last night enough?"

He made a low, growling sound.

"I'll bookmark the sports section. You can read it after the second alarm goes off," she called behind her.

The room was still dark. Roger yawned and touched himself. "When does the second alarm go off?"

"Now," she said. The clock radio blared as she shut the bathroom door.

"Aarrrggh," Roger groaned, burying his head beneath the pillow.

While brushing her teeth, Veronica questioned her decision to invite Roger over on a Sunday night, even if the sex had been outstanding. Roger being Max's friend didn't matter anymore—she and Max were history—but she couldn't understand why Max hadn't attempted to salvage the relationship. After their break up, he only phoned once, asking her if there was a chance for reconciliation. That was it. Following a private moment of rage at what she considered rejection, she indulged in a brief, perfunctory cry. Then she moved on, eventually agreeing to a friendly dinner with Roger after he called her repeatedly.

She retraced how it began. A few weeks ago, after the Yankees–Red Sox game, she let Roger steal a brief kiss before she hopped out of the cab in front of her apartment. She had toyed with the notion of taking him upstairs, but she was flying to Atlanta the next morning. That Saturday, following their margarita-fueled dinner date, Veronica took Roger home and put him through his paces. She kept him up and fully attentive to her needs throughout a long night of steamy sex. He was spent and silly when he crawled out her door the next day.

The following week, he called her every day. She'd finally agreed to meet him last night, after returning to the city from a visit with her mother. Roger showed up with a bottle of Cava and tickets for the Almodóvar film festival, a retrospective marathon at the Film Forum. Following the show, he took her to Blue Water Grill off Union Square. While they were nibbling appetizers, Roger presented her with a small, elegantly wrapped book of Neruda poems. The seduction was on and she enjoyed his performance. Although she was turned off by Roger's unquenchable thirst for wine, it hadn't gotten in the way of his sexual abilities, so for now, she'd let it slide. Roger was confident, handsome, and charming—a potential keeper.

After her coffee she checked in on Roger again. She placed the iPad open to the *The New York Times* on the edge of the bedside table as he snored lightly. His unshaven face was nestled in her pillow, making him look very masculine, yet boyish and vulnerable at the same time. She thought about running her fingers through his hair and then sliding under the covers again. But not today. She reset the alarm and hurried to meet her trainer.

When she returned, a steamy haze emanated from the bathroom. Roger was in the shower, whistling a Sinatra tune. Veronica went to the kitchen and prepared her power shake, filling the blender with fresh fruit, lecithin, maca, whey protein, spirulina, and some organic kefir. After drinking half the concoction, she padded back to the bathroom.

"Let's go, big fella. Chop, chop."

"Hop in here. I'll rub down those pretty muscles."

"I'll take a rain check. I've got a busy day."

"Please, baby. Let me hug you . . . just for a minute."

Veronica checked the clock. She had a few minutes to spare, so she peeled off her sweats and met Roger head-on under the pulsating showerheads. Ten minutes later, Roger was breathless and drained and leaning against the wall of the shower.

While she dressed, Roger sang the "doobie doobie doo" chorus from "Strangers in the Night." His briefcase was open and the contents were spread out on the side of the bed where he'd slept. While gathering the papers, Veronica picked up what appeared to be a sales proposal. With a fast-track career in the digital advertising division at Globison, she had to take a closer look. All she needed was one more sale to secure her bonus and put the down payment on the two-bedroom condo she'd been staking out in Tribeca for the past six months.

She glanced toward the bathroom. The door was closed and the water was still running, so she flipped through the file. She reached for a pad and pen, scribbled down the client's name, Layla Korindo-polos, and tucked the paper into her purse. After slipping into a tailored black Theory pantsuit and heels, she sorted through her closet shelves for a purse that completed her outfit.

She checked herself one more time in the full-length mirror, knocked on the bathroom door, and asked Roger to lock up on his way out. The door flew open and Roger greeted her naked, with a loaded toothbrush protruding from his mouth.

"Love was just a glance away, warm embracing dance . . ." he warbled.

"Have a nice day, Frank," she said.

Roger looked her over admiringly. "You clean up good, baby. I'll be out of here in a flash. And I promise not to try on any of your underwear."

"I'm sure they'll look good on you. Call me later," she said, heading for the door.

CHAPTER 10

Cassidy's stomach was already grumbling when her publisher and sales team paraded into her office to update her about their sales prospects and upcoming meetings. Although Cassidy's main focus was the magazine's editorial content, she was also a catalyst to her sales team's efforts to deliver ad pages. Her personality was magnetic, and she had an uncanny ability to make even the most uptight clients feel like they were chatting with a trusted friend. Cassidy was the magazine's secret weapon.

It was closing in on noon, so she rooted around for a bag of carrot sticks and nibbled them while reviewing the sales call schedule. *Same old, same old,* she thought as she read the list she'd seen repeatedly over the past two months. She stopped when she recognized a new name that appeared at the bottom of the page—Max's client, Layla Korindopolos, Director of Marketing for Peacock Beverages.

Cassidy tapped the document with her index finger. "Let me know about this meeting. I want to go," she said to her assistant as the meeting wrapped up.

She took a quick peek at her compact and applied a dab of Burt's Bees to her lips. Then she put on her sunglasses, tossed her Black-Berry and a plain envelope into her oversized bag, and glided out of her office onto West 56th Street. She picked up a salad at one of the ubiquitous New York City food outlets that serve everything from pancakes to sushi. Then she entered Central Park at the corner of 59th Street and Fifth Avenue and walked briskly toward the zoo.

Smoothing her dark pencil skirt, she took a seat on a wooden bench near the entrance. She jabbed a plastic fork into her green salad and washed it down with a chilled bottle of white tea. It was a picturesque spring day, and with Memorial Day approaching, Cassidy was ready for summer.

Throughout her twenties, Cassidy had taken a half-share in the Hamptons with a few select coworkers and friends. She enjoyed those long, lazy days at the beach and the usual brief flings. But this year she was looking forward to summer in the more relaxed confines of the Jersey Shore. She needed her private time to unwind from the grueling hours at her start-up magazine. *My Radiance* was her brainchild, and as the plans were finalized for the premier issue, it required her undivided attention. After dumping the remains of her lunch in the trash, she pulled out the envelope holding Max's debut, "The Guys' Guy's Guide to Love" column. She checked her watch before putting on reading glasses. Max had scrawled a note across the top of the page.

Cassidy, thanks for indulging my request to read this at the zoo. If you want an interesting perspective on male behavior, check out the monkeys and you'll see what I mean. I hope this column meets your expectations.
Enjoy, Max

PLEASE ALLOW ME TO INTRODUCE MYSELF . . .

My name is Rod and I'm a guy's guy. Like many of the men you see every day, I'm better looking than some and not as cute as others. You might have smiled at me on the street, let me buy you a glass of wine, or held my hand while walking through SoHo on a crisp autumn afternoon. Maybe you even slept with me. Like other men, I've made you laugh and cry, and at various times feel happy, mad, frustrated, inspired, depressed, and hopefully loved.

I'm sure you've wondered, and discussed with your girlfriends, what guys really think and talk about. What makes men such mysterious and fascinating studies in human behavior? This column is your key to answering those questions and demystifying men. I'll expose our strange ways and odd habits. I'll break down that smooth talker's moves—the guy you let undress you after one too many Pinot Grigios, only to find out later that he was married, gay, or had a foot fetish. And unlike other articles or books you might have read, I won't patronize you and remind you that most men are not deserving of your affections. No, instead I'm going to teach you how to win.

For the so-called players in this town, I'm their worst nightmare. I'll show you what makes these boys tick and how you can break them down and beat them at their own game. Maybe then they'll let out the inner-gentleman who is buried somewhere deep inside them—the man that you deserve.

I need to ask a favor. While I offer up the hard, cold truth, please don't shoot the messenger. This won't be pretty, but I'm here to help. Then it's up to you. So, if you're game, I'll be back next month, prying open Pandora's Box and sharing the secrets inside THE GUYS' GUY'S GUIDE TO LOVE. And don't be shy with your questions. Who knows? I might change my mind and disappear. Remember, I'm still a guy.

Until next time,

Rod

Cassidy laughed as she considered the column's potential. It matched her vision of adding value for her women readers by sharing a man's perspective. She'd have to sell her management on the concept, but as soon as the magazine's sales took off and there was a favorable response to the column, they'd defer to her recommendations. She read the column a second time, slipped it into her bag, and entered the zoo.

The Central Park Zoo houses two breeds of monkeys—the black-and-white colobus and the long-tailed, golden-headed and cotton-top tamarins. Inside the dim confines of the monkey house, the diminutive tamarins looked small, not weighing more than a few pounds. They gathered in small groups, nervously leaping from tree to tree in quick, jerky movements. When Cassidy stopped to observe their habitat, they became even more frenetic and called out at her in shrill whistles.

Their acrobatics amused the handful of tourists observing them. After a few minutes, Cassidy searched for the Angolan black-and-white colobus. The monkeys were covered in furry coats with bushy tails and wore sad countenances on their tiny faces. Two males, screeching at each other and swinging animatedly through the trees, caught Cassidy's eye. At the same time, a well-dressed woman approached with her young son in tow. The furry primates' trilling and moaning also captured the boy's attention. The little boy squeezed his mother's hand, pointing when the smallest monkey leapt to the ground and began masturbating rigorously.

"Mommy, what's he doing?" the boy asked.

Cassidy covered her mouth, choking back her laughter. The mother tugged her son's arm. The monkey faced her and sped up his movements. Another colobus jumped to the ground and joined the action. They were like dueling gunslingers, tugging at their private parts. The young boy hopped up and down, pulling his mother while she tried to drag him away. Cassidy followed them outside, still grinning. She called Max when she reached the zoo's exit and got his voice mail.

"Hey, it's me," she said. "I just visited your pals in the monkey house and I see what you mean. Is that all you guys think about? Don't bother responding. I already know the answer. By the way— you're hired."

CHAPTER 11

On the Wednesday morning before Memorial Day weekend, Max was awakened by shafts of bright sunshine filtering through his curtains. He rolled over and quickly realized that he had an erection. It had been a few weeks since he'd had sex and he was feeling both melancholy and horny.

The previous night, Max stayed home and listened to Muddy Waters and Bobby Blue Bland while poring over old photos capturing his time with Veronica. There they were, skiing in Aspen, gliding along the Caribbean Sea on a catamaran, and mountain biking through the woods of upstate New York. His eyes welled up when he studied the photo of her dressed to the nines for that industry party at the Puck Building. He crunched on the ice in his drink, contemplating a series of digital images that she'd let him take of her decked out in a black bustier, thigh-high stockings, and a garter.

Along with this morning's erection, Max nursed a hangover from the tumblers of dark rum he'd consumed. His head throbbed from the inside. Since Gloss had taken over at HHI, Max had felt the presence of an ominous, swollen cloud hanging above his head, but it was nothing compared to Veronica's departure. That felt like an endless heavy downpour from the same dark cloud.

Rolling onto his side, visions of Veronica's lush blonde hair and pinup body kept Max aroused. He let himself go, visualizing his hands running over her shapely thighs and taut stomach. He recalled her sweet taste, and as he touched himself he fell into a deep, sexually charged fantasy. Falling further into his erotic dream, he envisioned the subtle contours along the small of Veronica's back and her smooth, perfectly shaped derriere. He imagined her crimson nails slowly running down his spine, her brown eyes alive and her pillowy lips and soft tongue tasting like sweet candies. And of course, in this fantasy, she wanted him badly. At six fifteen, the radio alarm jarred Max into reality. He fell back on his pillow and stared blankly at the slowly spinning ceiling fan. He was caught off guard when an image of Cassidy bubbled into his consciousness—standing on the shoreline with the sun glistening off her hair, slowly unzipping her wetsuit. *Whoa, boy. Get a grip,* he thought, rolling over, looking down and then rubbing his face awake. He stared at the clock radio, remembering the eight o'clock account director's meeting with Gloss. Still hard as oak, he flung himself out of bed and scurried to the shower. He dressed quickly and burst out of his apartment, now clutching a Clif Bar in his right hand.

A few hours later, Roger stepped out of a cab following a wine-infused business lunch at the Union Square Café. No place in Manhattan had friendlier, more capable service or served a finer tuna burger. His clients loved the room, and Roger usually left with a closed deal. But today he failed to consummate an agreement with that annoying media planner who was always hitting him up for Yankees tickets. This twenty-three-year-old planner told Roger she wanted to reallocate most of the client's print budget into digital advertising and a robust social media program. Even for a smooth operator like Roger, selling print advertising had become a real challenge. And with mounting pressure to reach his quota, Roger's friendship with Max was becoming a factor in his success or failure. Unaccustomed to feelings of guilt, Roger's affair with Max's ex on the heels of their breakup somehow gnawed at him. And now Roger would have to go after a larger piece of Layla's ad budget, which would screw Max. Roger took out his iPhone. He wanted to call Max. He didn't know why, maybe to see if he still wanted to get together later that evening. But he dismissed the thought and took a cab back to his office.

Roger perked up when he saw his comely assistant, Gail, a young Korean American from Palisades Park, New Jersey. Having recently graduated Sarah Lawrence, Gail was taking the publication's traditional career path: working for a senior sales director to learn the business from the ground up. Gail's lithe frame was wrapped in a sleeveless black turtleneck and a short matching skirt. Her smooth features and shimmering black hair had not gone unnoticed by Roger, and today she was looking particularly inviting. Roger assumed she had a date.

After a long glance at her shapely legs tucked under the side of her workstation, he stopped at her desk. "Do we have a new time for the sales meeting? I'm out on Friday."

"It's at four. I sent you an e-mail about it yesterday." She looked up and smiled. "Need help with anything?"

"Hmm. Well, if you feel like stretching those legs and want something sweet from Starbucks, I'm buying. I need to tweak my projections. Lattes?"

"Sure. Grande skim with a shot of vanilla, right?"

Roger stood by his door, watching Gail shimmy down the corridor. She turned back and Roger smiled. When she reached the elevator, he stepped into his office and pulled up his sales forecast. His numbers were flat and that wasn't going to cut it. *Plates* needed revenue now if they were going to compete with the more established epicurean publications. Roger recalled Veronica's insistence that ad sales were shifting online for good. His paltry sales numbers were proving her correct.

When Gail appeared in the doorway with their coffees, Roger glanced up and down at her slender form. If she noticed his leering, she didn't let it show.

"I put the Splenda in," she said. "You better go. The meeting's on thirteen. Wait . . . your tie."

Roger looked down and grinned as she gently tugged at the knot. "Thanks," he said. "If they don't buy my forecast, you can have my office and the leather couch."

When it was Roger's turn to present, he lowballed the revenue from his potential deal with Peacock Beverages. He preferred keeping a few aces in the hole. Roger avoided committing to anything unless it was absolutely necessary.

"I'm looking at a five percent bump this year," he said gingerly from his seat at the oval table in the conference room. He guessed that in a challenging business environment, any sales increase would suffice. He smiled at the new publisher of *Plates*, but was met with indifference.

Roger referred to his boss as Buttwipe, a strong-jawed Ivy Leaguer and classic boomer who favored frameless glasses, rep ties, and starched dress shirts trimmed with white cuffs and collars. Buttwipe had remained chilly to Roger's breezy attitude since his recent promotion to publisher. *Fuck him*, Roger thought. *It's not my fault the smug-faced yuppie has to pay alimony and two mortgages. That's what happens when your wife catches you interviewing secretarial candidates doggie-style.* Roger looked at him and thought, *Hey, jerk wad, next time don't get caught.*

"Let's revisit those numbers, Fox. I want to hear more about Peacock."

Roger loosened the knot of his Hermes tie and cleared his throat. "Peacock Beverages is launching a line of new-age distilled spirits with all-natural holistic extracts. I've been meeting with their marketing director to discuss a major deal with us featuring promotions that match gourmet foods with their products. Our test kitchen has come up with some great ideas. Anyone ever try ginseng vodka with a light cream fusion whipped and drizzled over sorbet?"

"Sounds intriguing. But if these products are going to be so successful, why are you only committing to a few pages of advertising for the year?"

"This is a new line and the client hasn't sorted out her plan yet," Roger said, hoping Buttwipe's line of questioning would cease.

"Fox, if you expect us to invest in resources for developing recipes and production prototypes for a four-color ad insert, you'll need to increase your projection. Who's their agency?"

"Hammerhead, I think," Roger said.

"HHI? What's their budget?"

In his mind's eye, Roger saw Max's face. "Three or four million . . . maybe more."

"Then you need to get a bigger slice of that budget—a few million better. If you're in direct discussions with the Peacock client, that shouldn't be a problem. Add it to your forecast."

Roger nervously tapped his pen.

"Roger?"

"Yeah, I got it." *Buttwipe.*

After the meeting, Roger dragged himself to Starbucks again, this time ordering a venti-sized black coffee, no sugar. He felt himself slipping into crisis mode and didn't like the direction things were going. *Why did life have to get so damn complicated?* He walked slowly, and by the time he returned to his office, it was well after six. Most of the staff had gone. But Gail was still working, crouched in front of the bottom drawer of the file cabinet. Roger walked up and stood over her as she was yanking at his crammed expense folder. He leaned over to ask what she was still doing at the office and balanced his coffee on top of the filing cabinet above her. She jerked up suddenly, jamming her head into his crotch and causing him to splatter the hot coffee across his shirt.

"Yeooouch!" he exclaimed, doubling over. He grabbed his groin with one hand and pulled his coffee-soaked shirt away from his chest with the other.

Gail regained her balance, watching in horror as Roger hopped up and down in a crazed dance. *"Ohmigod!* I am so sorry. Are you okay?"

"Eieeeooow!" was all he could muster as he bounced back and forth.

Then he slipped on the coffee spill and fell forward, hitting his face on the corner of the file cabinet just below his eye. Gail put her hand on his back and then ran into the pantry, returning with a handful of paper towels soaked with water. Roger was leaning on the cabinet holding his hand on his crotch. A red welt appeared on his cheekbone as he rubbed himself, trying to neutralize the throbbing in his groin. Gail put the paper towels down and scampered back to the pantry, this time filling up a cloth napkin with ice. By now, Roger had pulled off his shirt and was examining his chest for scalding. He stumbled into his office and plopped himself down on the couch. Gail followed him inside. Roger grabbed the makeshift ice pack from her and placed it between his legs. He leaned back and lay moaning with his eyes closed. Gail crouched at his side, dabbing his chest with a wet napkin and holding an ice cube under his eye.

For the next few minutes, *"aaahhh"* was the only sound emanating from Roger. Gail closed the door and knelt at his side, nursing his burns and bruises. Roger breathed deeply as Gail placed her hand on his chest to calm him.

When the phone rang, she tried removing her hand from Roger's chest, but he gently pulled her back. "Please don't go. Check the phone on the coffee table, but stay here. I'm in pain."

"It's Max Hallyday," she said, reading his name and number off the consul.

Fuck, Roger thought. But before Roger could signal Gail to let the call go to voice mail, she hit the speaker button.

"Roger, it's Max. Wanted to see if we're still on for tonight. I can't wait to watch you work those women and . . ."

Roger clicked off the speakerphone with his foot. Gail began slowly moving her hand in small circles, occasionally running her nails across his nipples.

"Oooh, that feels good," Roger said, taking short breaths. He shifted his body toward her and the ice pack slipped off his crotch. A handful of cubes tumbled out of the napkin. Reflexively, she grabbed at the napkin, trying to prevent the ice from spilling out. While reaching for the napkin, she grazed Roger's groin and, surprise, surprise, Roger was now aroused.

He carefully reached down and gently placed her hand over his swelling erection. This time, she took him in her hand and began slowly massaging him. Roger pulled her close and kissed her, and she kissed him back, pressing her mouth on his and then twirling her tongue inside while tightening her grip on his crotch. Roger moaned and ran his hands over her breasts before expertly reaching around her to unfasten her bra. He freed her now-aroused bosom and took her pert nipple into his mouth. Once Roger was certain where this was going, he lay back and closed his eyes while she unclasped his belt buckle. Then his capable assistant put her head down and took command of their private meeting.

He met her bobbing head with his hips, and Gail pulled back and said softly, "Be right back."

She returned and tore open a condom, slipped it on him and then slowly glided herself down. When Roger felt her moist, warm grip take hold, he let out a groan. Within a few minutes, the meeting reached a very satisfying conclusion. Roger had always wondered what sex would be like with her, and it was even better than he'd expected.

Gail stood over him and tossed her hair back across her shoulders nonchalantly. Roger breathed heavily, but was smiling. The phone rang again, breaking the mood. Roger looked at her. She smiled while fixing her skirt, but made no effort to answer it.

He waited, and then said, "Could you please see who that is? It might be important."

She shot him a look and glanced at the phone. "Layla Korindopolos."

Roger sprang up like a jack-in-the-box. "Shit, I need to take that. We're having dinner." He groped for the receiver, almost knocking Gail over in the process. "Layla! I was just thinking about you. We're still on, right? Excellent. Meet you at the bar in an hour."

Gail quietly shut the door behind her and headed to the ladies room. When she returned, she grabbed her bag and walked down the corridor with her cell phone tucked under her chin.

CHAPTER 12

Layla waited for Roger outside the restaurant, sending e-mails from her BlackBerry. Although already attractive with her gently curved aquiline nose and smooth olive skin, when Layla displayed her ample breasts in her Prada dress with the plunging neckline, she transformed herself into a tasteful display of femininity.

When Roger climbed out of his cab and Layla saw his bruised face, she lowered her phone mid-text. "What happened? That's some nasty bruise," she said in a faintly disappointed tone before finishing her texting.

"This?" he said, pointing to the swollen area. "It's nothing. Last night a couple of frat boys were giving my friend's girl a hard time."

"Really?" she said, cautiously.

"Even in New York, sometimes you have to get involved."

"And you were helping a friend," she said, arching an eyebrow.

"That's what we do. We help our friends," Roger said, thinking about Max momentarily before getting distracted by her cleavage as he led her inside.

He needed to find out how much money she had in the budget for her new line. The ad agency, in this case Hornsby Hammerhead, was traditionally assigned the lion's share of the marketing budget for a new campaign. The remainder got doled out across opportunistic programs like Roger's. The plan was for Max to sell Layla a new ad campaign and then let Roger sell her complimentary programs. If asked, Max would support Roger and *Plates* as a good media vehicle to build her brand. But there was only one stack of money, and Roger needed to nail down a bigger cut right now. He couldn't escape the guilt that was gnawing inside, but this was business, and he needed to do whatever was necessary to survive.

After a second glass of Sancerre, though, Roger was finding it difficult to concentrate on anything except Layla's breasts. He didn't think she minded his salacious glances, but he did his best to maintain eye contact as she picked at her pan-seared tuna and he sliced up his New York strip steak. He kept the conversation light, volleying back and forth between business and her personal life. Roger learned that besides Layla being heir to a fortune, her mother had passed when she was a child. He could tell there had been a deep connection, and when Layla put her wine glass down and grew quiet after finishing her story about their final trip together to Athens, Roger knew it was time for a break.

"Could you excuse me?" he asked, pushing back his chair.

Roger wasn't sure where their dinner was headed so he needed to cover his bases. Once inside the men's room, he took out his phone and checked his messages. Max had called again. Roger stared at himself in the mirror for a moment, thinking. He sent Max a text, informing him that something had come up and they'd have to reschedule. Then he called Veronica, reminding himself that a good offense was the best defense. When his call went to voice mail, he pumped his fist.

After the beep, he paced back and forth across the men's room. *"Baby, Big Daddy here, and he's so looking forward to seeing your gorgeous face and tasting your sweet lips. And if you're a good girl, the big man's gonna treat you right. But if you misbehave, Big Daddy's gonna have to put his bad girl over his knee and . . . I'll let you fill in the blanks. Ciao."*

When he returned to the table, Layla's lips were painted a deep shade of red. Roger smiled inside and said, "May I ask you a personal question?"

"That depends. What would you like to know?"

"What it's like being Nikola Korindopolos's daughter?"

Roger had read about her father's hardnosed business tactics and mercurial personality. He refilled her wine glass.

"Despite all of the ranting in the press," she said, "my father has a big heart and does wonderful things for people. Of course, you never read about them."

"And what about you? Is it better being the daughter of a wealthy tycoon or do you sometimes wish that you could be . . . anonymous maybe? You know, just going about your life without the whole media empire thing hanging over your head. You're such a talented marketer, and if you don't mind my saying so, you're a very attractive woman," Roger said, carefully gauging her reaction.

She colored appreciatively. "Why thank you, Roger. That means a lot . . . especially from such a successful, good-looking man." She reached across the table and touched his hand. "It's nice when someone gets me. It can get lonely when everyone knows who your father is—and all they think about is his money. You're very sweet."

Wow! The girl can sling it, Roger thought. Now invigorated by the beef, red wine, and Layla's increasingly flirtatious banter, Roger decided to revise his plans. It was close to ten, and he'd promised to finalize the plans for his Memorial Day weekend junket to the Bahamas with Veronica. Earlier, she'd hinted that if it wasn't too late, he should stop by. But Layla was in no hurry to finish her meal or their evening, and he needed that budget. The instant Layla placed her fork on the table, Roger asked if she wanted anything else.

"I thought we'd have dessert . . . if you have time. I'm having so much fun and the food is outstanding," she said, gazing around the crowded landmark restaurant. "Don't you love having dinner with the pool right there? It's so New York . . . so romantic."

He stole a glance at his watch and then took a cursory look at the dessert menu.

"How about this one?" she said, pointing.

Roger nodded without looking up. A few moments later they were handed spoons for a crème brûlée. As Layla lingered over the rich custard, Roger watched her lick the burnt sugar off her spoon. He felt his phone vibrate, but ignored it and asked, "Could we take a few moments and discuss your partnering with *Plates*?"

"Of course," she said, slowly running her tongue along her lips.

"Well, I think we should expand the mail-in offer for the recipe guide and add two pages to a gatefold spread in the September issue.

Each month, we'll follow up with three consecutive ads on the right-hand page featuring a different flavor. Then we maintain momentum with another gatefold spread in *Plates'* gala year-end holiday entertaining issue and a launch party for the press and your distributors. How does that sound?"

Layla took a sip of water and dabbed the corner of her mouth with her napkin. "This has grown into quite the program. How much does all of this cost?"

"I'm sure we can work something out, but it's probably in the neighborhood of two million . . . for the pages and the party. Production of the recipe guide would be incremental, of course."

"You're aware of the funding we set aside for the advertising that HHI is working on?"

"Basically."

"So you're suggesting I cut their budget so I can pay for your program?"

Roger tried to blot out Max's now annoying image, thinking that he was doing the best he could to avoid the inevitable. "Is there someplace else you can shift funds from?"

"Not right now. I can't afford to produce HHI's campaign and do your program too. What do you suggest?"

Roger swallowed, determined not to think of his friend. "Start with my program. *Plates* can produce customized ads for you that can run in our magazine. And as soon as sales take off, you'll have the money to produce HHI's campaign. It's all about the brand, and this way, everybody wins."

"Everybody wins?"

"Sure, I mean, well—this way you can have a series of ads rolled out over the course of the launch. You'll just be starting with ours."

Layla stood up and pushed back her chair. "We need to talk more about this. I'll be right back," she said, straightening her dress and then stepping away from the table.

Once she was out of sight, Roger placed his elbows on the table and rested his forehead in his palms. After a few moments, he retrieved his phone. Veronica had called. He dialed her number.

"Got my message?" he began as soon as she answered. "Good. I

THE GUYS' GUY'S GUIDE TO LOVE

can't wait for the Bahamas. We're going to have a blast. I'm already packed and—"

"Roger, where are you?" Veronica asked, sounding annoyed. "I thought we were going to plan this trip together."

"I was stuck in a sales meeting all afternoon. It's been crazy."

"So where are you *now*? It sounds loud."

"Well, um, yeah," he said. "You were so right about digital advertising. Our numbers aren't great. Anyway . . . the whole team's out for dinner—to boost morale. You know, down and dirty beers and burgers and watching the game. The usual rah-rah nonsense."

"Really. Who's winning?"

He nervously searched the room, thinking, *It's the fucking Four Seasons. There's no Yankees game on television here.* His mind reeled, and he dropped the phone to the floor. Then he kicked it once for good measure before grabbing it and then hanging up. He spotted a waiter nearby. He peeled a twenty from his billfold and waved it frantically at him.

"Listen," Roger said. "I know this is a swanky place, but I need the score of the Yankees game. Like *NOW.*" He rubbed the bill between his fingers.

The waiter looked down and sniffed, but took the bill anyway and hurried off. Roger tapped his foot when he saw Layla making her way across the dining room. His heart raced, but Layla paused at another table. *Good, she knows someone.* His phone vibrated and his foot danced a pitter-patter rhythm beneath the table.

"What happened?" Veronica asked pointedly.

Out of the corner of his eye, Roger saw the waiter scurrying between tables with an excited look on his face. Seeing Roger holding his phone, he held up three fingers on his left hand and one finger on the right.

"Sorry, there was this big play at the plate. Some idiot knocked into me and I dropped the phone. Three to one."

"What?"

"The score. It's three to one. You wanted to know."

"Oh. Who's winning?"

With his eyes opened wide, Roger waved at the waiter again and mouthed, "Who's winning?" The waiter shrugged his shoulders.

91

Roger's facial muscles tightened and he blurted, "Yanks. They need this game, no matter who's winning right now."

"Are you all right?" she said. "You sound tense. Are you coming over?"

"Ah, I have to stay here for awhile," Roger said. "You're right, though. I'm pretty wound up. Maybe I should go home. Big day tomorrow. I'll call the car service for the ride to the airport." There was silence on the other end of the line. "You there . . . ?" he asked.

"I already took care of the car," Veronica said. "Go home and get some sleep. You're going to need your energy this weekend."

"Mmm. I like the sound of that," he said.

"I'm going to kick your butt all over the tennis court."

"Oh."

Roger turned and saw Layla walking briskly back to the table. He said goodbye abruptly, pasted on a smile, and waved for the check.

They strolled uptown under a light breeze toward Layla's penthouse on the Upper East Side. The walk calmed Roger down. He half-listened as Layla talked easily, once referencing all the nights she'd spent alone inside her posh apartment. He'd drop her off, knowing he'd done his business and shown her a good time.

When they reached her building, Layla placed her hand on Roger's lapel. "The conditions are perfect for a three hundred and sixty degree view of the city," she said. "Can I invite you up for a nightcap? I have prototypes of the new products. We can discuss those recipes."

She came closer and slid her hand to his shoulder. "The view truly is breathtaking. Promise."

Roger unconsciously picked his head up and then took a deep breath. He looked down and locked his eyes on her, considering the offer. She moved closer and he felt her firm breasts graze his chest. He hesitated for a moment, and then took her by the hand and walked her inside.

The view from Layla's sprawling apartment on the thirtieth floor was stunning. Layla motioned Roger to the wraparound sofa set covered with Fortuny fabric in the center of an impeccably furnished living room. She disappeared into the kitchen and returned with two unmarked bottles of clear liquor, crystal cocktail glasses, and a sterling silver ice bucket. Roger loosened his tie as Layla poured small portions into the glasses.

He inhaled the liquor's fragrant aroma. "Mmm, smells aromatic, like tropical fruits, with maybe a hint of ginger and orange zest?"

"That's persimmon mango rum with North American ginseng extract. It has traces of horny goat weed to promote male potency."

He took a sip and winked. "What's in yours?"

"A blend of vanilla, chamomile, taurine vodka with flower essences for enhancing fertility . . . and maca for a woman's desire," she said, clinking glasses. "Aren't they wonderful?"

Roger nodded and raised his glass. "Here's to Peacock and *Plates*!"

Layla added, "To a *satisfying* partnership."

"*Salute*," Roger said, smiling in agreement and neatly finishing the drink with one swallow.

"Would you like a tour?" Layla asked, taking his glass and placing it on the table.

His eyes lit up as he followed her. "This place is awesome and your views . . . I think I can see the Tower of London from here."

Layla guided him through the rooms, describing details of her artifacts and an impressive array of paintings, topped by a late stage Jackson Pollock and a small Dali. Roger followed her rump as it wiggled across the room. He wondered what life would be like waking up every day to a woman like Layla. She was no Veronica, but she was rich and relatively attractive. And, of course, she had those tits, he mused, turning off his phone.

"You have excellent taste," he said. "And you're so down-to-earth about having all this. Men must be falling all over themselves trying to get with you."

"Most of the ones I meet are either intimidated by my father's reputation or gold diggers. They're so obvious," Layla said. She squeezed his hand. "You haven't seen the bedroom."

There was a four-poster bed covered in reams of satin with a veil of finely spun silk draped between the posts. Layla flitted around the room lighting pillar candles. Roger half-expected half-naked servants to enter the room bearing silver bowls with hibiscus petals floating in water. When Layla finished she stood facing him, tilting her head back and pushing her bosom into his chest. Roger leaned down and kissed her. A few moments later, they were littering their clothing across the Moroccan carpet. Roger quickly undressed her down to a pink and black custom-designed bra-and-panties ensemble. He was hard by the time he unsnapped her brassiere, releasing her full breasts. They swayed free, her firm nipples quickly finding their way into his mouth. He eased her slowly onto her back and slipped on a condom. She was already wet when he entered her. He pushed himself deep inside, thinking *Google this*.

Soon Roger was covered in sweat. He pounded away, wondering how she could take it, but she just looked up, smiling. He sped up and finally exploded with a furious release. Afterward, she threw on her silk robe and slinked out of the bedroom. She returned brandishing a silver tray with macaroons and tall glasses of iced mint tea. Then she slipped her heels off and sat on the edge of the bed, feeding Roger and then tracing her nails lightly across his chest.

"Ouch!"

"Oh, so sensitive. What happened? Did I do that?"

"No, no. Someone spilled coffee on me today. It's just a little raw." She leaned over, nursing the area with soft kisses. Roger stared at her ceiling as she slowly slid her body down his torso, securing his penis between her breasts. Then, with a little grunt, she took him in her mouth.

Despite Layla's protests, Roger climbed out of her bed sometime after one. He felt her eyes watching him as he dressed. When he looked over, she smiled and ran her tongue over her lips.

"I really have to go," he said, notching his belt. "I've got a big meeting . . . in a couple of hours."

She followed him to the door and smiled as he rumbled down the hallway.

Back at his apartment, even after the hot shower, Roger was still wound up. He popped opened a can of Coors Light and sat naked at his computer. It had been a very long day, and by this time his tryst with Gail had been reduced to a vague recollection. As long as it didn't affect her performance at work, there'd be no problem. His bedding of Layla was strictly business, a means to an end . . .

survival. At least now his deal looked promising, but still, he felt used up and empty, and even a little bit cheap. He wanted to call Max, but it was too late. Then, after drafting an e-mail, he realized his folly and deleted it.

The beer steadied him, so he logged in online, clicking to his favorite dating site. He leaned closer and checked the green lights he'd received over the past two days. Tiger in Her Tank from Ozone Park looked long in the tooth and Talented Westsider peppered her profile with too many *I don't like's*. Roger deleted them and a handful of others. Then he saw a response from the woman Max had pointed out— Cassidy's friend, the one from Brooklyn who called herself Higher Ground. She appeared even prettier than the first time he'd seen her face. He quickly typed a short reply, including his phone number, and hit "send." Then he stumbled to his bed and passed out.

CHAPTER 13

Once the staff had secured the umbrellas into the cedar picnic tables, everything was in place for the first of Henry Goodson's lunchtime barbeques on the roof of his agency's Lafayette Street office. The open space provided a respite from the pressures of the ad business, and the employees looked forward to these relaxed bonding sessions. The showers had passed, and by midday the sun appeared high in the sky. Junior members of the staff wheeled out trays of burgers, hot dogs, and salads, plus the usual salty snacks and cold beverages, including a keg of Brooklyn Beer. The entire agency emerged on the roof at noon and began eating and socializing before taking off for the long weekend.

Although his amicable demeanor never showed any strain, the three decades of agency life had taken their toll on Henry. He was fielding another grueling phone call in his office when his assistant poked her head in the doorway and pointed to her watch. Henry acknowledged her with a nod while listening to his Bobalooie client vent about the failure of the agency's ideas during recent focus groups. Henry turned to the window. He couldn't recall a tougher time at the agency since he'd bought out his partner in the eighties.

"We need creative that moves the needle, Henry," his client said pointedly, "and we want your top account person assigned to our business. We can't expect you to keep managing the day-to-day details on our account."

"You're my top priority, Scooter. We'll get you new ideas by the end of next week."

Henry maintained a positive attitude, but covering the flagship account while still searching for Max's replacement reminded him that advertising was a game for younger players. Feeling tightness around his heart, he reached for the aspirin. He wasn't sure how much more client pressure he could withstand.

Cassidy scrolled through her BlackBerry during her cab ride to Lafayette Street. She stopped and clicked when she noticed an e-mail from a B. Banks.

Hi Cassidy,

Jimmy and I are attending the "Rock 'n' Read" next week. Hope to see you there.

Brenton Banks

She paused for a moment, considered her reply, and then decided to go with the bland *Looking forward to seeing you both, Cassidy.*

When she arrived at her father's office, her spirits were soaring. Earlier that morning, she'd put the final touches on the first issue of *My Radiance.* She was now ready for a three-day weekend at the shore to recharge her batteries. Climbing the narrow stairs to the roof in her white embroidered peasant top and faded skinny jeans, she found herself loosening from the tight grip of her busy morning. Hearing the laughter, animated conversation, and music, Cassidy quickened her steps. Her father was holding court at a table with a group of young creatives, retelling a tale about his working through a long, hot Memorial Day weekend when the agency was in its infancy. Cassidy smiled as she watched him entertaining the group in his white shirt and jeans. When he spotted his daughter, Henry raised his plastic cup and smiled.

"Where's the beer?" Cassidy asked. "We just green-lighted the premier issue of the magazine, so I'm officially on vacation for the next three days." She smiled and acknowledged the ripple of applause as her father and the crew greeted her.

After a few hugs with former coworkers, Cassidy grabbed a plate of food, took a seat next to her dad, and then easily engaged in light banter with the friendly faces around the table. Across the rooftop, an impromptu acoustic guitar jam began.

Henry placed his hand on his daughter's shoulder. "Thank God no one asked me to play the guitar. I haven't learned a new song since 'Stairway to Heaven.' "

"Oh, c'mon. No one seemed to mind the last time you played," Cassidy said. "How are you feeling?"

"I feel good, kid, but the doctors keep telling me to slow down."

"Then listen to them. You're all I have. Don't worry so much about the business. You've got a great team here."

"I guess I do," Henry said with a trace of resignation in his voice.

"Everything okay?"

"We're holding our own." Henry could sense that his daughter wasn't buying his usual upbeat response. "That's what I keep telling these kids so they don't leave. If there's any more attrition I might have a problem."

"Max shouldn't have left," she responded.

"Nonsense. Talented people need to keep moving or they get stale."

"Daddy, stop being so nice. That's your problem."

"No, baby. It's all connected. In the long run, it's best when the people who move on succeed. It reflects well on the agency."

Cassidy looked down into her beer. "So what's going on with Bobalooie?"

"They're a little uptight, but I'm keeping tabs on them. You know the drill." He shrugged. "You're only as good as your last meeting. We have to come up with a new campaign or they might start talking to other agencies. Who knows, even HHI could take a run at the account."

"Not with Max there. He'd never allow that." Cassidy locked her cornflower-blue eyes on her dad.

"He might not have a choice," Henry said. "But right now, I'm doing whatever it takes to keep this agency afloat. Then I'll find someone who can take over for me. I'm getting tired of the grind and was hoping that person was Max. But that's not an option now."

Cassidy nodded. "That girl he was seeing pressured him into taking the job."

"The good-looking blonde?" Henry said. "She must have gotten into his head. And if she's anything like what you've described, I'm not surprised. Women like that can make men start wars. He'll have to learn the hard way."

"Women start wars, too," she said pointedly.

"*Jealous* women start wars. But that's not you." He raised an eyebrow and then broke into a teasing grin, pushing a curl off her face. "Buy you another beer?"

CHAPTER 14

The skies were clearing as Layla stared out through the wall of windows toward Queens. That's where she'd grown up and her father had started out. She wished she could enjoy the fresh spring air, but her father's towering office building was sealed like a jar.

Her father took his seat at the head of the long dining table and tucked an embroidered silk napkin into his belt. "You look so relaxed," he said. "And that suit. It reminds me of your mother. Gold was her favorite thing in the world."

"Thank you, Papa," she said. "I love this suit, and Mom loved Gucci, too."

"She did," he said. "So, tell me, what's going on with your boozy drinks?"

"It's going well. Everyone has so many great ideas for them."

"You should make them with Ouzo," he said, adjusting a cufflink and then smoothing his mustache.

"We tried anise, but the other flavors tested better. I'm looking at a program with *Plates*, the new food magazine," she said. "They have the connections to help us get distribution in the top restaurants."

"*Plates*? What's that? I know *Gourmet*," Nikola said. A staffer rolled out a silver cart and served them red snapper with fingerling potatoes, tomatoes, and Kalamata black olives over rice.

"I've got my people looking into these digital media companies. Everyone's staring at their computer screens all day. Someone's got to sell them something," he said, tucking a piece of fish into his mouth.

Layla picked at her food. "That makes sense, Papa. The numbers support it. I've got some ideas for promoting our products online and . . ."

"I have a company in mind," he said.

"Which one?"

"Globison—their online division."

Layla's eyes grew wide. "Last week one of their sales people called me and made a great case for advertising with them. And they really know branded content and social media."

Nikola poured himself some wine. "See what you can find out about their financials," he said.

"They're putting together a proposal for me."

"That's a start," he said, tasting the wine and then wiping his mouth. "But this business—it's so cutthroat." His steely eyes pierced hers. "I'm looking forward to you joining me very soon."

She smiled wanly. "Papa, we've been over this. I have a great opportunity to build something of my own—"

He threw his napkin on the table. "I'm talking about working with your family."

Familiar with her father's temper, Layla chose her words carefully.

"Let me talk to this salesperson from Globison again. I'll see what I can find out about them," she said. If he insisted on sharing his empire with her, he'd have to do better—a lot better—than playing the daddy card. "I'm going to freshen up," she said, pushing away from the table. "I'll meet you upstairs at the helicopter."

Nikola clipped a cigar and then boomed at his staff, "Someone take these damn dishes away!"

CHAPTER 15

When Max arrived at Bette's office for their one o'clock meeting, the door was closed. Her assistant was at lunch. Max leaned over the desk and dialed Bette's extension.

She picked up on the third ring. "I thought I said no calls," Bette said sharply.

"It's Max. I'm here for our one o'clock. Wanna do this later?"

Bette cleared her throat. "Give me just a second."

When she opened the door, her face was whiter than usual. "Sorry. We just had our departmental meeting," she said. "You'd think after all of the new business the agency's won, we'd be hiring, not firing people."

Max took a seat on the couch. "So what happened?"

"They let three senior-level creative teams go."

"Why? Who the hell . . ."

"Who do you think? It was Gloss's meeting. He says there are too many high-level creatives who don't have enough billable hours to pay their salaries."

"Shit. What else?"

"We've been reorganized, so now the only account I'm working on is Peacock Beverages. They assigned my other remaining projects to some twenty-four-year-old blonde who's all legs." Bette glared in the direction of Gloss's office. "He's weeding out the people who built this agency."

"Probably thinks he can get by with junior people," Max said.

"Like on a major league baseball team—when a player's salary gets too high, they bring up some kid from the minors and . . ."

"Would you be upset if I told you to lose the sports metaphors?" Bette said. "I've got to come up with the right campaign for Peacock or I'm out." She crossed her arms, her eyes narrowing. "That tight-assed prick wants me gone. We both started out, at different times of course, at the same agency. Gloss was a little brown-nose account coordinator. Oh, I've seen how he screws people and believe me, he wasn't thrilled when he first recognized my face in the conference room. He's looking for an excuse. Has he said anything to you?"

"Not a word. I want you working on Peacock. There's no one else here who understands image advertising like you. And I can quarterback the team and get the ball into the end zone," Max said, forcing a smile. "Can I see the work?"

She nodded and picked up a stack of white foam boards filled with stock photography images and bold copy. "Okay, I call this first campaign 'Angel's Share.' The artwork combines celestial imagery with Eastern influences, and the copy borrows from mythology to describe the different flavors."

Max studied each board and then placed them on the coffee table. "Nice layouts. A bit ethereal, but beautiful images. We can present these. What about the others?"

Bette picked up a second pile of boards and spread them out. "These are the badass ideas. There are seven products in the line, so we came up with 'The Seven Deadly Sins.' And here are the seven models, each showcasing a different sin."

Max surveyed the retro B-movie graphics and a bevy of scantily clad, overly developed women depicted in a graphic novel style. *What was I thinking? I'm an idiot,* he thought while composing himself to address the creative director. "Interesting. I like the cowgirl outfit. Never thought of holstering a liquor bottle. But don't you think the leather-clad kitty with the whip and handcuffs are a bit much?"

"Something wrong with leather?" she quipped. "Max, these young guys have seen it all. They've grown up with online porn and those laddie magazines. You told me to go for it."

My bad. My very bad, he thought. "That's true, but I'm not sure about these. The sex is there, but where's the fun?"

"What's not fun about a nun pole dancing on a giant swizzle stick?"

"Was there a third idea?"

"Here," she said, handing Max the boards. He flipped through the stack, studying each one closely and nodding his head. The artwork was vibrant, colorful, and visually arresting. Bette had embedded a visual game into the layout of each ad centered on a flavor or key ingredient. Max read the few lines of copy that anchored each concept and spread the work on the table.

"I get it. What looks like snow-covered mountains with skiers are actually scoops of coconut ice cream. And in that one, the blueberries are scattered in the shape of a bear. But you have to look closely to see it."

"Right. That's my blue-bear-y. Get it?"

"Cool. So in this one, the mango is shaped like a fist. And here," he said, picking up another storyboard, "all those brown roots curled up at the base of these tree trunks spell out G-I-N-S-E-N-G. Has anyone seen these?" Max added, flipping through the boards a second time.

"No, I came up with the concept over the weekend. You like the copy?"

"It's great. You managed to highlight the holistic ingredients without overpromising or sounding preachy." He replaced the boards on the table. "What would you think of commissioning artists from the countries where the natural additives and ingredients are sourced and paying them to paint your concepts?"

"They create paintings for us and we turn them into ads," Bette said, nodding.

"And we'll use the images all over the website. They could work for viral videos, too." Max said. "That's where we can get into more details about the holistic aspects of the ingredients. Maybe even use the artwork for limited edition bottles." He put the boards down and rubbed his palms together. "So what do you call these?"

"Great advertising," she said, laughing. "I don't think we need a name. They speak for themselves. Hey, Hallyday, you're not that bad, for an account guy."

"Imagine that. We'll need to keep a lid on this. Keep working, but don't show these to anyone. I'll let you know as soon as I nail down the date for the client meeting," Max said. His phone beeped as he walked out. Gloss.

Back in his office, Max left a message with Gloss's assistant and then checked his voice mail. Cassidy had phoned earlier. Before diving into his pile of work, he returned her call.

"I still can't get over those monkeys. So surprisingly . . . charming," Cassidy said lightly.

"I knew you'd appreciate them. There's something about springtime that brings out the best in the male species."

"Yes, insightful. So, like I told you, we're going with your column— after a few tweaks of course," she said. "I really feel this can work. Hope you're working on the next one. Something with more . . . heat."

"Who am I, Jimmy Olsen?" he said, flipping his empty energy drink into the recycling can.

"Jimmy Olsen was a photographer; you're a writer, and I'm an editor with a deadline—okay? So how's the research going?"

"Roger blew me off last night," Max said, gazing at his e-mail.

"You better come up with something. The next issue goes to press in a week."

"How about an insider's view on hot monkey love?"

"Max, I'm serious. Don't let me down."

"Right," he said. Gloss's name lit up his telephone consul, dashing Max's hopes for a quietly productive afternoon. "Gotta go."

He picked up. "Kent, how are you?"

"Holiday, we need additional revenue next quarter, so I'm making a few changes."

Max braced himself.

"Holiday, are you there?"

"Yes, Kent."

"The numbers aren't looking so good, so we have to consolidate the creative teams. Your creative director for Peacock, the one with the pasty face—is it Betty?"

"It's Bette. Not Bett-y."

"Well, I'm afraid we'll have to let . . ."

"No way."

"Holiday, she isn't pulling her weight. And frankly, she makes too much money."

"She earns it. No one in this agency produces image advertising like Bette. I need her. *We* need her. "

"Have you set up the meeting with Bobalooie yet?"

"Kent . . ."

"I want that account, Holiday, and *you* need it, since *Bette's* jumbo salary just became your problem."

"Bobalooie's not leaving Goodson," Max said. "And Tooka Wooka's the new Bobalooie. They're working on a line of natural candies and gum with vitamins and antioxidants."

"Sweets rot their teeth, but kids are still keen for them just the way they are. I'm giving you a pass on the creative gal for now, but get me that meeting with your ex-client before I change my mind. Am I clear Hol-i-day?"

"Crystal, Kent. Crystal."

CHAPTER 16

Roger spent the morning hiding in his office behind a large container of coffee, finalizing preparations for his trip to the Bahamas. The lump beneath his eye had swollen and turned a deep reddish-purple, and he nursed an incessant hangover that made his head feel like it had been assaulted with a ball-peen hammer. He was avoiding Gail, even taking his own calls. At lunch he passed a deli and considered picking up a small bouquet of flowers for her, but instead popped into the Thomas Pink store and picked out a new shirt and tie for himself. He had been shifting against his chair back all morning due to a tight back from his late-night gymnastics with Layla. But now he could feel confident about submitting a revised sales forecast with a substantial increase built into her program.

When Max's number appeared on his phone, Roger shook off the guilt and reminded himself that Layla and Max would both benefit from his deceit. At least, that was the idea. Roger was doing them both a favor. They just didn't know it yet.

"Dude, que pasa?" Roger said. "How are things in the shark tank?"

"Oh . . . great. Never better," Max said dryly. "So what happened last night? I thought we were on."

"Sorry, man. Had a late meeting, then a sales dinner. Hope I didn't hold you up."

"I needed to pack for the weekend anyway. What are you up to later?"

Roger touched the mouse under his eye. "I'm pretty beat and I've got an early flight. I can meet for a drink."

"How about a run in the park?" Max suggested. "Work up a thirst."

"Running?" Roger shrugged. "What the hell? Maybe sweating out the poison will help."

"Good, and I'm up for another tutorial from the master," Max said, chuckling.

Roger drained his coffee. "Yes, we need to get you laid. Heard from Veronica?"

"Nah, but I've got her right where I want her. She's probably toying with some fool who's trying to impress her. She'll tear him up like a squeaky chew toy and move on to her next treat."

Roger held his tongue, and then said, "You sound like a man on a mission. Let's go for that run and compare notes. Maybe I can pick up a few pointers from you. Meet me at the entrance of the park across from Columbus Circle at six thirty."

Roger hung up and shook his head. *Max was so weak sometimes— about women, about work. He needed a lesson from the alpha dog.*

Roger waved to Max, who was sitting on the steps along Central Park's southwest entrance.

"Hey man," Max said, pointing at Roger's bruise. "What happened?"

"Tripped on the stairs. Can you believe it?"

"Nope," Max said, stretching his hamstrings.

"Okay, I got my ass kicked by a boxing kangaroo."

"That sounds more feasible. I'll bet some chick belted you."

"Let's go," Roger said, as they made their way toward the park's interior loop. "What's the latest on Peacock and your psycho boss?"

"Business is busy. Psycho is still crazy."

"As long as your clients are spending their money . . ."

They broke into a light jog when they reached the asphalt roadway. Central Park was an explosion of greenery. Not even the roar of rush-hour traffic could dampen the beauty of the park's rolling landscape, still glistening from a midday shower. The two men jogged easily and turned east, slowly climbing the park's outer loop. They passed the carousel toward the series of sloping hills behind the Metropolitan Museum of Art.

Max moved briskly alongside his friend. A droplet of sweat dripped from the bottom of Roger's sideburns. With his long strides, he usually outperformed Max in the five-mile road races they'd enter. But today, Max was feeling his groove. While sidestepping nuggets of horse manure left behind by the carriages that traversed the winding path, he began his inquiry.

"So, professor, what's your motivation for seducing all these women? What do you really want?"

Roger shook his arms, trying to loosen up. He glanced at Max, puzzled. "Are you writing a book on dating or something?" he asked.

Max felt his face turning red and looked away for a moment. "Is it about the hunt or the kill?"

Roger rolled his eyes. "I'm a red-blooded American who believes in God and puppies and Thanksgiving and well-built blondes. Something wrong with that?"

"Do they need to be blondes?"

"I like *all* women, but it helps if they're stacked." Roger cracked a smile. "All races, creeds, and colors are welcome in Roger's world. And if they wax, they get a check-plus."

Max laughed and picked up the pace. "You may be shallow, but you're inclusive."

"I'm real," Roger replied, unfazed. "If women can't deal with the truth, it's not my problem. I focus only on top-shelf ladies. Why? Because hot chicks are fun. Guys go out of their way, taking them to cool places—so they get lots of exposure. Makes 'em interesting and better in bed. Plus, time is a relentless prick. We're not young forever, so why bother with anything but the best?"

"So is this your way of living in the now?"

"I'm not sure about all that, but I don't want to wake up in my fifties and be hanging in East Side bars sniffing for women. But, ya never know," Roger said, turning as an attractive jogger ran by. "See that?" he said with a glint in his eye. "You need to pay attention. Women love this city, *amigo.* Know why?"

"Enlighten me," Max said.

"First, they come to New York because it gives them the best shot at getting a fair shake in business."

"Agreed," Max said.

"But, of course, that also means that a lot of misguided nutcases migrate to the city, too."

"So, what does that mean?"

"In New York, even if you're totally fucked up, at first people give you a pass. They assume that you're just eccentric. Eventually the crazies get found out. But by then it's too late. It's bad . . . spoils the gene pool."

"Because they never leave."

"*Exactly*," Roger said, laughing. "And second, look at these build-ings. Dude, New York's totally phallic. Women love living in the middle of . . ."

"A city of gigantic penises?"

"Think about it," Roger said.

Max couldn't stop laughing. As they approached the next hill, Roger was breathing heavily. Perspiration streamed down his fore-head and soaked through his heather-gray T-shirt. Max had bro-ken into a light cooling sweat. His muscles loosened as he pressed forward.

"So what does it mean?"

"It means Uncle Roger's going to follow his pecker and have as much fun as he can. New York women are savvy and successful. They're here for a good time, too, and they love to fuck. Is there a problem?"

"Relax. I'm just asking," Max said, bemused by his friend's Lothario Philosophies 101.

Roger's lips curled. "You know, there's a reason why your ex is your ex. You think too much. Don't take this the wrong way, but I'll bet she wants a guy who takes charge."

Max's stride became more determined. "Someone who takes what-ever he wants?"

"Something like that."

"Do you ever consider how anyone else feels?"

"Women in New York are independent. They have free will, they live with their choices, and they're as sexual as men. I haven't heard any complaints."

"Ever stick around long enough to find out?" Max retorted.

As they approached the crest of Cat Hill, behind the museum, Roger's pace began to slow. Max gestured with his head for Roger to pick it up.

"I thought you wanted a few tips on scoring," Roger said, straining now. "This is like final arguments with Perry Mason. Plus, it's bloody hot out here."

Max smiled as he veered onto the muddy cinder-and-gravel bridle path below the reservoir. Roger struggled to match him. A few horse-back riders galloped past, sending clumps of mud off their hooves.

Max sidestepped clops of manure and continued his questioning. "So it's all about taking whatever you want?"

"What's with you today?" Roger asked, slightly breathless.

"I want to know if you ever think about the consequences of your actions."

"I take what's available. If it's not available, I don't get it. Get it?" Roger said.

"Got it. Take whatever's available. Oh yeah—*right*," Max said wryly, stepping over a divot in the muddy trail.

Roger lumbered along, his energy now waning from the previous night. Max pushed ahead toward the drinking fountain at the reservoir. He heard thundering hooves in the mud closing in from behind. As he stepped to the side, he saw Roger slip and fall headfirst into the path of the horses. Max turned, grabbed Roger by the arm, and yanked him sideways, losing his own balance. Max landed on top of him, but managed to roll them off the path.

It was quiet for a moment as the riders assessed the situation. Max and Roger were both covered in mud, but neither appeared hurt. The handsome woman sitting high in the saddle of the lead horse looked down at them dismissively. Then she tugged the reigns and led the other riders away in a brisk gallop.

Max wiped his face and checked Roger. There was a large piece of mud stuck to the middle of his forehead and he was breathing heavily. Max picked off the chunk of dirt and threw it aside. "Your third eye was blocked. C'mon, let's get cleaned up."

Roger forced a weak smile as Max helped him to his feet. They walked slowly back to the stairs leading to the water fountain. As runners jogging around the reservoir converged on the fountain, a few looked bemused at the two mud-soaked men splashing water on each other. Roger pulled his shirt over his head and sat against the chain-link fence surrounding the reservoir. Max leaned over and stretched his hamstrings. Roger's eye was unerringly drawn to a pretty blonde in short black tights who stopped for a drink. Roger watched her as she held up her hair to sip some water.

"Incoming," Roger murmured, peeling mud off his shoes. As soon as the young woman finished drinking, Roger was ready with a line. "Excuse me, do you know anything about ankle injuries?"

The woman looked at him curiously, taking in Roger's naked chest and muddied shorts while considering his question. "I know a little bit. I'm a physical therapist," she answered. Then she relaxed into a smile and asked, "Are you all right?"

Roger looked back at her innocently. "I'm not sure."

A few minutes later, Roger nodded admiringly as he watched the woman depart in the direction where Max was stretching. Max smiled up at her and said something as she passed by that made her stop to talk. Roger saw Max pointing at him and then they both laughed. When the young woman finally bounded down the stairs and trotted off, her ponytail swung gaily behind her.

Roger stood up and approached Max. "Just so you know, I gave blondie my business card. I always keep a few on hand even if they get a little sweaty. Twenty bucks says she calls me this week."

Max put his hand out and Roger slapped it. "Deal," Max responded. Then he reached into the small pocket in his shorts, pulled out a woman's business card, and said, "Not if I call her first."

"Whoa! Nice one," Roger said, with a fist bump. "He's back! How did you do it?"

"Highlights at eleven, Roger. You ready for a cold one?"

They exited the park on West 96th Street, walked up Broadway, and stopped at a tavern across from Roger's apartment. The barroom was dark and musty, filled with groups of men watching the Mets game on a small television.

"Sierra Nevada," Max called out across the bar. "Rog?"

"I'll have a Steve McQueen," said Roger, picking off a hunk of caked-up mud from his leg.

"What?"

"You heard me. This guy knows how to make 'em," Roger said, nodding to the bartender.

"And a Steve McQueen . . . for my friend. A horse ran over him."

The heavy-jowled bartender looked at them and frowned. "You want that McQueen with Maker's, right?" he said to Roger.

"Yup." Roger turned to Max and brushed dirt away from his friend's shoulder. "A Steve McQueen is like a Manhattan. I like mine with a good bourbon and blackberry brandy. No vermouth and no bitters."

"I see why he died so young," said Max.

The bartender set Max's beer and the cocktail down on the bar. Roger raised his glass appreciatively and tapped Max's bottle before taking a drink of his syrupy concoction. "Now that is fucking good."

Max sipped some beer and asked, "What's the most important thing a guy needs to score women?"

Roger smacked his lips and made a mock salute with his drink, smiling. "Confidence. That's the key."

"And in this town, a little cash never hurts either," Max said with a laugh.

"*No romance without finance?* It's not just the money. Women dig men who believe in themselves and take risks. Remember Jack McRandy, the copywriter?"

Max nodded.

"Well, he was fired after his guerilla marketing team got arrested on their way over to Governors Island. They were planning to wrap a mega-sized pair of the client's adult diapers around the Statue of Liberty. Insane."

"Never happened," Max countered, shaking his head.

"True story. So, as the legend goes, after he gets canned, he packs up and moves to India and washes elephants for a year. When he comes back to New York, he's broke and has no job, but—and here's the thing—he acted like he didn't give a shit. The guy oozed confidence, and women were all over him and his tales about finding his spiritual path. Then he cashed in with a book about his travels." Roger leaned in. "Ever see his wife? She's from one of those countries in Eastern Europe where they grow models. Dude, it's all about the attitude." He jerked his head toward the park. "Look how easy it was meeting that blonde back there."

"Yeah, thanks for loosening her up for me," Max said, brandishing her card again and placing it on the bar. "How do you like them apples?"

When Roger reached over, Max covered it with his hand. "Twenty bucks."

"Fuck, I'll buy the drinks," Roger said, throwing a few bills down. "What I meant was, you did what came naturally. Nowadays it's tricky when you approach a lady without an introduction from a friend or business colleague who vouches for you. You might seem nice, but when she's separated from the herd, you're still a strange man to her."

"I *am* a strange man," Max said.

"Assume that when you're a new prospect to a woman, even if she thinks you're cute, you start at the bottom. Even if they'll never admit it, that's embedded in women's estrogen-fueled subconscious. They've all fallen for that guy who they thought was *the one*, but who turned out to be weird and scary."

"You really think that's where we start out?"

"Absolutely. We must atone for the sins of the jerks that have forsaken them. Women wear an invisible armor. They need it," Roger explained, swirling the ice in his drink, "because as soon as they let it down, they're vulnerable."

"To what?"

"To Uncle Roger's big-old wang dang doodle . . . and his boyish charm. That's why you have to smile and be nice and show her that you may be *the one*," Roger said, his fingers flashing quotation marks.

Max raised his eyebrows "So that's how Uncle Roger begins a relationship?"

"*Relationship?* I'm talking about a hookup."

"Ever think that you might be one of those guys?" Max asked.

"Which guys?" Roger stalled.

"The guys who make women feel guarded." Roger stared back straight-faced and Max chuckled. "Didn't think you'd get it. Roger, here's a test for you. What are four things couples need to have in common for their relationship to work?"

"Sex and money . . . and oh yeah, money and sex," Roger said. "That's four. I miss any?"

"You got two," Max said. "The other two are values and lifestyles."

"Sex and money I understand. What do you mean *values*?"

"It's easier to connect if both people had similar upbringings, like how their families view life and treat people."

"And lifestyles?"

"You don't need to do everything together, but if she digs five-star hotels and you're set on raising chickens in the backyard, there may be a disconnect."

"How about chemistry?" asked Roger.

"File that under sex."

"What if one person's rich?" Roger said, jiggling the ice in his drink.

"See values. It's more about what money *means* to them and how they manage it," Max said before taking another pull on his beer.

"So it's not only how much you have, but how you perceive money?"

"Bingo. Bartender, another Steve McQueen over here," Max said.

"Fuck values. I'll stick with sex and money. Anything else I've missed?"

"Well, you've convinced me that you really need help," said Max, laughing. "And it certainly doesn't sound like you're ready to settle down."

"I'm telling you that my wrangling days will soon be over. When I meet the right woman, I'll hang up my spurs. You'll see, *amigo*."

"Is that what a cowboy really wants?"

"Yep. But for now, I'll keep hitting the open trail," Roger declared, holding up his empty glass. "Gotta roll. Early flight."

"The fishing trip to Florida?"

"Tarpon and hopefully marlin, too. Whatever's cruising the Caribbean will find its way onto my dinner plate."

"I never heard of taking clients fishing over Memorial Day," Max mused.

"*Plates* has a special deal. And we've got the big boat. Remember, Gilligan?"

Max studied Roger as he sucked the ice from his glass.

"I don't recall it looking like a fishing boat."

Roger checked his watch again and cleared his throat. "Maximum, thanks for the run and for the whole saving-me-from-getting-trampled thing," Roger said, noticing his friend watching him. "The car's picking me up early. Need to pack up my pole and tackle. Have fun at the shore. Golf next weekend?" He held out his hand.

Max slapped Roger's palm. "Be careful of the undertow."

Roger gave him a puzzled look and said, "Yeah, see you next week."

Max watched Roger cross the street and enter his building. His stomach was growling, so he decided to stay and ordered a crab cake sandwich and another beer. Night was falling when he signaled for the check. He glanced up at the television. The Mets game was a blowout. Staring at the traffic through the grimy window, he thought about his friend's unique perspective. *Roger was either carrying a heavy emotional burden or content in his self-delusion.*

Max glimpsed back at the window and noticed Roger standing in front of his building at a waiting cab, lugging a garment bag, a carry-on case—and no fishing gear. Max tossed money on the bar and hurried outside. As Roger's taxi turned into the park, Max flagged his own cab, jumped in, and said, "Follow that car," cringing when he heard himself.

The driver, a gray-haired man with an impressive turban, smiled excitedly and declared, "Yes, sir!" He then sped off in pursuit of Roger's vehicle.

Max's eyes were riveted on Roger's cab as it headed east. When it exited the park, it closed in on Veronica's block. Max pushed back, closed his eyes, and said, *"Fuck."*

At the red traffic light, he pictured himself kicking down her door, wrestling Roger to the ground, and hammering a second black eye. The driver looked back in the mirror. Max's face was dark. He took a few deep breaths until finally his wave of anger subsided. Still, he glowered out the window thinking, *There's got to be a better way to handle a barracuda like Roger.* The driver glanced back again, awaiting directions.

"Turn around," Max said, as the light turned green.

He seethed all the way home, wishing he hadn't saved Roger from a well-deserved trampling. He slammed the door behind him as he entered his apartment. As if on a mission, he flipped open his laptop and began typing. An hour later, he forwarded his second column to Cassidy.

THE GUY TO AVOID—Part One

Last time we met I made a few promises. But you know about men and promises. In future columns, I'll give you behind-the-scenes looks into the lives of men in this city and the ways they get you into bed. But before I begin, you need to be honest with yourself. You're part of the problem. If you weren't so intent on having everything your way, right now, you'd be able to protect your heart from a guy who's made a science out of the art of seduction.

There are lots of good guys out there, but how exciting is that? We've all heard that nice guys come in last. But part of their cellar dwelling is because of you. It's understandable. People respond to clever advertising and slick packaging. And as smart and intuitive as you are, there's always that one guy who convinces you to break your rules. I'm not referring to "The One." No, I mean that OTHER one—"The Guy to Avoid." He's the game changer. The guy who cracked your pin code and hijacked your password. Deep down you knew that he was wrong for you, but you let him in anyway.

Maybe you met at a friend's party, or a business function, or in the parallel universe known as online dating. It doesn't matter. He sold you a bill of goods, sweet-talked you out of your panties, and was gone. Don't be embarrassed. It happens all the time.

Guys know him, too. We all have a friend like that. He's good-looking, quick-witted, athletic, and fun to be around. The social connector. And even if he seems to work half as hard as we do, he gets twice as much in return.

We know that when we're in his company we've joined an exclusive fraternity that gets us near the prettiest girls and into the hottest clubs. He's a cool guy, and although this isn't a man-crush, there are benefits to being his friend. That is, until we leave him alone with our girlfriends. Then we find out the hard way, too.

When you met him, it was the same. His eyes sparkled and his stories made you laugh. He seemed sensitive. He traveled, had a good job, dressed well, and lived in a great apartment that was clean and filled with really cool stuff. Your first date was short and fun. A second glass of Sancerre at a bustling lounge and then a quick bite to eat because you were having such a great time and he didn't want you to leave. At the end of the night, he leaned over and stole a kiss after hailing you a cab.

On the second date, he takes you to that hot new fusion place in MePa where the staff smiles at you approvingly and whisks you to a prime table. He takes charge of everything, picks a wonderful bottle of wine, and again keeps you laughing throughout dinner. There's no waiting in line at the club and the champagne makes you feel sexy, so you cut loose and grind on him a little on the dance floor. This is how a date should go. And then you give into his soft lips and deep soulful kisses in the back of the cab. But what flips your switch is the way he looks into your eyes and tells you how different he feels and how comfortable he is around you.

So you go back to his place, and when it feels right, he leads you into his room. You slip off your dress and you ravage one another all night. The next morning, after making love a second time, he cooks you breakfast. You're thinking that this is different and he might be "The One." Then, an hour later, you're sitting in a cab wearing the same clothes you wore the previous night, already wanting to call him. A day goes by and you wait, and then wait some more, but he doesn't call. So you phone him and your call goes directly to voice mail. This can't be happening, not to you. So you call again. No response. Later, your self-esteem reaches a new low while you type that e-mail—the one where your emotions get so tangled up that you're not sure what you can say without sounding like a pathetic fool. But he never replies, and finally the reality hits you in the gut. You've been had.

I'm sorry. Did that upset you? I'm sure it did, because I know how much you give and how much "The Guy to Avoid" takes. But you're too smart and work way too hard to let yourself be used that way ever again. And please try not to take it out on the next guy.

Hang in there with me and I'll break this down further when we get together again. And that's a promise. Maybe nice guys aren't so bad after all.

Until next time,

Rod

CHAPTER 17

Despite the gusts of wind blowing along the Garden State Parkway, Serena kept the top down on her Volkswagen Cabriolet. Cassidy curled up in the passenger seat with a jean jacket wrapped around her shoulders and a powder-blue bandana holding back her curly hair. Serena wore a short, butter-soft leather jacket and aviator sunglasses. She gripped the wheel firmly as she weaved in and out of traffic, never letting the speedometer dip below eighty.

"Should I call you Serena or Andretti?" Cassidy said, squeezing her armrest as the car swerved by an SUV with a college bumper sticker and a backseat loaded with short-haired young men. The driver leaned on his horn and the guy in the passenger seat motioned to the two women, fisting his hand and pumping it at his open mouth.

"Very nice. Can you believe them?" Serena said over the sounds of Bebel Gilberto blaring from the stereo. She looked up and pointed. "All these boys think about is sex, sex, and sex. *Dios mío*, what were You thinking when You created men?"

"Young guys have a hard time resisting a beautiful Latina like you," Cassidy said.

"But *I* can resist them, easily," Serena said, nonchalantly.

"Oh, come on. It's time you got back on the merry-go-round. It's been six months since you dumped . . . Jack? John? The one that turned out to be married."

"You mean Jeff, the well-hung architect. Oh well," Serena said, sighing. "This time I'm finding a guy who knows what he wants. No more projects," she said, passing a car with a "Palin for President" bumper sticker.

"Don't miss the exit," Cassidy said, struggling not to spill her bottled water as she drank. "Meet anyone interesting lately?"

"Not really. It's tough, and I'm so over the bar scene. The gym's the same, except the alcohol's been replaced by testosterone."

"True. How about that guy from your Bikram yoga class?"

"He's okay, I guess," Serena said. "Kind of hairy, though. He's got a back like Sasquatch."

"*Eeeooww.* Anyone else?"

"Well, there is one guy. I don't really know that much about him yet, but he's hot. *Caliente.*"

"*Caliente?*" Cassidy asked. "This sounds serious. Where did you meet him? Tell me everything."

"Okay, I confess," Serena said, laughing. "I saw him online."

"Ah-ha."

"Lately, I've just been inundated with men who aren't who they say they are. On the last few coffee dates, the guys were either ten years older or thirty pounds heavier than their photos." Serena shook her head in exasperation. "I would have given them a chance if they were only honest. Why do men lie?"

"It's in their DNA, like leaving the seat up. What about *caliente* boy?"

"He contacted me the day I was thinking of canceling my membership. I thought that's a sign. Usually, I just know," Serena said. "And I liked his eyes. They're this pretty green color."

"Sounds *guapo*," Cassidy said.

"*Muy guapo* and a great smile. His e-mail was short, but his profile had the things I'm looking for."

"Like what?"

"Like him not being a serial killer and . . ."

"No, really, what did you put on your profile?"

"Okay—I need a guy who can handle a strong, independent woman. It's tricky. The young ones have the energy, but nowadays, they're soft from sitting on their ass playing video games. I want a real man who's strong and secure, but not a workaholic. They get old fast and then try to define themselves by how much money they have. If I asked, they'd bring along their financial spreadsheets to review over coffee."

"Amazing," Cassidy chimed in. "And he's got to have something going on inside, right? He doesn't have to be Gary Zukav, but he can't be afraid to share his feelings."

"Exactly, and it's okay if he has a little edge, too, as long as he keeps his boyish charm," Serena said, gesturing again to the heavens as she changed lanes. "What's wrong with these guys? Aren't we girls easy to figure out?" she said, laughing.

Cassidy smiled. "And this guy—he said all that?"

"He said something even better."

"Like what?"

"Like wanting to be in a committed relationship."

"A guy said *that*? Does he have a twin?" Cassidy laughed. "What's his name?"

"Roger. It's my turn to write back. Then we'll see if he asks for my number."

"Roger?" Cassidy paused a moment. "Does he live in Brooklyn?"

"I think he lives in the city."

"You said green eyes?" Cassidy asked quickly.

"Yeah, why—have you dated him?"

"No," Cassidy said, shaking her head. "And I'm sure if you wanted him, I wouldn't stand a chance anyway. How do you know he's not lying like the rest of them?"

"I don't know, but if he is, then another one bites the dust . . . unless he has a big dick," Serena said. "Then at least I have a placeholder."

Cassidy bolted upright and snorted out her sip of water with a laugh.

"So how's your cute one holding up these days?" Serena asked, changing the subject.

"Still licking his wounds, but slowly coming around," Cassidy said, still brushing the water off her skirt.

"As long as that bitch ain't licking them, that's good."

"No," Cassidy said. "*She* wants distance."

"Good, the farther away, the better," said Serena.

A half hour later, Serena's car screeched into the gravel driveway of the beach house. Serena's dog, Chili, barked and scraped at the screen door. Cassidy grabbed her bag and looked over at the inlet's blue waters and exhaled. Inside the modest-framed house topped with cedar shingles, Alejandro lay on the wooden floor of his darkened room, finishing an hour-long self-Reiki session with his hands covering his midsection. Soft music was playing and a trail of incense smoke wafted into the hallway.

When Alejandro heard the car door slam and the sounds from the front of the house, he opened his eyes. After slowly rising, he inhaled deeply and stepped softly into the living room. Cassidy and Serena were outside unloading the car. Despite his help, it took a few trips to haul in all of their boxes, clothing, and shoes. While the two women settled into their rooms, Alejandro began prepping the fresh catch he'd bought off the back of a local party boat. Throughout their dinner of grilled fish and vegetables, Serena and Cassidy talked animatedly about work, and the three planned their long weekend. Alejandro dug into his knapsack and pulled out the free newspaper he had picked up on the boardwalk. He handed the paper to his cousin and directed her to a page he had folded back earlier.

Serena scanned the entertainment section that Alejandro had marked. "A Latin band and a limbo contest—sounds like fun."

Overhearing the conversation, Cassidy asked Serena for the paper and took a quick look. "Here's something at the bowling alley—a male Lady Gaga tribute band. And they're opening for Misstallica. Hard to beat that."

Serena laughed and shook her head. "C'mon, this limbo thing sounds like fun. Maybe Alejandro can win the beer and we'll have a party. I've seen him limbo."

"I play to win," Alejandro said, flashing a smile.

"*Por supuesta*, being obsessively competitive is part of the Y chromosome," Serena cracked. "You win, and we'll have a fiesta right here."

"Cold beer, hot nights. Works for me," Cassidy laughed.

After cleaning up, they walked out to the back deck. Alejandro shuffled down to the inlet with Chili in tow.

The two women lit a lantern and placed it on the wooden table. In the distance, the waves broke slowly upon the sand, creating a relaxing rhythm. Cassidy sipped her white wine and Serena held her sparkling water, both quiet at first as they listened to the sound of the waves. Subdued by the calm of the tranquil waters, they resumed discussions of their plans for the summer.

"Hey, I forgot to tell you. I convinced Max to write the column," said Cassidy.

"Awesome!"

"Yep. He's working for me now."

"All right. Girlfriend's got game. So have you . . . ? "

"Nope, this is strictly business. I don't take advantage of the staff," Cassidy said with a short laugh.

"Uh-huh. My guess is that's going to change."

CHAPTER 18

Max threw two bucks on the news counter at Penn Station and tucked *The New York Times* under his arm. He sped down the stairs to Track 2 where the Bay Head train was boarding. After he slid into a window seat, he sighed, hoping for a quiet commute. He checked his phone for messages and then narrowed his eyes when he saw two e-mails from Gloss. The train whistle blew, and an attractive young woman wearing a cotton sweater over a flowered dress squeezed into the car as the doors closed behind her. The stuffed oversized bags she had slung over her shoulders made her wobble as she walked. Her searching eyes spied the empty seat next to Max. She stopped in front of him and tried hoisting her heavy bags to the overhead carrier. Max stood up, and to her relief, offered to help. She smiled and thanked him. He secured both her bags, and she took the seat next to him, placing her tote on the floor.

Max returned to his sports section and the box score of the Yankees game. The young woman inserted a pair of iPod ear buds into her ears, unzipped her bag, and dug out a magazine. By the time the train pulled into the Newark Airport stop, she was relaxed and leafing through a thick issue of *Elle*. She took her time studying the splashy pictorial featuring the latest swimwear. Max scoffed to himself as he read a highbrow take on the latest Jack Black movie. He folded his paper and gazed out at the nondescript rubble of New Jersey's underbelly as the train chugged southward.

The train passed a string of backyard towns on its way down the shore. The young woman reached for another magazine and Max did a double take when he saw her flip open the premier issue of *My Radiance*. The cover featured a photo of a woman seated in a yoga pose with the headline, "Women Living in the Light." Max took a sidelong glance while she reviewed the table of contents.

He smiled when he saw his column listed on page fifty-one. He feigned reading his paper and continued watching the young woman leaf through articles about intuition, feng shui for the office, training for a half-marathon, and affordable weekend spa getaways. *My Radiance* focused on a woman's lifestyle and inner beauty rather than her outer looks. *Nice work, Cassidy,* he thought, as his fellow passenger continued making her way toward his column.

He tried not to let her catch him snooping, but she shot him a furtive glance when he leaned a bit too close. His heart beat faster when he saw the column's logo featuring a large black quill with a red, heart-shaped nib at the top of page fifty-one. He hoped his column would grab her attention. The woman picked up her head and gave him an annoyed look. He quickly turned to the window, but continued watching her from the corner of his eye. He thought he saw her smile as her eyes worked their way slowly down the page. After she finished, she rested the magazine on her lap and took out a package of Tic Tacs. She caught Max off guard when she held out the package of mints to him.

"Thanks. Do I need one?" he asked.

She smiled and said, "No, but you seem very interested in my reading material."

"Was I staring? I noticed that you were reading *My Radiance*. The editor is a close friend of mine. What do you think of it?"

"It's a good read—not the usual fluff they push on women. I can relate to the articles."

"Is that so? I've heard about this column, 'The Guys' Guy's Guide' to something or other. Did you notice it?"

"To love. It's called 'The Guys' Guy's Guide to Love.' "

"Oh. What did you think?"

"I liked it," she said.

Max let out a sigh of relief and the young woman eyed him quizzically before continuing. "Women are curious about guys, like what's on their minds, especially when it's about us. This Rod seems like a straight shooter."

"You think he's selling men out?" Max gave a searching look.

"Who cares, as long as he's helping women understand them," she said lightly. Max nodded in agreement.

"Well, thanks for the Tic Tacs. My friend will be pleased. She's really something, getting it all together to put out this magazine. I mean, she's really, you know, something and . . ."

The woman gave him a polite smile that said, *That's nice. We're done now,* before returning to her reading.

It was a ten-minute walk from the Asbury Park train station to the old Victorian house on the beach where Max kept a third-floor loft, facing the ocean. He threw his things on the bamboo couch and opened the windows and sliding door to the deck. He inhaled deeply and filled his lungs with fresh salty air. After unpacking, he put on some Bob Marley and opened a bottle of orange-flavored seltzer. He sank into his director's chair, watching the waves crash relentlessly to the shore as he mulled over his current state of affairs.

Before leaving his office, he'd e-mailed Gloss, updating him on his call to his former Bobalooie client. The client had been open to a meeting, signaling the first step in the mating dance between client and agency. Every time Max reminded himself that he was now working for HHI and only doing his job, he had to block out the image of Henry Goodson laid up in Beth Israel. Making a pact with a devil named Gloss served practically no purpose other than to drive the knife deeper into Henry's heart. Max wondered, *What the hell am I doing?*

When he dismissed that thought, the image of Veronica's face sprung up in his mind. *Why couldn't she just appreciate him and what they shared? Why did she always need more? Maybe their breakup had been inevitable.* He crumpled the empty plastic bottle, considering the very real possibility of her now being with Roger. Despite that—and maybe because of it—he wanted her again, one more time. His cell phone rang, breaking his train of thought. It was Cassidy.

"Playing golf today?" she asked.

"I haven't decided. Roger's not coming down this weekend. He's in Florida . . . fishing with clients. At least that's what he told me."

"On Memorial Day weekend?" Cassidy said.

"I know, it sounds . . . fishy, so to speak, but whatever. How's the house?"

"Great, we're off to the beach. Alejandro's here, too."

"Does he heal the fish?" Max said.

"He Reiki's the ocean," she clarified. "So how did your research go the other night?"

"Roger's even more dysfunctional than I imagined. I really don't think women will want to hear about this."

"Just tell them the truth," Cassidy said. "They can handle it."

"I'm still not convinced, but I did sit next to one of your readers on the train. She was smitten with Rod," he said.

"That's awesome. Was anyone else reading it?" asked Cassidy eagerly.

"Oh, the entire car was like a library. The conductor was so absorbed in the article about feng shuing your undergarments drawer that he forgot to announce the stop for the Rahway State Prison."

"Stop it," she said, laughing. "Hey, Serena, Alejandro, and I are going out tomorrow night. There's a Latin band playing at The Rows. Why don't you come by for dinner?"

"Sounds good. What can I bring?"

"Come by at seven. Just bring your sweet self, a bottle of wine, and your next column."

Max hung up and booted up his laptop at the wooden table facing the ocean. By the time he raised his head for a break, he'd finished another column. Then he grabbed his golf shoes and raced downstairs to his car.

CHAPTER 19

On Friday night, Roger and Veronica shared a light dinner in the sleek dining room of their luxury hotel in Nassau, Bahamas. The long week had finally caught up to Roger. He was quiet throughout the meal and let out an enormous yawn after the table was cleared. They stopped in the lounge for a nightcap before retiring. Inside their room overlooking the sea, Roger stayed awake long enough to attend to Veronica's needs. After she slipped out of her backless dress, he touched her beneath her red silk thong, running his hands and lips over her smooth skin. She moaned softly when he wrapped his large hands around her legs and held her tightly in his arms. She quivered and tightened before erupting. After catching her breath, Veronica returned the favor, bringing Roger to a thigh buckling orgasm with her mouth. Within minutes, he was snoring.

"Do you need all those clothes for a three-day trip?" Roger asked her as she unpacked the next morning.

"Worry about your own things," Veronica said.

After she'd changed into her silver snakeskin Versace bikini, Roger looked her over admiringly. They made a striking pair poolside, and heads turned when Veronica emerged from the pristine water like a toned, bronzed goddess. She toweled off, brushed her hair, and slipped on her shield sunglasses. Roger, in his navy surfer shorts, sprawled across a chaise lounge with his eyes closed while Veronica carefully applied lotion to her legs.

While Roger napped, Veronica reviewed the financials for the

condo in Tribeca she'd had her eye on. After recalculating her projected monthly payments for a second time, she was confident that
she could make the payments. She'd come a long way since hawking
health club memberships and selling cosmetics behind the counter at
the local mall to pay her tuition at Syracuse. Over the years, she'd
worked tirelessly, honing her commission sales skills. She had survived a variety of trial-by-fire work scenarios on her way up the ladder to Sales Director at Globison's online division.

She pushed the paperwork aside and opened the copy of *My Radiance* magazine she'd picked up at the airport. She flipped through the
pages, browsing articles and seeing which advertisers had purchased
space in the new publication. After checking her watch, she took out
a pen and slid the magazine on the small table.

When Roger awoke, he read the note she'd left him. Veronica was
taking a cardio step class on the beach. He sat up and ordered lunch
from the poolside café. It was twelve thirty when he tasted his first
cocktail of the day. When Veronica returned, her skin was glowing.
Even after a shower she was still perspiring under the broiling mid-
day sun. Roger ordered her a conch salad and iced tea, and then sunk
back into his recliner behind his Ray-Bans.

As he was dozing off, Veronica nudged his shoulder. "Are you
going to fall asleep on me again?" she said, startling him.

He shot up and then stretched like a giant cat. "Sorry, I'm so beat.
I've been working like a slave and they raised my forecast again."

"Poor baby. Break any new accounts?" she asked, patting her forehead with a towel.

"I think I've got enough pages to make my quota. How are sales?"
he asked.

"Paying for my condo," she shot back.

"Wow," he said, arching his back. "You're going through with it?"

"I am. As soon as I close one more account, my bonus kicks in and
I can make the down payment."

"Excellent! Mojitos to celebrate?" he asked hopefully.

"It's too early. Here," she added, handing him the tube of sun tan
lotion and displaying her shapely back to him. "Did you find out
the name of the company that's combining holistic ingredients with
alcohol?"

His jaw tightened as he squeezed lotion into his hands. "Not yet. Why?"

"No reason. I just like that idea."

Roger expertly coated her bare skin with his large hands and then stood up quickly, wondering what brought on her question. "Hey V, I need some exercise. I'm going for a walk. Why don't you hang out and relax here?"

"All right. Put something on that," Veronica said, pointing to the mark under his eye.

A warm wind blew off the water as Roger shuffled along the soft sand. His bruise still felt tender. Fortunately, Veronica had bought into his story about tripping on the subway stairs and landing on his face. He stopped and leaned against one of the palm trees lining the sand, wondering if New York's bustle and grind was burning him out. But then again, he was only eighteen months into what could turn into a lucrative position at *Plates*.

Feeling the gentle wind on his face, his thoughts drifted to Veronica and Layla. Roger wanted it all—the sex and the money, but something was missing. It didn't feel like either woman was right for him. He didn't believe that he could count on either Veronica or Layla if the chips were down. He needed someone with more substance—a woman who'd care for him once his playing days were over.

He kicked off his sandals and waded into the water, swimming out to meet a series of waves approaching from a hundred yards out. He ducked beneath two six-foot crests and then positioned himself to catch the next breaker. As the wave took shape, he began swimming toward the shore. Knifing his long arms through the water, he felt the wave lift his body. He thought he'd caught it perfectly. Then the bottom dropped out and the wave broke, crashing thunderously over his head.

He tumbled beneath the furious waters, a tangle of arms and legs. His body rolled and rolled until it hit something firm. His hand brushed against what felt like an ankle. When he emerged and looked up, he was staring at an endless pair of tanned legs, a white thong, and the underside of a pendulous pair of breasts nestled in a low-cut top. The sun was in his eyes, but he could still make out a head of long, silky brown hair fluttering in the breeze.

"I must have died and gone to heaven. Where are you from, angel?" he said.

"You okay, *chico*?" the woman asked, steadying him with her hand on his shoulder.

Roger picked up her accent and replied, *"Gracious para me ayuda. Muchas gracias."* He was unsure of his phrasing.

"De nada."

"De donde es usted?"

"I'm from the Bronx. Okay, *chico*?" she said, laughing. "You passed your Spanish exam."

"Excellente," he said, with a twisted smile. *"Soy Roger."*

It was close to an hour since he'd left Veronica by the pool. He'd been preoccupied by his thoughts, the waves, and now here was this stunning Latina. Roger picked himself up, his eyes riveted on his pretty new friend. They continued their small talk at the edge of the water. Roger decided that the universe had delivered her as a gift, so when she offered her number, he wrote it in the wet sand with a seashell, hoping he'd remember it. He was busy scribbling when he felt a shadow block the sun. He looked up and blanched; Veronica was glaring down at him.

"Hey . . . hey!" he said, "I was doodling when this nice lady came by. She's a foreigner and, uh, she doesn't speak English, so I was sketching an outline of the island for her. *Es una . . . mapa. Si?"* he said, dragging the small shell in a circle and then through the numbers.

"Looks like a phone number to me," said Veronica.

"No really, look—those are hills and see, here's the outline of the island."

"Um, sorry to interrupt," the young woman said. "Bye, Roger . . . and thanks for the Spanish lesson." She gave a little wave as she walked away, showing off her white-thonged, tanned derriere. He made a wistful face and stayed on his knees, watching her drift down the beach. Finally, Roger looked up sheepishly.

"So, she doesn't speak English?" Veronica asked. "I should cut your balls off. But first you're going to buy me dinner at that ridiculously expensive seafood place."

CHAPTER 20

Max's eyes lit up when Cassidy opened the door of the beach house wearing a pair of snug low-rise jeans, a bandeau top, and open-toed sandals. Max glanced down at her red toenails and the silver ring adorning her middle toe. His eyes followed her slender hips as she cut through the living room. Serena lay on the couch, reading a book about angels. Alejandro was sitting cross-legged on the floor, tuning an acoustic guitar.

"*Mi primo, no mas guitara ahora.* The fish stew. *Vaminos! Tengo hambre, Alejandro,*" Serena said, pointing toward the back of the house where a large pot simmered on a stone grill. "Max, here," she added with her hand out. "Let me put that wine on ice for you."

A half hour later, the four friends gathered around the picnic table devouring Alejandro's special dish. Max ripped a piece of crusty bread to sop up what was left in the bottom of his bowl while the girls debated the virtues of this year's open-toed wedges. He poured himself more wine, bored with the fashion talk.

"I thought you two were all about important issues for women," he said, "like in the magazine."

"This is important," they said, laughing.

Max glanced at Alejandro, rolling his eyes.

"Is that all you're eating?" Serena asked her cousin. "You've only had a spoonful of fish and a little rice."

"I need to stay lean for the limbo contest," Alejandro replied.

"Eat, Alejandro. Who cares about some contest?" Serena said.

"*I* care," Alejandro said, putting down his napkin. "And I'm going to win."

Max raised his eyebrows. "Okay, more for me then," he said, reaching for the pot. "I don't need to be skinny for any contest. We all know how I dance," he said, chuckling.

After a dessert of sliced mangoes, the four piled into Max's ten-year-old Mustang and drove to Bradley Beach. The Rows was set in a large mansion facing the sea. Its long outdoor deck was jammed with revelers drinking trays of shots, flavored drinks, and long-neck beers. The crowd was a potpourri of Jersey Shore chic with ultra-streaked hair, Snooki bun-tops, and overly tanned skin mixed with groups of summer transplants from Staten Island and the usual sprinkling of sun-bleached surfers.

With Alejandro in tow, Max worked his way to the main bar and ordered Coronas for Cassidy and himself, seltzer for Serena, and orange juice for Alejandro. By the time they returned, two burly twenty-somethings in graphic muscle tees were attempting to impress a bemused Serena and Cassidy.

"Nice meeting you, Flip—or was it Skip?" Serena said. "And good luck in A.C. Oh look, our boyfriends are here with our drinks," she said. Cassidy laughed as the two men gave Alejandro and Max the once over before skulking off.

"Let me guess—professional wrestlers on the junior circuit?" Max asked.

"The blonde had a tight butt," Cassidy said to Serena, ignoring his comment.

"And probably a pretty good take-down scissors kick," Max added.

They were standing outside as an amber moon began its ascent over the shimmering water. At ten o'clock, the band kicked off its set with a flourish of salsa beats, blaring horns, and sizzling guitars, igniting a rush to the dance floor. Serena took Alejandro's hand and led him in front of the band where they gyrated to a hot salsa.

Cassidy stood with Max at the bar, her hips shimmying back and forth. She smiled up at him. He took a swig of beer and rocked in place while Alejandro and Serena danced. "Look at those two," Max said. "Amazing."

"Come on," Cassidy said, pulling him across the dance floor. As she grooved effortlessly to the beat, he marveled at her gyrations. Max tried keeping up and reminded himself not to look down and count his steps. Serena slid over and showed Max a salsa move, and Cassidy paired off with Alejandro. When the next song began, the two women faced off and kicked the action up another notch. Max and Alejandro moved to the side and watched the ladies.

"Check out Cassidy," Alejandro said, nudging Max. "She dances like a Latina. *Bellisima.*"

Max shot him a quick glance and then pointed to the bar. "Let's get you hydrated for the contest."

Max stopped and looked back as they worked their way through the crowd. Two new guys had already moved in and were dancing with Serena and Cassidy. *Jeez,* Max thought. *They don't even look like they shave yet. What's she doing?*

The limbo contest began with separate elimination rounds for the women and men, with the two winners facing off for the overall title. In the women's competition, once the limbo stick had been lowered twice, half of the contestants had been eliminated. Within minutes, there were only three competitors remaining.

One of the girls—a pretty Latina with ebony eyes and bee-stung lips—stood with a group of drunken surfer boys who were carrying on loudly. In the final round, she managed to slip under the twenty-inch mark, and raised her hands in victory when the band played a salsa-tinged version of "We Are the Champions."

The red-faced announcer dressed in a white guayabera cotton shirt called for the male competitors and the congas erupted into a driving beat. Serena, Cassidy, and Max cheered for Alejandro as he slid easily beneath the limbo stick in his first three attempts. By the time the bar had been lowered to thirty inches, only Alejandro and one other contestant remained. Max watched Alejandro as he motioned confidently to the judges to lower the bar to twenty-four inches. Alejandro pulled at his shorts to make room for his legs and wiggled low to the floor, clearing the bar. The other competitor watched, shaking his head. Then when his turn came, he waved his hand in forfeit. Alejandro faced the crowd and grinned broadly, soaking in the applause.

The bandleader announced the final showdown between Alejandro and the pretty Latina for a grand prize of four cases of Brazilian beer. The two competitors were brought forward to face a cheering crowd. Max, Cassidy, and Serena edged closer as the two contestants faced each other and laughed awkwardly. The women in the bar screamed and whistled for Alejandro.

Max leaned in to Cassidy and said, "Hey, look around."

She looked back at him quizzically.

"I mean, can we get any cooler?" With an air of mock ironic self-realization, he added, "Saturday night. Cuban band. Limbo contest. Jersey Shore."

"And I can't think of a hotter way to kick off the summer," Cassidy responded cheerily.

Then Max turned and warily eyed the rowdy group of surfers as Alejandro and the Latina took turns effortlessly maneuvering their slender bodies below the bar. With every go-around, the surfers derided Alejandro and shouted obscenities, causing the young woman to look away uncomfortably.

One blonde, dreadlocked surfer who appeared to be their pack leader shouted, "You're going down, pretty boy," and his friends repeatedly chanted, "You're going down."

Max saw the tenseness on the young woman's face. He leaned into Cassidy. "She's toast now."

"Stop thinking about the beer," Cassidy said.

The Latina bent backward slowly and rattled the bar with her belly. But it stayed in place as she slipped beneath it. Alejandro motioned for the bar to be lowered and then turned to the surfers and gave a gracious smile. Max noticed the change in his body language. Alejandro was too relaxed.

"He's going to let her win," Max murmured. Then he called out in protest, "Don't even think about it, Alejandro; just win, dude!"

As Alejandro edged under the bamboo rod, a thrown bottle of beer suddenly exploded inches from his head, spraying beer on him. He slid under the pole anyway. Then another bottle shattered nearby.

Alejandro jumped away to avoid it. By this time, the crowd had erupted into a melee of fists and shouting and shoving. At the center was the group of drunken surfers, who were now absorbed by the frenzied crowd.

A team of black-clad bouncers charged the dance floor. As the action escalated, Alejandro grabbed the frightened Latina's hand and dragged her away. At the far end of the bar, Max motioned for Cassidy and Serena to escape outside, and then waded into the melee in search of Alejandro. With bottles and fists flying past his head, Max pushed combatants aside and moved steadily forward. He pulled a surfer off of someone he thought was Alejandro, but when he realized his mistake, a roundhouse right blindsided him, whacking him squarely under his eye and knocking him to the floor. By the time he turned over and picked himself up, order had been restored in the bar. The bouncers shoved the surfers outside just as the cops arrived amid a shower of flashing lights and blaring sirens.

Max touched the tender flesh under his eye and grimaced. He stumbled forward. Cassidy ran to his side, put her arm around his shoulder, and walked him outside.

"Are you all right?" she asked.

Serena appeared holding two cups of ice and a napkin. "You're going to have some shiner," she said. "Now look who shows up," she went on, nodding toward the door. "My *loco* cousin. And he's with the *chica. Dios mio!*"

"*Caramba!*" Alejandro exclaimed, seeing Max's face.

Max said, "Well, you won."

Alejandro smiled. "*Es verdad.* Thanks, Max. The beers are for you."

They stepped outside and stood around Max, making sure he was okay. Then the young woman who'd been hanging on to Alejandro tugged at his arm. He excused himself and walked her across the parking lot. Serena poked Cassidy when she saw the young girl reach around Alejandro's neck and begin kissing him.

"Slut," Serena said, frowning.

Max watched Alejandro, thinking, *It's been awhile. I could use some loving, too.* Then, as Alejandro pried himself loose and sent the pretty Latina on her way, Max smirked at Cassidy and whispered, "See? He's even prettier than her."

"Leave it alone," Cassidy said, trying not to laugh.

Serena narrowed her eyes. "Leave what alone?"

"Nothing," Max said, forcing a smile. "Oh, look. Here's Alejandro."

After collecting Alejandro's victory beer, they all piled inside the car. Cassidy asked Serena to drive and stay within the local speed limits. Serena nodded and then revved the Mustang's engine and tore out of the lot. Max and Cassidy were squeezed into the backseat. They listened to Serena and Alejandro talk animatedly in Spanish, apparently discussing the young Latina. A few minutes later, Serena skidded into their driveway.

After they unpacked the beer, Serena said her goodnights. Chili trailed Alejandro into the backyard, and Max trailed Cassidy into the kitchen.

"That's one nasty bruise," Cassidy said, holding an ice pack from the fridge to Max's face. "How do you feel?"

"Like I've been punched. And by the way, Serena needs driving lessons."

"Tell me about it," she agreed. "If you're up for it, we can take a walk on the beach."

"Okay, as long as there is no limbo involved."

"Let me get some ice and a blanket," she said.

"My head's killing me. How about a beer?"

Cassidy grabbed two cans from the refrigerator.

The ocean was calm when they reached the beach. They removed their shoes and walked near the water, cooling their feet in the damp sand. They spread their blanket on a small dune. Max popped open a beer and took a long swallow, peering up at the pale moon hanging like a painting over the Atlantic. He then turned the half-empty can into the sand and adjusted the ice pack under his eye.

Cassidy rubbed Max's shoulder. "That was brave, going out there for Alejandro." It was hard to tell the expression in Cassidy's moonlit eyes.

"Well, he didn't need any help. If anything, he should have rescued me from that crazy crowd," Max said, shaking his head. "He wins the prize, gets the girl . . . And he doesn't even *like* girls."

"I have news for you: he does. From the little Spanish I could make out, he was telling Serena that the girl wanted to get jiggy with him in her car, so he sent her home."

"*See*," Max said, pointedly.

"I think he's looking for something more than a quickie in the backseat."

"That's a change. Between him and Roger, it's like opposite ends of the world."

"Alejandro's not that different from you."

Max's eyebrows shot up. "What?"

"That win-win attitude. You've got that, too. Maybe it's because you guys are so competitive. You're already a winner. Look, you got the beer," she said, handing him his can. "And maybe when the time's right, you'll get the girl, too."

Max touched the swelling on his head again and winced. A tom-cat scampered past them into the fescue grass surrounding the sand dunes.

Cassidy followed the cat with her eyes. "Aw, so cute," she said as its tail disappeared into the light brush. "Where do you think he's going?"

"He's probably chasing sand mice," Max said, nonchalantly.

"Oh, I never knew there were sand mice."

"Yep, guys know about stuff like that. Sand mice." He opened the other can of beer and stared up at the sky. "Hey, what's that word for when the moon isn't quite full?"

"Gibbous," she said, sighing. "You forgot that I kicked your butt in Scrabble."

"That reminds me," he said, tugging a folded letter-size envelope from his back pocket. "Forgot to give this to you earlier."

"Your column?" She sat up. "Great. What's it about?"

"Love, sex, and tarpon fishing."

She laughed and leaned closer as he handed her the envelope. He faced her and smiled gently, and then suddenly found himself moving in to kiss her. At first she hesitated, but when his lips softly touched hers, she gave in to the kiss. When their lips parted, he raised his eyebrows.

"Whoops," he said.

"Whoops? That was a whoops?"

"Yeah . . . I mean, no. Of course not. I've been meaning to do that."

"Uh-huh. Always good to make these choices after beers and fist-fights," said Cassidy.

"Yeah . . . I mean no." He blinked at her and then fell heavily on the sand.

"Whoops," said Cassidy.

Max looked up and sighed. "Okay, maybe *that* was a whoops. Remember, I got clonked on the head a little while ago. But the kiss . . ."

Cassidy nodded. "That was sweet, Max. But we tried this before. Remember?"

He looked down and nodded.

Cassidy pursed her lips. "And we've got this nice thing going with our friendship. You know, editor-writer . . ."

"Boss-underling . . ."

"I'm serious," she said, giving him a prod. "We tried it the other way, and I like us this way." He forced a smile and ran his fingers through the cool sand.

"Besides, you're still getting over Miss Thong America."

"Talk about getting clonked on the head."

"Exactly." She wagged the column at him. "Let's stick with this for now? Okay?"

"You're the boss, boss . . ."

She stood up and extended her hand. "C'mon, slugger; you need some rest."

They walked slowly back to her place. After unsuccessfully trying to convince Cassidy that he was okay to drive, Max followed her inside. He was asleep on the couch by the time she returned with a pillow and blanket.

Serena was in the bathroom when she heard them enter the house. She'd already washed away her makeup. She studied her face and then shook her head, wondering how the hell she'd ended up spending her summer at the Jersey Shore. Talk about *la vida loca*.

THE GUYS' GUY'S GUIDE TO LOVE

She marched into the kitchen and grabbed a pint of chocolate gelato out of the freezer. After closing the door to her bedroom, she peeled back the wrapper. Her laptop glowed inside her darkened bedroom. She dug into the gelato and logged in online. Time to check out the guys. As she clicked through a series of headshots, she savored the chocolate. The parade of nondescript faces bored her, so she decided to reread that e-mail from that good-looking guy, Roger. After opening his profile, she studied his pretty green eyes. Then, holding the spoon in her mouth, she typed a short response and logged off. That night she lay naked under cool, fresh sheets. She stared at the ceiling and wondered, as she often had before, if this guy might be "The One." Then she pulled the covers tight, curled her arms around her pillow, and slowly drifted into a deep sleep.

Early the next morning, Chili nudged a wet tennis ball into Max's face. Max pushed Chili off and stumbled to the bathroom with the dog trailing at his side. His head throbbed dully and his mouth tasted of stale beer. He threw water on his face and then returned to the living room, noticing the sheet and blanket that Cassidy had put out for him. He kneeled down and scratched Chili's neck and belly before tiptoeing outside, gently closing the screen door behind him.

Cassidy was awake when she heard Max's steps along the gravel driveway. She could see him through her window and, as he tentatively backed his car onto the street, she smiled to herself.

CHAPTER 21

By the time Max returned to the city on Monday evening, the mouse on the left side of his face had turned purplish black. He studied it in the bathroom mirror and grit his teeth when patting it with a soapy face cloth. It throbbed and distorted his looks, but he thought it also made him look rugged and masculine.

He grabbed a Vitamin Water, booted up his laptop in his living room, and clicked on the television. After a little channel surfing, he settled on Bob Ross's *The Joy of Painting,* occasionally checking on the progress of a watercolor landscape while he typed. An hour later, he took another ice pack from the freezer, folded a towel over it, and tied it around his head. Then he stripped off his clothes and flopped into bed.

When he awoke, it was pouring rain. For some reason the alarm hadn't gone off at seven. He scrambled to the bathroom and checked his eye. Despite sleeping with the ice pack, the stain looked worse. After a hurried shower, he bolted out the door while unwrapping an energy bar. He forgot his umbrella and trotted between the raindrops along 34th Street before descending to the bowels of the subway.

Sitting behind his desk, he scanned the online editions of *Ad Snoop* and *Advertising Age* and checked the baseball scores. Then he opened his e-mails. An agency-wide announcement had been sent out the previous Friday informing employees that they were free to leave at four-thirty for the three-day weekend. Gloss had also sent two e-mails on Monday morning, marked urgent, asking the account directors to submit spreadsheets summarizing their projected revenue on their accounts. They were due on his desk at ten o'clock this morning.

Does this guy have a life? Max thought, glancing at the time and seeing it was already eight fifteen as he typed his brief response.

Preparing for major client presentation. Will review budgets with client tomorrow. Last week's numbers are accurate. He hit "send."

Gloss responded thirty seconds later. *Can't wait, Holiday. Need those numbers now.*

Max felt his blood rising. Ah, yes—anger. As the rush reached his brain, Max forwarded his reply. *Last week's projections are attached. Max.*

Gloss responded instantly. *See me now.*

Max printed out the revenue projections and chugged the remainder of his energy drink. He folded the chart under his arm and marched down the hall, oblivious to his coworkers gawking at his face.

"Guess she hits pretty hard, Hallyday," the smarmy director of the cat food account called out. Max ignored the jibe and slipped into the elevator.

When Max approached, Gloss's assistant raised his hand in a halting gesture, but Max stormed by. He protested, but when Max turned and raised his eyebrows, the assistant noticed the welt and backed down.

Max heard his voice trailing behind him as he opened the door: "Ah, Mr. Gloss is on the phone and . . ."

Gloss was seated at his desk in the dimly lit office in a dark suit. Hearing the commotion, he shook his finger and spoke into the phone, "That's correct. We're a branding company, not an ad agency. Yes, they're very different. It's all about building *your* brand. Great. Then I'll see you at Plaza Athenee at seven thirty. Cheers." After hanging up, he turned to Max. "Holiday, is that you causing problems?"

Max stepped inside and looked around. His eyes caught something new and he almost laughed when he spotted it—a framed photo of the Dalai Lama perched on the credenza behind Gloss's desk. Then Max remembered Gloss's efforts to score front-row tickets to see the Tibetan leader. He shook his head, thinking, *Talk about falling short of our heroes.*

"Good god, man." Gloss's eyes fixed on Max's bruise. "What have you done to yourself? You look as if you were dragged through a hedge backward."

"Thanks," Max said. "I won't bother making up a story about my eye. I had an accident with a wrench while changing a tire for an elderly woman stuck on the Major Deegan."

"That sounds like a blinking . . ."

"Here's my forecast," Max said, sliding an Excel spreadsheet across the desk. "I'll have a better idea where we stand with our billings after tomorrow's meeting."

"Hmm. Is the Korindopolos girl attending?"

"Of course."

"Maybe I'll drop in," Gloss said, narrowing his eyes as he stared at Max.

"Thanks, but it's not necessary. She only wants the people working on her business at her meetings," Max said.

"That's rubbish. What's your plan? What are you showing her?"

"We're presenting the *branding* campaigns for the new line."

"I see." Gloss tapped his pen sharply on Max's projections. "Holiday, do I need to remind you that if you don't sell some adverts soon, things could get sticky?"

"Right. If there's nothing else, I'd like to work on my presentation."

"There *is* something else," Gloss said, scrolling through the top page of Max's forecast. "Not enough revenue here, mate."

"Those are the figures I submitted last week," Max said. "The same ones you approved."

"Ancient history. There's bugger-all here," Gloss replied, removing his glasses. He stood and strutted around the desk, tucking his thumb under his suspenders. Now Max thought he looked like a barnyard cock.

"Let me put it to you this way," Gloss continued, puffing out his chest. "If your billings on Peacock don't show a significant increase soon, the only thing you'll be working on is the pitch for Bobalooie Bubble Gum. And if you value your job, you'll win that account *for your agency*! Do you read me . . . Hol-i-day?" Gloss said.

Max breathed slowly, acknowledging the burning sensation creeping up from his abdomen. "Peacock is planning to spend aggressively on this launch. And Tooka Wooka is finalizing a new line of *sweets* infused with vitamins. The confectionery market's shifting and this would be a great opportunity to align us with a first mover. Like I said, Tooka Wooka is the *new* Bobalooie."

"You're all mouth and trousers," Gloss scoffed. "Bobalooie is the category leader now. And advertising is a *right-now* business. They have a sizable budget and I want it here. In the meantime, get your Peacock client to open up her pocketbook or I'll have to cut back on your resources."

"Is that all?" Max asked stonily.

"You have two directives, Holiday. Sell something to Peacock and set that meeting with Bobalooie. That's all," Gloss said before returning to his chair and picking up the phone.

Max stormed back to his office and reviewed the creative brief again. He knew the agency that could successfully advertise a line of holistic drinks could distance itself from the competition for the foreseeable future. He dialed Bette. Her assistant answered.

"She just left for a meeting. Hang on. She left a note."

Max tapped his pencil, half-listening as she rummaged through some papers.

"She's with Mr. Gloss."

The blood drained from Max's face. "Have her call me as soon as she returns," he blurted. "And tell her not to leave," he added before hanging up.

After his beeline to Bette's office, Max took a seat on her contemporary red leather couch. While waiting, he pulled out his phone and checked his e-mail. When Bette finally appeared, her face was grim and tight. She closed her door and spat out, "That little fuck!"

"What happened?" Max asked, though he already knew.

"Gloss fired me," she said angrily. After a minute, her breathing slowed. She collected herself and asked, "What's with your eye?"

"Limbo accident. Tell me what happened."

She said nothing, but quickly checked the swollen patch beneath his eye again. Then she pulled out a package of tissues from her purse.

"He said the agency's going in a new direction and they need to create opportunities for the junior people."

"That's horse shit. I'll get this sorted out."

She took a deep breath. "No, Max, please . . . don't. It's over. I should have seen the signs. This damn business is all about being young and trendy. I've had enough. A friend of mine has been trying to get me back to Marin County to brand his new winery. That sounds pretty sweet right about now. I'll design bottles and labels and sip Pinot."

Max stood quietly, unsure what else he could say. "Has Gloss seen the Peacock ads?"

"Some of them. Sorry, I got nervous. He said that 'Angels Share' was boring. He didn't say anything when I showed him 'Seven Deadly Sins,' but he took the storyboards."

Max frowned. "Hmm. What about—?"

"He fired me before I could show him the one we liked."

"Did you leave the boards with him?"

"No, I was so pissed off I put them by the garbage along with 'Angels Share.' "

Max nodded. Bette stomped around the office stuffing personal items into an oversized leather bag. She stopped at her desk and stared at the computer screen.

"Bastards," she grumbled.

"What's the matter?"

"Check out these e-mails. News travels fast around here."

"What?"

"Here, look. This one says, 'Fuck you, no-talent bitch.' And here's another: 'Good luck job hunting.' I'm *so* out of here." She heaved her bag over her shoulder. "Take care, Max. Now you see what you're up against." She forced a smile before opening the door.

Max watched her walk down the corridor with her head held high. Then he shot out of her office in the direction of the plastic garbage cans where the creatives recycled their rejected work. After some rummaging, he returned to his office toting an armful of storyboards and then slid them behind his door.

CHAPTER 22

Gail had her back turned when Roger came shuffling down the corridor toting his usual vanilla skim latte. She'd cut her silky waist-length hair into a short bob that accented her pretty face and almond-shaped eyes. She was dressed sharply in a new ivory silk blouse with a tight black skirt and heels. Hearing Roger's approach, she shifted her chair in his direction. Roger muttered a semblance of good morning and plodded past her. He stopped by his door and turned back for a second look. "Gail. Your hair. You cut it all off. It was so . . . so pretty."

Her eyes froze him. Taking a step back, Roger added, "But it looks nice. Really nice."

Gail snorted and returned to her work. Roger slid behind his desk and pulled up his proposal for Peacock Beverages. He'd added two million dollars to the program, knowing that the only way Layla could afford it was by reducing HHI's portion of her budget. Roger didn't like screwing Max, but he had to protect his job. He'd even schedule a return visit to Layla's bed if it became necessary. It was business.

Just before noon, he placed his file on Gail's desk and flashed one of his trademark smiles. "We need to get this out ASAP. This is an important one for us." He'd emphasize *we* and *us* when he needed something right away.

A half hour later, Gail handed him the changes. He signed the document, handed it back, and without looking up, told her to send it out. When she walked off in a huff, he checked out her ass, wondering what was up with the attitude. He shrugged, pulled up his calendar, and was surprised that tonight was open. His squash game had been canceled and Veronica was in Chicago for a regional sales meetings.

His next meeting wasn't until three o'clock, so he ordered a sandwich. He kept his door slightly ajar so he could see Gail's legs, and then logged onto his online dating accounts. There were a few messages from hopeful ladies introducing themselves, but none that interested him. He sighed, and suddenly an incoming note appeared on his screen from the Latina in Brooklyn. The first time she responded she'd asked a few general questions about his interests and what he was looking for in a woman. He'd cut and pasted his standard reply from a similar thread to other women. It must have worked, because this time she included her cell number.

Serena was out of breath when she answered his call, telling him that she'd just finished teaching an hour-long core training class. They chatted easily, and after a few minutes of light banter, she threw him a curveball and asked, "Roger, are you a player?"

His eyes widened. "Absolutely not."

"Sorry, I had to ask," Serena said. "You seem nice. You have a smooth tone to your voice . . . like an actor. So I wanted to know if—"

"I'm really a doctor or I just play one on TV?"

"Something like that," she said, laughing. "I need to know if you're for real. Please tell me if all you're looking for is a hookup. Just be honest. Okay?"

Roger was surprised by her candor. "I'm as advertised."

"So, one woman will do?" she asked.

"I'm not like other guys—serial dating a bunch of different women. I know that with the right woman, a guy can go so much deeper—in every way. It's about quality. *That's* what I'm looking for."

"Hmm. I have to warn you," she said. "I remember everything."

"Then let's make this a memorable experience," he said.

"All right. So now that we've established that you only want to be with one woman, what happens next?"

He clicked to her digital photo. Her eyes were dark and exotic. He had to meet her. "Can I take you out for a drink?"

After a pause, she asked, "When?"

"Are you spontaneous?"

"I can be," she said. "What did you have in mind?"

"What are you doing tonight? I know it's short notice," he said.

"Where?"

Roger tapped his knuckles on his desk, mulling over his favorite meeting spots for his online hookups. "Do you know the Upper West Side?"

"I used to live off Amsterdam."

"There's this little French bistro near West End and—"

"Your apartment?" she asked.

"Um, it's in the neighborhood, but it's—."

"Have you taken other women there that you've met online?" she said.

"Um, maybe once, but . . ."

"Can we go someplace else?" she asked.

"Uh, sure. Where would you like to meet?" Roger said.

"Somewhere farther downtown," she suggested.

His mind quickly flipped through a Rolodex of lounges and restaurants.

"I know a cozy spot near Union Square," he said. "It's quiet—so we can talk."

"What time would you like to meet?" she asked.

"I can be there by eight. Does that work for you?"

"Yes," she said. Then, after another pause, "Roger?"

"Yes?"

"Did you read all of my profile?"

"A few times," he said. "Why?"

"Then you know that I'm punctual," she said. "And I'm sure you wouldn't want me waiting by myself . . . with a bunch of guys around."

After hanging up, Roger felt as if an older kid at the playground had taken his ball. This woman had struck a chord and it had been a long time since he'd felt this way. He might have even felt a twinge down below during their call. His internal line buzzed, jolting him out of his fantasy.

"Layla Korindopolos is on line two," Gail announced.

"Layla! How was Bermuda?"

"Fantastic. I'm tan and rested," she said.

"I'll bet you look fabulous. I want to hear all about your trip." Then he added, "Did you receive the new proposal?"

"It's spread out on my desk," she said. "And it's going to require lots of attention."

"That shouldn't be a problem," Roger replied.

"Good. Then why don't we discuss it over dinner?"

Roger thought it over. "Great idea. How about tomorrow?"

"I can't. I'm having dinner with a distributor," Layla said. "It has to be tonight. I hope that's okay."

Roger pursed his lips. "A quick drink?"

"It would be nice to have a light dinner . . . so we have time to discuss your program."

Roger rolled his eyes. "Let's meet at the W by Union Square. Does five thirty work for you?"

"Five thirty?"

"Six?" he asked hopefully.

"I can meet you there at six thirty."

As soon as he hung up, the line buzzed again.

"Veronica Sparks. Line one."

Roger punched the button and announced, "*Plates* magazine. Roger Fox at your service."

"Good. That's what I want," Veronica said. "I'm at the airport. I want to see you later."

Roger's eyes opened wide. "Why don't you get some rest tonight? We can hook up tomorrow. Dinner at The Dutch."

"You don't want to see me tonight?" she asked incredulously.

"Of course, but I've got a client dinner."

"What about later?" she said. "I bought something you'll like. It's tiny and cut really high on the sides. Looks great with stilettos."

His boxer briefs tightened. "I'll be there by ten."

"Okay, but for every five minutes you're late I'm putting another piece of clothing back on. By eleven I'll be wrapped in polar fleece and mittens."

"That's all the motivation I need. See you at ten."

After hanging up, Gail shot him a frosty look as he passed her on his way to the men's room. He splashed water on his face and ran his fingers through his hair, noticing a few strands of gray. He decided that they served as reminders for him to take a big bite out of life every day. He patted his bruise with a moist paper towel, thinking of everything he was juggling. He paused for a moment. Then he began to laugh. *Dammit, I'm the man. I'm Roger Fox.*

Although Roger dreaded his one-on-one meetings with Buttwipe, this time he brought along the goods to keep the slick-haired yuppie bastard off his back. His revised program for Peacock bumped up his sales forecast enough to put him in line for a bonus.

Roger took a seat next to the couch in the sprawling office and played it cool, watching his boss calculate his sales figures a second time.

"Looks like you nailed it, Fox. Can we book this?"

"The paperwork hasn't officially been signed," Roger replied. "But I'm meeting with the client later to massage the fine points. It's a slam dunk."

Buttwipe removed his glasses. "You're aware that without this program, your revenues are down. And you've almost burned through your entire expense account. This isn't the government. I'm running a business here, and you need to close this fucking deal. Can we book it?"

Roger raised his voice and blurted, "Sure, if you have to. Book it now."

"Roger, *I* don't *have* to—*you need* to," he said.

Roger threw up his hands. "I can't believe it. This deal is a major coup. I've put in some long nights pulling this proposal together."

"Yeah, I've seen Ms. Korindopolos. Get it signed."

Roger cursed under his breath and stalked back to his office. At five thirty, he grabbed his jacket and brushed his hair. Outside his office, Gail's coworkers were gathered around her desk, talking animatedly and laughing. Roger sniffed as he blew by them, failing to take notice of the birthday cake on Gail's workstation.

The lounge was already filled when Roger strode into the W Hotel. After spotting Layla seated at a table near the back, he quickly maneuvered through the crowd. As he approached, he looked down at Layla's tanned breasts bulging out of her black dress. She was dangling her Blahnik pump near the side of the table, revealing the *de rigueur* toe cleavage and spiked four-inch heels.

Keeping it real, Roger mused. "Layla. You're dazzling."

She beamed. "Thanks. I needed those few days."

Roger waved down the waitress and ordered two glasses of the Australian Chardonnay that Peacock imported. When the wine arrived, Layla swirled it around and held her glass under her nose. Then she drew a small sip and rolled it around her mouth.

"Mmm, this is wonderful . . . my favorite. So buttery, don't you think?"

Roger nodded and took a healthy swallow. "It's good. I'm getting hints of pippin apple and white peaches," he said. "So, how's the launch coming along? Is it on schedule?" He realized he sounded anxious, jumping into business right away.

"Yes, everything's on schedule," Layla said, her heel grazing his slacks. "I just came from a meeting with HHI."

Roger savored the wine. "Advertising. What a crapshoot. You never know what crazy ideas these agencies will come up with. That's why a branding program like ours is a strong bet, especially for a new product where you can't take any chances. By the way, did you take a look at my changes?"

Layla made a pouty face. "I did," she said. "You look nice in a woven tie. That color sets off your eyes. Did anyone ever tell you that they look like marbles?"

"Thanks," Roger said. He gave her an uneasy smile and began tapping his foot.

"Are we having dinner?" she asked.

"I can't tonight. I have plans I can't break. I hope you understand," he said. "I wish I could. Let's set up a dinner for next week . . . to celebrate our deal."

He braced himself, and her frown said it all. *Little rich girl likes having her way.* He peeked at his watch and shifted around in his seat.

"Wouldn't it be fun to go somewhere together?" she asked lightly. "You know, just hop on a plane and take off for the weekend?"

"Absolutely. I'd really like that," he said, tapping his foot faster now. "Let's plan that over dinner . . . next week. But I really need to get going."

The wait for the check felt eternal. When Layla excused herself to freshen up, Roger threw down his credit card. Outside, he hailed a taxi and held the door for her, assuring an unsmiling Layla that he'd call her tomorrow. As soon as the cab pulled away, he hurried along Park Avenue South.

CHAPTER 23

"Roger?" Serena said in a deep, sultry voice. She stood over his table in the lounge area at the dark, romantic, woody restaurant just east of Union Square. When he saw her, Roger's eyes lit up and he stopped scrolling through his phone messages.

"Hi, I'm Serena," she said.

He stood up and extended his hand. She glanced at it and exposed her cheek. His lips brushed her face. When she saw the deep bruise under his eye, she stepped back. "What happened?"

Instinctively, his hand shot up and covered the purple blotch. "Oh, this?" he said, moving his hand away carefully to expose the mouse. "It's nothing. Got hit by an errant golf ball."

She raised her eyebrows and then startled him by reaching over and touching his cheek beneath the bruise. "You need to take care of this."

He stood there sheepishly. "I'm seeing a doctor in the morning."

Serena had her game on—looking bronzed and fit, with just a touch of makeup and a deep shade of lip gloss accentuating her sensuous mouth. Her black pencil skirt was slit up the side, showcasing curvaceous hips and shapely legs perched in a pair of Jimmy Choos. She wore her tight white silk blouse with three buttons open, revealing a sideways glimpse of her black bra. Her black hair shimmered under the dim light.

Roger moved around in his chair, searching for his cool. He was surprised at how beautiful Serena was in person. His experiences with online dating had taught him to diminish his expectations of the women he'd meet in person from the professional photos featured in their profiles. Serena's beauty far exceeded the slightly out of focus picture she'd posted online.

"Are you all right?" she asked, studying him.

"Yes, yes. Of course," he said, holding back any "you're so beautiful" comments for now. "Can I get you a drink?"

"Cranberry juice and club soda with lime will be fine."

"They make a great mojito here," he suggested.

"And probably a pretty good cranberry and club with lime," she said with a smile.

"Right," Roger said, nodding to the waiter. After their beverages arrived, Roger set his phone down next to his drink. Serena looked at it and asked, "Are you expecting a call?"

Realizing his faux pas, he snatched it back and buried it in his pocket, wondering, *What's wrong with me? This chick is too smooth. Fuck it, I've been down this road before . . . a thousand times.* After a few sips of his Steve McQueen, Roger settled down, and over the next hour the conversation flowed easily. Although she didn't share much of her personal life, Serena was charming and attentive and quickly drew Roger out. He felt comfortable with her and talked openly about himself, laughing easily and never feeling pressured by her questions. And unlike many of the women he'd met online, Serena wasn't the least bit intimidated. She was self-assured in a non-competitive way that put him at ease.

He finished a second Steve McQueen while she nursed her cranberry juice cocktail. Roger asked her if she wanted another cranberry and club. Serena smiled faintly but declined. Their rapport was so good that he wasn't disappointed that she wasn't drinking alcohol. When his phone vibrated he carefully slid it out of his pocket and saw Veronica's name on the small screen.

"You need to take that?" Serena asked.

"Uh—no. No." Roger said, sensing her mild annoyance.

"It's getting late. I should be going," she said, reaching for her bag.

"Hang on. I'll be right back," he said.

On the way to the men's room, Roger stumbled when he turned the corner. While steadying himself, he heard the beep, signaling an incoming text message. He peered down at the screen, already knowing that it was Veronica.

Just called. Where r u?

On my way

U r late.

Roger began pacing. *Clients. I'll b there.*

Concerned.

?

Need 2 manage ur calendar better.

He looked up at the ceiling. *K*

U want me?

Of course!

Then y r u still there?

Roger rolled his eyes, thinking, *Guess I could have seen this coming.*

When he returned to the table, Serena was checking her face in her compact. "Sure you have to go?" he asked.

"Yes, I have an early day . . . and I can see you have things to attend to."

"Sorry," he said. "I've been on call twenty-four-seven with my crazy job."

After taking care of the bill, Roger walked Serena outside. He stopped in front of the restaurant and turned to her.

"Thanks for coming out tonight. I had a great time."

"Me too," she said, a bit too coolly.

"So . . . I'd like to see you again."

"Are you sure? You seem a little . . . preoccupied," Serena said.

"I know. I'm really busy with work right now, but I'd definitely like to see you again."

"Roger, I need to ask you something. You really seem to like those—what do you call them? Steve McQueens?"

He stiffened, took a deep breath, and stood tall. "Hey, I've been under the gun to make up for the shortfalls of my company's less successful sales people. I have a major responsibility and they rely on me. And, well, I'm a work-hard, play-hard type of guy," he said. Catching himself, he added, "I don't mean play like a *player*. You know what I mean. I have a lot of energy. That's all. Okay?"

She studied his eyes and then said, "All right."

The sounds of a high-pitched siren and the passing traffic broke the moment. Roger took her hands and leaned in, kissing her softly on the lips. Serena allowed him a quick peck, but it was enough to feel the electricity between them. As she searched his eyes again, he wondered what she was thinking. Then she surprised him, gently pulling him closer and kissing him again. Her sweet taste and soft mouth were intoxicating. She pulled back and smiled, politely declining his offer to hail her a cab. Then she turned and walked off into the quiet of the summer night.

"I'll call you," Roger said loudly, his eyes following her seductive stroll down 16th Street.

CHAPTER 24

"Holiday, when revenues aren't up to snuff, we make changes. It's nothing personal. The agency's assets travel up and down in the elevator every day and we need to pay for them."

Max glared at his office phone. He'd waited until after seven before finally getting through to Gloss, and this is what he got? "Kent, you fired my creative director," he said sharply. "And the client is coming in tomorrow morning."

"What time?"

"Ten, and she's always on time."

"Call her and see if she can stop by at two. I'll be available then. We'll have something new for you to sell her."

Max steadied himself. "What's that?"

"The 'Seven Deadly Sins,' Holiday. *Those* are adverts."

"Then why did you let Bette go?"

"Her executions were dreadful—too stiff. Boring. That was her problem. I have a new team mending her work."

Max squeezed the receiver. "That campaign is wrong. It's way too over the top for Peacock. You weren't supposed to see that concept. Bette was working on new ideas."

"Bollocks, man. I saw her campaign with all the nectars and the ingredients. It's shite. This agency only produces dynamic, memorable work that resonates with the pop culture. We don't present advertising that makes clients feel comfortable. Whether they're aware of it or not, that's not what they're paying us for."

Max couldn't deny the point, even though Gloss was using it to rationalize an irresponsible campaign.

"Your lack of vision. That might be where you're falling short, Holiday."

"Kent, do you have a problem with me? I think I can see that."

There was silence on the other end of the phone. "Holiday, you seem like a clever enough chap, but this is business."

"Then let me manage *my* account."

"That was the idea, but when things don't happen quickly enough, management steps in and *helps* you. That means you do things their way. Hang on," Gloss said. In the background, Max could hear the assistant reminding Gloss about his yoga class.

"Is there anything else, Holiday?"

Before he could stop himself, Max blurted, "Yoga, Kent?"

After a short pause, Gloss said, "Yes. Ashtanga—it's a private class, if you really must know. Clears the negative energy. You should try it sometime. Now give that new art director a call and see if he needs anything. You've got a long night ahead of you."

Max faced his harsh new reality. Things had never been this contentious at Goodson. As a division of a publicly owned holding company, the politics, rewards, and failures at HHI were magnified. And Gloss was proving to be a soulless corporate snake that managed through fear to keep people down. He was breaking things so he could fix them and creating chaos and drama to demonstrate his power. It was a game that required selling your soul to the devil and then thanking him for the opportunity.

Max needed a plan. If Gloss had the juice to fire a veteran like Bette, Max was vulnerable. He called Layla's office, and was surprised to find that her assistant was still at her desk, and doubly surprised that Layla's schedule was open from two to four the next day. He pulled out Bette's campaigns from behind the door and slipped them into an oversized portfolio bag. Then he called Henry Goodson.

CHAPTER 25

Garter belt or not? *Of course*, Veronica decided, snapping the black lace band to her thigh highs. She smiled slyly as she checked herself in the full-length mirror. Perfect. This was Veronica—relentlessly beautiful, in her zone, and ready for her man. While running a brush through her hair, she flashed to a memory of Max's deep blue eyes filled with pleasure whenever she'd suit up for love. And giving credit where due, when called upon, Max delivered. Sex was never their problem. He just failed to convince her that he had that X factor, the killer instinct she demanded in her man. His honesty and loving ways had not been enough.

Roger was different. He was more like her—aggressive and a realist. He knew that the best things in life needed to be taken. It made sense. She had to work hard for everything she had and found little reason to believe in abundance. There was only so much to go around. If it wasn't yours, it was somebody else's.

The digital clock on her night table glowed nine thirty. *Okay, Roger wasn't late yet, but where the hell was he?* Fruit spoils when left standing, and Veronica never allowed for that possibility. She flicked on the small lamp, stretched out on her bed, and began flipping through *My Radiance* magazine. The new issue was thicker than the first one and again laden with ads for high-end beauty and style products. Checking the masthead, she still couldn't believe that Cassidy Goodson was the editor. It was a long way from her stint as editorial assistant at *Face Front*. Cassidy was competent, but in Veronica's eyes, she didn't have the gravitas be an executive editor. Sure, she was energetic and bright. But could she run with the big dogs and break into the old boy's club that kept women down in major corporations?

Veronica skimmed through the diverse articles on yoga at the office, eco-tourism vacations, and investing in real estate foreclosures. They could wait. She wanted to read "The Guys' Guy's Guide to Love."

MASKED MEN

Your letters say that you want the truth about men. I'm warning you—it ain't pretty. But okay, here it goes. The modern man is weak and increasingly susceptible to temptation. Look at the newspaper and you'll see how men continue to succumb to their addictions of sex, greed, violence, and hypocrisy. It's time for women to rule this world in a better way—one man and one relationship at a time. And I'm here to help.

Fact: men lie—constantly. They do it to subdue the truth inside their poisoned consciousnesses. They hide. That's why you must confront and unmask your man. Think of their heroes—Zorro, Batman, the Lone Ranger, Spiderman. They all wore masks, and for good reason. To hide their identities. Okay, it's a metaphor, but it's true. For you to build a successful relationship, you need to unmask your man and make him reveal himself, even if he doesn't want to show you what's inside. Don't let your man get away with secrecy, because regardless of how much time you spend with him, you'll remain alone if you let him hide what's inside his heart. Why do men hide? Isn't it obvious? Because they're insecure and afraid they're not good enough for you. They do it because they can—because you let them.

But if you succeed in discovering his truth, you'll help your man become the person he wants to be—and the partner you deserve. Men need your help more than ever. Now, the good news: you can win. For the same reason a porcupine has quills and a turtle burrows into his shell for protection, women have been equipped with superior intuitive powers. While men waged wars wielding their brute strength and force, women were developing their sixth sense. And the more you trust your gift—the one that tells you "I just know"—the more you'll be rewarded.

Here's a way to supercharge that gift. Men aren't that complicated, not the way you and your friends think or hope they are. They're creatures of habit who spend most of their lonely lives thinking about sex, eating, sleeping, drinking, thinking about sex, watching sports, listening to music, playing sports and video games, thinking about sex, and repeating the cycle. That's about all. Don't believe me? Just ask.

An endless stream of available gratuitous sexual imagery, rump-shaking hip-hop videos, and the nihilistic drone of heavy metal music choke the minds and lower the vibrations of modern males. And the declining standards propagated by reality television have taken their toll. Men are caught in a web of misinformation that force-feeds their lowest common denominators. They've lost touch with our values and respect for themselves . . . and for you.

How can you make it work? Simple—ask questions. And then ask more questions, and in a gentle yet determined way, keep asking, until you've pushed aside their fragile egos and revealed the man inside. And remember, you have to listen to what he says, not judge him. Really listen or else he won't open up. Then it's up to you to decide if he is worthy of your love. Sound easy? It is. Whatever answers you receive, even if they're non-answers, the man is revealing himself. Find out how he feels about everything important in his life. If you stay on him, he'll be grateful because—more good news—men really want to open up to you.

When you call at eleven and he tells you that he's out with a few colleagues above the background noises, that little voice inside you might have its doubts. Start asking him questions. Which bar? What's the occasion? Who's there? And don't forget to follow up the next day, to make sure he was telling the truth.

162

I'm not suggesting that you jack up the poor guy the minute he walks through the door, but over time, you can ferret out the seemingly innocuous information that will tell you what makes men tick.

Listen to your man—really listen! Then, heed your gift of intuition. When you do, you'll know if he was out for an innocent night of beers and male bonding or trolling the bars in search of a little "something something" while you were curled up in your jammies watching *Glee*.

You deserve better. You deserve the best—so start asking questions. You'll be amazed at what you'll learn—the good and the bad. And you'll discover the man inside of your man. And if you're not satisfied with what you find in his heart, let him go. Your heart is too wonderful a gift to open up for anything less than an honest man.

Until next time,

Rod

Veronica returned the magazine to the night table and considered what she'd read. Then she stood up, slipped on her heels, and faced the full-length mirror. *Rod was right. She deserved the best and Roger needed to start paying attention. Now.* She glanced at the clock. Five minutes to ten. The fool. He should be here . . . on his knees. *I like that Rod*, Veronica thought. He's probably a hunk, too. She tuned her MP3 player to the Black Eyed Peas and danced her way down the hallway into the kitchen and uncorked a bottle of Prosecco. When the buzzer rang, Veronica pressed the intercom and instructed the doorman to send Roger up.

He knocked, but she didn't answer. *Let's see how much he wants it.* The bell rang and he called her, knocked again, and then turned the knob. He poked his head into the dimly lit living room and stepped inside. He called out for her again as he walked into the kitchen and heard footsteps toward the bedroom.

He grabbed a beer from the refrigerator. After a hearty gulp, he made his way toward the sounds coming from her bedroom. He reached the doorway and looked inside. Veronica was bathed in candlelight, standing tall in the center of the room with her hands on her hips.

He smiled. "Whoa, you look *awesome* baby."

"Where've you been?" she asked sternly.

"Ooh, baby. I love it when you take charge." He moved toward her, but she stopped him cold, shaking her head and wagging a finger.

"Where . . . were . . . you?" she repeated.

"Thinking about you. But as usual, I had to listen to some client yapping about food—pici pasta tossed with cockscombs, duck testicles, and truffles, if you really want to know."

"Which client and whose testicles?" she asked curtly.

He paused, yielding to her suspicion. "I was finalizing a program with the Peacock Beverages client."

"Really? And where did you go?"

"We had a couple of drinks at the W. I told her I couldn't stay for dinner." His eyes traced Veronica's form up and down. "You realize that you're making my pants feel tighter?"

"Good. How many drinks have you had?"

"Uh, a couple . . . two, I guess," he said.

"That's all? Your eyes are red."

He rubbed them. "And a glass of wine."

"So what does your client look like? I don't even have to ask if she's a woman. Is she attractive?"

"Not really. I mean, I guess she's all right," he said, taking another swallow of beer.

"What's that mean?"

"It means she's kind of short and has that Mediterranean look."

Veronica saw her opening and dug deeper. "Mediterranean look? What—does she look like a fisherman? Is she sexy?"

"V, it's a business relationship."

"Then why can't you tell me?"

Shifting his feet, Roger shot back, "Okay, she's got huge cans. Happy now?"

"Huge? Have you been sharing your peacock with her?"

Roger feigned a shocked look. "Of course not."

"I need to know where your focus is," she said, opening the drawstring on her sheer robe. "Roger, look at me. Do I have any reason to doubt you?"

His hand shot up in denial. "No way. You're the one, V."

"You're not interested in her *cans*?"

"*Noo.*" Roger said. "What's gotten into you?"

"Just asking. I know how women react to you," she said, losing the edge to her voice. She moistened her lips, tossed her robe aside, and placed her hands back on her hips. "See what you've got right here?"

He nodded, relieved that her questioning was over and the fun was about to begin. "Hell yeah. Be right back."

While Roger was in the bathroom, Veronica listened to her little voice inside and felt something was wrong. A few minutes later, Roger was crouched between her long legs, his lips and tongue caressing her thighs and around her moist crevice. She breathed heavily, attempting to work her way to orgasm, but it was taking longer than usual. Roger's ability to achieve an erection had been compromised by stress and the alcohol. He usually sprung up like a sapling so she reached down and took him firmly in her hand. After a few minutes of stroking, kissing, and massaging, he was barely hard enough to enter her. And then it was over after a few frenzied moments. Roger immediately collapsed in a heap and passed out. Veronica rolled onto her back and stared at the ceiling.

The next morning, she launched herself out of bed at six. Feeling the sheets rustling, Roger grabbed at her, but she slipped out of his hands and hopped into the shower. No workout today. She wanted to get to the office early and fine-tune the credentials presentation for the new client she was determined to win over. Scoring that account would ensure her bonus. Then she could make the down payment on her condo. After changing into her Armani pants suit and a lilac silk blouse, she made a final check in the mirror. She was perfectly coiffed, ready to take on the world. On her way out, she glanced down at Roger, disenchanted. His hair was sticking out and his head was buried in the pillow when she closed the door behind her.

CHAPTER 26

At two thirty-five, Layla strutted into the seventh-floor conference room wearing her black Chanel suit and a gold necklace. Max and Gloss were standing opposite each other with their arms folded.

Max clicked into his account service mode and greeted his client with a smile. "Layla, good afternoon," he said. "I apologize for the inconvenience." Seeing her staring at his bruised eye, he said, "No more basketball on Tuesday nights. Caught an elbow. I'm considering an eye patch. And maybe a parrot."

"Ahem," Gloss said.

"I'm sure you'd make a charming pirate, Max," Layla said, registering that this was the second man she'd seen that week wielding a black eye. "That's quite a lump."

"Ahem. Layla, this is Kent Gloss," Max said. "Kent, Layla Korindopolos, Director of Marketing for Peacock Beverages."

Layla smiled. "It's nice to meet someone who—let's see if I can remember the quote, 'knows a client's needs, better than they do.' Did I get that right?" she joked.

"Ah, the trades—a necessary evil. Managing the press is an art," Gloss replied, clasping her hand. "That one you mentioned was taken out of context. It's my pleasure meeting you. I thought I'd sit in on today's presentation. Make yourself comfortable while Max and I finish our discussion . . . outside."

Standing face to face in the hallway, Max and Gloss glared at each other.

"Holiday, you're not presenting that interminable advertising at this meeting."

"I saw your revisions," Max said. "Layla will never buy a campaign that objectifies women. We need to show her a range of ideas. We can't go into the meeting with only one campaign, and certainly not a campaign that has priests serving Jell-O shots and leather boys in studded collars lapping cocktails from chrome doggie dishes. How does that meet her objective of launching a high-end line of products with all-natural additives?"

"Just get in there and sell that work, Holiday," Gloss said.

After some small talk, Max kicked off the meeting. The new creative team snickered and made jokes while presenting their version of the "Seven Deadly Sins" campaign. Layla remained stone-faced. A cold silence had filled the room by the time the young art director held up the final storyboard.

"Is that it?" Layla asked evenly.

Seeing the disaster unfolding, Max pulled out a set of Bette's storyboards from the envelope and stood up. "Of course, the agency feels strongly about capturing the attention of the twenty-one to twenty-five-year-old target group with a provocative campaign like 'Seven Deadly Sins.' But we have another idea . . . just to show you the range of our thinking," he said, glancing at Gloss and ignoring the daggers shooting from his eyes. Max turned the "Angels Share" campaign toward Layla, presenting it as a work in progress. Based on the impassive look on her face, it was too little, too late. The well had already been poisoned, rendering Layla an unreceptive client.

"Well, at least you included what makes our products different," she said. "Is there more?" Max reached slowly for the other envelope with Bette's artist's campaign using the visual game for each flavor. He weighed his options, but before he could decide whether to present a good campaign at a bad meeting, Gloss shot up and waved his hand.

"That's it for now," he said with a sharp look at Max. We'll reconvene and discuss the work internally. Layla, we'll have something else for you very soon—you have my word."

Max stared at him, wondering why Gloss was seemingly going out of his way to screw up his account. *This is a smart guy. He must know what he's doing.* But at the time, Max was too pissed off to be sure.

Layla turned to a red-faced Max, and then Gloss. She rose, straightened her back, and began packing up. "Gentlemen, while you're reconvening, I'll explore investing in digital media and other promotional vehicles. So I suggest you work . . . quickly."

After a curt exit, the conference room cleared. Max and Gloss stayed behind and moved toward each other. Max watched the veins bulge in Gloss's neck when he barked, "Holiday, didn't I tell you not to show her those tiresome ads?"

"I know my client. I had to do something," Max said. "She despised that first campaign. You sold me out."

"Bollocks," Gloss growled. "Your client was quite clear about the possibility of reducing our budget. And if she does, you'll need to bring in another account that can pay your salary. Otherwise I'm not sure we can afford you. Am I making myself very clear?"

Max said nothing and walked out.

When Max returned to his office, there was a package wrapped in plain brown paper sitting on his desk. He peeled open the envelope and took out a handwritten note.

Hi Max,

Sorry again about your shirt. Thanks for contributing your valuable time to promote reading. Good luck this season.

Best,

Brenton and Jimmy Banks

Beneath a thin layer of tissue paper, Max unveiled a white polo shirt with the New York Giants football team's blue helmet stitched onto the chest. Max held it up and smiled. Nice. There was a business card in the box. Max took it out and read, "Brenton Banks, Esq. Mergers and Acquisitions."

Max opened his desk drawer and took out the envelope holding the two box-seat tickets for an upcoming Yankees versus Red Sox game that a magazine rep had dropped off for him yesterday. Max stared at the tickets—third row behind first base. He'd planned on asking Cassidy to the game, but instead grabbed the phone and dialed the number on Banks' card.

CHAPTER 27

On the Sunday morning of the Children's Literary Club of New York's "Rock 'n' Read" event, Cassidy emerged from the subway station at Columbus Circle into sparkling sunshine. The weather forecast for that afternoon had mentioned the possibility of thunderstorms, but at nine o'clock, the skies were a clear, vivid blue. Being a new event for the club, she wanted to make sure everything was set up correctly for the attendees filing in at one o'clock. Once all was arranged, she could step back and take in the festivities with everyone else.

The sound checks for the folk singers and children's authors went off without issue. Pretty soon the families began streaming through the roped-off entrance near the Summer Stage. Cassidy folded her arms and smiled, gazing at the excited children pulling their parents toward the stage. Although her friends had offered to help out, she knew how much Serena was looking forward to getting away for the weekend and how Max enjoyed golfing on Sundays. She told them she'd take care of this one, and she was pleased that so far everything was turning out fine.

By three o'clock, the clouds had moved in. The event was in full swing, with parents and children listening to readings from several well-known authors between musical performances. During one of the musical interludes, Brenton Banks appeared with Jimmy, wearing a Yankees cap and jersey. Cassidy waved warmly to greet them. Banks' navy short-sleeved polo shirt and jeans showed off his lean, athletic build.

"Having fun, Jimmy?" she asked.

The boy smiled shyly and held out his program to her. Cassidy leaned over and made out the scribbled signature of one of the ballplayers attending the event.

"Wow, a Yankee. Very cool," she said, sounding impressed. Cassidy felt Banks watching her as she chatted with the boy.

"Working today?" Banks asked.

"Actually, my part's done. I'm free now."

She pushed her hair to the side and they made small talk as Jimmy giggled and pulled on his dad's arm.

"We're going easy on the hot dogs today," Banks said, pushing the brim down on his son's Yankees cap. "How about an apple, J-man?"

The boy made a face and Banks laughed. "He wants ice cream."

As Cassidy pointed out the ice cream vendor, she felt a drop, and then another. A brisk wind picked up as the clouds suddenly burst open. Banks and Cassidy each took one of Jimmy's hands, and together they scooted under the plastic covering by the stands. But the wind picked up and tore off one of the sheets, spinning it across the event space.

Cassidy looked at the darkened skies and then at the staff rapidly covering the last of the stage equipment. "I should probably lend a hand," she said. She flagged down a scurrying staffer. "Do you guys need help?"

"Park staff's got it from here," the young man said.

"Excuse the pun, but it looks like they have things covered," Banks said.

She scanned the area. "Over here," she said, gesturing to a path leading to one of the exits. Banks motioned with his head. "I think this way is faster," he said, pulling Jimmy by the hand in the opposite direction. Cassidy hesitated, but followed them as they ran through the rain. Just then, the wind picked up speed and the sky emptied torrents of rain. Luckily, a staff member pulled up in a jeep, waved them inside, and drove them to the edge of the park.

While they waited under an awning near the corner of Central Park West and 86th Street, the heavy rain tapered into a light, steady drizzle. Banks directed Cassidy and Jimmy to wait under the awning and hailed the first available cab. He told the driver the address of an

uptown eatery that was popular for its kid-friendly menu and attentive staff.

"Hope you don't mind taking a side trip uptown. This place is for
real. I like to keep Jimmy close to his roots or else he might grow up
thinking that his ancestors ate pizza."

Cassidy laughed.

Once inside the restaurant off Frederick Douglass Boulevard,
Banks walked directly to the front, looked around, and then pointed
to a table, chatting easily with the hostess while they were being
seated. Banks positioned himself across from Cassidy with Jimmy in
the middle. When the waitress arrived, Banks gave her a high-wattage
smile and waved off the menus. He asked Cassidy if there were any
foods she didn't eat, and if she minded him ordering for the table.

She smiled. "No, as long as it's comfort food, I'll eat it."

Banks looked at his son. "It's the best. Right, J-man?"

The boy nodded, watching the other kids and their families seated
throughout the room. The waitress clicked her pen, waiting for the
order.

"He loves this place," Banks said before choosing an array of
authentic dishes prepared with a Creole flair for the table.

Cassidy watched as Banks helped Jimmy negotiate his drumstick,
coleslaw, and a small pork chop. He remained patient throughout the
meal, even when Jimmy scooped some of his mashed potatoes in his
hand. Banks gave him a look and then handed him a stack of napkins.
He had such a soft touch with the boy, his voice warm and rumbling.
Somehow he managed to feed Jimmy and himself and fill Cassidy in
on Jimmy's reading habits and karate class, all without ever taking
his eyes off her.

"I've been looking into schools for Jimmy, plus all the camps and
music lessons. The list never ends, but he's a great kid . . . even if he
eats with his hands sometimes, right?" Banks said, looking over at the
boy with mock sternness.

She smiled. "How do you do all of this?"

"All of what?"

"Come on, you're like super-dad."

He let out a huge laugh. "Hardly," he said. "I get lots of help and
make lots of mistakes, right Jimmy?"

"Lots," Jimmy said, fiddling with the drumstick.

Banks attentively refilled Cassidy's iced tea and handed her two packets of Splenda. "Need anything else?"

"I'm fine." *And you're real fine*, she thought. It felt strange, having a man take care of everything, but she kind of liked it, too.

When the plates were cleared, Banks looked at his son and smiled. "Ready for that ice cream, J-man?"

The boy nodded and then got up and pulled on his father's arm. "I wanna see the game," he said, pointing to the television near the restaurant's entrance.

"Okay," Banks said. "But stay where I can see you."

"He's a wonderful child," Cassidy said as the boy wandered off.

Banks wiped his hands with a napkin. "Yes, we're blessed. Unfortunately, all this shuttling him back and forth between his mom and me takes a toll. We weren't married that long and things weren't working out when all of a sudden Jimmy came into our lives," he said, looking in his son's direction. "He's growing up so fast."

Jimmy returned for his ice cream, and then Banks signaled for the check. He took a glance at his Rolex. "Wow. I'm sorry we've kept you so long."

Outside the skies were clearing as dusk settled on the city. Banks had a car waiting for her. Cassidy tried to protest, but Banks waved her off. He held her door and told the driver to be careful. Cassidy shook her head helplessly, but she didn't protest. *I could get used to this.*

He closed the door behind her and leaned over the window. "Maybe we can do this again?" he asked.

Cassidy's pale-blue eyes glowed with the pleasure of the invitation. "Thank you, Brenton. This was fun," she said, lightly touching his hand. "See you soon, Jimmy," she said, waving to the boy as the car pulled away.

CHAPTER 28

The two women shook hands, smiling politely while sizing each other up—the clothes, the hair, the shoes. While connecting her laptop to the projector on the conference room table, Veronica took a peek at Layla's breasts, wondering if Roger had seen them naked. Throughout Veronica's crisp, professional presentation, Layla peppered her with questions about Globison. Veronica, hungry for a sale, openly shared whatever she knew about the inner workings of her company.

After Veronica clicked to the last PowerPoint slide, Layla nodded her approval. "You make a strong case for investing our advertising dollars with you. Very impressive."

Veronica flashed a winning smile. "New-age spirits are the future, as is our digital advertising model. It's cost efficient and our program connects with your core target audience where they're spending their time. Shall we discuss next steps?"

"Of course there are financial considerations, but I like your program," Layla said, leaning back and playing with her Montblanc pen. "Since your approach is new to some of our senior executives, I'd like to learn more about your company's financials. Due diligence is necessary before investing millions with a new partner—even with an organization like Globison. In the meantime, I'll pull together a rough budget."

"Would you like me to show you what results our program delivers at different spending levels?" Veronica offered.

"That would be very helpful."

Veronica knew this was part of the dance. Ultimately, Layla would do whatever served the best interests of her brand. As soon as Veronica revised her proposal, Layla would squeeze her for the lowest price. After all, she was Nikola Korindopolos's daughter. And she'd negotiate with only one person's interest in mind. Hers.

"Thank you so much, Layla. This has been a pleasure." Then, unable to hold back her almost jealous curiosity, she said, "I love your outfit. And that bag's gorgeous. Who made . . . ?"

"It's custom," Layla replied, running her hand lightly across its supple leather.

"Of course," Veronica said. "I'll make the changes and have the new proposal in your hands shortly. You're going to love working with Globison." Then she pumped Layla's hand and strode out.

While passing the front desk in the lobby, a galvanized Veronica punched her boss's number into her BlackBerry. "I'm revising my forecast," she typed before spinning through the revolving doors into the bright sunlight. After she hung up, she immediately dialed her broker, announcing, "Let's move on that condo."

She clicked off the phone and dropped it into her bag. As she searched for a cab, she failed to notice Roger standing on the opposite side of the street, munching an apple. He'd been startled to see Veronica exit the building. He reached for his phone, held the camera open, closed one eye, and locked onto her image. Then he snapped two photos, slipped the device back in his pocket, and turned the corner.

When Layla returned from lunch, she considered Veronica's program. Despite her aggressiveness and somewhat transparent sales demeanor, Veronica had presented a strong case with the added value of providing details about her company's financial standing. As Layla walked toward her office, she glanced in at Cassidy's team setting up in the conference room. She frowned at her calendar, thinking, *Great. Another sales pitch.*

She checked her face in her compact and pasted on a smile as she entered the meeting room. Four heads turned her way at the same time, all beaming. A well-groomed woman with glasses waited for the others to make their introductions. This was the queen bee, like a star player who decided to ride along for this sales call. The woman looked Layla in the eye and smiled.

"Hi. Cassidy Goodson," she said, offering a card that identified her as the executive editor of *My Radiance*. "Thanks for making time for us."

Once everyone was in place, Layla folded her arms, expecting the usual boilerplate here's-why-you-absolutely-have-to-be-in-our-magazine pitch. But before the same young woman in the front of the room could begin, Cassidy gently motioned to Layla.

"Layla, if you don't mind, before we begin telling you about our new publication, could you take a few minutes and tell us about your new line, who you are targeting, and how we can assist you in the launch?"

Hallelujah, Layla thought. *Finally, someone's asking about my business.*

After Layla provided a brief overview of *Holy Spiritz*, Cassidy and her team asked questions concerning the source of her additives, if the flavors were organic, the relative importance of the women's market, and if she had considered a "green" positioning for the brand.

Layla nodded throughout the meeting, watching the team follow Cassidy's cues. She was impressed by the quality of their ideas and how easily the discussion flowed. Finally, the sales rep presented an overview of the magazine and its vision for helping women prosper and creating a better world. Layla was impressed, but braced herself for a sales pitch at the end of the presentation. She waited, but there was no proposal. Only a solitary PowerPoint slide stating, *HOW CAN WE HELP?*

Layla shifted in her seat. "So what's the catch?"

"There's no catch," Cassidy said. Then she scribbled something on her pad. "We'd like to spend some time with your brand before submitting our proposal. From what you've told us, you're going to need sampling and trial. Over the next ninety days, we're scheduling events to introduce our magazine to the press. That might be a great way to get your *Holy Spiritz* into the mouths of some respected tastemakers. Can I give you a call when we have a few dates locked in?"

Layla smiled warily. "Contingent on my purchasing a full schedule of advertising in your publication, I assume," she said.

Cassidy smiled again and shook her head. "I'm sure you'll need time to pull things together for your launch. We'd be happy to help you sample the products at our venues. After that, I know you'll want to partner with us."

That was it. No fine print. Nothing dependent on a sale. *I like this woman.*

"Hang on," Layla said, uncrossing her legs. "I'll be right back."

Cassidy gave her sales team her don't-ask-me look as they quietly waited for Layla to return. When the door opened, Layla strolled in, followed by an assistant pushing a cart holding seven bottles filled with clear liquid, an assortment of juices and mixers, stemware, and an ice bucket.

"Anyone interested in being baptized to our *Holy Spiritz*?" she asked, invitingly.

Over the course of the next half hour, the crew mixed and matched Layla's products in a variety of concoctions, laughing as they dreamed up names for each drink.

"Looks like we have a few winners," Layla announced after they ran out of ice a second time. "Brazilian Wax, Glamazon, and Happy Ending all passed the taste test. Nice work ladies."

Everyone laughed as Cassidy motioned for her team to pack up. She shook Layla's hand. "Thanks again. I'll call as soon as I have more information about our events. And we'll keep our eyes open for partnership opportunities for your brand."

Layla waved as the team filed out of the conference room and said, "Can everybody make it back to the dorm okay?" to a chorus of giggles. She thought, *Wow, that was actually fun.*

CHAPTER 29

"**M**eet me at the pistol range," Nikola said to his daughter.

"Papa, what's going on?" Layla asked, holding her cell phone to her ear as she hurried to her next meeting.

"Your information on Globison was excellent. We'll shoot and then talk over dinner."

It was the second time Layla's father had called—a sure sign that something was in the works. Roger had also phoned twice, leaving messages to find out if she'd read his revised proposal. His transparent behavior was disappointing. Deep down, she knew he was after her budget, but even that couldn't quiet her sexual pangs for him. She'd never let herself go like she did that night in his arms. But no one ever wanted her just for being Layla. It was always about her father's money, and now, hers. After allowing herself a brief recollection of their tryst, she deleted Roger's messages.

For the past twenty years, Nikola belonged to a private shooting club in Greenwich Village. Layla entered through the cordial dining room and walked directly to the pistol range in the back. Unlike most powerful business executives, firing live ammunition proved a better tonic for Nikola's mercurial personality than a leisurely stroll on the golf course. Layla declined the manager's offer of a pistol and the prerequisite gold-tinted glasses. She accepted the ear pads and then watched as her father methodically emptied his pistol into a small target twenty yards away. Before retrieving the target, Nikola greeted his daughter with a firm hug and a kiss on the cheek. His marksmanship had been exemplary, and he proudly pointed at the perforations around the bull's-eye.

"Today, I can't miss," he declared. "Where's your gun? You need to shoot something."

"That's all right. I'll watch you."

He motioned for a fresh target, took aim, and squeezed off another round. "So," he said, "I'm buying Globison."

"That's fantastic!"

"Then I'm selling it," he added.

"But why?" she asked. "It fits perfectly. You said you wanted to take advantage of the explosion in online advertising. Globison is the fastest growing company in the space."

Nikola furrowed his eyebrows. "Your father is a simple man. I shoot guns, and every so often I buy a company. I e-mail, but what do I know about selling advertising on the Internet? Maybe if I had someone to help me, someone I could trust . . ."

"But Papa, you saw the sales figures that I forwarded you. Their revenue is going through the roof."

"I know, but this digital media is different," he insisted, retrieving the target. "After the sale goes through, we'll spend a year cutting out the fat and then put the company back on the block. I'll make my money that way."

"But Globison is a gold mine," she protested.

"We'll see," he said. "Now, about you. How are the boozy drinks?"

Layla's head dropped as Nikola examined the bullet-riddled piece of paper. "They're fine, Papa. I'm having problems with my ad agency, so I'm considering other things—like promoting the new products online."

"Advertising agencies will say anything to get your money," he said. "But how can this be like working with your father?"

"Papa, please," she said. "It's something *I* need to do."

He took a breath and signaled for a fresh target. "This is what your mother would do—make me uncomfortable so I would give her whatever she wanted."

"Like having a child?"

He took aim and lowered his weapon. "Of course she was right about that, but . . ."

"That's why you loved her so much . . . and trusted her. So why can't you trust me?"

Nikola turned to her. "I'll tell you what; if you want me to keep Globison, join me. I told you I'd double your salary."

"I'm in the middle of launching *my own* products," she said.

"I'll let you run Globison."

She hesitated, then said, "Papa, I . . ."

"I'll give you a ten percent stake of the company, and if you show good results, I won't sell it right away." He adjusted the tinted glasses and sprayed another round in the vicinity of the bull's-eye.

She let his words sink in. This was different. She began calculating his offer and smiled inwardly. Layla never relished the idea of joining her obsessive, controlling father, but equity changed everything. It meant real money, real power. Although she loved her *Holy Spiritz*, she knew that her tireless efforts at Peacock would only make rich men of its owners. Her father was already rich. And he knew that everyone had a price. Even his daughter.

CHAPTER 30

When Cassidy entered her boss's office on the third floor of the magazine's headquarters on West 55th Street, the older woman greeted her from behind her desk with a sparkle of humor flashing in her eyes. Six large canvas bags of mail lay strewn across the floor next to her cluttered desk. Margo shifted like a hen warming her eggs as Cassidy stepped over the bags and took the seat across from her.

"You've got mail," Margo said.

"Excuse me?"

"Let me rephrase that. Rod's got mail."

Cassidy's light-blue eyes opened wide as she looked over the bulging sacks. "This is all for him? You're kidding."

"Rod's a hit with the ladies," her boss said.

"Are all of these letters?" Cassidy asked.

"I guess so, if you don't count the panties, half-naked photos, business cards, home phone numbers, and party invitations."

"I never . . ." Cassidy stammered.

"It probably was that column."

" 'Rising to Every Occasion.' "

"Well, you wanted something provocative," Margo said and drummed her red nails on the desk as if something were on her mind. "I think you know what I'm going to say next."

"You want more Rod," Cassidy said with a straight face.

"I think you're the one who'll be getting more Rod," she said drolly.

The original plan had been to publish *My Radiance* monthly, but when the first issue quickly sold out, the holding company turned up the heat. Cassidy's idea to seed the market by handing out free copies of the premier issue in New York and L.A. had been a knockout. Following up only three weeks later with a new issue had strained her staff, but it turned out to be a masterstroke. And with a "mini" empowerment-themed issue distributed to key retail outlets less than two weeks later, Cassidy and the sales force were exhausted but exhilarated. Unlike her days at *Face Front*, she didn't need to feature clichéd numbers or empty promises on the cover to sell her magazine. She happily rejected the "66 Ways to Satisfy Him in Bed," "Your 123 Secret Erogenous Zones," and "74 Ways to Say Goodbye" articles, and she planned to keep it that way.

"I guess he could do more," Cassidy said. "I just never thought he'd be so—"

"Is he hot?" her boss asked, lowering her reading glasses farther down and peering frankly at Cassidy's sudden change of demeanor.

Cassidy blanched. Margo wanted Rod to be their man-meat mascot. She wondered, *Max a star? Is this a good thing? Women FedEx-ing him their panties?*

"Well, he's attractive . . . in a real way. He's not some pretty boy, but he's got an amazing smile. And he's sweet—and has a cute body, and his eyes are this really gorgeous blue . . ." She trailed off, but then, realizing she was veering into dreamy schoolgirl territory, snapped back into her editor's voice. "Do we really need to use him? I thought he could write the column anonymously. Makes him more mysterious. No one needs to know who he is or meet him. If the press has any questions, they can ask me."

"Cassidy, this is your baby. I'm only here to make sure we deliver the profits. Rod's a success. We want more!"

Cassidy, realizing the truth, nodded. "Okay, I'll call him."

On the way back to her office she weighed the issue. The fortunes of *My Radiance* and Rod were now directly connected—more than what she'd had in mind when she talked Max into writing the column. When she sat down at her desk, she took a long breath and dialed his number.

"I was just thinking about you," Max said cheerfully.

"Really?" she said.

"Yep, I was thinking how awesome your editing has been. Even when you revise almost every sentence, I can still recognize my work," he said with a short laugh.

"We just want you to express yourself as clearly as possible."

"Right. Hey, I'm seeing the magazine everywhere."

Cassidy mindlessly started to doodle on her notepad. "Sales are strong. Your column about addressing a woman's needs really touched a nerve."

"Ha, ha. The truth is so many guys fail to see how much women give. These so-called players think that dating half a dozen women at once is the ticket. They haven't figured out that if they took the time to really know one woman, they could have so much more."

"That could make a great column, and that's why I'm calling. We've decided to speed up the rollout of the magazine. We need more of Rod. The new website's ready, so I'll need some short, bloggy pieces as soon as possible. I know you're busy, but what do you think?"

"My plate's pretty full right now, Cass. How many of these will you need?"

"I guess maybe ten or so, for now . . ." she said, casually.

"Ten? I have a day job."

"I know," she said. "But remember you said that you wanted to help women. You'll be releasing all of your bottled up emotions and . . ."

"*What?*"

The pencil slipped from Cassidy's hand. "I mean . . . now you have a forum for expressing yourself while showing women how to deal with guys like Roger."

"This isn't supposed to be therapy."

"It's not, but you're a guy," she said, switching to a more cajoling tone. "Don't worry. I'll help you pick the topics."

"I wasn't worried, but maybe I should be," he said.

"Just write about how guys view their world," she said. "And why women don't understand men and their strange behavior."

"Strange behavior?"

"You know—like those monkeys," she said. "Write about how men see their friends . . . and our friends, too, and why sports take up so much of their time, and why guys don't call after asking for our numbers. Come on."

He became silent, thinking between Cassidy's words, and then ran his hand through his hair. "You need this, don't you?"

"Yes, I need this," she said. "I know you won't let me down."

"That's what friends are for," he said.

The silence between them grew louder before Cassidy said, "Yes, Max, that's what friends are for."

After hanging up, she stared at the phone, reminding herself that despite Max's flashes of sensitivity and self-awareness, he really was still a guy. She looked down at her notepad and flushed when she saw what she had doodled—a seascape with a prominent lighthouse on the beach buttressed by two big boulders at its base.

CHAPTER 31

Summer was Roger's favorite time of the year. The days were long and hot, and the skirts were short and hot. With the July 4th weekend just around the corner and summer hours at the office, Roger was living in his own little acre of heaven. For many male New Yorkers his age, hedonistic lifestyles had been reduced to memories and replaced by marriage, kids, bills, and 9/11's reminder of life's impermanence. For many, it seemed like there was less of everything. But that meant there was more for Roger.

As he walked briskly through the park on his way to work, Roger's mind was fixated on doing whatever would be necessary to persuade Layla to sign his deal. He'd also be extra careful around Veronica. Catching her coming out of Peacock's building jolted him and reminded him of her unswerving ambition. And God—the gall of her asking those annoying questions about how he'd spent his evenings. She claimed that she wanted to know the real Roger. *The real Roger?* That made him laugh.

And how did that Serena get under his skin so quickly? They only met once, but she'd kept him off-balance and made him feel alive. It was obvious that she knew how to play the game, so he remained on his best behavior around her. When he had called to arrange a second date, she agreed, but at the last minute she rescheduled—twice. She had the distinction of being the only woman to cancel on him and get a bonus rain check. Serena was changing his rules with those full lips, those smoldering eyes, that sultry voice, and, of course, her perfect, heart-shaped ass.

When he arrived at work, Roger mumbled a quick, "Morning," to Gail as he passed by. He'd avoided her since their encounter on his couch.

An hour later, he called out, "Gail, we need to set up some lunches."

"Finish my review yet?" she responded. "HR is asking for it. Remember, today's my last day working with you."

"Oh, right," he said, pulling the blank form out of his desk. "Give me a few minutes."

Roger looked over the appraisal form, checking off what he considered positive ratings across the board. No sense taking chances. She'd earned high marks all around. When Gail stood at his door wielding her pad and pen, Roger motioned her inside. She took a seat and crossed her legs away from him. He watched her skirt slide up her thigh.

"Uh, Roger?" she said, raising an eyebrow.

"Right—your review. Here. I think you'll be pleased," he said, handing her the document. "You've done a fine job. More than I could have asked for."

She smoothed her hair away from her face and put on her glasses, pursing her lips as she slowly reviewed her appraisal. "You don't think I exceeded expectations for being proactive and helpful?"

Roger said, "I can't give you exceeded expectations on everything."

"How about my oral communications skills?" she said, gently swinging her heel.

"Okay, okay. Give me that," he said taking back the file and making the change. "Satisfied?" he asked, thrusting the papers back at her.

Gail scribbled her name on the bottom and smiled. "Thanks, Roger. This has truly been a learning experience."

"Good. Now, let's set up those lunches. Remember, Ms. Korindopolos is on Wednesday and Ms. Sparks on Thursday. I'll call Ms. Korindopolos. You get ahold of Ms. Sparks and the restaurant. And ask for Mario. He'll hold my table."

As Gail headed back to her desk, Roger checked his planner. Friday was the hearing in New Jersey for his DUI. He wasn't concerned. His mother's boyfriend, a prominent defense attorney in Monmouth County, was taking care of it. Still, it was an inconvenience—a wasted day in court instead of on the golf course. But golf could wait, too. The sales quarter was coming to a close and he needed Layla's signature on his proposal. He punched in her number with his Sharpie and greeted her with a chirpy good morning.

"Roger, if you're calling about your proposal, it's here on my desk."

"I called to invite you to lunch on Wednesday."

"Hang on. I'll check my calendar." She put him on hold for what seemed like an endless minute before returning. "Okay, I can meet you at one."

"Perfect," he said, pumping the air with a fist.

After hanging up, Roger stared out the window, saying, "And you'll sign that fucking contract."

At three, Gail poked her head into Roger's office. "Would it be okay if I took off a little early today? It's my last day on the floor and the girls want to take me out for drinks."

"We might need to change my forecast. Can you wait?"

"How long?"

"Until five fifteen or so?"

Gail stared through him. "Okay," she said coldly. "I can double check your lunch reservations."

"Excellent idea. Too bad I already sent in your review to HR. I could have moved up the check mark for completing tasks."

Gail narrowed her eyes, and with a downward turn of her lips, she stomped back to her workstation. Roger heard her slam something on her desk. He strained his neck to see what was happening outside his office and saw her on the phone. He turned back to his computer and the fantasy football preview he'd been reading.

With the phone to her ear, Gail glanced into Roger's office and saw that he was preoccupied. "I'm calling from Roger Fox's office again," she said. "It's about his lunch reservations." After hanging up, she made another call. At five o'clock, Gail stood in Roger's doorway. He was playing Tiny Wings on his computer.

She shook her head and said, "I'm out of here," before grabbing her bag and walking off.

Roger was standing in his doorway, hoping for a goodbye hug, but shrugged as he watched her march down the corridor. A short time later, Roger threw on his blazer and shut the light.

When he reached Central Park, Roger stopped at the traffic light and looked up to appreciate a glorious Manhattan sky painted with golden hues of a fading sun. Walking leisurely through the park, Roger phoned Serena. "If I remember correctly, you said you *could be* spontaneous," he said lightly.

"That's good. What do you have in mind?"

"Dinner."

"When?" she asked.

"Tonight."

"Oh, Roger, tonight doesn't work," she said. "I already have dinner plans."

"How about next Monday, then?"

"Monday?" she said. "That's not very spontaneous. Are you around this weekend? It's going to be beautiful."

"Can't. This weekend's not good," he said. "I'll be away. But Monday works. I'll even come to Brooklyn."

"Roger's coming to Brooklyn. Shall I alert the newswires?"

He laughed. This woman would not give him a break. "Okay, you got me. Pick a place, and I'll be there at seven."

"Why don't you come to my studio? I finish teaching my last class at six thirty. You can check out all the sweaty women."

"I love the smell of a woman's sweat," he said.

"Then you'll love hot yoga. The women are drowning in perspiration by the time the class is over. You'll think you died and went to heaven. Maybe you'll want to try it. Seriously. Yoga promotes clarity and truth."

"I'd like having a beautiful woman twist me into a pretzel," he said suggestively.

"Maybe someday," she said temptingly. "Hey Roger, I'm heading into the subway. See you Monday." Then she added, "I'm glad you called."

Roger hung up and picked up his pace, imagining Serena dripping with perspiration, standing naked in his bedroom. What was it about this woman that was making him so horny? What was so different about her? He wasn't sure. But when a leggy blonde in Lycra shorts jogged by and smiled at him, there was one thing he *was* sure about. It was summer in New York City and it was good to be Roger Fox.

CHAPTER 32

When her phone rang, Cassidy was finalizing the details on the sampling stations for *Holy Spiritz* at the upcoming *My Radiance* party. Not recognizing the number, she went against her instincts and answered. It was Brenton Banks, calling her for the second time that week.

"How's Jimmy?" she asked.

"That's actually why I'm calling. He's fine, except his mom insists that she take him to the 'Classical for Kids' concert at Lincoln Center tonight."

"Sounds great. What's the problem?"

"Someone sent me two seats for the Yankees–Red Sox game. They're right behind first base."

"Ah-ha. That is a problem."

"Yes, I was going to surprise Jimmy, but now I don't have the heart to tell him. So, I was hoping that if you didn't have plans—I know it's not much notice—but I thought you might enjoy going with me. I always remember when I meet a Red Sox fan living in New York."

"And I can't even say I'm rooting for the underdog anymore."

"They have a few more championships to win before they catch up to the Yanks," he said, laughing. "So what do you think?"

Cassidy checked her calendar. It was a rare Wednesday that she was actually free. *What the hell? Why not?* "Okay," she said. "Sounds like fun."

"Great. I'll take care of everything."

So Cassidy kicked back and enjoyed: ferry tickets from the East Side, beers and hot dogs, the car to P.J. Clarke's, and even the drinks after the game—though that was because the Yankees lost. It felt nice, letting him run things. Easy. But it felt strange, too. *When did you turn into such a girl?* she asked herself as they left the restaurant.

Banks' driver pulled up outside, as if on cue. "Can I drop you off?" Banks asked.

"Oh, that's okay," she said. "I'm going all the way to Brooklyn Heights."

"So? That's what cars are for," he said, smiling. "It'll give us time to review the box score again."

Cassidy knew that if she got into the car, she was going to end up in his arms and maybe his apartment. *This is one beautiful man. Rich, successful* . . . she thought, watching his riveting gray eyes.

She exhaled. "That's okay. I'm fine," she said. "Brenton, I had a great time. Thank you so much. I really . . ."

Banks stepped in close and kissed her. Cassidy leaned her head back and met his embrace. She kissed him in return, thinking how soft his lips were. Before things could go any further, she gently backed away, trying to maintain her composure.

"Good night," he said.

Cassidy smiled as she turned away, but she couldn't speak, even though her heart pounded and her inner voice was shouting, *"Wheee-heee!"* She did turn back, though, after a few steps and caught him watching her walk away. She wagged a mock-scolding finger his way and then smiled to herself while crossing Third Avenue.

She decided to walk a few blocks, wondering what life would be like with Brenton Banks. He was gentle, smart, hunky—and rich. Would she end up driving Jimmy around Westchester in a Range Rover? She tried to picture it. Cassidy Goodson, soccer mom. Rich soccer mom, she corrected herself—with a brownstone on Central Park North, a vacation house in Jamaica, and no crazy deadlines or a magazine to worry about.

He did mention that he made enough money for his ex-wife to quit her job at the law firm. Still, Cassidy wasn't sure if his money would make her world spin the way she wanted. But as she stepped into a cab by the Citicorp building, she heard that voice inside her head again, this time calling out, *"Woo-hoo!"*

When Roger arrived at his office, it was quiet. Gail had moved on to her new assignment, and HR still hadn't sent her replacement. Yesterday, Gail had stopped by to gather her things. While standing outside Roger's office holding a cardboard box, she made a point of reminding him about his lunches.

"There goes one great assistant," he thought, watching her slender hips slink down the hall one last time.

After deleting most of his e-mails, Roger took a cursory glance at his schedule. The following day he had another sales meeting, followed by his six-month review. He needed Layla's program to make his quota. She had to sign the deal today.

As twelve thirty rolled around, Roger straightened his periwinkle tie, slipped on his navy blazer, and checked his face in the small mirror on his door. His eyes immediately trained on the welt. It was still there, and now it had evolved into an unsightly ménage of greenish, yellow, and brown tints. He wondered if it would leave a mark, but forced the notion aside and smiled. *Time to make the doughnuts,* he thought, swaggering out the door.

When Veronica arrived at the restaurant, she moved ahead of a small group of patrons at the maitre d' station, tossed her hair back, and announced, "I'm meeting Mr. Fox."

"Mr. Fox, of course," the maitre d' said, looking up and eying her approvingly. "Right this way, please."

Five minutes later, Layla stood patiently behind two small parties waiting to be seated. She checked her BlackBerry and took a quick look in her compact before the maitre d' asked, "Yes, can I help you?"

"Good afternoon. I'm here to meet Mr. Fox."

"And you are . . . ?" he asked, as he double-checked his list.

"Layla Korindopolos."

"Ah, yes. This way, please." Layla followed him into the center of the intimate room, past the vases of fresh-cut flowers adorning each table.

"Here we are," he said, extending his hand to a table where a cell phone and a folder had been left next to a half-empty glass of water. A napkin lay open on the chair.

Layla, assuming the items were Roger's, said, "Thank you," and sat down.

"Yes," he responded, holding her chair. "I'll send your waiter over," he added before hurrying back to the front of the restaurant.

Layla heard a voice that she thought she recognized from behind her and turned around.

"Layla . . . hello. What a coincidence seeing you here."

"Veronica?" Layla said with a start.

Veronica smiled politely. "This place is always so busy. Looks like they got us mixed up, because this is where they seated me for my lunch date. I'll get the maitre d'."

"They must have seated me at the wrong table," Layla said.

"Please, stay here. I'll call him over. I'm sure it's a mistake," Veronica said, reclaiming her seat.

"Fine," Layla said with a sigh, sitting down tentatively. "Do you lunch here often?"

"Not really; lunch takes too long. I'm meeting someone I've been seeing," Veronica said.

"Oh, how nice."

After a few more awkward moments of silence, Layla asked Veronica the quintessential New York question. "So what does he do?"

"He works in media sales also."

"Really?" Layla said. Veronica waved at the maitre d'.

Seeing her, he moved fluidly between the crowded tables toward the two women. "Is everything satisfactory, ladies?" he asked.

"I'm not sure. We were both seated at this table. There must be a mistake," Veronica said.

"But I'm sure both of your names are on the reservation. Ms. Sparks and Ms. Korinidipiliz, yes?"

THE GUYS' GUY'S GUIDE TO LOVE

"It's Korindopolos," Layla corrected him. "Then whose table is this?"

"Of course that would be . . . let me double-check, but I'm certain it was for . . . oh there, excuse me . . ." He dashed away again, leaving the ladies alone.

Across the room, Roger was yapping into his cell phone as he followed the maitre d' through the maze of diners. He ended his call abruptly when they approached his usual table.

Roger's eyes widened when the maitre d' announced, "And here are the two lovely ladies who've been waiting for you, Mr. Fox."

Silence hung over the table as Roger's eyes darted back and forth at the two women. There was no way out. He licked his dry lips, smiled, and said, "What a nice surprise. I see my new assistant has made an error. Have you two been introduced?"

"Roger, please sit down," Veronica said, taking charge. "Layla, I'm sorry. They must have switched our reservations. Roger and I are old friends. Why don't you two stay and have your meeting?"

"No, please," Layla said, pushing away from the table. "Roger and I can discuss business some other time. I know how hard it is for couples with busy schedules to have lunch. Especially when they're both working on the same client."

"Layla . . . please. You can't think—I mean—don't leave," Roger said, his eyes shifting back and forth again. "This was obviously my new assistant's mistake. We're all friends here. Let's have a nice lunch . . . together."

Layla stood behind her chair. "Veronica," she said with a nod, and then, "Goodbye, Roger," before turning and striding across the crowded room.

Roger grimaced as Veronica gathered her things. She looked at him icily. "You really screwed that up."

"What does that mean?"

"It means you left business on the table."

"Whose business are you worried about, mine or yours?"

"It doesn't matter," she said. "That was sloppy." She grabbed her bag and stood up. "Goodbye, Roger. And for your own sake, get it together."

"Shit," he grumbled, tightening his fist on the table as she strutted away.

When the maitre d' returned, Roger explained what happened. "Mr. Fox, our deepest apologies. Can we interest you in lunch? It's on us. I'll have the chef prepare your favorite pasta al forno."

Roger took a deep breath and said sulkily, "Ask Sergio to make it al dente."

He quietly picked at his dish and left a cash tip. On his way back to *Plates*, Roger took stock of what had occurred. There had to be a way to turn things around. He told himself that business was like basketball—just a game. But Roger was shaken up, and it didn't feel like a game. His professional life was imploding. He had to do something. He grabbed his cell phone and called both women, but neither answered. So he kept trying. By the time he arrived at his office, he'd called Veronica three times. Finally, she took his call.

"You fucked her, didn't you?" Veronica asked.

"V, she's a client. That's all. I can't help it if she likes me. It's my job."

"Roger . . ."

"You're putting this all on me," he said. "How come you seemed to know her so well?"

"Um . . . my boss told me I had to reach out to new clients. I thought you and I could help each other."

"Right," Roger said dryly.

"Don't try to turn this around. I saw the way she looked at you," Veronica said. "You've had your paws on her *cans*, haven't you?"

"Come on, how can I even *look* at anyone else?" he said. "V, let me come over later. We'll talk about everything—our relationship. Then I'll take you to that little French bistro you like. I'm under a lot of pressure and . . . I really need to see you."

After a long pause, she responded. "Since when can't Roger Fox handle a little pressure?"

"I . . . I'm a bit confused." He waited for her response. Then he said, "Come on, we can pull this deal together."

After pausing again, she said, "All right. Come over at eight."

"Great," he said, exhaling.

He immediately phoned Layla. She'd be a tougher nut to crack, but it had to be done. Roger blew out a sigh of relief when she picked up.

"What do you want?" she asked in a chilly monotone.

"I'd like to apologize."

"Apologize for not telling me you were in a relationship?" she asked, raising her voice.

"I'm not!" he protested.

"Then why did Veronica say she was waiting for her boyfriend?"

"She said that?"

"Something like that," Layla said.

"We went out a few times and we stay in touch because we're in the same industry. But that's it. She's a friend, period," Roger said. There was silence, so he continued. "I'm serious. She's not right for me."

"Why not?"

Seeing an opening, Roger took a deep breath and began his riff. "I'm not into women who are all about their looks. Quiet confidence is more of a turn-on than someone who is aggressive and pushy. I try not to let on, but I'm kind of sensitive. I have to wear this damn mask to deal with the snakes in my industry. You understand." He pressed the receiver to his ear, listening closely for any change in her breathing. "And I'm really sorry about lunch, but it was a misunderstanding. Can I make it up to you?"

"Maybe I overreacted. What do you suggest?" she said warily.

"Dinner?"

"I'm very busy, Roger. I can do breakfast."

"Breakfast? Great. Breakfast it is. When?"

"Friday."

"Friday, Friday. This Friday? I have to be in Jersey by noon. How about . . ."

"Friday at eight. Can you make it?"

Roger stared at his noon court date on his calendar and tapped his foot. "I'll be there."

"Bye."

After work, he stopped off at the Hudson Hotel bar and ordered a Steve McQueen. It would be the first of four he'd consume over the next two hours. Forgoing dinner for a few handfuls of cocktail nuts,

Roger burned off his nervous energy flirting with a group of comely account executives from a midtown public relations agency. The women laughed as Roger spun a few choice stories that even made him chuckle. He bought their second round of black cherry mojitos, and then zeroed in on the pretty redhead when her girlfriends went to the bathroom. Roger moved closer and took out his business card, asked for hers, and said, "You've had a tough day. I'll bet you could use something sweet . . . a little sugar to sweeten your cup."

The young woman laughed when Roger puckered his lips. When he leaned in, she pulled back. She put her card to her mouth and pressed her lips on it, leaving a seductive crimson outline. Then she handed it to Roger. "If you call, you'll get the real thing and more," she said, before gliding off with her friends.

Outside the hotel, sweat soaked through Roger's shirt. He loosened his tie as he waited for a cab. Sitting inside the taxi, there was no relief from the heat and humidity. The tiny air conditioner only generated a whirring sound that pushed warm, stale air toward his face. By the time he arrived at Veronica's, his shirt was stuck to his back and his mouth tasted of cocktail nuts.

Veronica greeted him at her door in her office attire. "You're all wet. What happened?" As he came closer, she sniffed around his collar. "And you smell like alcohol and peanuts. Where have you been?"

"I had to take a client out for a drink."

"Roger . . . ?"

"Can I have a beer?"

"Why don't you take a shower? You left a T-shirt here. I'll order dinner," she said, pointing to her bathroom. A few minutes later, with his hair damp and slicked back, Roger waltzed into the kitchen wrapped in a towel. His eyes lit up when he saw a platter of sushi.

"Can I have that beer now?"

"Get dressed."

"Sure," he said, opening the refrigerator, popping the top off a bottle of Beck's, and taking a long swig. He sauntered back down the hall, stopping once to turn and wiggle his butt, pulling the towel back and forth across it. When he returned, he was wearing the T-shirt and his boxer shorts. He snatched a tuna roll off the plate and dunked it in the soy sauce before devouring it.

"Let's talk," Veronica said.

He wondered if she was going to bring up their relationship or their business first. His bet was on the business. He swallowed a piece of yellow tail, waiting for her move. Veronica put her chopsticks down and said, "I have an idea about Layla's business."

Roger looked up. Showtime.

"I know she's an important client for you, but I need this, too," she said. "There's a way we can both win."

A little stung by her predictability, Roger took the offensive. "First, tell me what you were doing at her office. Are you trying to steal my business just so you can close on that condo?"

"What are you talking about?" she protested.

"This," he said, dramatically opening his phone to the photos he snapped of her outside Peacock's offices.

"How'd you . . . ?" she said, raising her voice and speaking rapidly. "Okay, I met her at a credentials meeting. A half-hour meet and greet—that's all. My boss keeps pressuring me to network. I was going to tell you."

"V, you're the closer. Since when do you attend meet and greets?" Roger said coolly.

She stuck her chin out. "Well, it's obvious that she's interested in more than just your program. What's up with that?"

Roger shook his head. "It's like I told you. Layla's my client."

"So she's *your* client now? How convenient."

He quickly turned away, and then stared back across the table at her, waiting for her to continue her pitch. He didn't have to wait long.

"Okay," Veronica said, "if we want her money, we need to work together."

"Makes sense," Roger said. It really *was* all about the deal. Their relationship was a distant second, and the truth left him with a bitter taste. He wondered for a fleeting moment if Layla might be feeling the same thing about him now.

He pushed that thought aside. "So what do you have in mind?"

"More than anything, Layla wants her launch to be successful," Veronica said. "It's her baby, and she's got something to prove. When we met, she liked my program . . . a lot. She even asked me to show her what kind of sales it could deliver at higher spending levels."

"And?" he said, before finishing his beer.

"And that's how I help you. At the increased budget levels, I'll attach your program to mine . . . so we both win." Placing her hand on his, she continued, "I know this was going to be a big program for you, but have you closed the deal yet?"

Roger crossed his arms. "How much of your program goes to *Plates*?"

"Could be a million, provided she buys in at the higher levels."

"Why leave money on the table for me?" he asked.

"Because I care . . . and I'm sure you'd do the same for me," she said. "Consider it an act of good faith," she added with a smile.

"I want another beer," Roger said. He maintained his composure, but was seething as he yanked open her refrigerator. Her idea was a sham and she was positioning it as a favor. He saw the irony. It was the same rationale he'd been using to undermine Max. One good turn deserves another. Or, more appropriately, no good deed goes unpunished. Veronica was bamboozling him, so he needed to return the favor.

"Sounds like a plan, V," he said, flipping the top off the bottle.

"Really?" she said, surprised.

He tipped his beer back. "I've got an idea, too," he said, smacking his lips and replacing the bottle on her counter.

"What's that?" she said.

"I think we need to seal our deal in a special way."

"And how do you suggest we do that?" she asked, taking his hand. She squeezed it and nodded toward the bedroom.

After she clicked on her sound system, they undressed. Roger assumed the position, curled between Veronica's sun-kissed thighs. Most other men would envy him and where his head was buried, but Roger was having a little problem. Despite nibbling the soft fleshy mound between her legs and hearing her low moans, Roger was not responding.

"Oooh, I want you inside me. I need you. Fuck me now," she said. But he was still not aroused. Him! The great Roger Fox! *Because you've seen the real Veronica*, he told himself, *and she's a bitch. This is her fucking fault. Not yours!*

"C'mon, fuck me," she demanded, pulling him in close so they were facing each other. She played with his nipples, biting them gently. Roger kept trying, but it wasn't happening

"What's the matter?" she asked, sounding annoyed. "Too much to drink again?"

"I . . . I'm not sure. Today was stressful," he said, immediately wanting to take back the words. Roger never had problems performing, at anything. He treated sex the same as sinking a three-foot putt. It was muscle memory, being in the moment, not thinking—and certainly not about questioning himself. *Bitch!* When she reached for him again, he squirmed and felt panicky.

"You drank too much. And after all I do for you. I can't believe this," she said. Finally, she got up and wrapped herself in her robe.

"Give me a minute. I'll be fine," he said, trying to sound self-assured.

"Roger, look at me." He picked his head up as she continued. "This isn't working. I think you should go home and give little Roger some rest."

"But, I . . ." he began, realizing how pathetic he sounded and then throwing back the sheet. "Okay, maybe you're right. I'll go." He climbed out of bed, gathered up his suit, and plodded into the bathroom.

Veronica stood by, studying him with her arms folded. After he put his clothes back on, Roger headed to the kitchen and reached into the fridge. He took her last beer and shoved it in his pocket.

"Goodbye, Roger," she said.

"That's the second time you've told me that today," he said, and fumbled with the door before he closed it behind him.

CHAPTER 33

What did Roger say about writing his online dating profile? Max pondered, staring at his laptop, reading another batch of women's profiles. *Oh yeah, it was like marketing—supply and demand.* First find out what the target wants; then create a persona to meet their needs. Roger had said the trick was finding a way of making the profile truthful, even if you stretched the details a bit. Then, like a good method actor, you play the part with confidence. *Of course I love animals. I was at the Belmont Stakes last week.* Okay, this was Roger-speak, but Max had to meet a deadline for his next column.

He scanned profile after profile, compiling a list of the features most women were seeking in men. He was amazed by the consistency: successful, available, open, ready to commit, and honesty, honesty, honesty. Max wondered how Roger worked his way around that one.

Then Max laughed, remembering Roger's translations of the descriptions women gave themselves. Let's see—"athletic" meant no breasts, "average body" was code for *moo*, "seeking friendship first" translated to "ex-slut." Max filled out his own search criteria, keeping himself open to all races and religions. He put down twenty-five to forty as the age range for a potential partner. Since this was strictly research, he eliminated women with children, assuming they had enough to deal with. Then, he posted three photos of himself—one in a sports jacket, another in his surfer shorts at the beach, and a third taken at the Louvre. He chose Maximum1022 for his username, since his birthday was October 22. After a few more clicks, he'd reentered the online dating fray.

He padded to the kitchen, downed a tall glass of ginseng-infused iced tea, and skimmed an article in the paper about the Yankees–Red Sox series. By the time he returned to his laptop, there were already three green lights sitting in his mailbox. *This is too easy. No wonder Roger gets laid so much.* The first two were green card hunters from China and the Ivory Coast—one featuring a photo of Cameron Diaz as her *this-is-really-me* pic.

Max felt a little sad for these women as he deleted them. The third one was from a fifty-two-year-old woman from the north shore of Long Island with three kids. *Huh?* The phone vibrated as he logged off the website. It was Cassidy.

"What's up?" she asked.

"Just reading about the Yanks."

"Losers. Wow, did they take it on the chin the other night or what?"

"Were you at the game?"

"Um . . . I was actually," she said.

"*My Radiance* has a box at the stadium?" he asked, knowing full well they didn't.

"Uh, no. A friend got tickets somehow. Right behind first base. It was really cool."

First base? he thought. No way. Couldn't be Banks. *Could it?*

"What friend?" he asked.

"You wouldn't know him."

"Him?" Silence—a long silence, too.

"Max," she said finally. "I thought the advantage of our being *friends* friends instead of *special* friends was that we got to do whatever we wanted with whomever we want—without poking our big honkers into each other's business."

Max frowned. "Okay . . . boss."

"Okay then," she said lightly. "Are you working on something for me?"

He cleared his throat. "Yeah, I'm working on something . . . something different."

"I like the part about you're working on something. The part about it being something different, I'm not so sure about. What is it?"

"Well, what has your experience been with the online dating sites?"

"What's that got to do with it? Wait, is this about the 'Roger Method' to online dating?" Cassidy asked.

"He says those websites make him feel like a bear in springtime, swiping his big paw at the salmon swimming upstream."

"Oh, good—not the image, but that he's telling you how he also abuses online dating."

"It's not only about Roger. That's where the *different* part comes in," Max said.

"Oh?"

"Well, I thought we could add more realism to the story if I checked things out for myself." He braced himself.

"You signed up for one of those dating sites?" she asked.

"Sometimes us investigative reporters need to go undercover for our research. So I thought I'd sign up on a few popular sites. You know, to get you the real inside scoop," he said.

"Fine, but since you're not talking to Roger, I'll need to know what you're doing," she said. "Been on any coffee dates yet?"

"No," Max said. "I was thinking that a glass of Cabernet might be more conducive to ferreting out the truth."

"Max, please. There are so many women out there looking to meet a nice guy . . ."

"I thought since we were *friends* friends, I could write about whatever *I* wanted?" he said, walking into the kitchen. "This can be the guys' guy's perspective on online dating."

After a long pause, Cassidy said, "So . . . how's it going?"

"I just signed up, and to be honest with you, so far I'm a big dud, unless you count my admirers in the Xincai province."

"Where?"

"It's in China—the original Upper East Side. Manhattan's not the only place to meet women," he laughed, twisting the cap off a bottle of Gatorade.

"This calls for an executive decree," she said. "Give me your passwords."

"For my profiles?" he asked, laughing.

"I need to see this up close, in action."

"No way. I've got to protect my sources. Besides, you've already got your hands full with Mr. Behind-First-Base."

"Ha, ha. When can I come over?" she asked.

"Give me a week. I need to sort things out first. And no checking up on me. Promise?"

"Fine . . . I promise. But remember, *My Radiance* is about building women up, not exploiting them Roger-style. Okay, Rod?"

"I hear you," Max said. "I have to get back to work. I'm on a deadline."

After hanging up, Max signed back on to the dating sites, deciding he'd better get after his research before Cassidy became his online handler. With a week to play, he began browsing page after page in his quest for ladies interested in sharing a glass of wine with him. He bypassed sending little green lights, instead typing short personal notes to the handful of women whose profiles piqued his interest.

Max had been around the dating track, so he knew his way around the sites. But he had never realized how many intelligent, attractive, and educated women had posted profiles that read like resumes for love, complete with studio-quality photos. He was also surprised by how specific the criteria were for finding a man. No hair plugs, no kids, no couch potatoes, no bald spots, no fat, no obsession with the gym, no salaries less than $150,000, no one from New Jersey, no one who voted for McCain, no liars, no one not employed full-time, no baggage, *no, no, NO!*

This must be a different group than the women he explored with Roger a few weeks ago. Max wondered if their checklists were flexible guidelines or the entry point to a longer list of demands that would be revealed during a first date. After sending out a few notes, Max logged off and headed to the gym. When he returned, he had already received a few responses. He jotted down a handful of phone numbers and called three women. Two sounded smart and reasonable, so he invited them out for a drink, and they both accepted. *This is a piece of cake*, he thought. *Roger's got nothing on me.* In no time, his inbox began filling up with short messages and green lights, and by the time he signed off again, he'd set up a dozen introductory dates over the course of the following week.

He dove back into the online dating pool headfirst, jamming three quick dates into one night. That Thursday evening, he glided into a Midtown lounge to meet his first date. She was a dark-eyed, olive-skinned divorcee—from a starter marriage—now VP of Marketing at a cashmere importer. Max quickly learned the name of her boss, and over the course of the next half hour, why this guy was such a jerk. When Max motioned for a second glass of wine, she turned her drill bits on him. Why wasn't he married yet? Did he want kids? Where did he see himself in five years? How many times a week did he wash his sheets? She extracted everything through a tight smile and a stunning set of cosmetically enhanced teeth. Then, as if on cue, her phone rang. She mumbled something, hung up, and then stood. She told Max that it had been nice meeting him, and then shook his hand and strode out of the bar. Max frowned when the waitress finally returned with his glass of wine.

Things went downhill from there. He met his next date at a Starbucks on Park Avenue, a cavernous and still relatively undiscovered location for the coffee and laptop refuge. She was a pert Harvard MBA named Kim who didn't drink. She managed a hedge fund, played squash regularly, and twice mentioned that she knew all the words to "The Standard," in case Max had forgotten what school she'd attended.

When the question and answer period began, she asked Max about his job.

"I'm a VP at Hornsby Hammerhead," he said, thinking he'd score a quick check mark.

"Oh," she said, looking disappointed.

"You're familiar with HHI? Some people know us as Hammerhead" he added confidently.

"That's advertising, isn't it?" she said.

"Sure. It's a creative business."

"Is it true that advertising doesn't pay well?" she asked, taking a sip of coffee and checking her watch.

"Well, that depends. Once you become a VP, things come around and . . ."

"Max?"

"What?"

"I forgot. I have this presentation that I need to finish. I'm sorry. It was nice to meet you." She thrust out her hand and grabbed her tote.

Max checked his breath as he watched her walk away. His third date was at a bar off Madison Square Park. It began a half hour late—meeting ran over, she said, showing up all smiles. Max ordered her wine and a club soda for himself. He was determined to be on his game, having already notched two strikes on the evening.

"So tell me about yourself," Max said, this time going on offense.

His date, a perky blonde in a business suit and a short bob, did a quick double take, her face a cross between bewildered and bemused, as if saying, *"Doesn't he get it? I'm the one asking the questions."*

She said, "What would you like to know?"

After her clipped responses about where she lived and worked and what she thought of online dating, Max gave up. "You're very intelligent," he said, baring his neck to this alpha she-wolf.

She smiled, recognizing his surrender. Then, in an executive recruiter voice, smiled and asked, "Max, what three words best describe you?"

Max frowned before forcing a smile. This wasn't *like* an interview; *it was an interview.* "I guess I'm honest, open-minded, and . . . available. Emotionally, that is," he said, pleased with his response. "How about you?"

She frowned also. *You're forgetting again,* he read her expression. "Creative, fair, and trustworthy," she rattled off with a pasted-on smile.

"Are you in HR?" Max asked, finishing his club soda.

"Yes, for a bank. We put our candidates through a vigorous set of interviews. Sometimes up to thirty before *I make them an offer,*" she said, looking Max dead in the eye.

"Oh."

On the way home, he stopped off at a pub and ordered a pint of Guinness. Then he slid three bucks into the jukebox and chose five songs by The Rolling Stones. Twenty minutes later, he walked out of the bar to the sounds of Mick and Keith lamenting the chorus of "Beast of Burden." The classic song resonated in Max's mind as he shuffled down the stairs of the Eighth Avenue subway station.

Once home, he lay in bed and stared at the ceiling fan, his stomach a tangle of knots. *Maybe Roger's right about these women. He said they'd peel me like a grape. And why the hell are they so damn prickly? Maybe because of guys like him.* Then he rolled over and laughed. *Why bother trying to understand the unfathomable? Hey, as long as they're smart, successful, and beautiful. They must need us for something.*

CHAPTER 34

"**F**ind a half hour for her," Layla said to her assistant, cradling her cell phone as her stylist delicately snipped off her loose ends.

A few minutes later, the assistant called back, just as a light touch of styling gel was being applied. "Ms. Sparks is very persistent. She kept calling until I told her she could come in for a half hour on Friday."

"Thank you," Layla said.

Her stylist, Armand, turned her chair toward the window, where Manhattan's steely skyline jutted out like shark's teeth into a vast horizon. Layla's phone rang again. It was Max Hallyday, calling a second time to discuss their disastrous meeting. Max was a good ad man, but his agency had presented self-serving creative work that wasn't in her brand's best interests. For now, Layla would give Max the benefit of the doubt, if only because he showed potential as a bright, reliable steward of her business. After politely listening to his assurances about the new creative work under development, she dropped a bomb on Max's world.

"There's one more thing," she began. "I'm reducing HHI's portion of the budget. It should be temporary, but I'm exploring other options for the launch. I hope you understand."

"I see," he said quietly. "Our new campaigns tie seamlessly into digital promotions and social media. Something to keep in mind. I'll have them for you next week."

He'd accepted the news gracefully, and Layla wasn't surprised. That was how the business worked. He'd deal with it.

Handling Veronica was a different story. Layla sensed that there was something going on between Veronica and Roger, maybe in the past—but she wasn't sure. They were both beautiful, so in a way it was understandable. Even so, she'd let her guard down with Roger and he'd hurt her. Layla knew they were after her budget, but it didn't matter. She was a businesswoman, and she'd choose the strongest ideas for her brand regardless of where they came from. It would be nice if that Cassidy Goodson could jumpstart *Holy Spiritz* at her magazine events. Cassidy was a woman she could trust.

Then her father called. His deal for acquiring Globison was taking shape. If it happened, Layla would consider his offer: equity— real power. With a thriving market for online advertising, it was too lucrative to ignore. Decisions, decisions. She'd listen to her intuition, confident that the right path would reveal itself when it was time. But right now, Armand was doing her hair—beautifully.

When he arrived at work on Thursday, Roger was already tired and his head pounded like it had been whacked by a cow hammer. He frowned, remembering that he had another sales meeting, followed by the dreaded performance review. These sales meetings were being called far too frequently, but he knew that's what happens when business slows. The noose gets tighter and the pressure increases.

While his coworkers tap-danced through their forecasts, Roger nursed his coffee and subtly checked out the legs on the new hire sitting across from him in a sleeveless black linen dress. He watched as she first turned away, and then looked back and flashed a quick smile.

When it was Roger's turn to present, he included the pending deal with Layla in his forecast. Besides this program, none of his prospects had closed since the last meeting—and the year was now more than half over. Things weren't looking good. Being a former sports star, Roger viewed competitive activities, including sales, through the prism of basketball. When the heat was on, he'd enter his zone and score. *Plates* was a new publication, and its star players needed to step up and deliver before the game was over.

After Roger finished presenting, the conference room turned quiet. He heard a cough and someone fidgeting. *What's going on here? Don't these people know that selling takes time?* He looked over at Buttwipe. *Fucker's not saying anything.* Roger noticed him glancing at the new hire with the legs. That afternoon, Roger found out what was up during his performance review.

"Fox, you're not pulling your weight," his boss explained. As the conversation shifted into a more formal mode, Roger realized what was happening. He was being let go, and the woman he'd been ogling earlier was replacing him. Roger squirmed in his chair. He knew that if he didn't do something right now, it was over. He *had to* engage the smug asshole behind the mahogany desk.

"I can close Peacock Beverages. Then I'll make my quota," Roger said confidently.

"You've been promising that for over a month, Fox. Plus, you've already spent ninety percent of your annual expense account. You're costing us money."

"I need a little more time. I guarantee you I'll get it signed. If I can't, then go ahead and fire me. I can do this." Roger studied his boss's face. "Okay?"

Buttwipe's eyes bore a hole through Roger's forehead. He put his pen down and sighed. "I'm not sure why I'm doing this, but if you bring me a signed deal by the close of business tomorrow, you can stay. I'll even throw a few bucks into your expense account. I can't risk having someone representing our upscale epicurean publication seen wolfing down his lunch at a Sabrett stand," he said.

Roger decided that Buttwipe was the perfect moniker for the pile of yuppie goo that was cavalierly toying with his career. "I won't let you down," Roger said, half-smiling as he rose from his seat.

Once in the hallway, he mumbled, *"Douche bag,"* barely under his breath. He was so wound up that he failed to notice Gail sitting at her new workstation outside Buttwipe's office. When Roger saw her, his face turned beet red.

"Hi, Roger," she said cheerily. Then Gail bent down and slid her purse under the chair, making sure she aimed her behind in his direction. Clutching her pad and pen, she sashayed toward her new boss's office. She stopped at the door, turned back, and said, "Bye, Roger," before shutting the door in his face.

Roger shuffled numbly back to his office. He needed to call Layla and lock in their breakfast. He took a deep breath and dialed.

"Roger, I can't talk now. I'm on my way to a meeting," Layla began. "Are we on for breakfast tomorrow?"

"Yes. *YES!* I just called to confirm," he said. "And . . . there's something else."

"What's that?" she asked.

"Well, you've been so understanding, and I was wondering if there's anything else I could do . . . you know, to make this up to you? Anything."

Roger slowly counted to five, waiting for her response.

"Just be there tomorrow," she said finally. "We'll talk then." Then, after a pause, she added, "Thanks for calling."

Got her, he thought, hanging up. Even Roger was impressed by his performance. Time to make the doughnuts.

CHAPTER 35

Max adjusted his sunglasses and pedaled his road bike down Hudson River Park's asphalt path. He hoped the scorching sun and rigorous ride would clear his mind and help him sort through the events of the past few weeks.

When Layla had reduced his budget, Max knew that he'd lost any possible leverage with Gloss. And it was *all* about Kent Gloss. Gloss had played him like a vintage Fender Stratocaster. He could afford to, because as things stood, Gloss had no stake in Peacock. Gloss's predecessor had won the account for the agency, so there was no upside for him, no chance for him to shine. Kent needed something to break so he could step in and fix it. Knowing Max was a new hire lacking an internal support network, Gloss used the questionable ad campaign to turn the client against him, hoping to light a fire under Max about Bobalooie—because Kent *needed* Bobalooie. If Max could find a way to recapture Layla's advertising budget, things would be different.

With Bette out of the way, Gloss would assign a hand-picked creative director to the Peacock Beverages account. Max would take the hit for the budget cut, giving Gloss the rationale for replacing him when he was ready. Then, if he wanted to keep his job, Max would have no choice but to steal Bobalooie from Henry Goodson's agency.

When he called his former Bobalooie client, Max did not even have to ask for a meeting. His old client, Scooter—a third generation Wharton graduate—suggested they get together. Max considered taking him golfing, but decided that a long afternoon on the course was too much face time. So instead, Max met with Scooter at the agency, with Gloss conveniently stopping by for an introduction.

Henry's name never came up. To Scooter, it was all business—survival of the fittest. So there was Henry with the hyenas closing in . . . and Max part of the hungry pack. But what could he do? Like everybody else, Max had to survive.

And with all of the testosterone at Hornsby Hammerhead, he was experiencing another powerful feeling—lust. It had been almost two months now since he'd had sex, and Max was feeling strong stirrings below when he was around attractive women. And during this relentlessly hot summer in the city, there were beautiful women everywhere.

Like bats fluttering from a dark cave, Max's thoughts swarmed until they landed on the realization that he'd never loved Veronica. She was strikingly beautiful, but never satisfied. The times she'd let her hair down, she was a really cool person: open, vulnerable, and fun. Mostly, she was a moving target for his affections, impossible to keep pace with. But Max had hung in there, hoping she'd learn to relax and enjoy life. And his ego had constantly reminded him that losing her was not an option. He had needed to take charge and make it work, even if he realized in the end that it might have been driven by his competitive male nature. After all, she was the most beautiful woman he'd ever dated.

But it was time to face reality: Veronica was an endless climb—a mountain without a peak. And her heart had closed the door on him. But even if it was really over, Max was determined to come away with at least a psychic victory. He wanted to taste the good stuff one more time—and if he played his cards right, he'd get what he craved on *his* terms.

Max hardened as his thoughts moved to Roger and Veronica together. Like Roger, Veronica feared intimacy and hid her insecurity behind a sexually charged veil. She was driven, impenetrable—scared, maybe, down deep—and self-centered. Max took some comfort knowing that she and Roger would be lucky if they lasted even a few short months together. Their affair would end badly.

Thank God for Cassidy. She'd been Max's one shining light in a sea of darkness. *Should have taken her to the Yankees game,* he thought.

ROBERT MANNI

For now, he was on the clock to deliver the columns for her magazine. Max now identified with the women he wrote about who were mired in relationships with insensitive, narcissistic partners. He could no longer stomach trailing Roger. He'd have to generate his own material for the column.

As Max gazed across the water, he knew the time for waiting around and hoping for a solution had passed. Every day was judgment day, and nothing was going to change unless he heeded his father's advice to "make it happen." Henry was still laid up and Gloss was tightening the rope around Max's neck. Max pulled up his bike. He removed his sunglasses and faced south, watching the ripples of heat rising above the river as the Statue of Liberty cast its shadow over a passing ferry. Then he rode his bike in circles, racking his mind for a plan. *I've got to make the best of this Rod thing. And I'm going to nail Gloss's ass to the wall. I'm smarter than he is, and I'm better. And I'll stay true to everything I learned at Henry's side, but if I have to, I'll tap into the kill-or-be-killed credo I get at Hammerhead. And I'm going to win. And if V lands on my lap, I'm going to nail her, too. I'm going to win, whatever it takes, and on my terms.*

Although he wasn't sure how, when the time came, Max was determined to "make it happen." He slid on his shades and pumped the pedals back toward home.

212

CHAPTER 36

Hey gorgeous! Roger pecked onto the keyboard of his phone.
What do u want? Veronica snapped back.
Only u.
It's over.
Roger cursed as he texted. *What r u saying? We r a team!!*
2 late. I need more. Much more . . .
Seeing her words as punishment for his lack of performance, Roger typed furiously on the keyboard with one finger. *Been under pressure. Give me a break.*
I was going 2.
??
Her business card.
What?
Her lipstick kiss . . .
"Shit," he mumbled, recalling the redhead at the bar. *That was a joke. She's a client.*
Sooo weak. LOSER!
Roger stared at the phone. *Could the great one be losing his touch?* Stop thinking. Must keep moving—yeah, like a shark through dark waters. He ground his teeth, reminding himself that his relationship with Veronica was just a game. Still, he despised failing. Fuck it. *Fuck her! Just get the deal signed*, he thought, slamming the door on his way out.

Roger took a table in the back corner and sipped fresh-squeezed orange juice while waiting for Layla. At ten past eight o'clock, he became restless. After downing a second cup of coffee, he checked his watch again. Eight thirty and still no sign of her. His train was at nine-thirty-seven. He checked his phone for messages.

Roger—running late. My father needs help on a deal. Be there soon. L

Shit! He pulled out his proposal and reviewed it again. It looked good. All he needed was her to sign it and he'd be on his way. The waiter refilled his coffee cup as he continued his vigil, staring at the door and tapping his foot. Finally, Layla breezed into the restaurant in a white Chanel suit with black trim. He shot up to greet her, spilling coffee on the tablecloth.

They did the double air kiss and Roger sighed. *Got her!*

"Let's get you some breakfast," he offered cheerfully, waving at the waiter.

She raised her hand. "No, Roger. Really, I can't. I don't have time today. Just a decaf, please."

He hesitated, and then forced a smiled. "No problem. A decaf for the lady, and I'll have an English muffin and more coffee, please." As soon as the waiter sped off, Roger hunkered down to business. "I hope you don't mind our getting right to the proposal. It's here," he said, placing the papers on the table, "in case you have any questions."

"Roger . . ."

"I think you'll like the changes. I managed to cut back on production costs and . . ."

"Yes, about that, I . . ."

"And I've addressed your timing issues and scheduled a briefing with our creative team so we can begin the layouts for the recipe guide."

Layla waited for him to finish. "Roger, I'm sure you've taken care of everything. It's an excellent program."

The waiter slid the plate with the toasted English muffin in front of Roger. He slathered it with jam and nodded. "Great. Let's take care of this right now so we can get you on your way." He turned the document toward her, removing the top of his Porsche Design pen.

She looked into his eyes. "There's something else."

His eyes beamed. "Anything. Name it."

"No, it's—I can't sign off on your program. I'm leaving the company. Sorry."

Roger froze, pen hovering. "You're *what?*"

"I resigned. I had an offer I couldn't refuse, so to speak."

Roger's brain boiled as he scrambled for a lifeline that would save his job. "Who's taking your place? It's still a great program, like you said. Maybe there's someone else that will want—"

Layla sighed. "That's the other thing, Roger. The launch date has been pushed back for now and there's no replacement for me yet. I'm really sorry. I know how hard you've worked on this. But don't worry. I'm sure you can repackage the idea and sell it to someone else."

Roger's face turned red. "Oh sure, I'll turn it into a recipe guide for Ovaltine. That should do the trick. *I don't believe this,*" he said, pounding the table with an open hand.

Layla grabbed her bag and pushed back from the table. "I've got to be going. You take care, Roger."

Roger stared straight ahead while Layla strutted away.

At nine thirty, Roger raced through Penn Station to Track 14. Then, at nine thirty-seven, he jumped through the closing train doors and yanked his bag inside. With his chest heaving, he slumped into the seat and stared listlessly out the grimy window. An hour and ten minutes later, as the train approached Red Bank, he received a voice mail from his mother.

"Roger, darling. I'm so sorry, but Nick and I had a falling out, so he's not going to be available today to represent you. I'm sure the county will assign you a good attorney and everything will turn out fine. I'm on my way to Cape Cod for the weekend. There should be some food at home. Love, Mother."

Roger cringed as he entered the courthouse. Two hours later, he left without his license. It had been revoked for six months. He stood numbly outside, waiting for a cab to drive him to his mother's house in nearby Rumson. It had been a long week. He'd lost Veronica, his deal, his job, and now his driver's license. *TGIF.*

At eleven o'clock, Veronica paced the hallway outside Layla's office, peeking occasionally at her BlackBerry. She wasn't sure how Layla would treat her following their aborted lunch two days earlier. She'd brought her revised sales proposal and was hell-bent on securing Layla's signature. Yesterday she had fine-tuned her revisions and eliminated the section in the proposal for *Plates*. Roger was officially out of the picture, so he was out of the program, too. No loose ends. It was business.

When the door opened, Veronica centered herself. Fortunately, after an initial cool glance from Layla, the women got right down to it. A relieved Veronica expertly walked Layla through her changes, wondering why Layla had so many questions about Globison instead of the details of her program. When Veronica finally asked for the order, Layla thanked her and insisted that before moving forward, her legal team needed to review the contract. Still, it looked like a done deal for three million dollars. Afterward, Veronica paraded the entire six blocks to her office, floating on visions of herself ensconced in her new condo. She was so juiced up about the meeting that she even ducked into Barney's and set her sights on the fall handbag collections.

CHAPTER 37

Roger stared at the television in his mother's kitchen, gobbling a tuna salad sandwich. His head throbbed, so he crept upstairs after eating, swallowed three Advil, and lay down on his childhood bed. Within minutes, he fell into a deep, dreamless sleep. He awoke a few hours later and wiped away a string of drool that had seeped from the corner of his mouth. Still a little groggy, he opened the window and a warm and languid breeze blew into the room.

He turned on the television to a rerun of *Oprah*, with her legions filling the screen. He half-listened to the show about "players." Propped on his side, Roger watched the guest panel dissect the dysfunctional behavior of men who preyed on women. They didn't paint a pleasant picture. The women panelists were smart, attractive, and savvy to the wily moves of the *bad* boys. Roger laughed when one of the women described the infamous pick-up technique that relied on pointing out minor flaws in a woman as a way of keeping her off balance. At the break, he clicked over to *Leave It to Beaver*. This was more like it. He bunched up a pillow, rolled onto his stomach, and began feeling better until he saw the photo on the wall. It was Roger and his father at the golf club when he was a teenager. He turned away, shut off the TV, and padded downstairs.

Roger stood at the sink, munching down handfuls of potato chips and mulling over his weekend plans. He liked getting a break from the city, but *damn*! Stuck without a license, he couldn't drive his mother's Lexus. Roger toyed with the notion of taking her car out anyway, but with the way his luck was going . . . Maybe Max would drive down to visit his family for the weekend. Since his father's passing, Max kept a watchful eye on his mother and younger sister. He playfully boasted about his mom's cooking to Roger—about how she'd often fed his high school basketball team platters of homemade pasta after a weekend game. Roger had enjoyed many meals at her table and wished he could have shared the same warm relationship with his own family.

Roger had wondered if Max would join him for a round of golf or a bar crawl after he returned from the Bahamas. He'd sent e-mails, texted, and called a few times, but still had not received a response. Business had been crazy busy, though, so he hadn't given it much thought. But now, even weighed down by residual guilt, he'd welcome his friend's perspective on what had been a cataclysmic week. After wiping his hands, Roger dialed Max again and left another message. It was closing in on six o'clock. After slurping down a second Pepsi, he tucked his phone into his jeans and shuffled into the backyard. He walked across the three-acre spread toward the riverbank at the edge of the property and dialed Max again. This time, he picked up.

"Rog," Max answered dryly.

"Hey, bud! I'm at my Mom's. Coming down this weekend?"

"Nope. Working. What's up?"

"What's up? I was hoping to hang with my *amigo*. I see *cervezas frias y senoritas bonitas* on the horizon."

"Let me ask you something," Max said evenly.

"Shoot."

"You catch any blonde mermaids on that fishing trip?"

"What?"

"Think about it. I've gotta go."

Roger was jolted by the resounding click. *What the hell is his problem? Blonde mermaids? Veronica? No way he could know about her.* He shrugged and watched the river rush by. On his way back to the house, he stopped at the garage. Years ago, his father had attached a backboard to it. After rummaging around, he dug up a faded basketball inside the door. He wiped it with a rag and bounced it a few times. It needed air, but it would do. He took a short jump shot that clanged off the rim. His head still hurt. After tossing the ball up a few more times, he took a final shot that missed badly and then let the ball roll off the driveway.

There was no beer in the house, so he peered into the liquor cabinet with hopes of finding the ingredients for a Steve McQueen. He couldn't find any blackberry brandy, so he settled on a bottle of dark rum and a liter of cola. After throwing a handful of ice and a wedge of lime into a tall glass, he took a sip and smacked his lips.

Roger turned to the stack of vinyl records tucked beneath the stereo in the den—his father's odd collection of Sinatra, Montovani, and Herb Alpert, and the classic rock albums Roger played incessantly as a moody teen. After tossing aside Cat Stevens's *Tea for the Tillerman* with a scoff, he eliminated Pink Floyd (still light outside), Dean Martin (too Vegas), and Iron Maiden (too intense), before settling on Sam Cooke. While savoring his Cuba Libre, he grooved to "Chain Gang," "Cupid," and "Having a Party." He poured himself another tumbler of rum, this time adding only a splash of soda, and cranked up the volume. By the time the sun dipped below the horizon, the stack of albums was strewn across the floor. Roger had blasted Springsteen's *Born to Run* and then kicked off his sneakers and played air guitar to Jimi Hendrix's *His Greatest Hits*.

Energized from the sugar, Roger danced through the house. He turned up the volume even louder for "All Along the Watchtower," and then bounded upstairs to his room and began rummaging through the bedroom closet for his boxes of baseball cards. With the bottle of rum at his side, he plopped onto the floor and examined the piles of cards that he collected each year and wrapped in rubber bands.

Roger peeled the band off a collection from the seventies and the year Reggie Jackson hit three home runs in Game Six of the World Series. With a crooked smile, he recalled the times when his father talked about how they had watched this historic game together, with a three-year-old Roger bouncing on his knee. Ten years later, his father had walked out. Roger remembered pressing his face against his bedroom window with tears running down his cheeks as his father carried a suitcase to the car, where his blonde girlfriend waited in the passenger seat. After that, his father only returned for intermittent weekend visits. Sometimes he brought Roger to his golf club for lessons. Roger had never been as close to his mother, and after his dad left, she seemed even more occupied and distant. Then his father died of a heart aneurism during Roger's freshman year at college. Roger was in bed with a shapely premed student when he received the call. He listened quietly as his mother hysterically recounted the shocking news.

"Everything okay?" the coed asked after Roger hung up, noticing his now wooden expression.

"Sure," Roger said, pausing momentarily before returning to the bed. "Where were we?" he added, sliding next to her warm, half-covered body. The topic of his father rarely came up after the funeral. During the next school break, Roger came home to find his mother had removed any surviving family photos with his dad. Roger never mentioned the change.

Staring at the bent edges of his Catfish Hunter baseball card, Roger relived the memories. His eyes teared and his breathing turned to short sobs. *Dammit*, his father was out the door when Roger needed him—needed to throw the ball with him, needed to sort baseball cards with him, needed to measure his height against his, his shoe size, to know how grown up he was. His damn father. Gone. Off fucking his secretary, or whoever. Roger chuckled self-mockingly. *Like father, like son, right?* Banging some blonde until everything was perfect for a few seconds, then on to a brunette, or whatever color hair the girl of the moment had. *Jesus. No wonder.* He sat up, thumbed through the stack, and wiped a tear off the New York Yankees 1978 World Champions team card before taking two long swigs of rum from the bottle and scaling the card at the wall.

He sat with his legs crossed, whizzing baseball cards across the room. His face was twisted into a demonic smile as he peeled away the rubber bands and flung the cards. Soon tiring of this, he forced himself up in his stocking-clad feet and staggered toward the bathroom. Halfway there, he lurched, slipped, and fell face-first into the bedpost, and then onto the floor. He rolled onto his back and passed out.

He awoke at two in the morning. His head felt like it had been hit by a mallet. He stumbled to the bathroom and discovered a massive new bruise under his left eye, dwarfing the ruddy mark under his right one. He swallowed the remainder of his soda and stumbled back to bed. The next morning, he was greeted by the sounds of a woodpecker drilling a nearby oak tree. With a reverberating headache, he was in no mood for the bird's percussive assault. After shutting the windows, he drew the drapes closed, turned up the air conditioner, and then curled his long body back under the sheets.

Half a second later, it was mid-afternoon. Following a long shower, he ate two bowls of cereal and stepped outside onto the back porch, listening to the river burbling downstream. He watched an inning of the Yankees game and then threw up in the bathroom before depositing himself back into bed.

Sunday morning was overcast. Roger emerged from the house at noon clad in a T-shirt, surfer shorts, and dark sunglasses. His eye was swollen, but his headache had subsided. He pulled his old bicycle out of the garage, threw a backpack over his shoulder, and pedaled off. By the time he reached a half-empty beach, he was sweating profusely. Moving like a zombie, he waded into the ocean and immersed himself under the water. He spent the next half hour splashing around and resuscitating his spirits in the chilly Atlantic.

On his way home, Roger stopped at a supermarket and picked out a thick steak, a head of lettuce, Jersey tomatoes, and a six-pack. He felt better after eating, but later got sick from the beer and threw up again. He passed out on the bathroom floor. When he came to, he crawled to his bed and lay staring at the ceiling. Oddly, an image of Serena ordering her cranberry and club soda flashed through his mind. What would she think of him, curled up next to the toilet? What would anybody think? *Okay*, he told himself. *This is deeply fucked up. It is SERIOUSLY time for a change. Somehow.*

The next morning, blades of sunshine pierced the blinds and awakened him. He straightened up downstairs, pushing the vinyl albums into a pile. Then he dropped the needle onto his father's Jobim LP, *Wave*. He was determined that things were going to be different. It might get tough, but by the time he stepped on the Manhattan-bound train, Serena's deliciously big brown eyes were the only thing on his mind.

CHAPTER 38

"**I** need to get a look at these women you've met online," Cassidy said into her phone.

Max cradled his cell while skimming the sports section. "No way. I have more grill marks than a rump roast at a 4th of July barbeque."

"Already? What happened?" Cassidy asked.

"Roger was wrong."

"About being a big bear and scooping up salmon with his paw?"

"*Exactly.* These women are unbelievable. What I thought would be a few friendly glasses of Cava turned into the Spanish Inquisition."

"Oh, come on. Don't you get it?" she said. "Online dating gives women a sense of control. Like your alter ego wrote in that column. Men lie, so women have to find out if a guy's telling the truth. All these questions are just their way of making sure they're getting what's been advertised."

Max grimaced. "Well, that might be true, but I feel . . . *violated.*"

"Are these girls too much for the great Rod?" she asked, laughing. "Well, you can thank your running mate Roger for making them this way."

Max rubbed his jaw. "Maybe I met too many women, too quickly. I'm not blaming them, but it just seemed like they want instant perfection, and that's not how things work. And it ain't how men work."

"I know. A lot of women expect Prince Charming to ride down Fifth Avenue in a Ferrari and rescue them."

"But instead they get Sir Baldy from Jackson Heights rumbling into town on the 7 train."

"See, you're getting it," she said. "Women have it tough."

"Yeah, yeah."

"Well, if I can't see your profile, when do I get my column?"

"Soon. It's almost done."

Max hung up and drained a bottle of kombucha before returning to his laptop. He deleted the first draft of his column and began again.

NOBODY'S PERFECT

Your guy's guy has gone digital . . . for you, of course. I recently rejoined the online dating mosh pit and escaped with a few traces of dignity intact and a bruised ego. I never realized how strong and smart you ladies are. But, as any guy can attest—sometimes, ignorance is bliss.

You see, men join online dating services so they can pick up pretty girls while sitting at home in their tighty-whities. It's cheap and easy—a sex-line without the three-buck-a-minute tab to Candy the phone voice, who in reality looks less like Carmen Electra and more like your high school algebra teacher. But men quickly find out that online dating is not for the fainthearted, and that the cards are stacked high in the women's favor. After all, they can easily discover the truth about the men hitting on them online.

Guys can run, but they can't hide. Eventually, they have to come out of hiding and expose themselves. That could mean a proud display of male hunkiness, but most likely it will reveal those extra five years they somehow forgot and that incremental twenty-five pounds they gained over the winter from downing brews and wolfing nachos in front of a big plasma screen. I think you get the picture.

If you add fifteen percent in weight, age, debt, emotional baggage, and nostril hair, you'll come closer to the truth. So ease up on the guys. They have no idea that women are more evolved.

You're better at all of this than men are. And, come on, dating should be fun. Leave the checklist at home next time you go out to meet a prospective online suitor. No one's perfect, especially if they're looking for love on the Internet. We all make mistakes and we all have a past. Even you, Miss Lady. What matters is letting go and learning from the experiences—not worrying so much about the future. Now seems like as good a time as any for enjoying life and finding true love.

The idea that the perfect mate will show up at Starbucks with a strong jaw, a couple of million in the bank, and a special place in his heart for modern dance, Tuscany, and floral arrangements is a long shot. And when you look across the booth, wondering what your kids are going to look like, he's imagining how you'd look with a boob job sliding around the stripper's pole he's always dreamed about having in the bedroom.

This doesn't mean you should let men get away with their lies. All it means is that men and women share one common, undeniable trait—we're all human and we all need to be loved.

Until next time,

Rod

CHAPTER 39

After Roger signed the separation letter e-mailed from his now former employer, officially ending his employment at *Plates*, he spent a sweltering Monday afternoon in his apartment tying up loose ends and making arrangements to pick up his personal items from the office. He called a handful of executive recruiters, but none of his calls went well. His now ex-boss was away on business, forcing Roger into a humbling dialogue with an unusually chirpy Gail, who took her time e-mailing his remaining paperwork. When he called her with a question, she transferred him to Human Resources.

Despite his solid track record in sales, Roger soon realized that finding a comparable position would be challenging in a faltering economy. "What happened?" "Why were you let go?" and "Is there anything we should know about?" were the main interests of the recruiters' inquiries. None asked about his accomplishments or the revenue he'd consistently generated. The discussions always circled back to what had gone wrong. Dismayed, he flopped onto the couch and clicked on the television. He dozed off with another negative stock market report scrolling endlessly in red across the television screen.

At four o'clock, Roger pulled on a pair of faded jeans and a fitted western-style shirt. The mouse under his eye had now turned into a crimson-blue-black stain. He hid the bruise behind dark sunglasses before walking into the glaring sun.

Watching a troupe of break-dancing street kids perform during his subway ride to Brooklyn, he wondered what he'd do after his one-month severance ran out. Once in Park Slope, he walked along Seventh Avenue toward Serena's studio and boutique. Roger was impressed by the quaintness of the tree-lined streets and refurbished brownstones. The independent retail shops and cozy ethnic cafés checkering the avenue gave The Slope an authentic neighborhood vibe.

The sign outside Casa de Tranquilla was freshly painted white with aquamarine script set inside a band of small flowers. The boutique was on the ground floor. Roger ducked his head through the front door, where his senses were immediately greeted by wafts of soothing incense. The sounds of new-age-tinged South American music filtered softly through the space. A slender young woman wearing a lavender bandana with a Casa de Tranquilla logo studied his face. Roger nodded to her and smiled. The shelves were filled with oils; candles; boho-styled yoga wear; and clothing made from hemp, linen, and organic cotton. All the merchandise was branded with Serena's artful logo. The young woman asked Roger if he needed help and then pointed him toward the narrow staircase leading to the second-floor studio.

Tall windows framed the open room on two sides. Roger looked through the long pane of glass and saw Serena leading her afternoon yoga class—a dozen men and women in their late twenties to early fifties crouched on all fours like cats, all drenched with sweat. And on an already sultry summer day, the thermometer inside the room read one hundred degrees.

Another employee, wearing yoga pants and a tank top, was chatting with a little boy. She looked over at Roger and then told the boy to stay put while she went downstairs. Burrowing into one of the chairs against the wall, Roger watched the small boy straining to see inside the room. Roger chuckled to himself as he watched the boy struggle. Finally, he walked over, opened a folding chair, and placed it next to him.

"Wanna see what's going on in there?" he asked. The child ignored him. Roger tried again. "You like Doctor J?" The kid turned around and looked up at Roger. "You're wearing his number."

The boy glanced down at his retro New Jersey Nets basketball jersey. "No," he said before turning away.

"He's my all-time favorite player," Roger said.

The child pretended Roger wasn't there, no doubt having been trained not to talk to strangers.

"Yep. Julius Erving was the man," Roger continued, unfazed. For a moment, he remembered talking sports with his dad when he was a kid. "The Nets are moving to Brooklyn. Soon you can see them play right here. Would you like that?"

The boy nodded tentatively.

"Little buddy, what are you doing up here by yourself?" The boy didn't answer. Looking inside the room, Roger scanned the faces and asked, "Your mom in there?" He reminded himself it was a good idea to be nice to the kiddies. He'd seen some good-looking women pushing strollers around the neighborhood.

The boy pointed at the glass and nodded again. Roger stood up and smiled. "If you want to see her, stand on the chair. I'll hold it for you." The boy hesitated, so Roger playfully tapped the seat and said, "Let me know when you're ready."

Roger peered inside and watched Serena poised in front of her class. Her face was bathed in sunlight, creating a bright aura around her. Roger felt tugging at the bottom of his shirt. It was the little boy, who now wanted to see inside the room. Roger helped him up and pointed at a fortyish-looking woman with sandy-blonde hair and flinty eyes.

"I'll bet that's your mom in the gray top and tights. She looks like you."

The boy nodded and smiled up at Roger.

"Okay," Roger said, glancing at his watch. "The class is almost over. Hey . . . by the way, I'm Roger. What's your name?"

"Brady."

"Nice to meet you, Brady. You know there's a famous quarterback named Brady?"

The boy shook his head and Roger said, "Yep, and Brady is his last name. Tom Brady. One of the best."

The class ended and the participants began filing out. When Brady's mother walked through the door, she looked around for her son and saw Roger sitting with him. Seeing Roger's bruised face, she quickly grabbed her son's hand and pulled him to her side.

Roger looked over and smiled. "That's a good kid you've got there. Take care, Brady."

She nodded quickly before taking out her cell phone and tugging the boy's arm. When they reached the stairs, Brady turned back and waved to Roger.

———

Serena was patting her face with a towel, silently observing the exchange. "I see you met Brady. You make friends everywhere, don't you?"

He shrugged easily. "I'm in sales."

"So what did you think of my class?" she asked, now close enough to get a look at the purplish bruise and Roger's tired eyes. She was concerned. This was a far cry from the man she'd met at the bar near Union Square.

"I started sweating just from watching."

"The heat helps eliminate toxins," she said, examining his face. "What happened here? That's another very nasty bruise. Roger, you don't look well," she said, guardedly.

"This? A basketball buddy of mine threw an elbow. Looks worse than it feels."

Serena wasn't buying it. She wrapped her towel around her shoulders and began thinking of excuses to cancel their date. Alejandro came up from behind and tapped her on her shoulder, his shirt drenched from the class.

"Hey," she greeted him and turned to Roger. "This is my cousin, Alejandro."

"Hello," Alejandro said, extending a clammy hand.

"Roger Fox," Roger answered, wiping his jeans after they shook hands. "I saw you in the class. *Mucho calor*. Very warm in there."

"*Si perro soy caliente,*" Alejandro responded cheerfully. Roger gave him a yeah-sure-whatever look.

Serena saw the opportunity to collect her thoughts. "I'm going to hop in the shower. Alejandro, why don't you tell Roger about our classes?"

THE GUYS' GUY'S GUIDE TO LOVE

"Sure. Roger, do you like tea? I was about to make some yerba mate."

"As long as it's iced tea," Roger said.

Alejandro chuckled. "I can make it that way for you."

While showering, Serena decided she'd come up with an excuse to opt out of the date. She put aside her tight jeans, ribbed tank, and heeled sandals and changed into a loose-fitting Casa de Tranquilla branded cotton terry top with matching drawstring pants and a pair of Keds. She pulled her hair into a ponytail and checked her face in the mirror. She wanted to leave him with a pretty image, so she applied a touch of makeup. When she returned to the empty studio, Alejandro and Roger were standing by the open window sipping yerba mate.

"So what do you think?" Alejandro asked.

Roger held his nose and laughed before taking a second sip. "Kind of earthy, but it's not bad."

Serena caught Roger self-consciously turning his face to hide his welt when she approached. "I see Alejandro's introduced you to South America's favorite beverage."

Alejandro smiled. "It was nice meeting you, Roger," he said. "Gotta go walk the dog. Then I'm off to the shore."

"The Jersey Shore?" Roger asked.

"We're renting a house in Manasquan," Alejandro said.

"I grew up near there. You never mentioned that," he said, turning to Serena.

"Well, I guess not," Serena said. "Anyway, Alejandro, I'll see you before you leave."

After Alejandro left them, Serena motioned to the stairway. Outside, the skies were clear with a glowing sun still perched high in the sky. Serena led Roger toward a diner on the corner, unsure how to bow out of their date. If she couldn't conjure up something by the time they reached the diner, she thought she would suggest a cup of coffee and then tell Roger she wasn't feeling well.

Near the curb outside the diner, Brady's mother was chatting on her cell phone, waiting for the lights to change as her little boy yanked on her tracksuit. After a couple more hard tugs, the boy gave up and began spinning himself around like a top along the sidewalk. He teetered on the curb for a moment, apparently dizzy, and then toppled a few feet into the busy street and onto his butt.

"Roger, I'm not feeling all that . . ." Serena was saying when Roger bolted ahead. He moved quickly to beat the oncoming traffic and the light. He scooped the boy off the asphalt and safely onto the pavement.

"Whoa! Gotcha," Roger said.

"Brady!" the woman cried, nudging Roger aside. Roger backed away and made a crazy face at Brady, who laughed as his mother hauled him away.

For a moment Serena paused, taking in what just happened, and then looked up at Roger. "Nice catch," she said.

"Brady's a bud," he replied. "He would've done the same."

Serena smiled warmly at him. "Okay, hero. You've earned your dinner."

As they walked down the crowded avenue, Serena loosened the rubber band holding her ponytail and slipped her arm around Roger's.

CHAPTER 40

"**Y**ou're throwing a party to introduce Rod?" Max laughed into the phone. "Why?"

"We thought it would be nice to have a little celebration and give a select group of readers a chance to meet the man behind the column. Of course, we'll invite a few members of the press, too," said Cassidy innocently.

"Rod's not interested in meeting anyone right now," Max said, closing his Bobalooie advertising folder and pushing it to the side of his desk. He frowned when an e-mail from Gloss appeared in his inbox—his third that morning.

"Why not?" Cassidy asked pointedly. Eager to see a return on its investment, *My Radiance's* holding company had suggested the party. With her father in and out of the hospital for additional tests, plus the pressures of putting out another issue of the magazine, Cassidy's patience was running thin. "Your column's a hit and we need to leverage it. It's good business. You know that. Can you stop by my office tomorrow? I'll show you the edits on your column over lunch. Sashimi's good for the brain."

"Do they call them octopuses or octopussies?"

"I'll tell you when you get here. Say one o'clock?"

"Sure, if I can update my revenue forecasts by then."

"I thought you submitted them last week."

"Ancient history," Max muttered, wondering how long he could juggle the issues weighing down his professional and personal life.

"How about a column on the sex rituals of the male octopi?" he asked. "Talk about a player. They can reach places other guys can only dream about."

"That's not very funny, Cousteau. We'll talk about it at lunch."

Cassidy's office was on the sixth floor. Max stopped at the reception desk and was greeted by a young woman with tinted glasses and a bushel of hair held tenuously in check by a pencil. After checking Max out, she smiled discreetly and directed him to Cassidy's office. He was early for their lunch date, so he sauntered down the hall, taking in the inner workings of the start-up magazine. The cubes and offices were nondescript, but dressed up creatively by the employees with colorful photos of current pop culture icons.

Max drifted to the water cooler and heard women's laughter emanating from a conference room across the hall. His ears perked up when he heard, *"More Rod, please!"* There were cackles and hoots. *"After devouring his columns, I need to know whose rod this is. And if he's cute, I'll devour him, too."*

Cassidy's team was reading Rod's fan mail. The room erupted when a staff member held up a photo. "Check out the cowgirl! Chaps and lizard-skin boots. Yee-hah." When the laughter subsided, she began reading the letter in a low, sexy voice.

Dear Rod,

You're a straight shooter and I have something special for you to aim for. I'm yours and you will be mine.

Anytime, anywhere, and always,

Chantelle

"Isn't she clever?" The room again burst into laughter.

One of the staffers suggested a reader contest with an evening on the town with Rod as first prize. Someone suggested Cassidy might not like that. When Max heard Cassidy's name he leaned into the room, his eyes widening at the stacks of letters, envelopes, postcards, and lingerie spilling out from a pile of canvas postal bags. A dozen heads turned his way. At the end of the room, a woman dangling a sheer purple thong on the tip of her pencil said, "Sir, there's a meeting going on here."

Max felt his face turning red.

"Can we help you?" another woman asked.

"Sorry, wrong meeting," Max said. "I'm looking for Cassidy Goodson."

"Oh, Cassidy," she said. "Her office is straight down the hall."

"Thanks," Max smiled apologetically. "Sorry for the intrusion."

"No problem," a cute blonde replied, grinning mischievously. Max waved goodbye and turned back around.

"Nice butt," one of them said, causing a few giggles and "oh yeahs." He pretended not to hear as he stood a little taller and walked away.

Max reached Cassidy's open door and gave a little knock. She swung her chair around and motioned him in with one hand while holding the phone in the other. She made an "I'm bored" face, and then quickly finished the call and removed her glasses.

"Hey," she said, greeting him with a hug. Her office was immaculate, especially for a magazine editor. A vase of freshly cut flowers on her desk brought bright colors into the room.

"I want the names of all the women who've mailed in their tiny thongs to Rod," he said with a straight face.

"What in the lord's name are you talking about?" she asked, feigning ignorance.

"I peeked in the conference room. The lingerie . . . and all those letters . . ."

"That stuff always happens when a magazine gets hot," she said, grabbing her hobo bag.

"Women send in their underwear? Can I apply for a job here?" he asked, following her down the hall.

Like every other weekday, lunch at Nobu 57 was jam-packed with an energetic business crowd. Cassidy and Max sat at a small table along the wall, picking at a colorful platter of sashimi.

"It is octopi," Cassidy said, watching Max hold a sliver of purple and white between his chopsticks before sliding it into his mouth.

"And I don't want you thinking that I was keeping Rod's mail from you."

"But you were," he said with a laugh, refilling her cup with green tea.

"It's policy for my staff to screen all correspondence. All of our columnists get reader mail and . . ."

"Invitations from dominatrixes?"

"Men on death row receive marriage proposals," she said nonchalantly.

Max pursed his lips. "So when were you going to tell me how big Rod is getting?"

"All right, I should have said something. But it happened so quickly, and I didn't want this going to your head—like it has," Cassidy said, adjusting her glasses. With the exception of the clicking of chopsticks on the platter, the table became quiet.

Cassidy broke the silence. "Management insists that I throw an event for the magazine, and your column is an important part of our success."

"I thought we agreed that Rod would remain anonymous," he said, looking away. "Maybe I can just write back to a few lucky young coeds," he mused.

"*Max*," she said with a slightly raised voice. "I promise I'll do my best to keep the event manageable. I'll even give you a few letters when we get back."

Max stirred wasabi into his soy sauce with his chopsticks. "So who gets invited to this shindig?"

"A few hundred invitations are being sent to media buyers and some subscribers. And we have to invite the press, for PR. You know how it works."

"A few hundred? You must be kidding! I'll be a laughing stock."

"You're not a laughing stock to these women. I thought you wanted to protect them from guys like Roger. Wasn't that what you said?"

"Well, I . . ."

"Yes, you said that. And you'll be helping me." Cassidy's eyes were a clear, insistent blue.

"Again?" he asked, watching her and then softening. Max exhaled slowly and placed his chopsticks on his plate. "So when is this party?"

"A week from Thursday." She raised her hand for the check. "Don't worry. The party isn't all about Rod. It's to celebrate *My Radiance*."

"Since you put it that way, how could I refuse?" he asked, smiling.

"Um, there's one more thing," she said.

"Uh-oh."

"It's a good thing, actually. We agreed to set up a cocktail kiosk for Peacock Beverages. The *Holy Spiritz*?"

"What? Why?"

She put her hand over his. "Relax. My team calls on everyone. I made sure they didn't put the full-court press on, but Layla said— "

"So you're on a first-name basis now. Is she on your speed dial, too?"

Cassidy laughed skittishly. "Come on. This is good for you. She'll see how everyone loves her drinks and . . ."

"Everyone loves free drinks."

"Exactly. That way she'll want to spend more on her advertising."

Max bit back his lip, then said, "Whatever. This situation is becoming so inbred that we'll end up in line for the British throne."

"Trust me," she said with a little squeeze of his hand.

After stopping at Cassidy's office to pick up his edited columns, Max passed the same conference room where the meeting had taken place earlier. It was empty now except for the canvas bags, still packed with mail. Max looked over his shoulder to see if anyone was looking and then ducked inside. He dug his hand into one of the bags, grabbed a handful of envelopes, and stuffed them into his backpack before slipping out the door.

CHAPTER 41

In the weeks following Roger's first visit to Serena's yoga studio, they made a habit of taking long walks together. Serena often recalled that first walk, after Roger had scooped Brady off the curb.

When Roger opened up, Serena had discovered an inner vulnerability. For a guy, he articulated his feelings well when he chose to do so. There was no denying his striking good looks, especially when he flashed that high-wattage smile and when the sunlight flickered into his green eyes. And he'd shown a kinder, gentler side with Brady. Although Serena was going to maintain her guard, Roger was earning his chance.

One afternoon they stopped at a small family-run Mexican restaurant and were seated at a table along the window that was adorned by a small vase of roses. Serena laughed at Roger trying out his Spanish with the staff.

He flipped the menu over and then back again, moving around in his seat, "Virgin margaritas?" he asked. "There must be a liquor store around here."

"Roger, I told you that I don't drink," she said, causing Roger's face to turn blank. She smiled. "And it would be nice if you didn't either, at least while we get to know each other."

Throughout the meal, Serena asked him subtle questions. It was no easy task. At first, Roger skillfully deflected her inquiries with his sharp wit and a boyish smile. Serena remained gentle but persistent. By the time the table was cleared, Roger was discussing his father's leaving and his distant relationship with his mother. He even shared an edited version of his traumatic past week. Although he left out the part about getting drunk at his mother's house, he confided to her how a slip had caused the second black eye after she half-jokingly asked if he was into S&M.

Guys had become so needy these days that Serena wondered as Roger talked whether he would be low maintenance and give her the independence she needed. Would he continue sharing his feelings with her, or would he suddenly close up and turn into a control freak like most of the men she'd dated? And although she sensed that Roger had been with many women, it sounded like he was looking for a change. *Only time will tell*, she told herself.

Roger ordered a dessert they could share. She drove her spoon into the plate of chocolate flan.

"Hey, save some of that for me," he joked.

She smiled sheepishly. "Oops, busted."

They walked all the way back to Park Slope and she gave him a short but scorching kiss goodnight in front of her building. She knew he wanted more—they all wanted more—but he'd have to wait. She gently pushed him away before mounting her steps. He had lots more to do before she'd let him into her heart.

But Roger had shown her something. Since he still wasn't working, on many afternoons he'd take the long subway ride to Brooklyn to visit her. While she taught class, Roger would hang out with Alejandro, and to her surprise, the two men got along well. They sipped yerba mate through long straws while Alejandro shared his stories about surfing and spirituality. Although she never suggested it, one day Roger signed up for Serena's beginner's yoga class. At first he appeared tense and awkward, but he quickly mastered the downward-facing dog and warrior poses. Seeing how agile and limber he was for a big man, she guided him into the fish pose and a variety of stretches that helped open him up from the inside out. Serena was impressed by his effort, but was determined to keep things light until she felt more *comfortable*.

One sun-drenched afternoon, Serena was walking by a small room at the studio when she heard gentle new-age music. She ducked her head inside and saw Roger lying on a table. Alejandro was standing over him holding both hands across Roger's abdomen in a classic Reiki position. Roger's eyes were gently closed and he was breathing in a slow, steady rhythm. Serena smiled at Alejandro before she quietly closed the door.

Soon, Alejandro's Reiki sessions with Roger became a routine. He never brought it up and Serena never asked him about it. Changing Roger was never her goal. Facing down his demons had been his decision. She'd be there if he needed her, but he was a grown man and she had a business to run. Over the next month or so, though, Serena witnessed a noticeable shift in his demeanor as Roger became more relaxed. His eyes were clear and maintained a steady glow. His usual running commentary of cynical judgments had diminished, and his inner anger was cooling under August's blistering heat.

One afternoon, Serena stopped by after Alejandro finished giving Roger another hour-long Reiki session. Roger chugged a bottle of water. "Your cousin," he said to her, shaking his head. "I don't know what he's been doing, but I feel lighter now, and my mind is really sharp."

Alejandro looked at Roger as though he had heard these words many times before. "Roger, you're doing all the work. Reiki helps move the chi, or life force energy, through your body more easily. That's all. Over time, emotional and physical blockages usually clear away—like stones dislodged by a flowing river."

"Well, I definitely have more energy, and I don't feel as pissed off, despite everything that's been going on lately."

"That's great. What else are you feeling?" Alejandro asked.

"Like it's time to get back to work," he said, turning to Serena. "Like there's a lot more I have to give."

With the exception of a few cursory interviews, Roger hadn't had much luck rebooting his career. Despite all the phone calls, networking lunches, and correspondence he'd sent out, there were no solid opportunities on the horizon, and his bank account was dwindling. His contacts and connections blamed the lack of jobs on the economic meltdown and employers' summer vacations. Roger hadn't heard from Max in over a month and was now miffed at his friend for shunning him.

One morning, after returning from a long run in the park, Roger received a call from a headhunter.

"I'm working on an agency position—vice president level—and it matches your package at *Plates*," the recruiter said. "Want me to present you?"

"I'm not sure about going back to an ad agency—but all right," Roger said, not bothering to ask which agency had the opening.

"It's a good job, Roger."

"Why are they looking for an outside candidate?"

"They're shifting people around internally. Don't concern yourself with that. Just let me get you in there."

Roger thanked him and hung up. Two days later, the recruiter called back.

"Okay, they want you there at nine o'clock. You'll meet with Human Resources first. After you get your ticket punched, they'll send you to the hiring executive—an EVP."

"Thanks—which agency?"

"Hornsby Hammerhead."

Roger filled out a lengthy application and spent fifteen minutes chatting with a saccharine mid-forties blonde from HR who kept an eight-by-ten photo of her German Shepherd's face displayed on her desk. She led Roger to the elevator and directed him to Kent Gloss's office. Roger seemed to recall reading his name in the trades, but couldn't remember why.

The assistant wasn't at his desk, so Roger knocked on the open door before tentatively leaning his head into Gloss's office. When Gloss waved him in, he wondered why this guy was sitting in the dark with his suit buttoned all the way up. Gloss noticed Roger eyeing his set of soldiers as he entered his inner sanctum.

"A Hungarian artist hand-carved those for me. They're one of a kind," Gloss said, pausing as he waited for a response.

Roger picked up a soldier by the head and examined it. "Really? That guy must have some tiny tools to carve these."

When the two men shook hands, Gloss's hand disappeared into Roger's meaty paw. After Roger sat down, they quickly got down to business.

Gloss took a cursory glance at Roger's resume. "Hmm, lots of sales experience, and I see you had a stint at Goodson. Used to be a good shop once."

Roger paused and cocked his head. "Well, the old shop has managed to keep its old clients somehow."

Gloss curled one side of his mouth, seemingly holding back from saying something.

"Kent, can you tell me more about the position?" Roger asked.

"I need to make a change in the leadership on one of our most important accounts," Gloss began. "I'm looking for a self-starter— someone who can sell breakthrough creative. At Hornsby Hammerhead, we want account people who can persuade the client into buying top-shelf ideas. Provocative adverts that slash through the clutter. Convince me that you can do this."

Roger smoothed the back of his hair, thinking of the best strategy for dealing with this guy. Why all the posturing? Gloss sounded like another agency blowhard who talked a big game about selling the client wild ideas, but probably tucked his tail and did exactly what the client wanted. Roger decided to feed Gloss the rah-rah crap he wanted to hear.

"I can sell anything and manage any client. There's nothing I like more or do better than closing. That's my sweet spot. It doesn't matter what I'm selling or who's buying—ice to an Eskimo, portable heaters in Hell, or menorahs in Tehran. And I have the track record to back it up."

Gloss took off his glasses. "But can you sell these?" Gloss handed Roger one of the storyboards for the "Seven Deadly Sins" campaign. Roger examined it, recognizing Peacock's logo and the products, before handing it back. His eyes were steady, carefully taking in Gloss's expression until his salesman's instincts kicked in.

"It's a bit conservative . . . but sure. A new brand needs to make noise. No half-measures. But sure, I can sell this. I was expecting something more . . . visceral. Could we spice these up a bit?" Roger could feel Gloss taking it all in.

"You don't think that some of the images are a bit, shall we say, racy?"

"Nah, even the kids are bored with sex these days. Friends with benefits and all that. They all have ADHD anyway, and most young people are desensitized from playing violent video games. You see how their eyes glaze over. You gotta push 'em to the edge if you want to grab their attention."

Gloss leaned forward and peered at Roger excitedly through his designer glasses. "That's bang on, Fox. I like your attitude and I move quickly. So, let's have you come back—very soon. We'll discuss the account in more detail. What do you think?"

"Well, I'm currently weighing another offer, but this sounds intriguing. Let me know when you're ready for the next steps. I'm sure you understand, Kent."

"Yes, yes, of course. I'll have something put together by next week. Can you wait?"

"I might need to shift some things around, but I'll make this my priority." Roger paused. Then, changing his tone, he added, "Can I ask you something?"

"Of course. Fire away."

"I assume there's someone currently in this position. How would the transition work?"

There wasn't a flicker of hesitation in Gloss as he replied dryly, "I inherited a bad hire. I'll take care of it. No worries."

When Roger stepped outside, he shielded his eyes from the bright skies and removed his tie. It was another baking hot day, the third in a row. He took out his phone and considered calling Max, but then put it away. The following day, the recruiter called him twice before noon. Roger had been out for a run and returned his call after showering.

"Roger! You killed it. Gloss loves you. I think he's ready to make an offer."

"He is?" Roger replied nonchalantly.

"Yes, absolutely. Gloss is an all or nothing guy. When he wants something, he goes after it. No beating around the bush."

Roger didn't respond.

"Aren't you excited? Roger?"

"I appreciate the interest, but I can't take the job."

"What? HHI's a great agency and this is a top-notch position, reporting directly to Gloss. If it's about the money, I'll get you a major signing bonus and stock options."

"I know, but . . . sorry. I have to pass."

That was the last Roger heard from the recruiter.

CHAPTER 42

"And do not invite that dominatrix," Cassidy reminded her staff. She knew that once the avalanche of responses for her party poured in, a hectic schedule would prevent her from reviewing the list of confirmed attendees. When a magazine puts on a major event, no one can be sure who will show up. Many who'd RSVPed didn't attend, and invitations were frequently passed along to friends and coworkers, turning party planning into an exercise in futility.

The *My Radiance* gala was being held in a large second-floor space at Lincoln Center. The theme was East meets West, featuring a fusion of food and activities set to the beats of a world music band from northern Africa and hip-hop music spun by two local deejays.

Besides answering the question, "Who's Rod?" Cassidy and her planners were introducing the press and the advertising community to her new publication. As promised, her team set up a sampling station for *Holy Spiritz*. Cassidy received a courtesy call from Layla, thanking her again and sending her regrets that she wouldn't be attending due to her recent departure from the company.

The event was well stocked with swag and entertainment for the press. There was a raffle for freebies that included facials, manicures, and skin care products, and dinners at the city's top new restaurants. The grand prize was a trip for two to an upscale hotel and spa in Anguilla. Experts in feng shui, aromatherapy, fitness, and eco-friendly travel were situated at small tables throughout the venue. There was something planned for everyone, but by the overwhelming number of handwritten notes scribbled on the RVSPs, the majority of the women were attending for one reason: Rod.

Max arrived at Lincoln Center wearing his lightweight black suit and Prada loafers. When he entered the venue, music was blaring throughout the massive space. He quietly checked himself in as Max Hallyday. One of Cassidy's staff asked him to wait to the side while the crowd filed in. Max marveled at all the good-looking women streaming through the doors. While eyeing the ladies, once again it occurred to Max that he hadn't had sex for some time now. *Maybe tonight would be a good time to climb back into the saddle.* So to speak.

He smiled at a number of women giving him a cursory glance as they passed by in small groups. Max wondered if they were staring at the traces of his black eye. He hoped it made him look like a buff actor—like the tough guy with a good heart. As the room filled up, his self-confidence grew. *These women are here for me, even if they don't know it yet.* Maybe they'd introduce themselves once they found out who the man was around here.

Across the room, Cassidy scrambled around wearing a headset, carrying a clipboard, and snapping orders like a cruise director. Although she had a small, dedicated staff, *My Radiance* was a start-up effort and did not have the resources for managing an event this size. Cassidy was super organized and knew how to make things happen, but tonight would test even her adept skills.

She stopped at the check-in table and traced her finger down the list of attendees. When she noticed that Max had checked in, she tussled her hair and smoothed her tailored suit. Her stylish black-framed glasses and Sigerson Morrison heels accentuated her silhouette, giving her a naughty librarian look.

While questioning a member of her team about Max's whereabouts, she heard an unmistakably razor-sharp voice at the far end of the long table state, "Sparks. Veronica Sparks."

Cassidy spun around and saw Veronica preening in a short, gold cocktail dress. This was not what Cassidy had in mind at all. It was enough dealing with reporters and readers who wanted a piece of Rod without having the man-eating Veronica on the prowl—and on Cassidy's turf. Not tonight—no way.

As if she'd heard Cassidy's thoughts, Veronica looked over, smirked, and walked toward her. "Well, Cassidy Goodson. How are you?"

Cassidy smiled politely. "Hello, Veronica. I didn't think you still attended events like this. We thought you'd send someone."

"Oh, that's right, you're in editorial. Maybe you weren't aware that Globison cut a deal to sell the advertising for the digital version of *My Radiance*. If my team sells enough ads, maybe it can keep your print publication going. It's a tough market for magazines."

"We're limping along fairly well," Cassidy said, looking over the crowded room. "Still, I'm glad you're working for us. We need talented salespeople."

Veronica arched an eyebrow. "Well, we'll find out soon enough how much staying power the magazine has."

"I guess we will," Cassidy said, as a server offering a tray of hors d'oeuvres appeared at her side. "Meanwhile, we've got crab puffs!"

Veronica pasted on a smile. "I actually came to meet one of your columnists . . . the one named Rod. My team tells me he's what's heating things up for the publication. Is he here?"

"Uh, no. He's not being introduced until later. Much later."

"Hmm. I guess I'll have a glass of wine then. I assume it's organic. Maybe I'll have my palm read, too. You never know where your fortunes lie. This could be my lucky night," Veronica said, brushing by Cassidy.

Cassidy rolled her eyes as Veronica disappeared into the crowd.

Max ambled to the bar when he saw the banner for *Holy Spiritz*. After examining the drinks listed on the table tent, he told the barman, "I'm overdue for a Happy Ending. Make me a double." After a tentative sip of the cocktail, he nodded and took a long gulp.

Out of nowhere, Cassidy appeared at his side and grabbed his arm. "Max!" she said.

"It's Rod. Just Rod," he replied, looking her over. "You look fantastic."

"Thanks, Rod," she said, letting go of his arm. "Listen, I can't have you milling around and talking to just anyone. You'll spoil the surprise. Also," she added, nodding to his cocktail, "you can't be tipsy when I introduce you."

"Let me buy you a drink."

"I can't right now," she said, drumming her pen on the clipboard.

"But this tastes like vanilla."

"Max, I need you to come with me," she said, taking his arm again.

"It's Rod. C'mon, don't you want a Happy Ending?" he asked, following like a child being led to his room.

An old-school Michael Jackson song erupted over the speakers, and the crowd pushed onto the dance floor. The music was loud and the venue was in full swing.

"Let's dance," Max said, tugging at Cassidy.

"Since when do you dance?" she asked.

"Rod's an excellent dancer."

She had to smile. "That's good to know," she said. "Maybe later. For now, no getting lost, and please don't drink too much."

"Rod has nerves of steel. C'mon . . . one dance."

Cassidy just steered him to the side of the room and then prepped him about his introduction and handling of the press.

"So Rod just sits at a table and signs copies of the magazine?" he asked.

"And gets famous in the process. That's not such a bad deal, is it?"

Max shook his head in agreement, noticing her looking past him into the crowd.

Cassidy grabbed two bottles of water and handed one to Max. "Stay here. I'll have someone bring you some food. And Rod needs to be introduced carefully. By the way, you both look handsome tonight."

"Hide the women."

"Just stay here," she chastened. "We'll cut the music at nine for the introductions. Then we'll put Rod at that table with copies of the new issue. Don't disappear."

Max feigned a frown. "I thought this was supposed to be fun," he said, but she was already moving away, talking into her headset.

Five minutes later, one of Cassidy's assistants showed up with a plate of finger food, but Max had disappeared. After downing a second Happy Ending, he cruised the room. He stopped and checked his reflection on one of the mirrored panels. His hair had the *de rigueur* bed-head look, and the powder-blue shirt he wore open at the neck complemented his eyes. He looked around, guessing that the ratio of women to men was four to one. *Jackpot.*

Max put on what he thought was his most charming smile as he straightened his shoulders and injected himself into the circles of female conversations. If anyone asked, he said he was a consultant for the magazine. He considered having another Happy Ending cocktail, but switched to water.

At a few minutes before nine, Max returned to the general area where Cassidy had left him. Two members of her staff scurried his way, chattering into their headsets, no doubt telling Cassidy that he'd been located.

"*Ohmygod.* Cassidy has been beside herself."

"Anyone check the bar?" he asked.

"There you are," he heard Cassidy call from behind. She smoothed his lapels and took a quick look at his eyes. "Ready?" she asked, before paving the way to the microphone stand in the front of the room.

At exactly nine, the music faded and Cassidy switched on the mike. "Excuse me, everyone. I hope you're all having a great time at our coming out party for *My Radiance* magazine and all of you wonderful readers. My name is Cassidy Goodson."

As Max watched Cassidy work the group under a barrage of flashbulbs, he felt proud that she was making her dream come true. He realized how much sexier she'd become since they'd dated at her father's agency. Then he remembered her father and the upcoming pitch for Bobalooie. He sighed, thinking, *Might as well enjoy the ride while I can.*

Reality returned with a bang when Cassidy raised her voice and announced, "And of course I'm sure you've all been asking, 'Where is Rod?' Well, here he is."

Max took a breath and stepped forward, smiling and waving to the sea of women. They began clapping and whistling, and a few even shrieked as they surged forward to get a closer look. Max stood, surveying the scene like a conquering hero. He smiled broadly, and the women pushed forward again, enclosing him and Cassidy in an uncomfortably tight circle around the podium. Max grinned and lightly pumped his fist in the air, rather enjoying all the attention.

"Thank you, everybody," she said. "Now let's all relax and take it easy. We've set up a table for Rod where you can say hi and have him sign your magazines."

She led Max away from the hoard of mostly women following them across the floor. One woman grabbed at Max's butt, making him laugh. By the time they reached the back wall, Max had been pawed and pinched by faceless hands. He was relieved when Cassidy led him safely behind the table and switched the mike on again.

"Ladies, please. Rod will be happy to sign for you, but you need to make a line."

She saw the queue of women snaking around the room and cast a wary glance at Max signing a copy of the magazine with a flourish. *My God*, she thought. *He really thinks he's Rod.*

Max cheerfully greeted each woman who thrust a copy of *My Radiance*, their business card, or a few very personal items at him. Every so often, he glanced up, amazed by the cadre of women still waiting in line for him. As his admirers shuffled forward, a curvy brunette with a sprayed-on tan pushed her way to the front. She leaned over and in the process displayed a large pair of surgically enhanced breasts pouring out of her low-cut blouse. She beamed as she placed her business card in front of him.

She'd scribbled her phone number inside a red heart. "Hi Rod. I'm Mandy," she said, blowing her words through painted lips.

"Hi," Max said, doing his best to keep his eyes trained above her shoulders.

"You're a sweetheart for writing that column."

"Glad you like it . . . Mandy."

She pushed her card under his fingers. "You can call my cell anytime, darling. At night, I keep it on vibrate."

Max burst out laughing.

A half hour later, Max was glowing like a celebrity, still happily signing magazines, cards, and in one case, a coed's inner thigh. Cassidy took it all in, stone-faced as she stood close by with her arms folded. She walked behind him and put a hand on Max's shoulder. "Having fun?"

Max looked up and gave her a buoyant smile. "All this signing is hard work. My hand hurts."

"Yes, I can see how much pain you're in. Maybe we should wrap up the session."

He scoffed. "And disappoint your faithful readers? Rod's people need him." Then, waving a pretty redhead forward, he said. "It's okay, don't be shy."

Cassidy frowned and glanced at her watch. "That's it. We're cutting this off now," she said, running her finger across her throat to one of her staff.

"Hey, wait a minute," Max protested.

"You're letting this go to your head."

His brows drew together.

"Your *other* head," she added.

"Could it be the boss lady's a bit jealous?" Max laughed as he motioned to the next woman. He grinned as she pointed her camera at him for a photo.

Just then, a young athletic man confidently strode up to Cassidy. He was the Boston Red Sox's twenty-three-year-old third baseman, who'd just signed a mega contract with the team in town to battle the Yankees again.

"You promised me a dance," he said to her.

"I did," Cassidy said sweetly, ignoring Max's sudden frozen attention. "And you have excellent timing."

The well-dressed ballplayer brushed past Max and shot him a cocky look that said, "She's mine now, scribble-boy," and took Cassidy by the hand.

Before Max could say a word, they were on their way to the dance floor. As they grooved, heads turned to watch Cassidy and the handsome athlete dance. The music boomed, and as Max scratched out autographs, every so often his eyes darted to Cassidy dancing under the pulsating lights. And she looked fantastic, her body lithe and slender, moving gracefully in the young man's hard arms, her face flushed.

Max turned away as someone placed another copy of the magazine in front of him. "Look at you. Belle of the ball. Is that a cachet of thongs next to you?" It was Veronica. She stood over him with a hand on her hip, and for a moment he was Max Hallyday, ad man, all over again.

"I'm impressed—*Rod*," she said, taunting him. "Clever name, and smart to put your best feature forward."

He stared at her, but couldn't think of a response.

"Honey, what happened to your eye?" she asked, lifting a manicured hand toward him.

Max pushed back. "Got hit by a cheap shot. Never saw it coming."

"Oh, Max . . ." She smiled sadly at him. "That's water under the bridge by now, isn't it? It seems like you've been doing pretty well for yourself. Look at you. You're a rock star."

"I've had some help." He glanced toward the dance floor.

Veronica followed his eyes and saw Cassidy. "Max, with all these women lined up, you're hung up on her?" She laughed, tossing her hair. "Anyway, looks like Miss Perky's in good hands. He's as cute as Jeter, and he's loaded."

"Except he's twelve," Max said, before turning and giving her a puzzled look. "Miss who?"

Veronica reached over and gently touched his face beneath his bruise. "I'm saying maybe I was hasty about us," she said. "Let me make it up to you."

One last time—and this time, on my terms. The thought had beat like a tom-tom in Max's head for weeks. He glanced at Cassidy and the well-built ballplayer again and thought, *Fuck this. She's having her fun, so why shouldn't I?* Then he looked at Veronica, staring down at him and smiling salaciously.

"I guess I could use some air," he said, pushing away from the table.

A few minutes later, as a taxi sped them across the park, Veronica pressed her lips to Max's, expertly wrapping her tongue around his. Soon they stepped out of the cab in front of her building. Max looked up at the moon hovering sadly in the starless sky above the city and realized there was no turning back. They silently entered the elevator and waited for the doors to close. Veronica wasted no time and kissed him again. As the car ascended, she slid her hand down and began unzipping his pants.

Max closed his eyes, thinking, *There's probably a special place in Hell for guys like me, but at least I'll have Roger and Gloss for company.*

The party was winding down by the time Cassidy and her third baseman exited the dance floor.

The burly ballplayer wiped the perspiration off his face. "Cosmojito?"

Cassidy spotted Max's empty table, said, "Hang on a sec," and waved over one of her staff members. "Where's Rod?" she asked.

The young woman was a jumble of headset, clipboard, and two PDAs. "Gone, I think," she replied tentatively.

"Gone? Gone where?"

The girl shrugged. "With some woman."

Cassidy dropped her head back. "What woman?" she asked, though she already knew.

"Um. The tall one? The blonde? The one in the gold dress that looked like a . . ."

" . . . Victoria's Secret model?"

"That's the one. Want me to find him for you?"

Cassidy sighed. "Forget it. I'm sure he's got his hands full by now." She turned to the Red Sox player and considered him. "So, congratulations on your deal. Did I read twenty million?"

"That doesn't include the incentives," he said with a self-satisfied grin.

Cassidy felt the stares of the pack of young women swarming nearby, eyeballing the athlete like he was a hunk of dark chocolate. She looked around and then pointed. "The bar's that way."

"Awesome," he said. "Can I get you something?"

Cassidy exhaled. "I guess I could use a Happy Ending right about now."

His eyes lit up. "Wicked awesome. Let's par-*ty*," he said, clamping an arm around her waist. They slowly made their way toward the bar as the women converged around them.

CHAPTER 43

The next morning, Max squinted under brilliant sunshine as he walked on the path bordering Central Park's Great Lawn. His suit jacket hung over his shoulder and his wrinkled shirt remained untucked. Reaching for his tortoiseshell sunglasses, Max recognized a familiar figure loping along in running gear out of the corner of his eye.

He cringed when he saw that Roger had seen him. Roger cupped his hands to call out, "Hold it right there, *amigo*. You're busted for breaking curfew."

Max put his head down and moved faster.

"Max! Hang on!" Roger said, trotting toward him. When he caught up to Max, he placed a hand on his shoulder. "Hey, dude, wait. Uncle Roger won't take your lunch money."

Max spun around. "I guess my girlfriend and my client were enough for you."

"Whoa, relax." Roger looked Max over. "Looks like somebody's been out partying all night and doing the walk of shame," he said lightly.

"You need an edit button, Roger. For once can you just leave it alone?"

"C'mon, I'm just busting balls," Roger said, striding alongside Max. "I haven't seen you in ages and you don't return any of my calls. What's up with that?"

"What are you doing out here?" Max bristled. "Shouldn't you be at work stealing someone's clients?"

Roger pulled up. "If you're talking about Peacock . . . you're right. But you were having a meltdown, and you said that there was plenty of money to go around."

"*After* I sold Layla an ad campaign."

Roger shrugged in acknowledgement. "Anyway, I got fired."

"Really?" Max stopped to look at Roger.

"Really."

Max exhaled. "Well, what comes around, I guess."

Roger frowned. "Dude, I fucked up, okay? I admit it. But that's ancient history. I had a meeting the other day that we need to talk about."

"I'm late," Max said, brushing by him.

"It's important."

Max spun around. "Well, I just came from a meeting of my own . . . in Veronica's shower."

Roger took a step back, and then lowered his head and his voice. "Listen, I've changed . . . like you said. And there's something you need to know."

"Save it. There's nothing to discuss. I've already taken care of the business, and her. But since you're doing me so many favors, here's something for you," Max said, balling up a fist and hitting Roger squarely in his solar plexus. "Like you say—that was for your own good."

Max started walking away, leaving Roger stunned and hunched over, his hands holding his midsection. Max looked back. "Oh, come on. I didn't hit you that hard, ya big wuss," he said before walking on.

Watching him go, Roger caught his breath and murmured, "Okay, maybe I deserved that."

CHAPTER 44

Roger strolled north up Broadway, ambivalent to the wave of white-collar workers marching past him, Starbucks cups in hand and iPod ear-bud wires dangling around their necks. When he reached West End Avenue, he stopped at a deli. Standing outside, he sipped his fresh-squeezed orange juice from the straw rising from the clear-lidded top. He had stopped to admire the colorful array of flowers for sale that he'd barely noticed before, despite his walking by the display for the past five years. After his encounter with Max in the park, Roger realized it was impossible for Max to understand him. Words were not going to be enough to convince his friend that he was changing.

That afternoon, after e-mailing yet another batch of resumes, Roger plopped onto the couch and phoned Serena.

"I know it's not much notice, but if you're available Saturday night," he said, "I'd like to cook dinner for you . . . at my place."

"Oh—"

"Trust me. I'll take care of everything. You eat fish, right?"

"I do," she said. Then, after a pause, "Okay, I'm not going to the beach this weekend. What time is good?"

"Great! Let's shoot for eight."

For the next two days, Roger floated on cloud nine with an image of Serena at his side. Of course, on Roger's cloud nine, Serena was wearing only a pair of high-heeled mules and a few puffs of vapor. After a month of polite hugs and brief good-night kisses, it was time to take the relationship to the next level. But after his career implosion and failed attempts at intimacy with Veronica, Roger had some nagging doubts about his sexual . . . *performance*. Since it was time for his annual physical anyway, he phoned his doctor.

On the morning of Roger's appointment, there was a heavy downpour that drenched him even before he stepped onto a cross-town bus. He stood crammed in the aisle, mentally rehearsing his story so the doctor would write the prescription for his mojo.

At the doctor's office, Roger took a seat in the waiting area and thumbed through a stack of magazines. He opened a copy of *My Radiance*. Its cover featured a fresh-faced model wrapped in a sarong. He scanned the table of contents, flipped to page fifty-seven—*The Guys' Guy's Guide to Love*—and began reading.

THE GUY TO AVOID—Part Two

We all know him. He's the guy we just can't resist, even if you're a guy and he's one of your friends. He's a bit taller and better looking, his words flow as naturally as honey from a comb, and everything seems to fall the right way for him. And I'll bet if YOU were a guy, you'd want to be just like him and have your way with all those silly girls you know. And so we're drawn to him like moths to a flame, and eventually our wings are singed. Because, ladies, it's all about him, and if you don't figure that out early in the game, you'll find out the hard way. And I know that no matter how clear a picture I paint of this sociopath, a lot of you will succumb to his charms anyway. He's that good at what he does. It's understandable, because we all want to know why his world seems like a cooler place than the one we're faced with every day. He has a gift, and he uses it on you.

We're infatuated by his clever comments and his version of the truth. He weaves his verbal tapestry effortlessly. He's funny and clever and looks right into your eyes while flashing that trademark smile. Pretty soon, ladies, you're in his apartment on your back. And then before you know it, your heart's been broken. You might take it out on the next suitor that comes calling. Let him pay for that other guy's sins while he moves on to the next woman. So it becomes this vicious cycle of who can get what from the opposite sex until it grinds down our collective innocence like grist for the mill.

Not a very pretty picture, is it? Remember, ladies, you asked for the truth. So what can a nice girl like you do to protect herself from this testosterone-fueled guided missile shooting through the city? I can share a few pointers about him, but ultimately, you're on your own. First of all, he sees all of you as fair game. He prefers the good-looking ones. He says that beautiful women are more interesting because they're taken to the best places, unlike some of their less physically gifted sisters who spend too many Saturday nights at home on the couch becoming even less interesting.

Oops. That hurts, doesn't it? This is what he believes and his behavior reflects these twisted, cynical thoughts. But when he's with you, he makes you feel like you are the prettiest girl in the room. He focuses on you like a prowling jungle cat hungry for those pretty gazelles that run so fast and taste so good. So he stays close and listens and watches until he makes his move. And when he's done with you and that body you worked on all winter in those torturous Pilates and spin classes, he licks his lips and moves on, temporarily satiated until the next pretty one comes along.

He's always one step ahead of you. He goes the extra mile, putting two profiles on those online dating sites—he says it casts a wider net. He deletes the leftovers and keeps moving. With the time he invests in hunting, he knows your habits and what you respond to. He talks freely about how awesome his last girlfriend was and how they're still friends, and oh yeah, it was totally his fault that the relationship didn't work out. But he knows better now, because of what he's lost. And yes, ladies, he's ready for a committed relationship. At least that's what he says. Just don't gain any weight, have a painful period, let your boobs sag or any gray hairs show, and never back off on giving him that oral sex he craves. Because, if you do—he's gone. He knows all about those Seven S's and making deposits into your love bank. He meets women everywhere—in knitting classes, cuddle parties, baseball games, at the office, wherever. And he knows what it's like to live in New York—no matter how confident you act—and how alone and insecure you sometimes feel.

Now don't get mad. You asked. So protect yourself, and keep asking all those questions that reveal men. I don't mean what school he attended or how much money he makes at that hedge fund he manages. I mean you need to find out how he treats people, like his family, and how he deals with adversity. Then you'll see what's inside, and that's what really counts. Do whatever you feel is necessary to find out if he'll respect the most important relationship in his life: that special relationship with you.

Until next time,

Rod

"Rod, my ass!" Roger said, startling the elderly woman seated beside him. *It should be Dick. So this is how he's helping with her damn magazine. No wonder he's been avoiding me.*

By the time his name was called, Roger was beside himself, but his rage worked in his favor. After the avuncular physician finished his examination, he asked Roger about his level of stress and those nasty facial bruises. Roger explained that he'd been having problems at work and was under social duress. He swallowed and said he needed something to relieve his sexual anxiety. The doctor looked at him skeptically, but then opened his glass cabinet and took out a small trial packet and handed it to Roger.

"Roger," the older man said, peering at him through bifocals. "This is medicine. This isn't for partying. If you feel you need to, take one before sexual activity. But besides you needing to calm down, you're in excellent health. Is there anything else bothering you? You seem troubled."

Roger shook his head and closed his hand around the small envelope. On his way out of the doctor's office, Roger ducked back into the waiting room and snatched the magazine. He rolled it up and then walked under the clearing skies through Central Park. When he reached Broadway, Roger passed that same deli again—the one with the flower display along the sidewalk. He looked over as a warm gust of air ruffled the flower petals, creating a shimmering palette of color.

When he arrived home, he stood in the kitchen and flipped open the copy of *My Radiance* again. This time, he chuckled to himself when he read the part about online dating. He closed the magazine, resting his hand over it, and stood quietly. Then he booted his laptop and logged on to his dating sites. He hadn't been online for over a month, and his profiles were now filled with e-mails. Without bothering to open any of them, he checked "select all" and deleted entire caches.

He pulled up the desktop folder where he stored all the women on the services that he'd had sex with, like pelts taken after a hunter's kill. He studied the faces: the record company executive with the D-cups, the feisty stylist with pink streaks in her hair, the personal trainer with the spanking fetish, the voluptuous Jamaican attorney with chocolate-drop eyes, and all the rest. They were right where he'd left them. Roger realized he'd been blessed by meeting so many beautiful and intelligent women, all looking for the same thing—the right guy. But Roger had been a phantom, an elusive man who appeared to be there, but was never really available. He did the one thing he could do to make it up to them. After taking a deep breath, he deleted them all. Then he pulled up his Saint in the City profile and deleted that, too. Finally, he pulled up MrLucky. He dangled his index finger over the delete key before deciding, *Nah, I'll just peek in every now and then. A little Roger-porn, staring at all the girls I could have nailed. I'll bet even Dr. Phil says it's okay to look.*

The next morning, Roger stopped at an indoor farmer's market on Broadway and glided down the aisle feeling like Pepé le Pew preparing for his night of love. He grabbed a package of pumpkin ravioli, thinking, *Pumpkin fuckin' ravioli?* before placing it back on the shelf. He quickly filled his basket with fresh broccoli, a honeydew melon, and two bright pink tuna steaks. On his way to the checkout counter, he grabbed a pint of dark chocolate sorbet. The next stop would usually have been the wine store, but since Serena's decree at the Mexican restaurant, he hadn't had a drink. Although he sometimes missed the jangling of ice cubes and late night action, he'd ignored all calls from his former wingmen Jim Beam, Jose Cuervo, and Steve McQueen, believing that he might be better off without their company. On his way home, Roger stopped at the deli with the flower display. Roger stared at the flowers quietly, thinking, *Might as well go all the way,* before picking out a bright bouquet of spider mums, lilies, and hydrangeas.

That afternoon, he slipped his cleaning woman an extra twenty dollars in advance for doing the windows and giving some special attention to his bathroom. He wanted Serena to feel welcome and comfortable. After the cleaning woman left, he prepped the food and set the table. He wiped dust off a vase he found under the sink, filled it halfway with water, and arranged the flowers. Then he moved on to the bedroom to fluff the pillows. While searching for matches to light some candles, he found the remainder of a joint sitting in an ashtray on the bookshelf. He lit a match, but then blew it out and replaced the ashtray on the top shelf. Finally, he put on the sterling silver beaded chain with the moldavite pendant that Serena had given him when he graduated to her intermediate yoga class. She told him that the stone promoted self-awareness and personal transformation. Standing in his living room, he purveyed the results of his housework and laughed at himself, wondering if he'd morphed into the dreaded metrosexual.

Standing in front of the bathroom mirror, Serena brushed her hair and checked herself one final time. Her face became even more desirable when she added a light layer of red lip gloss and a trace of eyeliner. She knew tonight was going to be special. She'd put Roger through a stricter regime than she had other men, but it had never been about wanting to change him. She was beyond that. She'd been supportive, and he'd demonstrated more discipline than she'd expected. He was attending her yoga classes regularly and seeing Alejandro for Reiki sessions twice a week. He ate better, too—more fruits and vegetables and less meat—and she hadn't seen him take a drink since that first night. As a result, his body was changing. He was leaner and more fit—he said from running in the park—and his green eyes were luminous. The best thing, though, wasn't physical. His energy had become lighter and he was fun and more playful to be around. And he was helpful—he loved walking Chili, and never asked anything of Serena. He encouraged her to expand her business and even offered to help put together a better licensing deal for her spa's line of clothing.

So tonight, she was going to let go. Serena was pleased that keeping the relationship light had not scared Roger off. That was good to a point, however. She decided that if she didn't turn up the passion, they might be destined for the friend zone. Until now, that had been fine. But not tonight.

On her way out, she checked herself one last time in the full-length bedroom mirror and adjusted her flowing white skirt. Her black stretch tank top fit perfectly, showing off her breasts and tanned arms. Underneath, she was wearing a matching see-through bra and her sexiest pair of Tonga panties. Her heeled sandals accentuated her shapely legs. She dabbed her favorite scent on her wrists, behind her earlobes, between her breasts, and on the back of her knees. Finally, after adjusting her hoop earrings, she brushed her hair off her face and was on her way.

Roger appeared anxious and almost shy when she appeared at his door. While giving her a tour of his apartment, he stumbled on the ottoman in the living room. To Serena's delight, his home was clean and uncluttered. Even the bathroom smelled fresh, and she gave him a mental check-plus for that.

"Nice view. So much light. And the flowers are so pretty," she said, smiling.

"*Mi casa es su casa,*" he said, gesturing to the couch. "How about a cranberry juice and club soda?"

Roger seared the tuna like a chef competing on *The Next Food Network Star,* and they flirted throughout the meal as Stan Getz played

THE GUYS' GUY'S GUIDE TO LOVE

his sultry saxophone in the background. After dinner, Roger gathered up the dishes and carried them to the kitchen. They stood at the counter, waiting for the tea water to boil.

"Sorbet?" Roger inquired.

Serena hesitated. "What flavor?"

"Huckleberry fusion."

Serena shook her head. "No, that's okay."

"Just kidding," he said, smiling while taking out the pint of chocolate sorbet from the freezer. He filled a spoon and offered it to her. She leaned closer, gently holding his wrist as she savored a mouthful of the dark, cold chocolate. Seeing her lick the spoon clean, he dug it into the pint again. She moved closer, and after another taste, she smiled seductively and took the spoon from his hand. This time, she fed him. Roger gobbled up the sorbet and moved closer, kissing her—gently at first, and then more hungrily. When the kettle began to whistle, Roger flicked the stove off and looked into Serena's eyes.

"Let's go," Roger said, taking her by the hand.

"Aren't we watching the movie?" she asked, following him and then holding back when they were halfway across the living room.

"Really?"

"Let's see if we like it," she said, letting go of his hand and sitting on the couch.

Roger sighed. "Okay, sure. Be right back," he said, before ducking into the bathroom.

Roger brushed his teeth and then opened the cabinet above the sink where he'd placed the small packet from his doctor. He tore the seal, and to be sure, shook both blue tablets into his hand. Uncertain what might occur, he decided to hold off on the meds until they were well into the movie. He didn't want to be sitting next to Serena wielding a massive hard-on as they watched a foreign film with subtitles.

He was standing over the toilet holding the pills when the kitchen phone rang. *Shit!* He'd left it on speaker. He couldn't take the chance that some former flame might call. Roger placed the two pills on top of the tank and scurried out to catch the call. He missed it, but luckily it was a telemarketer. Trotting back through the living room, he looked over to where Serena had been sitting. The couch was empty and the bathroom door was closed.

Serena brushed her teeth and turned to the toilet, giving Roger a demerit for leaving the seat up. She saw the two blue pills sitting on top of the tank. She picked them up and examined them. She knew what they were. Roger's sudden knocking on the door startled her, and the tablets slipped from her hand, splashing into the bowl.

"Uh, Serena?" Roger asked, leaning in closer to the door.

"I'll just be a minute," she said. The two blue pills stared at her from the bottom of the toilet. She looked down at them, shrugged, and flushed them away. Then she applied another dash of gloss to her lips and smiled, thinking, *Oh, baby, you won't need those when I'm done with you.*

When Roger returned to the bathroom, the pills were gone. *Damn! I left them right there.* Then, the unthinkable: Did she take them or, worse, flush them? He threw up his hands and walked back to the living room where Serena was curled up seductively along the couch.

"Come here," she said, gently scratching her nails along the couch.

Shit, she thinks I'm a total pussy. Worse yet, now it's a challenge. I'm her mercy fuck!

He nodded resignedly and sat down beside her. Before tonight, *The Motorcycle Diaries* would have held their interest. Picking up on his fidgeting, Serena rubbed Roger's shoulders. By the time the movie's protagonist had packed for his trip, Serena and Roger were soul kissing and slowly exploring each other's bodies. Roger touched her face as he kissed her, and she ran her tongue over his lips. When he cupped her breasts, Serena's nipples were already hard and pressing against her bra. She slid her hand across his chest and unbuttoned his shirt.

They entered his bedroom, leaving a trail of clothing in their wake. Serena's sensuous kisses and confident touch rendered Roger hard as oak. As they rolled onto his bed, Roger yanked at the covers and reached at his night table for a condom while Serena unfastened her skirt and lay on her back.

Roger slid his head between Serena's smooth thighs. After a few minutes, Roger entered her easily, and she greeted his body with breathy moans. Once settled deep inside of her, he knew this was a perfect fit. After a deep orgasm, Serena mounted him and pushed her breasts toward his mouth. Roger let himself go, calling out her name in the darkness before exploding.

Roger lay at her side, holding her and gently stroking her hair. Neither spoke as shafts of moonlight shone through the half-open window. Roger's breathing became slow and rhythmic as he lay facing her. Soon they drifted into a deep sleep.

When he awoke, Serena's head was resting on his chest. He kissed her eyelids softly and after a few moments of touching, they made love again. As the sun peeked through the curtains, they explored each other's bodies and newfound scents. Afterward, they lay on their backs basking in the glow of new love.

Roger propped himself up on one arm and touched her cheek. "How 'bout some breakfast, Roger style?"

"I just had my breakfast," she said, her eyes deep and warm.

"You like cereal?"

She crinkled her nose.

"I have some that's chocolately good," he said, smiling.

Serena reached her arms around his neck and kissed him.

CHAPTER 45

"**D**o I ask Max or Rod for an autograph?" the bubbly blonde asked from behind the health club's juice bar.

"Huh?" Max said, surprised by the question and then bemused to be spotted like a celebrity.

"Don't be shy, Mr. Guy's Guy. I just saw a photo of you."

Max unscrewed the cap on his protein drink. "In the post office?" he asked, before taking a swig.

"No, silly. Here."

She opened the morning paper to a feature about the travails of relationships in the city. At the bottom of the page, there was a photograph of Max at the *My Radiance* party. He was seated at the greeting table, pen in hand, staring into the impressive cleavage of Mandy from Long Island. In bold, the caption read, "The Look of Success?" An accompanying blurb described one Max Hallyday, advertising executive, moonlighting as the relationship Svengali for New York's rough-and-tumble dating scene.

"Not that photo. Does anyone still care about this?" Max scoffed and leaned his elbow on the counter to get a closer look.

"Looks like you do," she said, pointing at the picture and giggling.

Max picked up on the flirtation in her eyes and paused a moment before taking a pen from the counter. He scribbled something, pushed the newspaper back toward her, and said, "Thanks for sharing."

She looked down to find Max had drawn a devilish moustache on his face and crossed out the word "success," replacing it with "trouble." The blonde burst out laughing.

"See ya around, Rod!" she called out to Max as he sauntered out of the health club.

As he walked down the corridor toward his office, Max again picked up on the stares from the female employees. Along with their murmurings and laughter, he felt they were mentally undressing him. After closing his door, he booted up his computer and was greeted by another batch of e-mails crammed into his inbox from friends, business colleagues, random women, and of course, Gloss. Everyone wanted something. Max thought about it.

Okay, Gloss and Roger are after the money. V and all these women are determined to hitch a ride on Rod's success. And what about Cassidy? She dances her way into the arms of some meathead ballplayer and is guilting me about Henry while I'm writing all of those columns for her. So what does good old Max Hallyday get in return? A power-mongering boss sticking his head up my butt and a best friend who steals my client and my woman. This isn't what I signed up for.

Max crumpled up his coffee cup and threw it at the trash, missing the basket. There was still an hour before his first meeting, so he began sifting through the cache of e-mails. They'd been pouring in steadily since his name found its way onto the newswires. His e-mail address and contact information were easy to track down. He was a stationary target—a sitting duck. *Might as well enjoy it.*

He skimmed over the morning's collection of e-mail first. Digital photos of women in various states of undress made up at least half of the correspondence. He was amazed by the directness of the women and the graphic nature of their stated desires. They all wanted Rod. Max realized, *I've become a commodity, a piece of meat.* It dawned on him that what had begun with his schoolboy snicker was being replaced by the seductive game of fast-found celebrity.

Max mused, *What to do with all the e-mails and e-vites?* He chuckled as he started a new desktop folder on his computer. He dragged and dropped the women he'd found most appealing into the cache, a sort of fantasy desktop harem. *"I'm a baaad man,"* he thought, adding pretty faces to the growing accumulation of prospective conquests.

An hour later, Max fidgeted inside a cavernous main conference room listening to a cultural trends expert that HHI had hired. During the question and answer period, Max's thoughts drifted back to the women—his women. He was a free man in the prime of life and there was no one holding him back from hooking up with whomever he chose. Except for "nice guy Max." He'd have to put that part of himself aside for now. These women wanted a phantom named Rod, and what was so wrong with introducing him to them?

After the meeting, Max phoned a sultry model/actress type with bedroom eyes who'd sent him racy photos, a few of which featured her decked out in a sheer black teddy. She gushed throughout the call and agreed to meet him at eight o'clock in the bar at the new Hotel Gansevoort. It was so easy. Over the next hour, Max set up a series of drink dates, jogs in the park, coffee talks, and lunches.

In a heartbeat, his relationship with New York's women had changed. To the new Max, these women were now fresh, succulent oysters waiting to be devoured. Drunk with his Rod-power, Max decided that it was time for him to show Roger how it was really done. He laughed as he slipped on his shades and strolled out of the building to grab lunch.

When he returned, there was a new e-mail from Kent Gloss. Max clicked on it. *Call me.* He frowned as he dialed.

"Holiday, I saw that photo of you again . . . not that I make a habit of reading *Page Six*."

"Of course not."

"Let me get to the point. I really don't care what you do in your spare time, mate, but it's bad form when it sheds a negative light on the agency. Do you read me Hol-i-day?"

"Loud and clear, Kent."

"By the way, try to think of a way we can put that column of yours to good use."

"You mean like pitching the Match.com account?"

"That's bang on, Holiday. There might be hope for you yet. But right now, you've got bugger all since the Korindopolos girl flew the coop. You need revenue to pay that big salary of yours."

Gloss was right. Layla's decision to join her father put Max and her account in jeopardy. When she informed Max of her impending departure from Peacock Beverages, she assured him that he'd done a wonderful job and offered vague assurances about the account's solid

standing with Hornsby Hammerhead. Max knew better. Her departure was like blood in the water for the agency sharks patrolling the
waters for loose accounts to swallow.

Max twisted in his chair as Gloss continued. "And Holiday, let's
be sure we're on the same page about Bobalooie. Your former client
spoke very highly of you during lunch. Said you were the best ad man
he'd ever worked with. And since he's agreed to open up the account
for competition, you'll need to leverage that relationship for all it's
worth."

"He said we could show him a few ideas. That's all. He didn't say
it was a pitch."

"Are you daft?" Gloss asked. "When the client looks at your creative, that's a pitch—and you're going to make it happen. Now, my
sources tell me that Henry Goodson's been having health issues. Let's
hope he pulls through. I've heard good things about the old bugger.
But in the meantime, see if you can move up the date of *the pitch* so
Goodson doesn't have time to develop a new campaign. You understand, Holiday. This isn't personal."

"It's business. Right, Kent?"

"Exactly. Good, now get cracking. You need this one, mate."

"Sure thing," Max replied. He hung up and kicked over his trash
can.

There was no way out. Once Max had arranged lunch with his
former client, the wheels had been set in motion for Gloss's full-scale
assault on Bobalooie. Max felt as though the train transporting his
soul to hell had pulled out of the station. A wave of guilt poured
over him.

Then a voice inside whispered, *Things will work out. You've got a plan,
and Cassidy will never know a thing.*

Max knew he was dreaming.

He stayed in his office the rest of the day. It was approaching seven
when he checked his voice mail a final time, jotting down notes from
business calls and invitations from his admirers. Halfway through
the messages, he heard Veronica's voice.

*"Hey, it's V. Just called to see how you're doing. I saw your picture in the
paper again today. You looked cute, even though you were staring at that woman's tits. My god, what a cow! Max, I really had a great time the other night.*

I don't know what got into you, but WOW. You were so intense. I thought I'd have heard from you by now. I was hoping you were free for dinner. I want to tell you about my condo. Call me."

Max wondered if it had been better, knowing it was the last time he was making love to the most beautiful woman he'd ever been with. The night with Veronica had been about sex—lusty, primal, and exhilarating. It was not the psychic victory he'd hoped for. Following their lovemaking, it quickly became all about Rod—how much he was being paid for "The Guys' Guy's Guide to Love" and how he needed to leverage his success—like dumping *My Radiance* for a better deal with one of Globison's more established media properties. In typical Veronica fashion, she persisted about her desire to arrange a meeting between Rod and her management. Max realized that nothing had changed. Business was business. If the circumstances had been different, he might have responded to her offer. But now this affected Cassidy, and that was a line he couldn't cross. She was the one who created Rod and envisioned the column's potential.

Max's mind then flashed to images of Cassidy dancing under the hot lights with that baseball player, spiraling to her slurping body shots off his pecs. He shook it off, but ultimately Max's final evening with Veronica provided only one clear epiphany—closure. He exhaled and deleted her message.

CHAPTER 46

Veronica was standing tall in her burnt-almond monokini on the edge of the diving board. The skies had remained clear throughout her week off at the Hamptons house where she had rented a half-share. By Sunday, her skin had turned a deep bronze. Earlier that afternoon, a scattering of dark clouds had moved in steadily toward the rarified air above Bridgehampton, but it appeared to be kept at bay for the time being. As she bounced evenly on the stiff plank, the men watched intently and the women attempted to avert their eyes. Veronica locked into her dive and prepared to launch her trim form majestically over the pool.

She had turned thirty-four two weeks ago and was eager to take the next steps for mastering her world. Everything was falling into place. After she had deposited a sizable down payment into an escrow account, her condo deal was finally under contract. Roger had become irrelevant after she'd learned that he lost his job. She assumed it was only a matter of time before he came around looking for her shoulder to cry on, begging for another chance. She hoped that he knew better. Her deal with Peacock Beverages was looking rock solid, and seducing Max again had been child's play.

The moment she pushed off the board, someone called out her name. She instantly felt her trajectory skew off course. The distraction caused her to twist her body as she hit the water. She surfaced, miffed, and climbed out of the pool, searching for the culprit who'd interrupted her show. It was that annoying woman from the brokerage firm renting the bedroom across the hall. Why was she always in Veronica's way?

"Veronica, there's a call for you. Your real estate broker. I thought you'd want to take it."

Veronica's glare bore a hole through the woman's forehead as she brushed past her into the kitchen.

"What's up?" Veronica asked curtly, picking up the phone.

"The builder's run into some unforeseen material and transport costs."

"You've got to be kidding."

"No, the final numbers are going to change . . . a tad," her realtor explained.

"And how much does a fucking tad cost these days?" Veronica asked.

"Just under ten thousand. That should be the last of the changes."

"This is bullshit," she said. "You said my deal was set in stone."

"With the price you were quoted, the contract accommodates unforeseen changes like this," he said. "Tribeca is very desirable. Even if you wanted out of the deal, with all the fees, it would cost you. Veronica, our clientele understands this is part of the process. It's a very fluid market right now and . . ."

"Oh, shut up—and thanks for ruining my weekend," she snapped before hanging up. It was approaching five o'clock. Time to pack for the bumper-to-bumper drive back to the city. Returning poolside for her bag, she checked her BlackBerry again to see if Max had returned her calls, but her inbox was empty.

The next morning, the skies burst open early, and it rained incessantly until noon. During Veronica's executive staff meeting, the sale of Globison's digital division to Nikola Korindopolos's conglomerate was announced. Initially, the news stunned her, but then Veronica envisioned a move up the ladder in the larger organization. Bigger pond, bigger fish. Following the ominous mention of "additional forthcoming announcements," the meeting ended abruptly without questions.

While her colleagues squirmed, fearing a scenario of mass firings and layoffs, Veronica licked her chops. This could definitely work out. Her deal with Peacock Beverages was ready for signature, so she'd start off on the right foot with her new company. After leaving her office at six, she treated herself to a deep tissue massage at an East Side spa. Following her appointment, she ducked into Barney's and purchased the beaded clutch she'd been eyeing—the one that matched her silver mini dress.

That evening, she sent Max a seductive text message, inviting him to dinner. She wanted to take him somewhere romantic and close to her apartment so she could tempt him into joining her for a mind-blowing dessert. After checking her phone three times, she plugged it into the charger and turned in for the night. While reading her e-mails at her desk the next morning, her divisional president called, asking her to stop by. Veronica checked the mirror before striding confidently to the elevator. The president motioned her into his office and told her to shut the door. Veronica arched her back and pushed her hair to the side so it tumbled onto her shoulder.

"Veronica, you've been doing a wonderful job," he began. "The company's been sold, and when new people take over, there are usually management changes. Let me get right to the point: I'm being reassigned."

"Oh, I'm so sorry," she said casually.

"The new company wants a senior vice president to work directly with Nikola Korindopolos," he said while Veronica arranged her hair again. "The company usually doesn't put someone so young into this role, but in this case, they're making an exception so . . ."

Veronica's head swelled with the image of her being anointed the youngest senior vice president in the history of the division. "I—I don't know what to say. This is so beyond anything I . . ."

Her boss put up his hand. "Veronica, there's someone coming in to fill that job. You'll be reporting to . . ."

"Wait, this can't be right. I thought that you said if I made my numbers, I'd make SVP this year."

"I put in a good word for you," he said ruefully. "There's not much else I can do."

Veronica breathed rapidly. "So . . . so who is this new person?"

After clearing his throat, he continued. "Actually, you know her. That should be good for you. It's Layla Korindopolos."

Veronica's face went gray.

"It was just announced in the trades that she's leaving Peacock Beverages and joining her father's company," he continued. "It's nothing personal. You've done a fine job, but that's how the business works."

Veronica's hands became tight fists and the rush of blood to her suntanned face turned it purple. After a string of questions all beginning with *why*, her boss looked at his watch and told Veronica he had an appointment with Human Resources. When he extended his hand, she turned without shaking it and walked toward the door.

"By the way, she starts tomorrow," he said, as Veronica stormed down the hallway.

CHAPTER 47

Cassidy's thighs burned, but she continued peddling. Her spin class reminded her of her personal life: she was working hard but seemed to be getting nowhere. She had so much on her mind and no clear answers to all the issues that gnawed at her. Her primary concern was her father. He'd been in and out of the hospital several times now, but the doctors couldn't get a handle on exactly what was wrong with his heart. Every test came back with mixed results and a need for more analysis. If his health didn't improve, she'd have to find a way to keep his agency solvent. Sweat flew off her face as she pumped her quads harder now, deaf to the blaring music and lost in her thoughts.

At least *My Radiance* was a smashing success, but at what price? The first few issues sold out at the newsstands, and her team was working twenty-four-seven to meet the deadlines. And the momentum for Max's column was building. *These women, all these crazy women, wanted more Rod.* She climbed higher on her haunches, responding to the trainer barking commands at the class. *Did I really push him into Veronica's arms? Dammit!* Max had avoided her since the party. Could she blame him, really? She was the one who wasn't letting her hair down. That was until she let that hunky ballplayer whisk her onto the dance floor. *What was I thinking going off with that himbo? Sure it was my choice, and with that chiseled boy toy, I might have overlooked the narcissistic attitude and limited vocabulary, at least for a while. But the groping and grabbing was so annoying. And predictable. And then his whispering in my ear that*

*he usually didn't date older women, but was making an exception because I was
so hot. Buh-bye.*

As the cool down began, she let up on herself. *With all those women
to choose from, Max had to go back to her? Sure, she's attractive, but men are
constantly checking me out, too. I can't walk down Sixth Avenue at lunchtime
without heads turning. And yeah, maybe I wanted Max to see a little of that.
Okay, maybe that was childish, but all I did was dance. He LEFT with her. Victoria's Strumpet.* She puffed her cheeks and shook her hair to the side,
peddling with a slow, steady cadence as the class wound down. She
thought about Brenton. *The hunk. The very rich hunk.* What about him?
She was attracted to him; that was for certain. *What woman wouldn't
be?* But Cassidy knew herself too well. She'd never be able to open
her heart to anyone else until she and Max worked out whatever was
between them. And Brenton Banks deserved better.

When the class ended, Cassidy was still feeling amped up. She'd
burned off a few hundred calories and what little fat was left on her
already lean physique, but she still didn't have any answers—just a lot
of questions that would continue eating at her unless she took action.

After showering, she walked outside and checked her phone. Banks
had called, following up on the e-mails he'd sent her. She scrolled
through her other messages and then dialed Max.

"I can just about hear you," she said over a blare of horns in the
background.

"Sorry, I'm in the back of a car stuck in traffic heading into the
Holland Tunnel," Max said. "Focus groups tonight in Jersey City.
The planning team wants to find out what the bridge and tunnel
crowd thinks of *Holy Spiritz.*"

"I read the trades. Sorry to hear your client took another job."

Max didn't respond.

"So what's that mean for you?" she asked.

"Now I have to find a way to hold onto the account and see if I can
convince her replacement to put the money back into the ad budget. I
forwarded a recommendation telling them how to best allocate their
funds during the brand launch. Who knows? Maybe someone will
read it and do the right thing."

"What if it takes awhile to find a new pers—"

"It means my boss will burrow his head a few more inches up my butt. I'll need to find a way to pay for my salary or I'll be fed to the hammerheads."

"Oh, sorry. Do you want me to call Layla and see what I can find out? She really likes us and—"

"*No.* But thanks. You've already done enough," he said, realizing he sounded annoyed. Outside, the engines revving in stalled traffic and the nonstop honking seared Max's brain. "Layla was my client. I can handle it," he explained, fidgeting around the backseat.

Cassidy stopped to take a sip from her water bottle at the corner of 55th Street. "You know, I thought meeting her with our team would help you," she said, trying to sound reassuring.

"I know, sorry. Things are all screwed up. That's all. I'm really under the gun."

"I haven't seen you since the party," Cassidy said, as another series of horn blasts shot through the receiver, long, loud, and off-key. She knew it wasn't the right time or place for this conversation, but she'd already let it slip.

He cringed but didn't say anything. The honking outside was relentless, and his driver was jabbering into his headset.

"I can't hear you, Max," she said. "Were you saying you were sorry for slinking out of the party without saying goodbye?"

He stared through the window, feeling trapped. "No, I was saying that if that jock patrols third base like he moves around the dance floor, he's headed back to the minors."

"Sorry, I didn't catch all that. I think we need to talk."

"About what?" he asked innocently.

"Everything."

"That covers a lot," he replied. "Should we begin with my dysfunctional childhood?"

She ignored that. "I missed you after you disappeared from the party. Did you get home all right?"

Silence.

"Did you hear me?"

Max hesitated and then held the phone outside his window for a moment. "You're breaking up," he said, rolling his eyes at himself.

"I looked for you," Cassidy said louder, "but you'd already *left.*"

Silence. Then, "Why are we having this conversation now?"

"We don't *have* to have this conversation at all," she bristled. "And stop acting like you can't hear me."

Horns blared again. "What can I say? You were dirty dancing with your *special* friend, with the jock rot."

"Well, I didn't sleep with him."

Max frowned, thinking, *I'm an idiot.*

"I can't hear you," she said.

"I didn't say anything. We're going into the tunnel now," he said, as the signal began cutting in and out.

Cassidy stared at the phone angrily, wanting to hurl it into the street. But then she shook her head and hung up. *What am I doing?* she asked herself. *We're not even dating and I'm filleting the poor guy like a king salmon.* She let out a short laugh and walked up Fifth Avenue.

CHAPTER 48

Veronica was out of bed at five and covered with perspiration by six o'clock, as her trainer put her through another high-intensity workout. Most days she felt exhilarated after this brutal regime, but today she was troubled by what awaited her at work. During the cab ride to the office, she chided the driver as he flew down Second Avenue in a futile attempt to catch all the green lights. Stopping for her morning coffee, she eschewed her usual decaf for a grande skim latte.

When she stepped off the elevator, it was quiet. When she passed the vacant corner office she'd been scouting, to her surprise, she heard a voice inside. When she looked in, Layla was sitting behind the desk on the phone.

Hearing Veronica's heels, Layla turned. "Well, I'm glad someone's committed to this business," she said, hanging up. "How are you, Veronica?"

"Hi. I'm fine," Veronica said, shifting in the doorway. "And congratulations. I was so happy when I heard you were joining us."

Layla raised an eyebrow.

Veronica stepped inside cautiously. "Can we talk?"

Layla glanced at her watch and then motioned to the chair. "I've only got a few minutes. What's on your mind? We've got a lot of work ahead of us."

"Of course. I'd like us to book that Peacock deal," Veronica said, measuring her words, "and include that revenue into our forecast."

"I signed off on it before I left the company, but it's now up to whoever takes my position to decide. I'll make a call, but then you'll need to close it," Layla said, now studying Veronica. "So, tell me how you see your role in the new organization. What would you like to be doing?"

Veronica crossed her legs away from Layla, processing the question. "I've consistently increased sales for the division," she said, "so I see myself as a strong number two, until the opportunity presents itself to run my own division. I'm sure you understand."

"Of course," Layla said politely. "We'll need good people to grow. As long as we do well, so will you." She gave a tight smile. "Anything else?"

Veronica shook her head and smiled coolly. By the time she returned to her office, her coffee was cold and she felt a knot in her stomach.

Layla plunged into her new job focused on learning the digital media business. She maintained contact with Peacock to continue the dialogue on the deal she left behind, knowing that her replacement could nix the program. Still, it was three million in revenue, too much to leave on the table. She'd keep tabs on it until Peacock hired her successor. Putting this one on Veronica would remind her who was running the show now. Keeping Veronica hungry was good business. She was capable, and for the time being, useful.

Layla summoned Veronica constantly, hounding her for updated sales forecasts and detailed market analysis. She peppered Veronica with endless questions about the accounts in the sales pipeline, including her progress on the Peacock deal. But since no one had taken Layla's place at her former employer, there was no one Veronica could connect with to close the deal.

Veronica kept herself afloat on a trickle of smaller programs, but spent too much time fuming about the money she'd already spent from the hefty commission that she hadn't nailed down yet. The escalating costs for her condo and her compulsive shopping had created a mountain of debt. And after their wild night in bed, Max never returned her calls. Veronica wondered if she'd been used.

The mounting tension and negative energy was draining and

created havoc on her personal upkeep. She caught herself nibbling on those sweets that made her face break out. Her mounting bills forced her to cancel sessions with her trainer. One morning, she stared into the mirror and discovered a gray hair. She cursed as she yanked it out with tweezers. Three days later, two more had taken its place. Every time she saw Layla parading down the hall with what had been Veronica's former staff hanging on her every word, she felt nauseous. With her passion for her job waning, she began showing up at the office later and leaving before six.

One morning, Veronica peeked outside her office and noticed a diminutive man standing in the hallway, talking animatedly into his cell phone. He stood slightly over five feet and was wearing an expensive suit and highly polished shoes. When he turned her way, Veronica recognized Nikola Korindopolos and decided it would be a good time for her to take a slow walk to the ladies room. She smiled a "good morning" as she passed by, sensing his eyes following her as she swayed down the corridor, stopping once to bend over and fix her shoe. She took a glance back, and he casually looked away. When she returned, he was still there.

She stopped and took a deep breath. "Hi. You're Mr. Korindopolos, aren't you?"

He smiled proudly. "Yes, and you are . . ."

She extended her hand. "Veronica. Veronica Sparks."

"I can see we have a bright future for this company," he said with a laugh as he looked up at her. "Very nice meeting you," he added before excusing himself.

Veronica glanced at Layla's closed door before continuing her waltz down the hall.

At one, Veronica grabbed her sunglasses and walked to the elevator. Layla had been on her ass all morning, asking for revisions on a presentation she was giving to one of Veronica's clients. When Veronica entered the lobby, Nikola was standing near the revolving doors again on the phone. Veronica walked steadily toward him, and as if on cue, he turned, smiled, and ended his call.

"Good afternoon, Ms. Sparks."

"Oh, Mr. Korindopolos," she said, arching her back. "It's Veronica, actually."

"Veronica. A beautiful name," he said. "And such a beautiful day. Do you have lunch plans?" Her eyes lit up, and he continued, "I like to learn about my new company from the people who are making it so successful. Care to join me at the 21 Club? We'll be back in an hour . . . or so."

"Love to," she said, taking a quick look around.

"Good, come. My driver is here," Nikola said, gesturing to the door.

The lunch stretched past twothirty. When Veronica passed Layla's office, she felt her cold stare. There was a pile of messages waiting on her desk, including three from Layla. After evading Layla's interrogation about her mid-day disappearance, Veronica walked her boss through her latest projections.

Layla found a typo on the Excel spreadsheet—a rarity for Veronica. She shook her head and said, "I'm worried."

What a troll. Without Daddy, she'd be working for me, Veronica thought, packing up her projections.

"One more thing," Layla said.

Veronica looked up.

"We need more revenue from the *My Radiance* deal. That's a hot little publication."

"I'm meeting with them next week. They're a real pain, though. Totally disorganized."

Layla gave Veronica a puzzled look. "Really?"

"Really," Veronica shot back.

"Well, if we want to keep our deal with them, we'll need sales. Don't you agree?"

Veronica pursed her lips, but held her tongue. On her way out the door, she heard the phone ring and Layla say, "Hello, Papa."

Friday morning, Layla poked her head into Veronica's office. She was on the phone arguing with her real estate broker.

"Is this a good time?" Layla asked.

Veronica quickly ended the call. "Yes, of course."

Layla stood over her. "Do you have lunch plans?"

"No. I have a few deals in the works . . . that you'll like," Veronica said, hearing herself suck up.

"Stop by at one," Layla said. "I have a table at Docks."

Over lunch, Layla skewed the conversation to Veronica's take on the shifting sands of digital advertising and its keys for success. Veronica's brain felt like it was being emptied. And she couldn't help but notice the weight Layla had shed around her middle and how attractive her new hairstyle looked with her new, narrower silhouette.

"I wasn't sure why you asked me to lunch," Veronica said, after the plates were cleared.

Her words hung in the air. Layla moistened her lips and smiled. "I'll get the check," she said. "Have you ever been to our offices, where my father works?"

Veronica blushed and said, "No."

Layla watched her eyes and then signed the bill.

Outside, Veronica tried to keep calm. If she could close the Peacock deal and get that commission, she could handle reporting to Layla—at least for a little while longer.

The elevator opened on the top floor and Layla led the way down the long hallway to her father's offices. Layla stopped at the double doors with the logo featuring the interlocking letters *KE* and *Korindopolos Enterprises* in script underneath.

"He's not here today," Layla said, glancing at Veronica. "Let's go inside anyway. It's important that you see the full extent of our operation."

Veronica entered and the door clicked shut behind her.

Layla took the seat behind her father's mahogany desk and waved Veronica to the chair across from her.

"So," she said. "Here's the bottom line. Veronica, I know that you understand our business, and you work hard. And sometimes that doesn't seem to be enough for women like us. Am I right?"

Veronica shifted in her chair. "Women like us?"

"That's right. I understand taking an extra step or two when it's necessary . . . like trying to push the deal through with Peacock any way we can," Layla said, leaning back and forth in the chair. "But there are limits."

"But . . ."

Layla waved her off. "I really don't care what goes on between the sheets with you and an operator like Roger Fox. I'm talking about stepping over the line. I may sit in one of those nice little offices down the street, but that's temporary. *This* is headquarters for my father's business," she said, extending her arms. "That means this is *my* headquarters. This is a new beginning for this company—*my* company—and I can't allow any extracurricular activities taking place between a woman with your talents and my father. He's not some two-bit salesman. Do you agree?"

Veronica leaned forward. "Layla! You have to understand . . . he asked me to lunch. I had to go. But, I promise you, *nothing* like that would ever—"

"Veronica, there's one more thing," Layla said, with the corners of her mouth turning up. "You're fired."

CHAPTER 49

Park Slope's Seventh Avenue Street Fair was even more crowded than usual. Summer was coming to a close. Bands played, meat sizzled, women in linen dresses powered their babies in high-tech strollers along the street, and—since Park Slope was still technically Brooklyn—a few young girls snapped their gum while on display in their tiny tops and short-shorts. A line of vendors hawked an array of arts and crafts, the usual beaded jewelry, Day-Glo posters, black T-shirts featuring Biggie Smalls and Tony Montana, and rows of tube socks.

Roger followed the slow-moving throng on his way to Serena's studio. He was taking her hot yoga class, followed by a Reiki session with Alejandro, and then dinner. After passing the umpteenth booth selling hot peppers, sausages, and funnel cakes, Roger stopped at a small stand where a Latin American woman was slicing the side of a pig soaking in its juices on a hot metal platter. Roger watched and then asked a question about the food in Spanish as the woman reached in with her tongs, pulling soft hunks of meat from the bone. She dropped a small piece of fatty pernil onto a little paper plate and held it out for him. Roger politely declined and bought a bottle of water instead. He chugged from the bottle and poured some down the back of his neck before continuing down the crowded avenue.

Since Roger's funds started shrinking, casual Middle Eastern fare and an indie film had replaced dinners at Cipriani Downtown and late night bottle service at clubs in the Meatpacking District. But his nerves had settled and his concerns about his streak of bad luck had dissipated. Spending more time with Serena kept him grounded, and it didn't feel like he was missing out on the action in a city overflowing with beautiful women.

She'd been the difference. Roger had never met a woman so independent, yet attentive to his needs. She was a strong, loving partner who skillfully handled his recharged sexuality. She kept him satisfied and always wanting more.

Roger's eyes were shielded behind a pair of amber aviator sunglasses when he recognized a familiar face at the kiosk for the ASPCA. Cassidy, standing by a shaded pen filled with puppies, was handing out literature. Roger hadn't seen her in close to a year. Cassidy had always treated Roger coolly, but whether she approved of him or not, they were connected by Max. And although the subject had never come up, he was uncertain what she knew about his relationship with Serena. And now he'd invested too much of his heart to let Cassidy blow things up. Faster than his inner voice could say, *Danger, Will Robinson*, Roger took a breath and moved toward her, deciding it was time to find out the score.

When he reached the booth, Roger gazed down at the puppies. After a brief deliberation, he reached in and picked up a tough-looking brown and white mutt.

Cassidy, clad in denim shorts and a white tank top with her hair pulled under a powder-blue bandana, hurried over. Not recognizing Roger, she pointed to the little beagle-spaniel mix. "That one's a charmer. He needs a name."

Roger grinned. "He looks like a Max to me. Did you know that Max is the most popular name for dogs?"

"Roger," Cassidy said, turning. "What are you doing in Brooklyn?"

"My yoga class," he said, stroking the dog's head.

"Why am I having a hard time believing you?"

"I take hot yoga at Casa de Tranquilla."

Cassidy's jaw dropped. "It *is* you then."

"What do you mean?"

"You're the guy . . . the Roger my friend Serena told me about," Cassidy said. "She seems so happy that I figured it couldn't possibly . . ."

"Be me?"

"Sorry, it's just that she likes guys who are faithful, and that's not really your thing."

"It's my thing with her."

Cassidy looked at him skeptically.

"I'm on my way to see her now. After class I have a Reiki session with Alejandro," he said, stroking the mutt under its chin.

"Really?"

"Really. I've changed."

She raised her eyebrows.

"Well, I'm chang*ing*." Roger laughed and scratched the dog's belly. "I just stopped by to check out the puppies."

"And we know how Roger likes checking out the puppies," Cassidy said cheerily.

"Okay, I probably deserved that."

"That one could use a nice home," she said, ignoring his comment.

"Me, buy a dog?"

"Adopt him," she said. "You can name him whatever you want . . . even Max."

"He does have that same sad look on his face," Roger said, holding the puppy in front of him. The little dog yelped and then piddled on Roger's chest. Cassidy laughed as he turned the dog sideways.

"See, he likes you," Cassidy said.

"I can see that," Roger said, handing the dog back to her. "You don't want me taking care of a puppy." He brushed off his shirt, reached into his pocket, and peeled out a twenty. "Here's a contribution."

She studied his face, smiled briefly, and said, "Thanks."

Roger nodded. "By the way, Max isn't talking to me. He's very busy these days, although somehow he finds time to write about me in your magazine."

Cassidy blushed. "Those columns aren't necessarily about you."

He rolled his eyes.

"We're educating women about guys *like* you."

"Hide your daughters and bolt the doors. Fox is in the henhouse."

"Maybe Serena needs to hide," Cassidy said.

"Please tell me she doesn't know about those columns."

"That's something to consider next time you're checking out the puppies."

He studied her eyes and asked, "So, how's Max?"

She pushed a wisp of hair aside. "We haven't spoken much lately," she said. "He's under the gun at HHI so he e-mails his columns to me."

It was Roger's turn to arch an eyebrow.

"Ever since his photo was in the paper," she said, "he's been acting differently. He's been like . . ."

"Like me?"

Cassidy placed the dog back into the pen.

Roger said, "Maybe Max needs a puppy." He noticed the crease in her brow. "What is it? Veronica?"

Cassidy didn't respond.

"It'll never work out," Roger said.

"Think I care?"

"I'll bet you think he'd be better off with someone else . . . maybe someone like you."

Her eyes dropped momentarily.

"I'll talk to him," Roger said.

"Roger, seriously, stick to taking care of Serena."

"She's my number one priority. In the meantime, I'll take one of these T-shirts," he said, grabbing an extra large off the pile. "I hope your dad is feeling better."

The afternoon breeze shifted and blew gently at their backs. Roger leaned over and surprised Cassidy with a gentle hug.

She looked at him curiously as he walked away and then called out to him, "Don't forget what I said about Serena."

He turned and laughed. "Hey, by the way, I like what you did with your hair. It looks real nice," he said, before disappearing into the crowd.

CHAPTER 50

Max rolled over and found himself staring into waves of auburn hair. He tried, but he couldn't remember her name. He pushed the covers aside and tiptoed naked to her bathroom, hoping he might slip out before she awoke. But when he returned, she was propped up on her elbow. The sheets had been pulled aside and she was tempting him with her milky white skin and the neatly trimmed strip gracing the welcoming mound between her long legs.

"Good morning, sunshine," she said, raising her lips into a luscious smile. He hesitated but then felt a stirring, so he slid next to her and lightly massaged the insides of her thighs with his hand. As her breathing quickened, he guided her onto her back. After slipping on a condom, he entered her again. An hour later, while strolling back to his apartment, he debated whether she was worth a second date. He reached into his pocket for her business card. *Oh yeah, Cheryl.* Then he tossed it in a trash can. She was too tall anyway, he decided, and she reminded him of that cheerleader in high school who threw him over in favor of the captain of the football team.

Last night had been the first time he'd broken his rule about not staying overnight. It was all about the sex. He didn't want to get involved or wake up to make small talk with a woman he really didn't know. But last night they consumed too much champagne, and after doing the deed, he passed out.

The thrill of Max's neo-celebrity was wearing thin. He quickly bored of the attention and needs of his cadre of female admirers. He'd almost lost count of the number of women he'd bedded since the *My Radiance* party. And he'd learned that his perspective on casual hook-ups was different than Roger's. For Max, it was work. For Roger, it was all pleasure. He'd brag about camping out overnight at his conquest's apartment before moving on. Max recalled Roger's wink when he declared that, "Breakfast is the most important meal of the day," and "After a good morning fuck, nothing beats a hot shower and one of those big, fluffy towels."

But Max really wasn't enjoying himself. He loved sex, but in his heart, he was a serial monogamist. Falling in love with the right woman had always been his goal. Unlike Roger, Max viewed emotional intimacy as a prelude to sex. He had to feel an underlying connection with a woman. But recently, it had been wham, bam, and out the door. Sure, not every woman Max met hopped into bed with him, but he was astonished by how willing the women were about having sex, and how so many aspiring models and actresses were willing to trade the short-term use of their bodies for connections that could help their careers. Max made it clear that he didn't have all these show biz contacts, but it didn't seem to matter. These women's dreams were fueled by hope. And despite his newfound celebrity and a parade of one-night stands, Max was lonely.

After showering, he hurried off to another internal update with Gloss on the Bobalooie pitch. The presentation was less than two weeks away, and Max had been tasked with pulling everything together. It was the kind of new business rainmaking opportunity most people in Max's position would fight over. Winning a new account does wonders for your advertising career. But Max was torn. On his way to work, he blasted The Killers on his iPod. When he reached Fifth Avenue, his phone vibrated.

"You son of a bitch."

"Huh?"

"You heard me, Max Hallyday."

"Cassidy?" he asked.

"Did you read *Ad Snoop*?"

Max froze. *Ad Snoop* had broken a story, Cassidy said, about Hornsby Hammerhead's secret pitch for the Bobalooie account. Someone had tipped them off to put the squeeze on Goodson—no doubt Gloss's handiwork.

"It's one thing to behave like a D-level celebrity—some wannabe player who sleeps with skanky, second-rate models—but when you go after my father's business—while he's sick—that's when I step in. How dare you?"

"Calm down and let me explain."

"Don't you tell me to calm down, you . . . you . . ."

"Dog?"

"You bitch! Kent Gloss's bitch. After all your complaining. I guess it's easier laying down for him."

"Please, let me explain," he said, holding the phone farther away from his ear.

"No, let *me* explain," she said. "As much as *My Radiance* means to me, I won't sit back and let thirty years of my father's hard work go down the drain, especially when he's back in the hospital."

"Again? I didn't know he . . ."

"Of course you didn't. I'll quit and go back to the agency and protect that account from HHI . . . and from you."

"Cassidy, don't. *My Radiance* needs you. Don't do it . . . please."

"Worried about your column?" she asked. "From what I've read recently, the way you're carrying on, your ideas will dry up at the same time as your . . ."

"It's not what it looks like. You've got to trust . . ."

"The guy you're writing about now is a soulless predator and doesn't even sound like he's having fun. At least Roger was being himself. He's a fool, but he doesn't know any better. But you do . . ." she said. "*You're a bastard!* And I was so proud of you. But you had to blow it. And with my father's agency. Is this how you repay him?"

"Cass, I'm working on something and— "

"Just stop talking." Then, after a prolonged silence, she said, "Goodbye, Max," and hung up.

His phone vibrated again. "Cassidy, please . . ."

"Holiday? You're late," Gloss said. "We're finalizing the plan for Bobalooie. Get up here NOW."

After work, Max hurried across town to meet Brenton Banks at the Yale Club. They were finally getting together after rescheduling their previous appointment at the last minute. He was curious about Banks and his business, and also anxious to find out if it had just been a coincidence that both Banks and Cassidy were seated in the same section at the same Yankees game.

Max arrived at the club's dining room at six thirty, sipped sparkling water for a half hour, and finally greeted Banks at a few minutes past seven. Banks was nattily dressed in a midnight-blue designer suit and a silver tie. He had a powerful grip that Max tried to match when they shook hands.

Banks ordered Stoli on the rocks. Max opted for Stoli also, with a slice of orange. While waiting for their drinks, Banks said, "Thanks again for those Yankees tickets."

Max's ears perked up like a German Shorthaired Pointer's. "Did Jimmy enjoy the game?" he asked innocently.

"Actually, as it turned out, his mom had other ideas for that night."

"Oh," Max said, letting the word hang in the air.

"I ended up going with a friend," Banks said. "Hope you don't mind."

Max looked him in the eye. "Not at all, as long as it wasn't a Red Sox fan."

Banks hesitated slightly, and then smiled mysteriously before turning to the waiter who had their drinks.

Max swallowed and felt his stomach tighten. *That's it, then. Had to be her.* He decided to change the subject, and politely asked about Jimmy and how he was doing in school.

"You know, Jimmy's reading skills have really picked up. Not that he had a problem, but now he really digs it. Maybe it had something to do with your stories."

"That's good," Max said, letting the compliment pass. He thanked Banks for the polo shirt, and Banks informed him that he was a long-time Giants season ticket holder.

"Play any ball in college?" Max asked, before biting into his orange slice.

"First base at Grambling," Banks began.

Oh great, another infielder, Max thought, leaving the rind on the napkin.

"I had hopes for a pro career," Banks continued, "but after my knee popped sliding into home, it was on to business school." Banks signaled for another round of drinks. "If you wouldn't mind, can I ask you a few questions about the advertising business and your agency?"

Max checked his watch, but then nodded instinctively, smelling potential business. "Sure."

"Tell me how you land a client and the best way you'd invest their money," he said with a short laugh.

Max knew the drill. He took a breath and described the relative merits for clients working with smaller independent boutiques versus those aligned with large advertising holding companies. He explained the importance of choosing an agency that listened and understood the client's business, matching their brand's needs with the right agency partner, and the benefits of building an enduring relationship.

Banks nodded thoughtfully. "So it's kind of like dating and taking the time to understand a woman."

"Uh, I guess you could say that," Max replied, thinking of Cassidy and trying his best not to narrow his eyes.

Max then talked about his team's determination to win at Goodson. They'd crafted a clear communications strategy and effectively serviced the Bobalooie brand with an ad campaign that fueled annual double-digit sales increases throughout the account's tenure at the agency.

"To win, an agency needs to exceed its client's expectations by paying attention and investing the time to learn everything about the client's business. There are no shortcuts, and that's the kind of partnerships we created," Max said.

Banks nodded, weighing Max's words. "It's rare to meet someone in your field who's so passionate and knowledgeable. Sounds like you had the perfect relationship."

"Yeah," Max replied.

"If you don't mind my asking, why did you leave?"

Max cleared his throat. "HHI is a great agency."

Banks swirled the ice around his drink.

"They have incredible resources," Max continued. "Anyway, we all have to keep moving, I guess. Advertising has no rules. It's a *relationship* business, even though many people forget that there are rules for relationships."

"Well, thanks for the insights."

"Uh-huh," Max said, peeking down at his watch, wondering, *Why am I spilling my guts to this guy?* "So Brenton, you're an attorney. Any particular areas of specialization? "

"My JD's in business litigation, but these days I'm in charge of our mergers and acquisitions team," Banks said. "We work mostly with consumer products and media companies. The reason I asked all those questions is that I'd be curious to get your perspective on a deal I'm working on."

"Oh?" Max said.

"Yes . . . you might find it interesting."

Banks spent the next half hour discussing his practice and a few deals he was involved in. Max listened, and then Banks unknowingly dropped a potential solution to Max's problems right into his lap. It was all Max could do to keep from coughing his vodka onto Banks' three-thousand-dollar suit.

Banks signaled for the bill, saying, "I'll take care of this."

Outside, the two men shook hands and agreed to talk in a week before climbing into separate taxis.

While his cab crawled in traffic, Max twisted in the backseat. He knew. There was no real proof that Banks and Cassidy were together at the Yankees game, but it was becoming a pattern, and Max just knew. *Why does the guy who could be the key to working my way out of this jam have to be sitting in MY seats with Cassidy? Okay, the universe is fucked up, but somehow, some fucking way, I can make this happen.* He sat quietly for a few moments before leaning forward and clapping his hands together loudly, proclaiming, "Yeah!" The driver glanced back through the rearview mirror and barked something that sounded like cursing in a foreign language that Max didn't understand. Max was still smiling to himself when he leaned back into the seat.

CHAPTER 51

"Where are we going?" Roger asked, holding Serena's hand as they entered Brooklyn's Prospect Park Zoo.

"Over there," she said, pointing toward the Children's Corner. A carousel turned to the pumping sounds of carnival music. The children squealed, riding the brightly painted wooden horses. A warm breeze whispered through the trees as Roger and Serena approached a wooden bench. Chili curled up on a patch of grass at their feet.

She took Roger's hand. "Roger, how do you feel about us?"

He shifted as she waited for his response. Then, with a steady voice, he said, "I really care about you."

"Sometimes I'm not so sure."

"Huh?"

"Is there someone else?"

His eyes turned serious. "No—why are you asking me that?"

She turned his way. "Why do you still need to go on those online dating sites?"

Roger pulled back and scrunched his face. "I don't know what you're talking about. I deleted my profile."

"Really?"

"Yes," he protested.

She held his gaze and said, "Then who the hell is MrLucky?"

Roger's face turned red. *Say something,* he told himself, but he couldn't come up with the right answer. "Oh. That's an old profile. I forgot to remove it."

Serena steadied her gaze. She wasn't buying it. "Then why does it always say you've been on the service within the past twenty-four hours?" she asked.

Feeling set up, Roger looked away to avoid his embarrassment. Checking in online had remained his one guilty pleasure, someplace where he could sit in the dark and just look. The pressure of losing his job and committing to one woman—even someone as wonderful as Serena, had unnerved him. He kept searching for a clever response, but instead blurted, "They billed my credit card again."

Serena's eyes turned cold. "That's such bullshit. Why are you doing this?"

He took a breath and said, "Okay, look. I took my other profile down. I must have forgotten about that one." She tried holding onto his hand, but he pulled it free.

"Roger, this is important. Please sit down," she said calmly as he stood. Serena reached for his hand and guided him back to the bench.

"Baby, I'm sorry. I've been an idiot, but I was only looking. Really," he murmured. Then his head shot up. "Hey, what were you doing on there anyway?"

Serena's face flushed. "Um—I'm not. I was canceling my subscription."

"Oh, sure. *You* were on there, so you're turning it around," Roger said. "And checking up on me. Nice."

"Roger, look at me. I don't need to go on that site anymore, and I thought you didn't either," she said calmly. "There are a lot of pretty women that would like to date a man like you. And that's the problem. People can get lost on these dating sites. If you keep your profile active, there will always be someone else to check out. It never ends." She squeezed his hand. "You either want to be with me or you don't. Which is it?"

He considered her statement. Did he still need his little outlet, his escape hatch? Did he want to slide back into his old life, his old habits? If he did, now was the time. Inside he knew the answer. He took a deep breath and looked into her eyes. "I have everything I need right here. I'm in love with you. I'll cancel the damn membership."

Serena smiled softly and placed her other hand on his. "I love you, too, Roger. But you need to give me your word . . . never again, at least not on my watch."

He pulled her up to his chest and wrapped his arms around her. Then he caught himself from rolling his eyes and said, "Promise."

A slow squeak, followed by the lingering scent of Chili's fart, broke the tension.

"I guess we're all in agreement then," Roger said with a laugh.

The next morning, Roger stood in the lower level of the subway station. His face was dripping with sweat as he peered down the dark tunnel searching for an F train. Except for the rumble of the occasional train shooting by on the other track, the only other sounds at this hour came from an elderly man seated on a folding chair playing the "Theme from the Godfather" on his accordion. In the quiet of the station, there was no escaping the tune.

"Hey . . . my friend," Roger said while peeling off a five dollar bill and stuffing it into the man's open case. "An offer you can't refuse. How about a little Sinatra or some Bobby Darin?"

Grabbing the cash, the old man grinned and then broke into a jaunty version of "Beyond the Sea." Roger gave him the thumbs up, but the roar of an approaching train drowned out the song. Roger shook his head. "Can't win in this fucking town," he said, stepping inside.

He stretched his legs across the half-empty car with the Darin song playing in his head until the steel wheels screeched into the next station. A blonde and a brunette dressed down in casual Sunday attire scooted inside and took the seats directly across from Roger. As the train pulled out, the two women chatted animatedly. They were way too perky for Roger. There was a copy of *My Radiance* magazine sticking out of the blonde woman's tote. Roger's eyes fixated on it all the way to the next stop.

Finally, the young woman looked down at her bag. After deciding that Roger was sane, she said, "Excuse me, but is something wrong?"

"Oh, sorry," Roger said, looking up. "I was checking out your magazine—*My Radiance*. I work at an ad agency and the media reps keep telling me about it."

"Which agency?"

"Uh, Goodson, on Lafayette Street," he said. "You ladies work in advertising?"

"We work at HHI," the blonde said proudly.

"Hammerhead. I know somebody there," he said.

"Really, who?"

"Max Hallyday," Roger said.

"Oh Maaax," the brunette said with a smile. "Everyone knows him. All the girls read his column."

"Of course. What do you think of it?" Roger asked.

The women turned to each other and the brunette responded, "I really like it. It's so honest—like he's telling us how guys really are."

"You think it's true?"

"Most of it."

"So what kind of picture does he paint of the men he's writing about?" he asked.

"Assholes!" the women said in unison, breaking into laughter. "There's this one guy he really trashes. What a loser."

Roger's ears turned red, but he held his tongue.

"Max is like this star now, always going to all these parties," the blonde said. "He even has a blog." Nudging her friend, she added, "She's got the hots for him. Right, Julie?"

"I just said he was cute."

Roger grimaced. "Thanks for sharing. Nice chatting with you two."

"Here, take the magazine," the blonde offered. "I finished it."

Roger nodded and shoved it in his back pocket. "Thanks, I know just the place to read it."

The two woman laughed as the train pulled into his station. Roger stood by the door, watching the blonde checking him out.

"Hey, what's your name?" she asked.

The doors opened and he smiled at her. "I'm the guy to avoid . . . parts one *and* two."

CHAPTER 52

V eronica tossed her mail on the kitchen counter, not bothering to turn on the lights. She walked stone-faced into her bedroom, changing into a pair of athletic shorts and a Syracuse T-shirt. She lay on her bed, gaping at the ceiling, her mind twisting through a garbled rehash of the day. When the late afternoon light softened and the room turned dark, Veronica sat up and rubbed her eyes before slowly returning to the kitchen. She flicked on the lights, twisted open a bottle of Perrier, and began sifting through her mail. There were bills and the usual catalogues from Bloomingdale's, Bliss, and Victoria's Secret. She tossed the bills on the counter and picked up the new issue of *My Radiance*. After glancing at the cover, she grabbed her sparkling water and scrunched her legs up on the living room couch. She leafed through the masthead and table of contents before settling in on page seventy-two and the latest *"The Guys' Guy's Guide to Love:"*

A DISH SERVED COLD

Here's a question men sometimes ask each other: Would you want to know when it's the last time you're making love to the most beautiful woman you've been with in your entire life? Ask any man and he'll tell you about that special woman he loved and lusted after who now only exists in a lost moment in time. The one who would have stayed at his side if he knew then what he knows now. But he didn't pay attention until it was too late, and now she's gone. Would he have wanted to know the truth when he was making love to her that final time?

As shallow as the question appears, this notion can launch bar room debates among men in any corner of the world. Whether they're sipping Manhattans at P.J. Clarke's, drinking punch on the sandy floor of the Rum Bar in Turks and Caicos, chugging beers around a keg in a musty college frat house, or savoring scotch under the dim lights of the Opal Lounge on Edinburgh's George Street, it makes no difference. If you're with a group of guys, and especially if there's alcohol on hand, this timeless issue will set their tongues wagging. And the endless deliberations over the variables—how old am I, how old is she, and are we married—only add to the banter.

How would you, the woman, feel if you knew the man was aware that it was the last time? Would you be turned on by his passion or put off by his desperation? Would he ravish you with such fervor that the beauty of the moment would be lost to a sense of impending doom? For a man, the last time he makes love with the woman of his dreams can be a bittersweet precursor to his own end.

And it's not only about the physical aspects of the moment. It's about everything that was shared—the trust, the dreams, and the caring. It's about the puppy he surprised you with on Christmas morning, the cherry pie you baked for his birthday, and that snowman the two of you built in the quiet following the blizzard. All of this transformed the sex and the lust into, well . . . love.

And who knows what the universe has in store? That might have been his one chance to harness all of life's beauty incarnated into one person. Looks are subjective, but a man knows when he's captured a shooting star that can carry his dreams across the sky.

Before you judge, think about it. Are you that different? Like anything else it depends on the individual. But take it from a man who had the elusive opportunity to experience knowing when it was the last time he was making love to the most beautiful woman he had ever been with. In this particular instance, it was a premeditated plan to sleep with someone that I did not plan on seeing again. Was it better knowing? I can't say for sure, but for me, that final time did nothing more than bring closure to what was the wrong relationship. You can relate to that. Was it revenge? No, it was worse because I finally realized that we weren't really in love in the first place.

Until next time,

Rod

Veronica sucked air through her mouth as Max's words "weren't really in love in the first place" sank in. He never meant to start up again. She slammed the magazine on the sofa, thinking about the time she'd invested trying to turn Max into a powerhouse. *But he wasn't so bad, was he?* When they were a couple, he was respectful and reliable. Unlike most of the men she dated, Max was honest. And she missed the freedom that came from trusting a man. Was she really that much of a power bitch? When she was with Max, she could let her guard down. With him, things were easy. He made her laugh. He'd been faithful. And he was capable. What else did she want from a man? Maybe Max didn't share her take-no-prisoners attitude, but so what? He still made things happen. Why did she throw their relationship away? For a Roger? The magazine fell to the rug. Veronica's breathing quickened and her body shook. She put her face into her hands and cried. *He never even loved me.*

Stepping out of the shower, Roger heard a group of teenagers on the playground behind his building. He squeezed his head out of the bathroom window and looked down to find a group of young men shooting baskets, joking, and trash talking. He grinned and phoned Max.

"It's me, *amigo.*"

299

At first, his greeting was met by empty silence. Then, "I'm on my way out."

"Bullshit, you're watching *ESPN* again," he said, catching the sounds of the television blaring in the background.

"What do you want?" Max asked.

"Well, first of all, you don't hit very hard, so all is forgiven. How 'bout coming by and shooting some hoops? I'll give you a few ideas for that column of yours, too. That's a good deal, don't you think?"

"They're not about . . ."

"They *are* about me. I've read them. *Okay?*" Roger said. "The guy to avoid—parts one and two—and your online dating conquests. Come on. You're sullying my reputation. So, if you don't have some chippie lined up, meet me in an hour at the courts behind my building and I'll give you something to write about."

"I just told you—"

"Just this one favor. After that . . . if you want, I won't bother you. I know how busy you are these days."

After a long pause, Max replied, "One game."

Roger pulled on a pair of cut-off sweatpants, laced up his Converse All Stars, and dug out the basketball buried at the bottom of the closet. While he was on the floor reaching around, he discovered a bag of his old high school basketball jerseys all rolled up together. After squeezing into one, he looked into the mirror and laughed. His old number, twenty-two, was wrapped around him like a sausage casing. He threw on an oversized T-shirt over it and bounded down the stairs.

He stood patiently by the side of the court, waiting until the group asked him to play. After missing his first two jump shots, Roger went on a scoring binge, and pretty soon his play became as dominant as the old Roger. After two more games, the teens called it a day. Roger was pumping in jump shots by himself when Max walked around the corner wearing a New York Knicks jersey.

"Hey, superstar!" Roger called out.

"So what are we playing for?" Max asked curtly.

Roger bounced the ball at him and said, "We could play HORSE, or how about OUT . . . for a couple of sawbucks, of course?"

"You're on," Max said. "You must have a stack of twenties put aside with my name on it."

"It's OUT then. Here, you go first," Roger said.

They'd played the game a hundred times. The rules were simple. If your shot goes into the basket, the other player has to replicate it. If he misses, he gets a letter.

"So what's this about a new idea?" Max asked, hoisting the ball up to the basket from fifteen feet away. His shot clanged off the rim.

Roger bounced the ball and then fired from the top of the key. It swished through the net. "It's about you being honest . . . with yourself," Roger said.

"I don't know what you're talking about. But at least you were right about women. They're a piece of cake once you get your game down."

"Dude, I was wrong about women. Just like you are now. And if I know you like I think I do, I'll bet you're not having that much fun," Roger said as Max's shot careened off the backboard. "And that's O."

"What do you mean?" Max asked, shooting Roger a look as he rifled the ball back to him.

Roger caught the ball and then spun it on the tip of his index finger. "Rumor has it that you're a big player now. Maybe bigger than I was."

"*Was?* Are you going to shoot?" Max asked as Roger began dribbling the basketball between his legs.

"Let me break it down," said Roger. "First, I don't care what you write about me. I know who I am, and who I was. You thought I was using women, but you were wrong. They all have free will and they love sex. They're just like us."

"Huh?" Max said. "What's with the 'who-I-was' nonsense? After you screw your best friend's ex and then steal his business, all of a sudden you're a new man. I thought getting canned might wake you up."

"It did. And I only hooked up with Veronica *after* she dumped you. You knew she wasn't right for you. You even wrote about it in your column," Roger said, now spinning the ball with his hands. "I'll bet she was thrilled when she read that. Dude, you didn't love her. You were into how cool it felt sleeping with someone as hot and sexy as V. That was your big conquest and you kept going back for more."

"Shoot the damn ball," Max said, frowning.

Roger took a few steps and swung up a fifteen-foot hook shot that hit the backboard and dropped through the net. Then he tossed the ball crisply to Max. "I know I should have stayed away. But you were looking for the right relationship, and Veronica wasn't it. I know it sounds bad, but maybe I *was* doing you a favor."

Max gave him an icy look as Roger continued. "It was the same with Peacock. You weren't on your game, and with Layla's budget at risk, you were leaving money on the table. I thought that with all your problems, you'd need time to come up with the right campaign. So, if she shifted more of her cash to *Plates*, I could keep things on track."

"You've turned rationalizing asshole behavior into an art form."

"Did you want Layla spending her money somewhere else—like with Veronica?"

Max grimaced as he shot the ball. It missed badly, hitting the top of the backboard and bouncing to the side of the court.

"She was after Layla's budget, too," Roger said. "That's O-U, by the way."

"Stop covering your ass."

"Dude, I busted her leaving Peacock's offices," Roger said. "She offered to cut me in on her deal. I know I was wrong about a lot of things—and I'm sorry—but you have to believe me."

Max looked at him impassively. "I'm not surprised," Max said. "Veronica and I were done, so she was doing her thing. That's what she does. But what's this about you *changing*, and why now? Like everything else with you, it's way too convenient."

"I think losing my job and having time to rehash all of the shitty things I've done got me thinking," Roger said, holding the ball. "And, I met a woman."

Max rolled his eyes.

"Yep, you pointed her out to me . . . online. Serena de los Reyes."

"I don't believe it," Max said, laughing. "Which one of your dual personalities did she meet? And what happened to your legions of wanton women?"

"I deleted them."

"Roger, don't screw with Serena," Max said.

"I really dig her."

"Why should I believe you?" Max asked.

"I know I always wanted to get laid before moving on," Roger said. "But when I met Serena, everything changed. She wants more from me, and now I understand why. I'm learning, and things *are* different now, and it's good. Really good."

Max bounced the ball away from Roger's grasp and gazed warily at him. This was sounding like a bad episode of Dr. Phil. *What's next? Is he going to chest-bump me and tell me that I'm the man?*

"And maybe I learned a few things from you, too," Roger said.

Max gave him a dubious look. "Like how not to be a jerk?"

"What I'm saying is that you're a great guy, but now you're *trying* to be someone else."

"Think I can't handle the women?" Max said, throwing the ball back to him with two hands.

"That's not what I said, but you're not this stone-cold swordsman that your alter ego wants to be. It's not you," Roger said with a shrug. "But . . . you've got this hot shit column. Maybe you should read the articles again. And maybe there's a woman who's had your back, but because you're so busy chasing tail right now, you probably hadn't noticed."

Roger dribbled the ball between his legs again before taking his T-shirt off, revealing his old school jersey. Max leaned back and laughed. The release felt good. Debating Roger was no fun. He was slipperier than a guest on *Hardball.*

Roger turned around, facing his body away from the basket. He set himself, leaned back, and took aim before flipping the ball with both hands over his head and through the net.

"Your turn," he said, tossing the ball gingerly to Max.

"I can't believe you still have that jersey."

"Listen, *amigo,* I know you're the big stud now, but I don't want to see you make the same mistakes as me. You need a woman who can give you what I've got now."

"I'll get right on it," Max said, as he set up to match Roger's over-the-head shot. "But if you want me to take you seriously, tell me something I don't know."

"I turned down your job . . . at Hammerhead," Roger said as Max flipped the ball over his head toward the hoop.

It hit the rim squarely and bounced off the court. "What?" Max snapped.

"You don't know everything, dude," Roger said, retrieving the ball. "Yeah, I interviewed with Kent-fucking-Gloss. He wants to replace you, but I told him no thanks. Now I'm collecting unemployment and taking shit from you."

Max stood frozen. He had no comeback.

"And," Roger continued, pointing to his face, "my black eye looks better than yours."

"Oh yeah? Which one?" Max countered.

"Listen, while you're out there shooting your stuff, there's another one of those S's you should know," Roger said, bouncing the ball hard now.

Max looked at him blankly. "Yeah?"

"*Score,* buddy. Gotta know the *score.*" Roger flipped the ball through the basket again and sauntered off the court bouncing his ball. "By the way, you owe me twenty bucks."

CHAPTER 53

"**A**ren't you going to introduce me to him?" Max's date asked from across the table.

He sighed. She was gorgeous. A dark-skinned Latina from Queens, all of twenty-two, and she was the newly crowned Ms. Ring Card Girl at one of the boxing websites. Despite her amazingly fit body and curves in all the right places, at five-feet-one with a multicolored tattoo adorning her lower back, the young lady's future in modeling beyond motorcycle and booty magazines was limited. She needed the right contacts and a few favors. Although her amazingly round silicone breasts were pushing out of a barely there tank top, Max was still distracted by Roger's ambush on the basketball court.

"I haven't met Howard yet, but if I do, I'll mention you," he said.

"I thought you were on his show?" she asked, shaking her streaked hair off her face.

"Not yet. How do you know so much about my schedule?"

"Max, we have the same agent. He tells me everything, and I've only got a small window to make it. Do you know how many pretty girls out there are trying to do exactly the same thing as me?"

"You're young, smart, and beautiful. You have nothing to worry about."

"Thanks, but I need exposure."

Max cleared his throat. "If I can get you on his show, are you going to strip and tell him you've had sex with a woman?"

"I will and I have. So what? I make my living with this body, and I work my ass off making it look good," she said. She traced the pointed tip of her boot up Max's leg and said, "Doncha' think?"

Max nodded.

"So, are you going to help me?"

"Of course," he said.

"Good." She stood up and checked her diamond watch shaped like a boxing ring. She straightened her pleated leather mini skirt, shook out her hair, and then leaned over and rested her hand on Max's thigh.

"I'll freshen up. Wanna go back to your place?" she asked, brushing her fingers over his crotch.

"Check, please."

The sex was vigorous, maybe a bit too much so. Max's lower back ached after it was over. When the young woman asked him to spank her, he laughed. After she brought it up a third time, Max obliged. He play-acted, verbally admonishing her and splaying an open hand across her full buttocks until they turned an angry red. Each time she pleaded for more, he slapped her ass harder. He found himself grinning as he play-punished her for being a naughty, naughty girl.

While making love, his thrusts became so intense he thought he'd break her. But her thighs were firm and her spirit strong. If anyone was in danger of buckling under, it was Max. While he sweated and breathed heavily, she stayed up on all fours, displaying herself to him like a prize. She begged him to hit it hard and fast, and when he did, she told him to take off his condom and ejaculate across the winged tattoo spread along her lower back.

After a shuddering orgasm, Max laid face up, empty, exhausted, and feeling dirty. He enjoyed getting off, but the aftermath was no longer fun. He was having trouble compartmentalizing all of the sex and realized that he wasn't cut out for this lifestyle. As soon as the young woman left his apartment, Max yanked the soiled sheets off his bed.

After a long shower, Max pedaled his bike downtown, swerving through traffic to catch the lights. Visiting hours were almost over at the hospital. Upon entering Henry's room, Max saw the older man sitting up in bed, watching a baseball game. Although his face was pallid, Max saw clarity in his eyes. After exchanging pleasantries, Max spoke frankly to his former boss.

"I want to come back," he said bluntly.

Henry's eyebrow ticked upward. Max observed him switch into his business countenance. "I don't think that's a good idea, son."

Max looked down and pursed his lips. "I'm sorry about what happened. I had to make a call and I couldn't . . ."

"I know, but please, don't bullshit me," Henry said. "You didn't have a choice. That doesn't mean I wasn't pissed off when I read about it." Henry coolly eyeballed Max. "And it doesn't mean I'm going to sit back and let my largest account walk out the door."

Max said nothing, letting Henry vent. He'd come around if he planned on keeping Bobalooie. After a brief staring contest, Max said, "I know you're upset, but this is your business . . . and I can help. Remember when you said that the most important thing in the ad game is building relationships?"

"Of course," Henry said. Then, with a hint of a smile, he added, "So, you have a plan?"

"I do."

"That's good. Let's hear it."

Fifteen minutes later, Henry exhaled and looked around the room. He rubbed his goatee and said, "For now, I can only pay what you were earning before you left."

"It's not about the money."

"Who are you kidding?" Henry said. "And just so we're clear, if this *doesn't* work out, I won't be able to afford you."

"No problem," Max said. Then he nodded to the television. "Want the sound back on?"

"Why not?" Henry said, crinkling his eyes. "I'm sure Cassidy will be happy that there's no need for her to leave her job. I wouldn't have let her come back anyway, but you know how determined my daughter gets when she wants something."

"I know. If it's okay, Henry, I'd like to keep this just between us . . . for now," Max said.

Henry nodded. "I understand. You take care. I'll be out of here soon."

On the way back to his apartment, Max pedaled across town and turned onto the bike path along the Hudson. He stopped next to Chelsea Piers and stared across the water toward New Jersey. For the first time all summer, he felt good about himself. When he reached his building, he locked his bike in its storage slot and then scooted up the stairs. There was something else he needed to do. He booted up his computer, took a deep breath, and began typing.

The next morning, Max arrived at the office at six twenty. He threw his bag down and rode the elevator to Kent Gloss's floor.

"Holiday?" Gloss said, squinting his eyes when he saw Max in his doorway. "I'm surprised you're actually awake at this hour. Are you here to tell me that you've got things organized for the pitch? Frankly, I'm still not convinced you're the right man for this. Don't take it personally, mate."

"I don't."

"Anyway Holiday, I reckon we could use a little showbiz to liven up the presentation and I . . ."

"Kent . . ."

"Balls, Holiday! What is it now?"

"I quit."

"Nice one. What do you want?"

"I'm giving you my notice," Max said, matter-of-factly.

Gloss's neck turned a burning red. Spittle flew from his paper-thin lips as he blurted, "What the fuck do you think you're doing, Hol-i-day?"

"Going back to Goodson," Max said, plucking the British general off Gloss's display of antique soldiers.

"Are you mad?" Gloss roared. "Holiday, you just made a very big mistake. Now, put that down and get the hell out of my office." He picked up the phone. "You're history."

"See you at the pitch. And by the way, it's Hallyday . . . *mate*. Maybe you'll remember that when you read it in *Ad Snoop*." He flipped the small figurine in the air and caught it, placing it facedown on the miniature battlefield before walking out.

After e-mailing his resignation, Max quietly packed his belongings and bid a few coworkers goodbye as they made their way into the office. Gloss had already contacted HR to make sure Max wouldn't stay the customary two weeks. *Perfect*, Max thought. No more e-mails, then, either. At ten o'clock, he walked out of Hornsby Hammerhead smiling and trying not to hum that dopey song from *Working Girl*.

The following day Max moved back into his old office at Goodson. An art director working on the Bobalooie account greeted him with, "Man, you really *are* crazy."

"Why's that?"

"You left HHI to come back *here*? Didn't they tell you—the pitch is next week?"

"Yeah, but I have faith in your creative talents," Max said. "We'll be fine."

Max phoned Scooter, his former Bobalooie client, to inform him about his returning to Goodson, but his call went directly to voice mail. A few hours later, he called again with the same result. Max turned his chair toward the window, wondering.

That afternoon, he met the creative teams in the conference room for the first of a marathon of meetings leading up to the pitch. This meant spending August's glorious last weekend indoors, ironing out the details of the agency's presentation.

Over the next six days, Max was up at five thirty and in the office by seven. Each day he tried reaching Scooter by phone or e-mail, but there was still no reply. After a few more attempts, Max finally spoke with a secretary, but she was vague about the whereabouts of his former client or when he was due back in the office. Max weighed the possibilities and then sent one last e-mail stating that he was looking forward to seeing Scooter at the pitch.

On the eve of the presentation, Max worked quietly in his office, jotting notes on the hard copy of his presentation. It was almost midnight. Max had kept Henry posted on the presentation by phone, but he still hadn't returned to the agency. And Cassidy was ignoring Max's calls. He'd finished another column and typed a quick note to her. Then he stared at the screen for a long moment before hitting "send."

He was feeling wound up and anxious, until finally a quiet settled over him. Returning to Goodson had been his decision. No guilt about the past. No worries about the future. It was time to step up and lead the agency into battle. This was his chance.

He checked his e-mail one last time. There was a message in his inbox from Scooter's assistant, informing Max that he'd left the company. For an ad agency hanging onto its lead account by a thread, changes in key client personnel were a bad omen. New management usually meant choosing a new agency. Max pounded his fist on his desk. He cursed as he reread the note and decided not to tell Henry. There was nothing he could do anyway. This was on Max's watch, so he'd deal with the new client in the morning.

Following a restless night, Max was behind his desk again by seven. After a final run-through, Max and the creative team took a car service to Bobalooie's offices to set up for their presentation. At nine o'clock sharp, the clients filed into the room. Max searched the group for new faces, quickly picking out a woman who he thought to be the new contact. She looked vaguely familiar. Max approached her, and as they shook hands, she introduced herself as the new VP of Marketing.

After exchanging business cards, she asked, "Where's Henry Goodson?"

Max smiled and informed her that Henry was still recovering, but sent his best. As soon as everyone was seated, Max stood in front of the group and began his introductory remarks. After an overview of the business, the creative strategy, and the current advertising, Max introduced his creative director. He studied the new client as the campaigns were presented. She remained predictably poker-faced throughout the meeting, occasionally scribbling a few notes. The final ad campaign featured kids blowing bubbles that transported them across the galaxy. This time she smiled.

From Max's perspective, the presentation and creative ideas were on target, but he wasn't sure it would be enough to keep the account. Scooter's enthusiasm and support were missed, and Max knew that decisions about choosing an agency often came down to chemistry or prior relationships. Following a brief Q&A session, the new client told Max they would make their decision by the end of the week.

Outside in the foyer, Kent Gloss and HHI's twelve-person team had mobilized. The contingent included a trio of little people dressed in colorful, matching attire. They break-danced, spun rhymes, and blew bubbles, delighting everyone passing through the lobby.

Max tried slipping by unnoticed, but Gloss spotted him. "Holiday! Oh, *Holiday!* How'd it go up there?"

Max turned. "Hello, Kent," he said evenly. "The client made a point about despising rap music."

"It's hip-hop, mate," Gloss corrected. "So where's Goodson?"

"Too busy for this sideshow," Max replied.

"That so?" Gloss sneered.

Max's eyes locked onto Gloss's. The two men stared defiantly at each other, neither wanting to blink first.

"I'm going to bury you, mate," Gloss said. "I'm your undertaker."

Max smiled. "Undertakers don't bury people, Kent. They stand around watching other people do their dirty work," he said, before turning and walking away.

While his creative team traded jibes in the backseat, Max remained somber during the ride back to the agency. The first thing he did was conduct an online search of the new Bobalooie client. He frowned when he found an article about her in a trade publication. It was from two years ago, announcing her promotion at a rival agency. Kent Gloss had been her boss.

Exhausted after a long week's work, Max dropped into his office chair and emptied his mind, believing an idea would come to him. *What would the Dalai Lama do?* he thought cynically. Then a twisted smile formed on his face. He looked up the number for *Ad Snoop* and then reached across his desk and grabbed a handful of tissues. He rolled his eyes for doing such a dumb detective show thing, but held them over the receiver anyway and then dialed the publication's news desk.

"I'm calling from Kent Gloss's office," he said

"Oh—do you want Mr. Crimmins?"

"Mr. Crimmins?" Max asked himself aloud.

"Yes, our bureau chief?"

"Crimmins, of course—what was I thinking? No, that won't be necessary. Mr. Gloss isn't available right now, but he said it was very important that *Mr. Crimmins* knew that the Bobalooie pitch went extremely well, and it looks like the client is going to award the business to HHI."

"Well, congratulations. Are you sure you don't want me to put you through?"

"No, no. Just give him the message, and . . . there's one more thing," Max said through the Kleenex.

"Oh?"

"Did you ever secure those tickets Mr. Gloss requested for the Dalai Lama benefit?"

"Let me check . . . Yes, we have them here—and they're in the first row! Would you like me to messenger them over?"

"Oh no, that won't be necessary, either. Mr. Gloss has had a change of heart. As a tribute to *His Holiness*, he's requested that you find someone deserving to give his tickets away to—what did he call them? Ah yes, the *little* people—someone in the mail room or the typing pool."

"Typing pool?"

"Well, maybe one of the janitors. Mr. Gloss is very insistent."

"Are you sure?"

"Absolutely. He feels very strongly about this."

'That's very admirable of him."

"Yes, but of course this has to be done anonymously. You understand."

"I'll take care of it personally."

"God bless you."

Then Max leaned back in his chair, and like sinking the game-winning basket, balled up the tissues and tossed them in a Roger-like jump shot into the trash.

When Max arrived at work the next morning, Henry Goodson was seated behind his desk, reviewing a stack of mail.

"Welcome back," Max said. "How did it go?"

Henry looked up at him over his reading glasses. "Fine."

"Great. We gave it our best shot at the pitch."

"I know," Henry said. "I'll call the all-hands meeting."

"Okay," Max said. "Do you want me to fill you in on the pitch?"

Henry waved Max off. He put his head down and returned to his paperwork. Once back in his office, Max slid behind his desk and checked his voice mail. Scooter had called again, this time leaving a number. Max made a wry face and said, "Gee, thanks." When he clicked open the online edition of *Ad Snoop*, the headline screamed, "HHI Blows Up For Bobalooie." Max folded his hands behind his head and smiled.

CHAPTER 54

"There's a new column from Rod in there," Cassidy said to her assistant. "Why don't you take a look while I get organized?"

The doe-eyed young woman balanced a cardboard tray holding two skim lattes as Cassidy perused her e-mail and printed out the correspondence requiring immediate action. After safely maneuvering the coffees onto the table adjacent to Cassidy's desk, the young woman collected the copies spitting out of the printer.

Cassidy was dressed down for casual Friday in a pair of vintage jeans, sling backs, and a desert rose cotton blouse. She was looking forward to leaving the office early and driving down the shore with Serena for Labor Day weekend.

Seeing the uncomfortable look on her assistant's face, Cassidy said, "What's wrong? You don't like the column?"

The young woman picked her head up, but said nothing.

"What?" Cassidy asked.

The assistant handed her the pages. "You need to read this."

Cassidy took a long sip of coffee and began.

INSIDE JOB

You never seem to know when something special is going to end. And this column marks an ending of sorts, because this is my last one. I hope that it will also mark a much richer beginning for all you wonderful readers, and for me, too.

I've spent the past few months filling you in on the wily ways of the men in New York. I've tried to focus on the guys who take advantage of your bodies, minds, and hearts. These men have proven themselves unworthy of your affections and representative of a weaker sex. Let's face it: men are afraid. We're not strong the way you need to be every day of your life. We don't have to deal with makeup, $400 visits to the hair salon, $600 shoes, less pay for equal work, having our bodies compared to strip club dancers after they've been lasered and waxed and starved . . . and that's just the beginning. And there are a helluva lot more available women out there than men. Truth is, it's never been a level playing field, and men get off easy. But you love us anyway and believe we can change. It's so unfair. We should worship you.

But sometimes the finer points in life can be boiled down to different perspectives. I recently read that more than thirty percent of women believed that if their dog were a man, he'd make a great boyfriend. When I asked a female friend how this could be possible, she explained that a dog would always be happy and affectionate when he sees you, and will always give you his unconditional love. When I mentioned this same statistic to a guy, he wondered aloud if the new criteria for dating a woman included sleeping curled up on the corner of the bed and getting his belly scratched, because that's about as far as the physical stuff goes. The same article states that more than a third of men ranked "always being in a good mood" as the number one quality they seek in a woman. You're probably thinking, what's the point? Well, once again, it seems like men and women see their worlds very differently. And that's why communicating and listening to one another is so important.

So what did I learn about myself during my research of the urban male womanizer for this column? For one thing, no matter how insensitive their behavior is, these men aren't trying to hurt you on purpose. They're desperate, and usually unhappy. I'm not suggesting that you give them a pass and forgive them unconditionally for their heartless indiscretions. No—I only suggest that you try to understand that men are driven by their egos. But if you show them how to share love, you'll enrich their lives and maybe build that special relationship that we all seek.

I hope I've provided a few tips that can help you protect yourself while you're steering your relationship in the right direction. I've told you how men live, eat, drink, lie, and get off. Now it's up to you to change the world. What makes me so sure about this? Because over the course of writing and being recognized for this column, I started behaving like the men I was reporting on, like an undercover cop that falls under the spell of the drug gang he's been sent to infiltrate. I slid onto a sexual carousel with a surprising number of willing women who enabled my bad behavior. And like the men I was studying, I eventually found myself barren inside. This wasn't the real me.

Now, I'm neither envious nor judgmental of these guys. And that's the point. For men and women to come together, we need to pay attention and do our best to understand our differences. I'm not suggesting you let men get away with all the bad things they do, but if you can relate to the pain gnawing inside these men, you might see them differently. And surely you deserve something better. You deserve the best.

You're probably wondering what happened to me and why I've decided to bring this column to a close. It was simple. Living a lie led me to the truth. There's a woman who helped make my dreams come true. She's been there all along, but I was too caught up in my self-centered world to notice how wonderful she really is. She's strong and kind and she's never put me down,

THE GUYS' GUY'S GUIDE TO LOVE

even when I acted like a fool. She's never judged me and she always listened. She's my best friend and everything I need in a woman. Now I know better. The heart wants what it wants.

Ladies, I've done my best to share everything I know about men with you. And I was the one who got an education. Now it's my turn to learn how to handle the truth.

Farewell and good luck,

Rod

At the bottom of the page, Max had added, *Cassidy, we need to talk.*

Cassidy's face flushed and her heart raced. When she looked up, her assistant was gone.

Cassidy speed dialed Max. "I read your column."

"What column?" Max replied casually.

"Stop joking," she said. "What do you want to talk about? Are you still after my dad's business?"

"Cass, I should have said something."

"About what?"

"About quitting my job."

"*What?*"

"Two weeks ago. I'm back at Goodson."

"Why didn't you tell me?" she asked, softening her tone.

"I thought it would be better to keep it between me and your dad while I was working on the pitch," he said.

"You went back so I wouldn't have to leave the magazine, didn't you?"

"Of course not. I . . ."

"You did," she said. "And you did it for my father . . . thank you."

"There's something else—in the trades about Bobalooie."

"What happened? Is my dad there?"

"He's here, and he's called an all-hands meeting for one o'clock. Why don't you come down? We're having food and drinks before the long weekend . . . and a few announcements."

Cassidy checked her watch. "Serena's coming over. She's driving us to the shore. I guess we can stop by," she said. "Can't you just tell me what happened?"

"Why don't you do the driving, and maybe read my column again," Max said with a laugh. "Aren't you upset that I won't be writing for you anymore?"

"Let's talk about that later."

After hanging up, Cassidy typed an e-mail to Brenton Banks. She kept it light and to the point. Before she hit send, she read it a second time and then deleted it. *He deserves better. He's a good man and so good looking.*

She picked up the phone.

"Cassidy, great to hear from you. Guess what? We just closed that deal. Six months of haggling and nitpicking are finally over. I can finally take a break and move on to something else. I think I'm taking Jimmy to St. Barth."

"Sounds great, Brenton. Congratulations," she said, knowing she sounded perfunctory.

"Thanks . . . you okay? We still on for dinner next week?"

She made a wistful face and said, "That's why I'm calling."

Banks took it like a man, just as Cassidy expected. After she hung up, she thought about his soft kisses and imagined what he would look like naked—in his ten-million-dollar apartment. Max had better keep bringing his A-game.

Roger was stretched out on the couch with his legs propped up on the coffee table, wearing a ratty pair of camo boxers, his faded Yankees cap, and a three-day stubble. The Friday before Labor Day wasn't the best day to look for a job, so he flicked on the television and flipped channels before staring at an *Oprah* rerun. The phone rang and he heard a familiar voice on the line.

"What are you doing at home? It's fucking beautiful outside."

"Max?"

"Is that *Oprah* I hear in the background?"

"Hell no," Roger said, turning the television off and flinging the remote across the couch. "What inspired you to call? Looking for a rematch? I'll just throw old number twenty-two back on and pop open another can of whoop ass."

"I have a job lead for you."

Roger pushed himself up. "Yeah?"

"Oh yeah," Max said. "We're having an all-hands meeting down here at Goodson at one o'clock. Why don't you stop by and I'll fill you in? After *Oprah*, of course."

Roger scoffed. "Did you say Goodson? What the hell are you talking about?"

"Oh—I forgot to tell you. I'm done with HHI."

"What?"

"Listen, I'm slammed right now, but get down here. I promise it'll be worth the trip."

"If this is another recon mission for that damn column, forget it."

"And if you want a ride down the shore—bring your stuff." Max laughed. "I almost forgot; there's one more thing. Another one of those S's."

"*Shit.*"

"Far from it. This could make you a *star*."

CHAPTER 55

"No problem. I picked up a new radar detector," Serena said, walking alongside Cassidy into a coffee shop on Montague Street to buy bottles of water.

"You've already gotten two tickets this summer," Cassidy said. Then she froze.

Veronica was the last person they expected to see staring out the window of a booth, with her hair bunched on top of her head. She was dressed down in a baggy T-shirt and gym shorts and wasn't wearing makeup. In front of her was a plate anchored by two scoops of tuna salad on iceberg lettuce and a pot of tea.

Serena nudged Cassidy and said under her breath, "*Mira* . . . she looks like shit—for her at least."

"Two bottles of water—and this," Cassidy told the cashier when Serena handed her a dark chocolate bar. Cassidy handed over the cash and craned her neck to check if what Serena had told her was true. "That can't be her," she said. "She lives on the Upper East Side."

"I'm telling you, it's her," Serena insisted. "God, all she needs is a scrunchie. Look, she's got a yoga mat. I'll bet she took a class next door, although I can't imagine why. That place sucks. What's she doing in Brooklyn?"

"Let's go," Cassidy said, tucking her change into her jeans.

"No. I want to see," Serena said, taking off down the aisle. Cassidy shook her head and followed. Veronica looked up, and then quickly turned away. It was too late. The two women were already standing at her booth.

Veronica looked at them warily. "Hi. What are you guys doing here?"

"We live here. What are you doing here?" Serena said.

Cassidy forced a tentative smile and motioned her head to Veronica's workout bag and rolled up mat. "Hello, Veronica. You come all the way to Brooklyn for yoga class?"

Veronica's eyes lacked her usual fire and there were hints of fine lines at the corners of her mouth. Something had happened to this girl.

"This place is known for its tuna platter," Serena said, looking down at her untouched plate.

Cassidy poked her with an elbow. "I thought you hung out in Manhattan."

"Actually, I live here now—right down the street, off Joralemon."

"What happened? You gave up the glorious Upper East Side?" Serena asked.

Veronica paused and said, "I lost my job and wanted a change. You know how it is," she added, staring at Serena.

"Oh . . . right," Serena said.

"That's too bad," Cassidy said.

Veronica touched her hair. "Globison let me go after selling the company. With this economy there's not much going on right now, but I have a few options," she said. "Maybe I'll try something new. Anyway, I'm renting in a brownstone. It's okay. I like the neighborhood, although I really don't know anyone. So how about you guys?"

"We live in the hood," Serena said.

"But we're going down the shore for the weekend," Cassidy chimed in.

"Really?" Veronica said. "My aunt lives in Spring Lake Heights. She's always telling me to forget the Hamptons and come visit her."

"The Hamptons, right. Manhattan Beach," Serena said. "The shore's more laid-back."

"But we like it," Cassidy chimed in. "It's all part of the same ocean."

Veronica fiddled with the plastic wrapper on a package of Saltines.

"Um, forgot something. Be right back," Cassidy said, guiding Serena toward the ladies room.

"What?" Serena protested while being shuttled ahead.

Once inside the ladies room, Cassidy said, "I know this sounds crazy, but it's a long weekend and—"

"You *are* crazy," Serena said. "That bitch isn't coming with us. And since when are you so forgiving of *Victoria*?" Serena asked.

"It's the new me," Cassidy said. "What's the big deal? Life's too short and she's a whipped pony."

"I really taught you well," Serena said, shaking her head and then smiling. "She did sound like she was telling the truth . . . but if she comes anywhere near Roger, I'm kicking her *puta* ass."

Cassidy gave her an oh-come-on-now look and Serena said, "All right, what the hell?"

When they returned, Cassidy mentioned the surfing contest.

Veronica's eyes lit up. "Sounds like fun. Maybe I'll take the train down to my aunt's on Sunday. It would be nice to get away." Then she smiled at the two of them and said, "Thanks."

CHAPTER 56

"**N**ice work, son," Henry said, pulling up a chair. "You had me worried, but you came through."

Max thanked him and took a seat on the couch.

"We'll send your announcement and a photo out to *Ad Snoop* today," Henry said. "I'm sure your buddy Gloss will enjoy them."

"Thanks, Henry," Max smiled. "Uh, there's one more thing. I'll need the right team to manage the accounts."

"That can be your first decision. You have anyone in mind?"

"I'd like to hire Roger."

"Fox?"

"Yes."

"Hmm . . . Fox? Well, he's sharp and he's got the personality," Henry said, stroking his goatee, "but he's a piece of work. You think he's the right fit?"

"He's coming into his own. It's okay. I'll keep an eye on him."

"Well, I did agree to let you manage things your way . . . but this one's on your watch," Henry said.

"I won't let you down," Max said, shaking his mentor's hand.

"I know," Henry said, with the old spark glinting in his eyes. "Now get out of here. I've got to prepare my little speech."

The eighty-person staff assembled on the roof under clear September skies. Henry Goodson emerged from the doorway in a navy blazer, carrying faded newspapers under his arm. He walked to the center of the patio, motioned Max to his side, and faced his people with a warm smile and a commanding presence.

"Hello, everyone," he began, as the nervous chatter quieted down. "It looks like a glorious weekend, so let's get right to why we're here. This truly is a fine group of individuals, and I'm proud to have the privilege of working alongside all of you. You've done a fantastic job protecting our most important account. A special thank-you goes out to Max and his team for all their hard work." Then he unfolded one of the newspapers and held it up for everyone to see.

"It says, 'Dewey Wins!' and although none of you were around then, Harry Truman was elected president that year." He unfolded another paper and pointed to the front page. "Here's one you might recognize: 'Gore Wins Presidency.' " Henry looked around. The murmurings were followed by quiet.

"The point is, sometimes conclusions are made after only part of the story's been told. There's one more I'd like to show you. It's hot off the presses from this morning's ad column. It says, 'Hornsby Hammerhead Wins Bobalooie Account Following a Decade at Goodson.' See what I mean?"

Looking into the puzzled faces, he continued. "Let me tell you what's going on. First of all, I just received a call from our friends at Bobalooie. They are still reviewing the creative work that the competing agencies presented, and they were quite upset after reading today's headlines. They believe the press leak came from someone at HHI."

Max smiled as he looked out across a beckoning New York City skyline.

"But more important," Henry said, clearing his throat, "earlier today, I attended a meeting with the Board of Directors of Tooka Wooka Confectionery. For the past few months, Tooka Wooka has been in talks to purchase Bobalooie Bubble Gum. That deal was finalized this morning. What did I know about Tooka Wooka? Not enough. But then Max Hallyday came to see me a few weeks ago, offering an introduction to Brenton Banks, their lead counsel and investor. It's a long story, but Max had developed a relationship with Mr. Banks. We all met several times. Mr. Banks was impressed with Max and our agency's work so we discussed the potential of our playing a key role with his newly merged organization. And today I'm delighted to announce that Tooka Wooka has appointed Goodson their agency of record. That's for their entire portfolio of brands—including Bobalooie. HHI is out. In fact, they were never in. Nice work, Max, and congratulations to everyone."

Roger let out a hoot and grabbed Serena, who was standing between him and Cassidy. Cheers emanated across the rooftop and Goodson's staff buzzed about the changes. Max turned, his eyes locking on Cassidy. Then Roger pushed through the crowd, raising his hand and slapping Max a high five. When things quieted down, Henry waved and called for everyone's attention.

"There's one more thing," Henry said, surveying the scene. "I've decided to take a little time off to figure out what I want to do with the rest of my life. I'll stay involved with the agency—that is, when the trout aren't jumping upstate—but I'll no longer direct our day-to-day operations. I've offered that role to someone who's proven that he can lead. So, I'm pleased to announce Max Hallyday as the new President of Goodson Advertising."

Max grinned and walked toward Henry, pulling his shoulders back and soaking up the applause. Henry put his hand on Max's shoulder and looked on him proudly before turning back to the cheering crowd. He told everyone they could leave whenever they wanted to get a jump on the weekend. As if on cue, the music came on. After greeting and thanking everyone, Henry and Max walked together across the rooftop.

Max bounded down the stairs to his office and checked his messages. Scooter had called again, urging Max to contact him immediately. Max checked the time and picked up the phone.

"Max? That you buddy?"

"We missed you at the pitch," Max said.

"Sorry about that. I just read about the decision in the trades."

"We'll bounce back somehow," Max said, rolling his eyes. "So what happened with you?"

"Long story," Scooter began. "I wasn't crazy about those guys at HHI. Especially that creep Gloss. After you left the agency, he called me."

Max pushed back in his chair, now listening closely to his former client.

"It's funny. He invites me to a round of golf at Winged Foot. Of course I said yes—couldn't pass that up. Anyway, we're out there and I'm shooting a decent round, but the entire time Gloss keeps trashing you and Goodson. When we stopped at the turn for a sandwich, I couldn't listen anymore so I figured that would be a good time to tell him that I was leaving Bobalooie."

"I'll bet he loved hearing that," Max said.

"Oh, he was thrilled. So immediately he whips out his BlackBerry and then says he needs to get back to the city for a meeting. Before I could even tell him about my new job, he's driving the cart off the course. What an a-hole."

"So where did you . . . ?"

"I just started my new gig. That's why I called. We're in the market for a new agency and I thought you guys could use the business."

"*Scooter,*" Max said, now in his friendly voice. "You still haven't told me where you're working."

"You're familiar with Peacock Beverages. I'm replacing Layla Korindopolos."

Max leaned forward. "You're kidding."

"I know you managed Peacock at HHI. That's why I'm calling. I thought you'd like to see the account at Goodson. Interested?"

"Count me in," Max said, laughing. Then, thinking about it, he changed into his serious business voice and asked, "Scooter, what kind of budget are we talking about? I'm sure there's been some talk about the brand going entirely digital."

"Oh yeah. I saw some of the proposals. In fact, my predecessor had signed off on a huge online advertising deal." Max gulped as Scooter continued. "But then I read that proposal you sent in that had a nice blend of online and offline ideas. Nice job. So I killed the deal. You're right. This is booze, so initially we need to build an image for the brand and do lots of sampling. Then we can do a deep dive into digital and social media. So that's another three million we can put back into your budget. Provided you're interested. What do you think?"

Max cleared his throat. *"Absolutely!* Why don't I come by next week?" he asked, sliding open his desk drawer and pulling out the folder marked "Peacock Beverage Artist's Campaign." He stared down at the storyboards. "Maybe I'll bring along an idea for you."

"You can have something that quickly?"

"You know that I always make things happen for my favorite client," Max said.

"Hey, Max, one more thing," Scooter said. "That name, *Holy Spiritz*. I'm not sold on it. It might create problems. Think you guys can come up with something else?"

"Damn right we can," Max said. "Congrats on the new job."

After the call, Max drummed his pencil on his desktop, mentally ticking off what else he needed to do before leaving for the weekend. First, he dashed off an e-mail to Brenton Banks, thanking him for his support and for the opportunity to manage his business. He sent his best regards to Jimmy, and informed Banks that he and his son would be receiving tickets for a number of Yankees games during the post-season. Then he rubbed his hands together and typed an e-mail to Kent Gloss.

Kent:

While awaiting the decision on the Bobalooie pitch, I wanted to wish you and the agency good luck. But then I read that HHI has been awarded the account. My heartiest congratulations on a hard-fought battle. You've consistently demonstrated that special quality—almost visionary—of knowing what's going to happen in our business before it occurs. Bobalooie's a great account, and I'm sure you'd agree that they deserve the best agency.

Good luck,

Max Hal-ly-day

Max grinned and hit "send." When he looked up, Roger was standing in the doorway.

"Hey man, nice going," Roger said.

"Come on in . . . and grab the door."

Max spent the next few minutes telling Roger about the call from

Peacock, and how he envisioned the new Tooka Wooka account fitting into the agency, stressing how important it was to have someone managing it that he could trust.

"I could use some help," Max said. "Sound interesting to you?"

"You want me to manage Peacock Beverages?" Roger asked.

"Nah. I'll get someone else for that," Max said. "I was thinking that you could manage Tooka Wooka. It's the biggest account in the agency."

"Candy?"

"You told me how you're such a sweet guy now. That is, unless you'd rather take my old job at HHI."

"No way. This sounds great."

"Roger, tell me I'm doing the right thing," Max said with a sobering look at his friend.

Roger held his gaze and then glanced away momentarily. He turned back to Max and said, "It's cool. You can trust me . . . really. Some men change. Right?"

Max studied Roger. "Evolve. I said evolve."

He stood up and extended his hand. "Gotta go find Cassidy."

Roger pumped his hand and gave a fist bump. "Glad to see you finally woke up, too."

Most of the crowd had dispersed by the time Max reemerged onto the open rooftop. Cassidy was catching up with one of the art directors when Max spotted her. He watched her quietly for a moment before she returned his gaze. She smiled as he walked toward her. The art director gave Cassidy a quick hug and then disappeared down the stairway.

"I'm glad you came," Max said when he reached her side.

"Me, too," she said. "You know, I'm really happy for you. So is my dad."

"Why don't we celebrate tomorrow night at the beach?"

She gave a sly smile. "Is that a good idea? I mean, now with you being made president of the agency and Rod's success, you've got a lot going on in your life."

"What?"

"You won, Max. You got what you wanted, and you did it your way. Isn't that enough?"

Max scuffed his foot on the roof's surface like a horse trying to count. "This is just the beginning. I haven't won anything, really. And the column was your idea."

She touched his arm. "You're going to have a lot of new responsibilities now. All of these people will be looking to you for leadership, for your guidance. Their careers are tied to you."

"If everyone pitches in and does their job, we'll be fine. As long as the creative is strong and strategic and we nurture our client relationships, we'll keep growing."

"You already sound like my father."

Max faced her and held her hands. "Remember when Alejandro won the limbo contest?"

"Of course. You were a hero."

He raised his eyebrows.

"And a drunk," she said.

He frowned. "The point is, you remember. And that night you said, someday, when it was my turn, I'd win the prize . . . and get the girl. Well, that's what I want."

She studied his eyes. "What are you saying?"

He smiled. "Remember my last column?"

She blushed a little and nodded.

"About the woman who was helping make my dreams come true? The one who never judged me and was always supportive?"

"Yes, but I'd like to hear more," she said, holding her breath.

"Well, she's beautiful inside and out, and she's the only one I want to be with."

"You really think that's a good idea?" she asked.

"I do," he responded. And he kissed her.

Cassidy kissed him back, and then softly stroked his cheek.

"Seriously?"

"Not another S word."

"What?"

"Sorry, nothing."

"Well, if you want things to change for us," she said, "I need to know that it's going to be the best it can be—right from the start."

"It will be. I promise."

She looked deeply into his eyes and slid her arms up around his neck. "You're not getting out of writing that column so easily."

"What does that mean?" he asked, holding back a smile.

"It means that it's over when I tell you it's over. Do you read me, Hol-i-day?" she said, pulling him toward her and kissing him again.

Max held her close, smiling over her shoulder at the rows of buildings cutting across the city skyline. "That sounds *way* too familiar."

EPILOGUE

The construction crew for the Jersey Shore Surfing Championships created a beehive of activity outside Max's loft. Max awoke before Cassidy and watched her sleeping peacefully, still feeling the passion from the previous night's lovemaking. He carefully removed her hand from his shoulder and crept out of bed.

The morning sun shone brightly and the sky was clear blue when Max looked down from his deck at the workers putting up a large plastic banner and dragging thick electronic wires from the national sports network van across the hot sand.

Max heard Cassidy call out, "Hey, what's going on out there?" and peeked back inside. She was sitting up with her hair tousled, holding a sheet over her breasts.

"Good morning," he said, leaning over and kissing her. "They're getting ready for the contest. I wonder if Alejandro knows how big a deal this is."

"Serena says he's been obsessive about training. He really wants to win."

"Of course."

Cassidy yawned. "When does it start?"

"At one."

"What time is it now?"

"Eight fifteen. You can go back to sleep, but try not to snore. They have an ordinance in town about powering up your lawnmower before nine," Max said as he lifted the sheet to peek at Cassidy.

"Shut up and come here," she said, reaching her arms around his neck. Max slipped out of his shorts and climbed under the sheets, snuggling close to her. Within minutes, they were making love again.

Alejandro carried his board down the wooden steps onto the beach, stopping to recite the Reiki Master credo: *"Just for today . . . I will let go of anger. I will let go of worry. I will act with kindness toward every living thing. I will earn my living honestly. I will give thanks for my many blessings."*

After applying a final coat of sex wax to his board, he pulled on his rubber top with REIKI stenciled across the back and chest. Then he dragged his surfboard into the ocean and paddled out to the deep waters.

There were twenty surfers competing in the finals. After a series of eliminations, today's contest featured the top qualifiers. While waiting for a practice wave, Alejandro recognized a familiar face in the water—the tattooed guy with blonde dreadlocks from the brawl at the limbo contest. He was skimming along on his board near the jetty. When he saw Alejandro, he pushed his long braids off his face and glared. Alejandro acknowledged him with a nod, but received a frozen look in return. He shook his head and then spotted Max, Cassidy, Serena, and Roger making their way across the beach.

Max unfolded his blanket and watched as the national cable and local news crews began filming their opening segments. The former pro surfer reporting the contest faced the camera and announced, "Here's how our scoring works. Points are awarded for the best five rides based on the size and difficulty of the waves and the skills demonstrated."

The participants were announced, and Max, Cassidy, and Serena groaned when they recognized the surfer with the dreadlocks. With a loud bang, the pistol sounded to kick off the event, and the crowd cheered. It was early September, so, as usual, the wind had picked up overnight, blowing directly offshore and rounding the waves into optimal contest condition. A man-made stone jetty was positioned on their right, providing even more opportunities for the surfers to drop the hammer on their rides.

Max and the crew cheered as Alejandro quickly piled up points on a series of explosive rides. When the scores were announced, he was among the leaders, along with a well-known competitor from Cape May and the tattooed guy, whose lack of skills were offset by his risky moves. Alejandro waved when the announcers playfully referred to him as the Reiki Master. His fluid display made him look like he was in command of the rolling seas, and soon he had the crowd on his side.

At three o'clock, the scores were tallied, eliminating all but three surfers. Alejandro was tied for the lead with the surfer from Cape May, followed by the tattooed guy, who remained within striking distance. Their final ride would determine the winner, and there were only fifteen minutes left in the competition.

Max watched Alejandro and the surfer from Cape May nod to each other while waiting for their last breaker. The tattooed surfer paddled nearby and spit in the water after witnessing the exchange. The crowd buzzed as the clock wound down. The three men searched the horizon for their final wave. Alejandro was the first to pick up an approaching series of swells and paddled furiously toward the jetty to catch the break.

Max raised his binoculars and watched the surfer from Cape May holding back as Alejandro made his move. But the tattooed guy closed in from behind, challenging him for the wave. As the barrel formed, Alejandro stood up, catching the crest of the wave as it slashed off the jetty's point break. The tattooed guy appeared out of his blind spot, forcing Alejandro to shift his course to avoid a collision. While cutting Alejandro off, the tattooed surfer's board shot out from under him, sending him thrashing toward the jetty. Alejandro dove in after the fallen competitor and emerged a few moments later with an arm wrapped around the blonde surfer. He pulled him along determinedly through the breakers and away from the jagged rocks.

He helped the surfer out of the water and they both fell onto the beach. The first-aid team quickly ran over. Alejandro turned when he heard the crowd cheering and watched as the contestant from Cape

May majestically rode a ten-foot swell toward the shore. The gun went off, ending the contest. Max, with Serena close behind him, was the first to arrive on the scene as Alejandro looked down at the stricken surfer coughing up seawater.

The surfer looked up, and, breathing heavily through his mouth, forced out, "Hey man, thanks. Sorry about that ride."

"No problem," Alejandro replied.

After the medical crew checked them over, Alejandro asked if he could share Reiki with the fallen surfer. The man nodded as Alejandro knelt down and placed his hands gently across his crown. Soon the press surrounded him and began peppering Alejandro with questions. He shook his head in an attempt to keep them at bay so he could do his work. By now, the others had arrived. Max stepped in and asked the reporters to give them space. Ten minutes later, Alejandro finished up the abbreviated Reiki session. The tattooed surfer slowly reached out and gently tapped his shoulder. He acknowledged him with his thumb up.

The next few minutes were spent with Alejandro responding to the reporters' questions about why he'd abandoned his chance of winning the contest, and about Reiki. The winning surfer from Cape May came by and put his arm around Alejandro before holding their hands up together to the cheering crowd.

Max patted Alejandro on the back. "I guess winning isn't everything."

Alejandro smiled, listening as the television reporters described Reiki for their audiences. He turned to Max. "That depends on how you define winning."

Max smiled back. *"Es verdad."*

Later that afternoon, Max stood on the deck with Roger and Alejandro. Cassidy and Serena had offered to pick up fresh fish for a celebratory dinner at their house. Max arranged three director's chairs in a semi-circle facing the ocean.

Roger toasted Alejandro with his iced yerba mate tea. "Hey man, you get props for saving that moron."

"He was my teacher; he taught me that this was just a contest."

Max raised his eyebrows, but had to smile.

"That's pretty deep, dude," Roger said. "I might have let him sink."

"You see, Alejandro, Roger's *evolving*. He's a work in progress. And maybe he needs a few more Reiki sessions," Max said. "Hey, let me ask you something. Roger, you've heard this, but let's hear what Alejandro has to say."

Roger waved his hands. "Oh, please. Not again."

"Just chill. Okay, here's the question. Is it better knowing when it's the last time you're making love to the most beautiful woman you've ever been with?"

Alejandro took a sip of tea, thoughtfully processing the question. He looked out at the ocean and listened to its roar. "You hear that?"

"It never stops," Max said. "Now tell me what you think."

"I have a story for you. It's an ancient Buddhist tale about the tiger and the strawberry," Alejandro began. "Then I want to return to the beach and catch one more wave.

"A young man is walking through a forest when he's confronted by a group of tigers. He realizes that if they catch him, the tigers will eat him. So he flees, and the largest tiger bolts after him, chasing him up a steep hill. The man runs as fast as he can. He sees a cliff up ahead and thinks that if he can only make it to the cliff, he can jump onto the path below that leads to the river where he'll be safe. He keeps running, but when he finally reaches the cliff, he looks down and sees a half dozen tigers waiting below.

"The young man realizes his life is over. He's overcome with anxiety and internally debates the best way to die. He stops next to a row of strawberry bushes. He bends down and picks the freshest, most beautiful strawberry he's seen in his entire life. While standing quietly, the ground rumbles as the tiger races toward him. He carefully admires the strawberry's bright red color and inhales its fragrant bouquet. Then he places the strawberry in his mouth and bites into a fruit so sweet and delicious, it's unlike anything he's tasted in his life. Although this is his final moment, he savors that strawberry and feels more alive than at any other time in his existence."

The three sat pensively before Roger broke their silence by chugging his iced tea. "Wow, I know how that dude felt. It's like I told you," Roger said to Max. "You only pick out the most delicious strawberries."

"And you've certainly sampled plenty," Max said.

"And I've been chased by quite a few tigers with French manicures," Roger countered.

Max chuckled and walked Alejandro to the door. "You did good out there. We'll be the judges for your final wave."

"Thanks, Max. Now I can't lose," he said, as Chili followed him down the stairs.

The beach was empty. Max and Roger watched Alejandro carry his surfboard across the sand. Chili curled up peacefully on his towel.

Roger looked at Max and hit him on the arm. "Hope you were listening."

"I thought you changed."

"Hey, just because you're going to be my boss now doesn't mean you can't learn a few more tricks," Roger said. "Remember, Uncle Roger always keeps a few up his sleeve. And don't tell me you understood that story."

"There's a difference between living in the moment and knowing what the moment means," Max said.

"Yeah, right," Roger said, leaning back in his chair. "Wow, those waves are sweet," he added, pointing to a series of breakers. He picked up Max's binoculars and scanned the shoreline. "Hey man . . . you're not going to believe this. Here—tell me if that's who I think it is."

Taking the glasses, Max focused in on a woman walking along the edge of the water. She was wearing a heather-gray hoodie over very short denim cut-offs that showed off a pair of impressively toned legs. Her lush blonde hair blew behind her as she glided up the beach.

"My God . . ." Max said.

"Lemme see," Roger said, snatching back the glasses. "Yep, that's Veronica. And she's stopping to watch our boy catch waves. And here comes Chili. Uh-oh. She's sitting down."

"You still want her? I mean, after she dumped you?" Max asked straight-faced.

Roger lowered the glasses. "Man, she still looks sinful. But, it's like I told you: I've moved on to higher ground." He raised the binoculars again. "And you, *amigo*?"

"I was able to walk away."

"Good boy. So, was it better knowing it was the last time?" Roger asked.

"The sex was awesome, but we weren't meant to be. Maybe Alejandro's right."

"Not sure about that. When it comes to women, he's clueless," Roger said, zooming in on Veronica's legs. "Man, this has the makings of a train wreck. I'm not sure if I can look away."

Max extended his hand and Roger gave him the binoculars. Max focused on Veronica as she watched Alejandro knife through the crest of a curl.

"I think our boy just caught that elusive wave," Max said. "You know, Rog, you still have a few things to learn."

"Tell me, brother."

"My column for instance," he said, returning the binoculars.

"What about it?" Roger asked, taking the glasses.

"Well, *amigo*, the bottom line is, there is no 'Guys' Guy's Guide to Love.'"

"Huh?"

"You heard me," Max said. "All these questions women have about men are all about them hoping that there's more to us than what they see. But there's no mystery. It's all a myth. What they see is what they get. But what guy would be crazy enough to tell them?"

"Yo, he'd need a set of balls," Roger said, laughing and turning to his friend.

"Face it," Max said. "Women are self-sufficient. They can do it all. And if men don't keep pace, they'll become commodities."

"Necessary evils—like Route 22 in North Jersey," Roger said.

"Yup. The truth is, women are the new men. And guess what? We'd be lost without them," Max said. "It's funny. All a guy wants is a woman who'll accept him for who he is—even if he still leaves the seat up occasionally. It's that simple."

"Makes you wonder why relationships get so damn complicated."

"You need to ask a woman that." Max chuckled.

Roger trained the binoculars back on Veronica and then at Alejandro, who had just finished his ride. He carried his surfboard toward the beach under the waning sunlight. Veronica was waiting for him with a welcoming smile.

"Whoa, dude," Roger said. "V's definitely back."

Veronica turned to face Alejandro. While he was toweling off his glowing body, she said something that made him laugh. He smoothed his wet hair and pitched his board upright in the sand. Chili sidled up to them and circled a few times. Finally, Veronica bent down and ran her hands through Chili's speckled fur. Then she looked up invitingly at Alejandro, who bent down and began stroking Chili's back.

"Poor sap doesn't stand a chance."

"Maybe. It's up to him, I guess," Max said, taking the binoculars and placing them on the railing. He turned toward Roger. "Hey, I almost forgot. There's another one of those S's."

Roger laughed lightly. "Jeez, let's see . . . super? No, no wait, how about . . . studly?"

"Nope."

"Strong?"

"You're still thinking like a guy."

"Hmm . . . spiritual?"

"Uh-uh."

"Serious?"

"Nah."

"Sincere, supportive, successful? How about . . . shocking?"

"You know, Roger, we all have our issues, but men and women aren't that different. We're searching for the same things in life. And when you get to the heart of it, everyone needs to be loved. So why do men and women keep analyzing each other when the truth is so . . . *simple*," Max said, smiling.

"You know something, *amigo*?" Roger said. "We've heard that somewhere before, but for once, you're right," he added with a wink.

As the sun began its slow descent toward the horizon, the two men leaned back and laughed. Then Roger held up an open hand and Max hit it squarely.

338